FULLY AUTOMATIC

JADE C. JAMISON

Copyright © 2014 Jade C. Jamison

Cover image © 2010 Deliormanli, iStockphoto

All rights reserved.

ISBN: 1495409813
ISBN-13: 978-1495409813

The characters and events portrayed in this book are fictitious or are used fictitiously. Any similarity to real persons, living or dead, is purely coincidental and not intended by the author. Characters and names of real persons who appear in the book are used fictitiously.

When Brad caught Nick outside the apartment after work, he asked him to take a walk. He was still wearing his work coveralls, but he needed to feel everyone out. "How you feeling? The past few weeks have been pretty emotional. You holding up okay, man?"

"Yeah." Nick shrugged. He was quiet for a little bit but then said, "Things have been a little weird, though."

"Yeah. I was thinking about calling a meeting."

"You think that would help?"

Brad took a deep breath. "Honestly? I have no fucking idea. But...I hate the idea of waiting for the next time, you know? I'd like a promise from Ethan that we're done with this phase of our lives."

"You don't really think he'd make a promise like that, do you?"

"No. Wishful thinking."

They walked in silence for a minute and then Nick said, "You know what's going on with Val and Ethan, right?"

A ringing started in his ears, and he felt dread as a shiver tickled his spine. He knew he wasn't going to like what Nick had to say, but he needed to know. "What?"

Nick stopped walking and Brad turned to face him. "I'm only telling you this because it's only fair to you. I'm not sure what all is or was going on between you and Val, but I don't want—anyway, uh...Ethan proposed to Val."

It felt like the air had been knocked out of his lungs. "What?"

"Ethan asked Val to marry him. I, uh...don't know if it's totally official yet, but..."

Somehow he had the presence of mind to say, "Don't say anything about me and Val to Ethan. That shit's over."

"Yeah. No way. It's not like she was cheating on him."

Brad felt like he was going to throw up. He grew quiet, walking back to the apartment with Nick, but his mind was trying to find a way to deal with the worst news it had ever received...

Thanks to Bullet, *I made some wonderful friends. One is a lovely young woman named Christina who, like Valerie, fronts a rock band.* Fully Automatic *is dedicated to Christina Giordano and the awesome guys in Impact Event: Chad Holbrook, Alex James Knoll, Ryan Meisenheimer, and Dylan Freidman. I send you love and wish you success!*

FOREWORD

I can hardly believe it's been a year since I started writing *Bullet*, the book that pulled me out of obscurity and into the Amazon bestselling author's club! This past year has changed my life, in some ways, very unexpectedly. I am not complaining, not by a long shot. It has been fun!

When I wrote *Bullet*, it was meant to be a standalone book. Yes, I loved the characters and knew them well, but I hadn't had any other plans for them. Readers begged for more, and I listened. So, here it is—the fourth book in the Bullet series and one that many readers have waited patiently for—*Fully Automatic*, the same story, only told from Brad's point of view.

Only it's *not* the same story. Yes, you're going to read a lot of the same scenes from a different perspective, but there's more to the story than that. You're going to learn so much more about Brad. I know I did. I loved Brad from the moment I began writing his character, but there were some things I didn't know. For instance, I knew he was driven to succeed—I just didn't know how much until his back was against the wall.

Let's talk about that, though—the male perspective. This book was tough on me for multiple reasons. Oh, yeah, I bawled like a baby, because when Brad hurt, so did I. But it was even harder. I've written books from dual perspectives before, but that didn't seem as difficult, because I still had the female perspective as my anchor. Writing from the male POV, I doubted myself from time to time. Sure, I love Brad and I know him, but I wondered—did I really know what I was talking about? Then it got worse. Several times I questioned myself, thinking, "Sure, readers *think* they want this book, but they're gonna hate it!"

Well, there comes a time when we as writers must let our babies go and send them out into the cold, cruel world. That time has come with Brad's story. Now that I've made it through this arduous journey, I believe it is the story you wanted to read. I don't think you're expecting everything I've given you, but I believe you'll love it anyway. Why? Because you love Brad, and I'm pretty damn sure you're going to love him even more by the time you put the book down.

So I'm giving this book to you now, my labor of love. I hope you love it as much as I have grown to.

Peace, love, and rock on,
Jade, January 2014

CHAPTER ONE

MMM...THIS GIRL was so sweet. And she was so different from all the other girls Brad had ever dated. She was innocent and almost shy when it came to matters of a sexual nature. Unfortunately, Brad found that to be quite a turn on.

They shouldn't have snuck off into the bathroom, but it had been Leah's idea. She'd wanted to be alone with him away from the party. Her brown eyes had twinkled as she grabbed his hand and pulled him through the crowd. They walked upstairs where there weren't as many people. The bathroom was empty, and she pulled him in by the hands. When he asked what they were doing (unable to stop the grin plastered on his face), she locked the door and slammed him against the wall, sticking her tongue in his mouth.

Maybe that meant she was ready. He'd been telling her *no pressure* for the last three months since they'd started dating. Yeah, he'd love to be her first, but her dad was an elder at one of the churches in town and she was a good girl. She wasn't like a lot of the church girls who were hornier and nastier than regular girls. She loved her father and wanted to obey him, even though her body wanted Brad.

She made it hard, though…figuratively, yes, but literally too. His balls were already aching, because he knew he'd have to wait until he was home and in bed to find some relief. She was being aggressive now, something she'd never done before.

Still…he wasn't gonna quit kissing her back until she asked him to stop. He couldn't help the hard on and wasn't going to say anything about it. He hoped it didn't make her uncomfortable, but he couldn't will it down. She felt so good, smelled so sweet up against him, and the tips of her fingernails against the back of his neck were driving him crazy.

She pressed herself up into him, and that was when Brad was pretty certain he was going to get lucky. He'd never pushed his luck with her, but now he felt bold enough to try, so he kissed down the side of her neck. He'd rarely tasted the flesh there before. She sighed and he felt her hands move down his neck and then his chest and then his blood started pumping harder, taking a dive below.

Jesus. He knew he was going to have to ask her if she was sure it was what she wanted. Hell, he *should* have been asking if she wanted to find a bed or something, but he was feeling too desperate by this point. He'd just have to make sure he was gentle with her.

He felt her fingers on the front of his jeans, unbuckling the belt buckle. At that point, he could feel his cock throbbing. He was afraid by this point there'd be no stopping him. But she kissed him hard on the lips and unzipped his jeans.

He couldn't simply let her do it, not without making sure. He stopped the kiss and tried to tune out his cock. It was trying to take over the last rational thought in his head. "Leah..." He shook his head when she opened his eyes. "You wanted to wait..."

She grinned at him, flashing her white teeth. "I have a surprise for you."

The girl was gorgeous, even though he'd kissed all the soft pink lipstick off her lips. She batted her eyelashes and snuck her hand inside his underwear. He couldn't help the groan in his throat. He tried analyzing what her surprise could be, and he could only figure she got on the pill. And what an asshole he was. There was no way he was going to suggest a bed at this point, not now that her hand was wrapped around him. All he could manage was "You sure you want to do this?"

She smiled again, her tongue between her teeth. She nodded and began to kneel down. Brad hadn't thought it would be possible, but his cock felt like it was swelling further. It was going to explode.

There she was, though, on her knees, and she pulled his dick out of his pants, wrapping those sweet little lips around him. "Oh, my God." He'd tried to refrain from what she called *taking the Lord's name in vain* since he'd started dating her, but he wasn't thinking anymore. And she didn't seem to mind. In fact, he felt her giggle, and the vibration from her lips added to the crazy pleasure he was feeling. Fuck, he was so close. He knew it was because he hadn't had sex in a long time, and he'd planned on it being an insane amount of time before ever going there with her. But there she was, bringing him to ecstasy. He ran his fingers through her blonde mane while her mouth sucked on his cock, each motion bringing him closer to the top. He sucked in a deep breath of air through his teeth and then *bam*. He lost his load, and he didn't even have the presence of mind to figure out if she was swallowing or not…at first. But then he realized she was and that made the next pump that much more intense. Even the guy banging on the door telling them to hurry couldn't ruin it.

It was fucking intense, and it felt like Brad's brains had drained out his dick. He felt lightheaded and leaned his head back against the cool tile on the bathroom wall. His slack jaw hung as he tried to catch his breath. He felt Leah lick up his shaft and he realized he was too sensitive now. He thought he was going to lose his fucking mind.

Bang! Bang! Bang! "Seriously. I gotta take a piss, dude."

"Fuck off. There are two more bathrooms downstairs."

Leah stood up, a twinkle in her eyes. She kissed Brad's chin and said, "Yeah. Fuck off."

Brad opened his eyes and grinned. He knew his eyes were wide, because he'd never heard his girlfriend swear like that. The worst he'd ever heard her say was *damn*.

The voice outside the door said, "No, fuck you." The guy banged on the door once more, but Brad was sure he was taking his bladder elsewhere.

Brad took Leah's face in his hands and kissed her. It was gentle but full of meaning. He wasn't ready to say it to her, but he was falling hard. He didn't know that he'd ever felt this full inside because of a girl before, but she made him feel whole, happy, and now she'd made him feel more like a man than he ever had before. He hadn't asked, wasn't going to, but she'd decided to move their relationship up a notch that night. He could barely believe it. He hadn't even planned to invite her to go to the party, because he knew there would be booze there, and she didn't approve, but Ethan had been talking about it all day long. She asked about it, and Brad couldn't lie to her. She'd begged to come along, and he couldn't tell his girl no.

And now she'd just gone a little further than they'd ever gone before. Brad hadn't even touched her breasts yet. He'd felt her bare back, played with her bra strap until she'd asked him to stop, and now she'd actually given him a hell of a blow job.

He felt like he was regaining his senses. He pressed his forehead to hers, drinking in her brown eyes. "So what inspired *that*?"

She smiled at him, her eyes squinting with happiness. "I don't know. Just...Madi and I were talking the other day, and she's done that...a *lot*. I guess I just wanted to make you happy. You've been so patient with me..."

This girl. God. Wow. "You're worth it, okay? I will wait as long as you need me to." And probably longer.

"Did you like it?"

He chuckled. "Did I like it? You kidding? Fucking amazing." He sucked in a quick breath. "Sorry." He tried—normally, of course, and not in the heat of passion—to control his cursing around Leah as much as he could. She'd never said anything about it, but she was so innocent, so pure that he felt like being his normal self could corrupt her chasteness. He didn't want to mar her, physically or psychically, so he tried to watch his mouth as much as he could.

She smiled. "Yay! I can't wait to tell Madi."

He couldn't help the frown. "You're gonna tell her?"

Her smile faded. "Oh. Yeah. I guess I shouldn't."

"Not because you don't want her to get you in trouble, Leah. It just feels like it's something that should be between you and me only, you know?"

She smiled. "Yeah, I see what you mean." She giggled. "Still, it's a big first for me."

Brad laughed and kissed her again. "You are something else." There was more pounding on the door, and he realized his jeans were still unzipped. He had to find the energy to start moving again, because Leah had to be home by midnight, but he didn't want to leave just because some asshole couldn't find another bathroom. "Give us a minute, will ya?"

"Brad?"

Brad recognized the voice. "Yeah."

"We gotta go, man."

"What time is it?"

"Time to split before I fucking kill somebody."

That didn't sound good. "Be there in a minute." He kissed Leah one last time. "Guess we need to go, but…" She had a twinkle in her eyes, and she raised her eyebrows in anticipation of his next words. "I promise you…when you're ready, I want to make you feel like a woman. I want you to feel like you were born for it."

She blinked and then smiled. But then she whispered, "I've heard it hurts. Bad."

He pulled her close and whispered in her ear. "I'm not talking about losing your virginity." He kissed the side of her ear and then pulled his head back, his hands still cupping her head. "I'm just talking about when you let me touch you." She blushed and giggled. "I want you to feel like I just did. But that will wait until you're ready."

Her cheeks remained a soft pink. "Okay."

Brad had only had success once thus far, and it was thanks to his dad's advice. He didn't see his father much nowadays, but the man was still the best father Brad could have asked for. His father had told him that all women were different, but the tongue could level the playing field. It took a lot of patience and what his dad called "indirect stimulation," but it had worked, and Brad was amazed. He could tell the girl's orgasm was nothing like his had been—hers was long and sustained, whereas his was out of this world but *bam!* and then done. He wanted to try again with Leah, because she was a girl he really cared about. He'd told her no pressure, though, and he'd meant it.

"Come on. Let's get out of here." He tucked himself back in his pants and zipped up. He took Leah's hand and walked toward the bathroom door. When he opened it, he halfway expected someone to be there waiting to come inside. But the coast was clear, and they walked down the hallway toward the stairs and descended them.

The closer they got to the ground floor, the more bodies cluttered the stairs. Some of the people were talking, while others were embraced and in various stages of making out. Apparently, Brad wasn't the only one to get lucky that night, but he was one of the first. It was loud downstairs, music blaring from the speakers of the stereo in the living room, and Brad figured the only thing saving the kid hosting from having the cops show up was the fact that his parents' house was in the boonies. He had no idea where the kids' parents were, but he wasn't going to question it.

One step before they got to the floor, Brad shouted at Leah, "If you see Ethan anywhere, let me know." When his friend had knocked on the bathroom door earlier, he'd sounded ready to snap. Brad knew what that meant—it meant he had to get his friend out of there and pronto. He was probably fighting with his girlfriend again. Those two were volatile, like oil and water, and Brad would breathe a sigh of relief when Ethan grew tired of the stupid girl. He had no idea what Ethan saw in her. The girl was a slut and had hit on him once or twice—*after* she and Ethan had started dating. Brad had turned her down, but it had eaten at him, and he'd considered telling his friend more than once. Instead, he'd hinted around that maybe his friend's girlfriend wasn't so nice. Ethan seemed to know but didn't care.

Brad and Leah walked through the noisy, crowded, smoky living room, slowly making their way through the crowd that halfway parted as they moved between bodies. He held her hand tighter as the crowd pressed in. He couldn't see Ethan anywhere and decided to make his way toward the living room. But then Leah squeezed his hand and he heard her voice. He turned to look at her and she said, pointing with her other hand, "He's over there."

Brad looked at her finger and followed the invisible line extending from it away toward the front door. But Ethan wasn't quite that far. He was standing beside the closet door next to the door leading outside. He was opening the door to the closet and he looked beyond pissed. Brad took that as a signal. He'd seen his friend like that enough to know he was ready to beat the shit out of someone—and that meant he was risking another night in jail.

He had no idea how much his friend had had to drink, nor if he'd taken anything else to feed his buzz, but he *did* know he'd promised Ethan's mom that he'd try to keep him out of trouble. He pulled Leah through the crowd, this time not waiting for people to part. Instead, he shoved his way through. He knew that meant people would be spilling beer on themselves or the floor when the motion from his jostling made their arms sway, and their tipsiness kept them from being able to balance their cups enough to keep the liquid inside.

Ethan's expression was one of both anger and hurt, and he was getting ready to reach inside the closet when Brad got there. Leah was behind him and wasn't able to see inside, but Brad was close enough that he could. Inside the closet, the coats were pushed to one side and Ethan's girlfriend Heidi stood beside them, a guy leaning back against the wall, Heidi's hands on his chest. The guy, who looked to be a year or two older than Ethan and Brad, had a cocky grin on his face, but he was still fully clothed. Heidi's skirt was hiked halfway up her thighs, but she too was dressed. She was almost pouting at Ethan. "What the fuck are you doing, Heidi?"

Brad couldn't hear the girl's response, but it didn't matter. Anything coming out of her mouth would be bullshit. "Come on, man. Let's get out of here."

"No fuckin' way." His friend's green eyes narrowed as he clenched his jaw. "I'm gonna beat this motherfucker senseless first."

Brad placed his open palm on Ethan's chest. "Don't do it, man. It's not worth it."

"Says you."

Heidi's blue eyes twinkled. She got off on this shit. Ethan was feeding her, making it worse, but the guy didn't see it. Ethan reached in the closet and grabbed the guy by the collar, starting to pull him out. Brad knew he had to intervene or it was going to be a bad night. He pushed Ethan in the chest while shoving the other guy back, and he wedged himself between them as best he could. He was up close and personal with Ethan and stared in his eyes. Man, Ethan wasn't even there. How the fuck could he rationalize with him while the guy was in an animal state?

He had to try. "Let him go, man. Just let it go." Ethan's eyes flashed again but something registered. Brad could see it in his friend's eyes. His words were pointed when he said, "She's not worth it." Surely, Ethan knew that. He'd bitched and moaned for months about how he was pretty sure Heidi was being unfaithful, but instead of ditching the girl, it had made Ethan all the more insecure and clingy. But Brad thought maybe this time he was getting through to his friend. Again, he repeated himself. "She's just not worth it."

Ethan let go of the guy's collar but then, as though it were a last-ditch effort, he lunged at him. Brad managed to hold him back nonetheless. He thought maybe it was a ploy so that Ethan could save face. Ethan valued his reputation as a scrapper and a bad ass, so he couldn't *just* walk away from a potential fight. Instead, if his friend stopped him from beating the shit out of some guy, he could later say his plan to pummel the dude into the ground had been thwarted.

Ethan strained against him, but it wasn't anything he couldn't handle. Brad pushed back, forcing Ethan farther into the living room away from the closet. He turned his head and yelled. "Heidi, if you know what's good for you, you and your lover boy will get the fuck out of here *now*." He turned back to Ethan. His friend's eyes didn't show it, but Brad believed he was getting through to him. "We're getting out of here." He turned to make sure Leah was with them and he nodded his head toward the front door. She nodded back and followed as Brad pulled, pushed, and dragged his friend until they were outside.

On the deck in the cool air, Brad could see the glint in Ethan's eyes under the porch light, but he wasn't struggling anymore. "Deep breath, man." Ethan's jaw was clenched and Brad knew one of two things would happen—either Ethan would start trash talking or he'd say nothing. When his friend marched promptly to the railing on the deck and leaned over, throwing up probably most of what he'd drunk that night, he figured he'd say nothing. "It's late. We need to get out of here."

Leah's voice sounded panicked. "It's not midnight yet, is it?"

Brad smiled and wrapped his arm around her shoulders. "Not even close. I'll have you home way before your curfew." She grinned back at him and stood on her tiptoes to give him a sweet kiss on the lips. "Coming, Ethan?"

His friend shook his head as though to get his bearings and walked toward them. Aside from the shit that had gone down that evening, Brad had the two most important people by his side now, and nothing could get him down.

CHAPTER TWO

BRAD WAS DOODLING in his notebook, trying to stylize the word *Bullet* so it would look good on the cover of a metal CD. He curved the letters, much like he'd seen done in other logos, but past incarnations had looked like blood dripping and, on another one, he'd tried to make the *t* look like a handgun. It didn't matter yet anyway. He and Ethan still had to settle on two other members and start writing music. Brad had already written two songs in secret, but he had no idea what they'd sound like once the whole band was together. In the meantime, he and Ethan played covers of some of their favorite tunes to sharpen their skills.

Part of the problem too was Ethan enjoyed partying too much, but now that toxic Heidi was out of the picture, Brad hoped he could get his friend to focus better.

So Thursday morning in early April, he sat in government class doodling. He realized his teacher would have preferred it if Brad had been taking notes, but Brad figured the guy should be happy Brad was paying any attention at all. Drawing helped him focus on the man's words, and right now his teacher was droning on and on about the president's vetoing power. Brad was so ready to be out of school. He was just hanging in there until graduation, maintaining passing grades until he could walk away, done. He had friends going on to college, some to tech school, others going into the military, and even others venturing out into the unknown, but Brad had one dream, one goal—that was to make his band. He'd already been in one other his sophomore year in high school, but it had fizzled when the drummer and vocalist had gone to college at the end of the year and—since then—Brad had focused on becoming the best guitar player he could. Ethan tried talking him into being in the school band, but he wanted no part of it. Ethan played bass drum for the marching band and he enjoyed it, but Brad thought playing in the school band would just distract him from what he really wanted to do—and that was to be part of something big. He dreamed of being in a metal band. He would even sing if need be, but music was his life, and he would only be happy if he could make that dream a reality.

The bell rang and he left class, walking down the hall to his locker. He dropped off the notebook and textbook and then looked around for the two people he spent most lunch breaks with—Leah and Ethan. Ethan showed up and nodded his head. Brad was somewhat surprised. His friend had handled his breakup with Heidi surprisingly well. But he was afraid it was the calm before the storm. He knew his friend well enough to know that he could be self-destructive, and he expected a cascade of shit to come crashing down in the next week, whenever Ethan finally managed to completely lose it. He'd either track down closet guy and beat the shit out of him or go on a complete bender. The problem was that Brad had been trying to hide Ethan's out-of-control behavior from June, the guy's mother, but Brad was afraid the gig was about up. Bad enough Ethan had wound up emptying a bottle of Vicodin that had been prescribed to June a year earlier. All Brad could figure was that either June was such a mess that she couldn't see Ethan for what he was becoming or he and Ethan really *were* good at hiding it all.

He was pretty sure June had the blinders on, though. From what Brad knew, her life had been a continual mess, and Ethan just happened to suffer from collateral damage. Brad and Ethan had partied together hard earlier in high school, but Brad soon realized it wasn't simply fun rebellion or a need to get loose and crazy for Ethan. Ethan seemed to need to get lost once in a while, to drown in oblivion, but he always managed to come up for air and be stronger for it. Still, Brad worried about it sometimes, but the times he'd bring it up, Ethan wouldn't talk. It was better just to support his friend and be there to pick up any pieces that might fall to the ground.

For now, though, Ethan appeared to be lucid and calm, and he hadn't said shit about Heidi or the guy they'd caught her getting ready to bone. It was almost as though Ethan had managed to get it all out of his system that night. That his friend hadn't talked about her, called her, or asked around about her made Brad think that maybe Ethan had grown up some in the past year. He could only hope. He nodded back at his friend. There was no sense talking. The halls were always noisy and chaotic between classes, but especially right before lunch. He looked around and then he saw her—beautiful Leah, rounding the corner. She saw him too and smiled, waving her tiny pale hand, the bracelet around her wrist wiggling back and forth with the motion.

God, she was a sight. Her long blonde hair framed her lovely pale face that was enhanced with the light makeup she wore, and her warm brown eyes always made him think of a deer—innocent, not quite willing to trust or relax. She was thin but filled out, thanks to her involvement on the school's dance team. He'd never been with a girl who'd had as firm a body as hers—and he liked it. Today, she wore as short a skirt as she could get away with, which was barely halfway up her thighs. From what Leah had told him, her dad was pretty strict about what she wore. She couldn't wear as much makeup as her friends, and jewelry had to be modest. Body piercing was out of the question, although Brad didn't think she would have been interested in it anyway. She couldn't wear anything revealing—no bare midriff, no super short skirts that would lend themselves to a peek, no low-cut tops. Brad felt honored just having been able to touch her bare thigh or her back underneath her shirt. She'd let him move a little but not much. Her dad had influenced her heavily, and Brad respected that. He didn't want her dad bearing down on him one night with a shotgun.

It wasn't like Brad couldn't get laid. He was no slut, but he'd had enough sex to know there would always be a girl out there willing to part her legs. And he had no intention of pressuring his girlfriend. He cared for her a lot, and if they were going to consummate their relationship, it would be when Leah felt completely ready and not a moment before.

She made her way through their crowd of classmates flooding senior hall and slipped her hand in Brad's. She'd already put her books away and had her purse over her shoulder. She stood on her tiptoes and raised her voice in Brad's ear. "Where we going today?"

He shrugged and looked over at Ethan, and the three of them walked outside. Once they were in the fresh spring air, Brad asked, "You guys just wanna get something from the gas station and hang at the park to eat?"

Leah smiled. "Sure."

Ethan said nothing but nodded and ran his hands through his reddish brown hair. They walked toward Brad's little white car, what he called his *tin can*, and got in, Ethan in the backseat. The first time he turned the key, the car sputtered but didn't catch. Brad drew in a deep breath. He'd live if his car needed more repairs, but it was damned inconvenient, and he was sick of sinking money into it. He had a weekend job at Super Lube, changing oil in cars in record time, but he wanted to spend his money on important things, things related to his dream, not keeping a piece of shit car on the road. He spent a little money on Leah too but not much. She was pretty low maintenance, and his mom loved having her over for dinner, so Brad rarely had to spend lots of money on dates—the movies once in a while, the price of admission for school dances, but nothing outrageous.

The second time, though, the car started up and he gave it extra gas to make sure it didn't die. The music was on the loud side. The radio station was playing a Mudvayne song, but Leah wasn't as big a fan of metal as he and Ethan, so he turned the radio down and grinned at her as he slid the car in gear and pulled out of the parking space.

By the time they got to the gas station, Brad could smell the smoke wafting up front from the backseat. Leah didn't say a word, and at first Brad couldn't tell if it was a cigarette or pot. He felt relieved that it was only a cigarette, but he could never be sure with Ethan. He and Leah both opened the front doors but Ethan didn't get out. He held a five-dollar bill out the window to Brad and said, "Just get me a Dr. Pepper and a Snickers, would ya?"

"Great lunch."

"What're you having? Nachos or a hot dog? Like that's so great?"

"Better than all that sugary shit."

"Yeah, well, I'm gonna need it to survive English this afternoon."

Brad saw his friend's eyes and knew he'd taken something on the drive. Yeah. The last thing he needed was more shit in his body, but there was no arguing with him. He shook his head and draped his arm over Leah's shoulders. The two of them wound up getting a sub sandwich to split, chips, and drinks, and then the three of them drove to the park a couple of blocks away. They found a table partially shaded by a tree, but the sun was warm and pleasant and there wasn't even a hint of a breeze. Leah sat completely in the shade but wore a pink cardigan over her beige dress. None of them said anything at first, instead just eating, but Brad finally asked Ethan, "So, what'd your friend say?"

"Who? About what?"

"Nick, right? One of your drummer friends from band?"

"Oh, yeah. Yeah. He wants to come over this weekend. He said he could set up his drum kit in your garage and jam some with us... 'see if it's a good fit,' he said."

"Cool. And I told you about Zane, right? He said he's in."

"Not even gonna try playing with us?"

"Nah. I've known him for a while. He played in another piss ant band about a year ago, and he's seen me play. He said he doesn't give a shit as long as we don't play pop or country. He's in. He misses playing in a real band. And he's good. Trust me. He'll be a good fit."

"I trust you, man." Ethan's eyelids were getting heavy and he rested his head on his forearm. Not good. Brad didn't want to have to drag his friend into the nurse's office.

Leah distracted him, though. She rested her hand on his forearm. "What are you doing tomorrow after school?"

He shrugged. "Probably laundry."

She lowered her voice and leaned closer to him. "Your mom working?"

He grinned and looked in her eyes. He could see Ethan out of the corner of his eye, and his friend didn't seem to be paying attention. "Yeah..."

"Can I come over for a while?"

"Like you have to ask?"

Further talk about his band was quashed by the look in his girlfriend's eyes and Ethan's continuing state of intoxication. For now, he was okay with that.

CHAPTER THREE

LEAH HADN'T EVEN gone home after school that Friday. She went home with Brad. They spent a couple hours watching videos on YouTube, because she'd been asking about his band and the kind of music he wanted to play. She had never seen his old band, and she didn't listen to a lot of the music Brad did. She was more a Top Forty kind of gal, but maybe Brad could change that.

He had to turn it off after he saw her lip curl at a Chelsea Grin video.

By then, it was close to dinner, so he found the leftover spaghetti in the fridge and threw it in the microwave. They ate in the kitchen and continued their conversation about his band, but he could tell by the look on her face that Leah was a little hesitant about the music Brad wanted to play. She must have known before, based on the music Brad played all the time.

When they were done eating, she asked to hear him play. That made him feel better. So they went to his bedroom.

His guitar was in there, for starters, and it wasn't like she'd never been there before. But the only times she'd been there before were when Brad's mom had been home. Still, he wasn't thinking much about it. They'd kissed and snuggled on his bed before, but he'd never gone further. He respected her wishes, but still...she'd ignited a fire in him when she'd wrapped her pink lips around his cock, and he hadn't been able to think about much else since.

It didn't matter, though. Unless and until she said she was ready, he would keep his hands—and his dick—to himself.

He knew she didn't like music as heavy as he did, so he played some of his new music on his acoustic guitar and he skipped over the solos. He also kept the vocals calmer than he would have were he onstage. He couldn't help but feel some pride when she said she liked the songs. He wondered what she would think when they were plugged in and loud, but he thought maybe she could acquire a taste for his music. Love could maybe help her appreciate it more.

Love?

Yes, Brad knew that was what he was feeling. He'd never felt this way before, never been drawn to a girl like Leah until now. She seemed so perfect for him, so right, and even though there were so many differences between them, that was okay. Those differences seemed to smooth out and not matter when he was with her.

He grinned and set his guitar on the floor, propping the neck against the foot of the bed, and he turned back to her. "So...you really like the songs?"

"I do." She smiled back and after a few moments said,

"Are you going to play them like that?"

"What do you mean?"

"You know—kind of quiet like that?"

Oh. He knew where this was headed. "Why?"

She placed her index finger on his t-shirt at chest level and swirled it playfully. "I really liked it. I...imagined you playing a louder song."

Yep. He was right. "Well, it'll definitely be plugged in onstage. And, yeah, lots louder. Can't help it, Leah. It's in my blood."

She smiled then and there was something in her eyes. God, how he'd love to know what she was thinking. She acted like she was going to say something, but then Brad heard a door downstairs shut. "Brad!" his mother's voice carried up the stairs. "Honey, I was called into work early, so I'm gonna go change, but can you put the groceries away, please?"

"Yeah, be there in a minute, mom." He'd known his mother would leave between six and six-thirty, but he hadn't expected to not see her at all. He touched his nose to Leah's. "Be right back."

"I can help you, you know."

He smiled as he stood. "Okay." He held out his hand and waited for Leah to slip hers into his, and they walked down the stairs. When they got to the kitchen, Brad found five plastic grocery bags on the table.

"What do you want me to do?"

He looked through the bags and handed one to her. "That all looks like fridge stuff. Would you mind putting it in there?"

"No problem." While she took care of the one bag,

Brad put away the canned and boxed goods in three of the bags. As the two of them worked on putting away what was in the last bag, Brad's mom walked in the kitchen wearing yellow scrubs.

"Oh, Leah. I didn't know you were here. How are you?"

"Great, Mrs. Payne. How are you?"

She grimaced. "Busy, unfortunately." She walked over to Brad and kissed him on the cheek, standing on her toes since her son was quite a bit taller than she. "See you tomorrow, bud."

Brad smiled. "See ya, mom."

"See you, Leah." His mother grabbed her purse and headed out the door. Brad couldn't help but smile as his mother walked out. He knew she was the reason he had the dark hair on his head. His father had light brown hair too, but his mother's was almost black and so was his. In fact, he suspected he looked more like his mother all the way around in the face—dark eyes, dark hair, full lips. The facial hair changed all that, though. Body-wise, he was more like his father—tall and solid. Unlike both his parents, though, Brad was planning to be tattooed—*a lot*.

He turned to face his girlfriend. "So, where were we?"

She grinned. "You were playing songs for me."

"Not boring you, was I?"

She shook her head, almost acting shy. He smiled and kissed her forehead, then took her by the hand to lead her back to his room. Leah sometimes had a tendency to act demure even when she didn't need to, but it was one of the things she did that endeared her to Brad. When they got to his room, they sat back on the edge of the bed where they'd been before, but Leah held onto his hand. He was going to grab for his guitar but instead looked in her eyes. And he could tell she didn't want him to play music for her anymore. Her eyes told him that much.

Still...she didn't realize how difficult it was becoming for him to engage in hot and heavy make out sessions with no release. He would never pressure her, and he would find ways to take care of himself later, but every time they got involved in a heavy kissing session, he found himself worked up beyond control. The blow job last weekend hadn't helped, because now his mind raced back to that night. He didn't want to ask her to do it again, but it was all he could think about.

It didn't matter. He couldn't resist her, and he could do what he'd been doing—taking care of himself when she was gone. So he leaned over and cupped her cheek in his hand. She tilted her head into his hand and closed her eyes. She inhaled a slow breath and then looked at him. She searched his eyes as he moved his face close to hers and met her lips with a kiss.

It was unlike any other kiss they had shared before. There was something about it that felt a little steamier, a little more intimate, and Brad tried not to think about it. It was then, as his tongue explored her mouth, that he finally let go and let the emotion wash over him, the one he'd been denying, the one he'd felt sure couldn't be real.

He loved this girl.

Yes, he'd cared about other girls before, but not like Leah. Leah was beginning to feel like a part of him, like something he wouldn't be able to live without, like air. He knew he was too young to feel that way, too inexperienced, but he couldn't help the feeling. It was there, and it was strong, and there wasn't a damn thing he could do about it.

So he just let himself feel it. He believed she could feel it too, because something tonight was different. He felt her hands on his chest, but they weren't resting there. Her fingers were curled just enough that he could feel her fingernails through his shirt. She was tense, but not in a nervous way.

If he was reading her signals right, he knew what to do. His hand was already on the back of her head, his fingers entwined in her hair, the base of his palm resting on her neck, and he moved his hand to ease her head to the side. He ended their kiss and moved his lips to her neck, just inches below her ear. She let out a breath, one he could hear, and that confirmed that he was on the right track. He could still feel her fingers digging into him as he moved his lips down her neck to below her chin.

He didn't know if he should say anything or simply move and let her say something if she wanted him to stop. He was sure he was on the right track, though, and so he was going to move forward, but he'd take it slow. He could tell she liked his lips on her neck by how she was responding, so he wanted to keep making her feel good.

That meant moving his hands, and he knew if she didn't like it, she'd say something. They'd only been dating a month the first time he'd tried, and she'd stopped him, telling him she wasn't ready. He'd respected her request since, keeping his hands in acceptable places, but when she'd given him that blow job almost a week ago, it had felt like all bets were off—like she was ready to move forward.

So he let his hands glide down her back, and when he

got to her waist, where her pink t-shirt met her jeans, he paused. She was kissing him, her breathing a little deeper, a little more jagged, and she moved her hands to his shoulders, then his neck. One hand stayed pressed against his neck, her nails pressing against the flesh, and the other hand wound its way through his hair. He'd started growing it out at Christmas. He'd kept it short all through high school to keep his mother happy, but he'd decided he was a man now and could do what he wanted. His mother hadn't said a word, not at first, when it started covering his ears, not when his bangs hung in his eyes. She'd finally caved and asked him during spring break when he was going to get his hair cut, and he told her he wasn't. She'd shrugged and frowned but hadn't said another word. He was glad now, because Leah's hand in it felt good.

He slid his hands up underneath the back of her tee where he could feel the warm flesh just above the waistband of her jeans. She didn't say anything. A good sign. So he thought he'd try moving a little higher. Still not a word, but as his hand inched its way up her back, she pressed her breasts into him. But she wasn't telling him to stop.

Another deep kiss and then his hand reached her bra strap. He tried to remain calm. It was time for the moment of truth. He felt around the back of the strap to make sure it hooked in back and discovered it did, so he slid his other hand up to meet it. Still nothing. He was sure if she'd wanted him to stop, she would already be protesting. Still…he wasn't going to go fast, wasn't going to press. He wanted her to want it; he didn't want to pressure her.

She kissed him harder back as his fingers worked the

hooks on the bra apart, and when he got it undone, he let it go. She didn't object, so he splayed his hands out over the area where the bra had been holding her, moving one hand up between her shoulder blades.

Time for another moment of truth. He moved his lips back to her neck and kissed her again. Not a word except for a soft sigh. That triggered his confidence. He was definitely on the right track. She felt so good too, and he could feel himself getting hard. That made him mad at himself because he wasn't doing this for him. It was for her. He wanted her to feel like a woman, feel ultimate pleasure because of him, and so he had to hold his steed back. Tonight was *not* about him. Not now anyway. It was only about sweet Leah. He pressed against her, urging her to lie back, and she did, her head resting on his pillow. He lay beside her, feeling more sure now but even now wanting to take his time. One of his arms held him up as he brought his lips back to hers, but the other rested on her belly, right about where he imagined her navel to be, and after another deep kiss, he slid his hand underneath her shirt. Still no resistance, and so, over the course of the next few seconds, he took his time gliding his hand up to the bottom of her bra. It remained on, but it was loose now. He felt his pulse increase, because he was further than he'd ever been before, and he was pretty sure she was going to let him.

Another deep kiss and he moved his hand under her bra. Not only did she let him, but he could feel the tight nipple against his hand. He was touching her with his picking hand, not his fretting hand, so he could appreciate the sensation of her smooth, soft skin. His fretting fingers would have been worthless—calloused and lacking some of the sensation his picking fingers had. He was gentle, taking his time touching her—not squeezing or pinching. Instead, he swirled a finger around the nipple, and she shifted underneath him. He paused a moment, trying to read the cue. No, she wasn't asking him to stop. He figured it out as her fingers tightened their grip in his hair.

Uncertainty gone, he brushed his fingers down the slope of her breast so he could pull her shirt up. He stopped kissing her and looked down on her. Her eyes were closed, but she looked so beautiful. He started pulling her shirt up to her chin and then she opened those lovely brown orbs. Her pupils were wide, and she looked more desirable than he'd ever seen her. "Take yours off too?"

Goddamn. No wonder his fucking cock was swollen beyond belief. Apparently it knew more than he did.

No. He wasn't going to. Not tonight. He wouldn't take her virginity. She would have to ask him to, and they'd have to be prepared.

He did want to make her feel incredible, though, and he wasn't going to stop. He nodded at her and pulled his t-shirt over his head first. She placed her hands on his chest. Wow. That felt better than he'd thought. He gritted his teeth together and hoped he didn't look scary to her. He was fighting some pretty powerful urges, so he plugged into the thought he'd had earlier—the one in which he realized what Leah meant to him. With that thought foremost in his mind, he pulled her shirt up her body, and she sat up a little so he could get it over her head. He looked in her eyes that had turned dark with desire, and he grabbed the front of her bra right between the two cups and pulled it away from her body. She moved and bent her arms so that he could take it all the way off, and he set it on the bed behind where he was going to lie back down again.

He had to be careful. Seeing her halfway nude made him want to plunge into her, but he had to restrain himself. So his lips met hers again, his motions intentionally soft and slow, and he took his time moving his hand to her breasts again. Then he kissed her neck and moved to a nipple. She gasped again but he could see her shift once more. She wanted this, wanted him to make her feel alive, and he wasn't going to let her down.

He started kissing back up toward her face. "God, you're perfect," he said as he cupped her breast with his hand. Then he kissed her again, slow and hot, and decided to go for it. He trailed his fingers down her abdomen, stopping when he got to the waistband of her jeans, and then he pushed the button through the buttonhole. She thrust her fingers into his hair again and kissed him back hard. Yeah, Brad tried not to smile, but it felt so good knowing she wanted him. He still didn't want to rush. He wanted to make sure that *she* was sure she wanted it, and he'd only know for certain if he gave her plenty of time to tell him *no*. So when he got to her zipper, he took his time pulling it down. He could tell her breathing was a little harder. She was definitely warmed up. He slid his hand inside, on top of her panties, making a pass, and he could feel her tilt her pelvis almost imperceptibly. She was definitely feeling the urge. So he slid his hand down farther, pushing a finger in between her jeans and panties. It was tight but he could tell her panties were wet. A good sign. So he kissed her one more time and then pressed his forehead to hers. He knew it was a risky move, taking her out of the mood and making her be rational, but it was a chance he had to take. When she opened her eyes, he said, "I'm not gonna take your virginity, Leah, not tonight, but I want to make you feel good. Can I do that?"

She was breathless. "Uh-huh." A slight nod, almost an urgency in her voice. He leaned over to kiss her one last time. Then he sat up and helped her slide her jeans off her hips and down her legs. She kicked her sandals off and then he let her jeans drop to the floor. She was wearing hot pink panties, nothing fancy, but they were snug on her and accentuated her shape. He felt himself wanting to rush again but wasn't going to. He pulled on the sides and she tilted her ass up off the bed while he slid the panties off her. Then, without haste but a little more quickly, he pulled them down her thighs, over her knees, and she bent them so he didn't have to move down the bed to pull the panties the rest of the way off.

He leaned over and kissed her belly next to her navel, drawing the flesh into his mouth some. Then he trailed his tongue down toward the bush between her legs, stopping at the mound. He kissed her flesh again and then changed position so he was between her legs. He'd only ever tried oral on a girl once before and while it hadn't ended in utter failure, he hadn't been able to make her come. He figured it was because he'd been fingering her before and had managed to that way. Since then, his dad had given him some suggestions, and he planned to put them to good use.

She was a little nervous—he could tell. He didn't think there was any way to alleviate her anxiety. She'd never had a guy touching her before, so she'd have to go through it sometime. Brad realized too that that might mean he wouldn't be able to bring her to orgasm because of her inexperience and nervousness too, so he hoped he could help her enjoy herself. He kissed her inner thigh and then lifted that leg so it draped over his shoulder. He slid his thumbs up her slit to part her open and there she was. His dad had told him to not concentrate directly on the area women raved about—the clit—but to work all around it at first, especially with a girl with less experience. He'd told Brad to wait until she started tensing up and then move in for the kill. Patience too, he'd advised, and start slowly. Don't increase the speed for a while either. Brad thought he could do that. He didn't mind taking a long time to build her to the breaking point.

So he started, doing just what he'd planned. He stroked his tongue slowly against the sides and she seemed to like it okay, but nothing was happening. It wasn't like his dad had told him, so he decided *fuck it*. He moved his tongue to her clit—easy to find. He did decide to take one bit of his dad's advice, and that was to move slowly. He didn't want to overwhelm her, and he wanted her to enjoy it. After a minute or so, that's when he heard her breathing change. She was taking in deeper breaths and every gulp of air became audible. She moved her hands back into his hair, and he felt himself growing hard again. He tried to ignore his own excitement as he focused on her, and he kept up the steady pace, increasing it a bit. After a few more minutes, she started taking deep breaths, lots of air into her lungs, and he was sure she was close. He decided then to go for broke and he sped up. She made a slight noise one of the times she was gulping down air, and that's when he knew he was on the right track and that an orgasm was likely. He wasn't going to stop then. A few more seconds and he felt the muscles in her thighs get tighter. He kept his hands on them but again focused on what his tongue was doing and then her thighs started to squeeze against him and she let out a small groan. He knew what that meant—what he did now mattered more than ever. So he kept up the same pace, focusing on the same spot, and her groans became cries, music to his ears.

After the longest time, her fingers started pushing on his head. "Stop."

He paused. "You sure?"

"Yes." Her voice was light and sounded like a pant.

"You okay?"

She continued to breath hard, her chest heaving. "I think so."

He crawled up to lie next to her. Part of her hair was matted to her forehead. He pushed it aside with a finger and kissed her on the nose. "You sure?"

Her cheeks and chest were pink but she looked like she was glowing. Success. There was a twinkle in her eyes, and she managed a small smile. "Yes. I'm starting to wonder what I waited so long for."

He chuckled and pulled her into an embrace. He let her sleep for a while, her naked body resting in his arms. After a long while, his dick softened back up but his balls ached. That was okay. He had a remedy for it later. He could hardly wait until she was ready…but he *could* and *would* wait, for as long as she needed.

CHAPTER FOUR

TWO WEEKS LATER, Bullet was formed. Brad had never felt this good about a band before. Somehow, he, Ethan, Nick, and Zane fit together. The song-writing process was fluid and nothing short of amazing. They all had the same vision for the band but different influences and inspirations, so the cohesiveness was almost instantaneous, while the music they were making already sounded different. Brad thought it was fresh and new, and he couldn't wait until they had more songs written and could play a few gigs.

Leah watched them perform their first two songs. He sang one and Ethan sang the other. They hadn't settled on a permanent singer, but Ethan seemed to do well when he was sober. The rest of the time, it was better to just let his friend become absorbed in his guitar while he covered the lyrics on all the songs. They started practicing every night after school, except Friday, because that was Brad's night with Leah, and since he worked on Saturday and Sunday, they practiced for a couple of hours Saturday night, but not as much as they would have liked. Ethan started calling Leah *Yoko* behind her back until Brad told him to shut the fuck up.

He and Leah still saw each other as much as they could, and they continued to engage in sexual play, but they hadn't fully consummated, and Brad wasn't going to force the issue. She'd gotten really good at giving him head, and he had plenty more surprises for what he could do for her. He knew the first time for a girl could be painful, and he didn't want to go there with her until she was ready.

A couple weeks later and the band had four strong songs. Brad started talking about playing some shows and then putting together enough money to record an EP. He started mapping out his plan with the guys and then Ethan said, "Dude, my grandpa's making me go to college this fall."

"So?"

"So…it's not here. I'm gonna have to move."

"Seriously?"

Ethan frowned. "Yeah. It's just for a year, though. He made me promise to go for a year, and then if I still didn't want to, he wouldn't make me."

"He can't make you *now*, man."

Ethan sighed. "He's already paid the tuition, and he's going to give me all the money I want while I go. It's either that or…"

"Or what?"

"He takes back my truck and my guitar."

"He can't do that."

"Technically, he can't, but he's done a lot for mom and

me. I can't just tell my grandpa to fuck off."

Brad sighed. He knew Ethan's grandfather was a cool dude. He'd been the only good man in Ethan's life. Brad wished the man lived closer where he could have actually had an influence on him. Brad had known Ethan for a long time, and the guy's mother made one shitty choice after another. He didn't understand how she'd wound up having such a great father. Ethan had never said, but Brad suspected Ethan's parents had just been plain bad for each other, and Ethan had been caught in the middle of many a bad thing. Ethan's dad leaving hadn't helped, either, because June had managed to bring home plenty of men who were as bad, if not worse, than Ethan's dad had dreamed of.

Still, he couldn't hold his friend back. He'd wanted to have a band with his best friend for the last couple of years and now that everything was starting to gel, it was upsetting to have it pulled right out from under him. But he knew his friend and knew Ethan would never choose to go to college on his own. Maybe it would be good for him. He'd have to focus and apply himself, something he'd rarely done in high school. The guy was smart—Brad knew that much. Maybe Ethan's grandfather saw potential. "So how often could you come home?"

Ethan shrugged. "I dunno. Maybe once a month? And then after the year was up we could hit it hard?"

Brad shrugged. "Maybe."

Zane said, "Yeah, I have to do the college thing to."

"You have to too?"

"My dad said he's tired of me being a loser. He says my hair's too long, and I'll never get a job looking the way I do if I don't get an education." Yeah, Brad knew Zane's dad hated the hair—he'd commented about Brad's before too. Zane's wasn't as bad, though—his black hair barely went over his ears, and against the guy's olive complexion and dark blue eyes, he would have thought the guy's dad was giving him tips on how to attract girls.

Brad felt his heart sink. He'd been considering doing a few things—playing here and there—without Ethan for the year, but he couldn't do it without a bassist too.

"Yeah, but…Ethan and I are going to the same school."

"Where you goin'?"

"Western."

Brad thought for a few minutes. Well, that wasn't so bad. It was close. At least it wasn't out of state or on Colorado's eastern slope. Zane said, "But I don't want to do more than a year either. If my dad sees I'm just wasting my time and his money in school, I think he'll change his mind. He wants me to be like my sister. She'll be a junior in college next fall, and she's on the dean's list and getting scholarships 'cause she's so smart." He laughed. "I told my dad to send me to Juilliard, and he got pissed."

He hoped the disappointment didn't show on his face. He'd been hoping to be discovered in a year; instead, they'd just be getting started. "Well, can we at least do some of our writing through email and stuff?"

"Yeah, man. And we'll come home once a month too."

Zane said, "We get a week off at Thanksgiving and a month off at Christmas too."

Nick hadn't said a word till that point. "Come on, ladies." Nick tended to be the quiet one, but when he talked, he usually made them laugh—or at least tried to.

Even his demeanor didn't demand too much attention—his short dark brown hair made him the odd man out of the group, and his blue eyes took in every little detail. He might have seemed quiet, but he didn't miss a thing. "We're not breaking up. We're just cooling off for a while."

Brad shook his head. While he appreciated the humor, he didn't care for the setback. So, he'd have to rearrange his plans. Maybe he could spend the next year working his ass off and buying all the things the band would need. They needed better amps and shit like that. He'd make a list and prioritize what they needed most and start checking things off one at a time. What was going to make things worse, though, was that Leah was going to be attending Colorado Christian University in the fall, and that was somewhere in the Denver area. If she'd been around, it wouldn't have been so bad. He had a lot of thinking to do. His band was his dream.

One year. They had one year, and if Ethan and Zane decided school was what they wanted to do in after that year was up, then the band would never be their thing...and he'd have to start from scratch again. That was it, though—one year. He hoped he'd be able to wait.

One week before graduation, he and Leah were lying on his bed, having finished another hot and heavy session. She was swirling a finger on the few random hairs that had decided to sprout on his chest. He was running his hand over her hair, feeling full and alive. The closer he got to graduation, the more he dreaded it. He knew she wouldn't be leaving for college until August, but it made him sad just the same. Still...he was going to enjoy their time together while they had it. He tried not to think about it.

Leah lifted her head to look him in the eyes. She too looked sad. She must have been thinking what he had. "Hey." She looked down at her finger again. "There's something I need to talk to you about."

He didn't like the sound of that and sat up a little. "What?"

She blinked. "Well, you know I'm going to college this fall."

"Yeah." It was as though she'd been reading his thoughts.

"You know what I'm going into, right?"

"Political science. Isn't that what you said?"

She nodded. "I'm going to double major in prelaw."

"Okay."

Her face changed and she looked even sadder. She blinked again. "I really like you, Brad, and I've loved our time together."

His heart sank. He already knew where it was going, even though he didn't want to believe it. She *liked* him? When he fucking *loved* her? How the fuck had he missed this? He clamped his jaw, hoping to hold it together while she talked. "Where's this going?"

"That's what I mean. My dad's decided we're all going to move to Lakewood. He's already found a house there. I'll still be living in the dorms, but my family will be close by."

He sucked in a breath. "Are you breaking up with me?"

"Uh, well…"

"You are."

She was quiet for a moment before she said, "Well,

yeah, but it's not because I don't like you."

He had to be cool. He just nodded. "Okay."

"Brad, you know we can't be together, right? We're so different."

Now he couldn't believe what he was hearing. He knew she was still wet between her legs from what they'd been doing earlier, and now she was dumping him like he'd meant nothing to her. "If you feel that way, why'd you go out with me in the first place?"

At least she acted like breaking up with him wasn't something she wanted to do. He'd give her that. "Because you're sweet and good looking and I liked you."

He felt deflated. He'd just been fun for her to finish out the school year. And now she was ready to dump him. He felt like a pile of dog shit, and he wasn't going to beg her to keep seeing him until she left. If he wasn't wanted, he wasn't going to force himself on her. But after all they'd been through. What a fucking idiot he'd been. He'd never felt that way about a girl before, and he needed to make sure he never would again.

He couldn't remember what he said after that, but he pulled her to his chest and held her close. He'd hold his head high at graduation and put his heart into his band. But right now it felt like a large hand was squeezing his heart, making it impossible to breathe. He had to find a way to make it through that first.

CHAPTER FIVE

UNBELIVABLE. BULLET ALREADY had thirteen solid songs by mid-July, and they'd played a couple of shows in small venues. They hadn't played to huge crowds, but they were already gaining a bit of a fan base.

Okay, so about ten people had told Brad they loved the band. It still did his heart good to know he was moving people with his music.

He hadn't dated since Leah. She'd come by his house the day her family had moved in June and kissed him on the cheek. It felt like she was branding him, the kiss hurt so much. If he hadn't loved her as much as he did, he'd have been pissed at her.

He knew he should be going wild now, fucking everything he could find, but he couldn't. He needed to let her go first before he could see someone else.

Still, he tried. He and the band went to a party one night after a show. They'd been drinking and a girl had cornered him. The beer made it a little easier to allow himself to be kissed and groped. But then he found out the girl's boyfriend was on vacation. He wouldn't have minded a little one-night stand, but no way was he going to help a girl cheat on her boyfriend. No way. Not after he'd seen what it had done to Ethan—another excuse to get drunk and high, but even more because of what it had done to his dad before that.

Brad loved his mom, but it had taken him a long time to forgive her for that. He'd never asked, and neither of his parents had ever outright told him, but he knew. His dad had left his mom because she'd been fooling around on him. Brad's older brother had already moved out of the house. Brad had been eight at the time, his brother twenty. Brad had wanted to stay with his dad after the divorce but had never asked outright. His mom kept the house and his dad found a little apartment to start out with, so he'd never even asked for custody. By the time Brad started high school, though, he'd managed to forgive his mother her indiscretion and his dad his failure to ask for his son. His dad had been an active participant in his life, so he couldn't hold anything against the man. He'd been a great dad. And his mother had been a good parent as well, tending to his every need, including helping him through biology, a subject he'd grown to detest. Once she and his dad split, she'd gone back into nursing, something she hadn't done for years, getting a job at the hospital. Once Brad was in middle school, she began working mostly nights because of the shift differential. She earned significantly more working crappy night shifts than she had working day shifts. It was around that time that Brad had started finding forgiveness for her, because she was willing to work her ass off to keep him fed and clothed, and she trusted him alone by himself. That said a lot.

Of course, over the years, Brad had done a lot to earn that trust. He did plenty of chores around the house, had never hosted a party there in his mother's absence (even though it would have been so easy to), and stayed out of trouble at school. Sometimes, he felt like he was the parent and his mother the child.

So when his mom called to ask if Brad could pick up her and one of her friends from the bar because they'd had too much to drink, he wanted to tell her to call a cab. But he couldn't bring himself to do it. It was a Thursday night and he and Bullet had already finished their rehearsal. He'd sat down on the couch, ready to veg to whatever he could find on the television, when she'd called and asked. There wasn't anything on he was dying to see anyway, so he got in the car and drove to the bar where his mom said they'd be.

She was standing out on the sidewalk in front of the bar, smoking a cigarette and chatting with some guy. She didn't see him, so he pulled into a parking space. He walked half a block and then had to tap on his mom's shoulder to get her attention. "Oh, hey, son. What are you doing here?"

He didn't roll his eyes, though he'd wanted to. "You called me and asked me to pick you up."

She smiled at the man across from her. "Just a second." She led Brad a few steps away by his elbow. Her voice was low. "Actually, son, I'm going to stick around. I'll find a ride. But Misti still needs one. Could you please give her a ride?"

"I might as well. I'm here."

His mother looked behind him and then raised her

voice. "Misti!"

A thin woman with dark hair looked up at them. She'd been sitting on the curb next to the stop sign. Brad figured that meant she'd been totally wasted. But she'd been doing something on her phone. She stood and slid her phone into the back pocket of her jeans and walked over. Brad noticed his mom had walked back over to the guy she'd been talking to earlier, leaving Brad standing by himself as the other woman joined him.

"Brad, right?"

He nodded. "Yep."

"Misti. I work with your mom." She held out a hand. She didn't seem too trashed.

"Nice to meet you." The woman had dark hair that ended at her shoulders, so it was longer than Brad's but barely. She had dark eyes to match her mane and she had prominent dimples. She didn't even have to smile for them to be evident. He shook her hand and then turned to his mother. "You sure you don't need a ride?"

His mom threw the cigarette on the sidewalk. "Yeah. I'll catch a ride later."

He was pretty sure his mom was doing the *middle age crazy* thing. After she'd broken up with the lover who'd destroyed her marriage, she'd been discreet. Brad knew she'd seen guys now and then, but she'd been subtle. The last month, though, she'd been going out a lot, and if Brad wasn't mistaken, she was gonna get laid tonight. He told Misti, "My car's over here," and started walking that way, lost in thought. He hadn't been with anyone since Leah, just couldn't bring himself to, and the funniest part was that he and Leah had never fully consummated their relationship. She was still a virgin the night she'd broken up with him, and so Brad didn't even want to think about how long that meant he'd gone without.

So the atmosphere was ripe when the woman named Misti—who was not his mom's age but much older than Brad (he guessed somewhere in her thirties)—got in the passenger side of his car. Before starting the engine, he asked her where she lived so he could head in the right direction.

He turned on the radio and a Godsmack tune was playing on the station. He turned the volume down, knowing most people could barely tolerate hard rock and heavy metal, but she said, "Oh, I *love* these guys."

He grinned. "You can turn it back up if you want."

"That's okay." She leaned her head back against the seat. "I don't know if you remember me, but I was at that jewelry party of your mom's in February."

Brad shook his head. "Sorry. I don't remember. There were a lot of people there for that."

"Yeah." She looked out the rolled-down window. "You have air conditioning?"

He laughed. "You're lookin' at it."

She chuckled and they were quiet for a few moments. "I noticed *you*, though."

Brad wasn't sure about the vibes he was getting from his mom's friend, but he looked back at her. She might have been older, but she was pretty. He wasn't sure how to respond, so he said, "What?"

"I noticed you, Brad. You're a kid, sure, but you are one good-lookin' guy. I think you'd just started dating that girl at the time, and your mom would come into work, saying she thought this girl was the one for you…until she told us you'd broken up with her."

He was feeling a little pissed that his mom felt the need to chat about his love life as though she were a gossip magazine. "I don't want to talk about it."

"Oh, I'm sorry. I didn't mean to upset you."

"It's…fine. I just don't want to talk about it."

She was quiet for a few minutes, and the radio station started playing a Foo Fighters song. "I don't want you to talk about it either. I just wondered if you'd be interested in hearing an offer."

"An offer?"

"Are you seeing anyone right now?"

Holy shit. His instincts were right. She was hitting on him. He was torn. Part of him wanted to continue to mope and feel sorry for himself, but the rest of him really wanted to feel a woman's body up next to his. It had been way too long. No, he didn't want anything emotional. He wasn't ready for that. But if this woman was offering a no-strings-attached fuck, he thought maybe he could be on board with that. Still, he didn't want to seem too eager, in case he was misreading her. "Why?"

"I think you might be a little fun, Bradley Payne." He took a deep breath but said nothing. He wasn't sure what to make of it. She turned the radio down a little more and asked, "How old are you, Brad?"

Fuck. She was honestly considering him, and he couldn't believe that he was giving it serious thought as well. He couldn't help the smile that crossed his face. This much older woman wanted to make sure she wouldn't be convicted of statutory rape. Well, he'd turned nineteen in

March. She had nothing to worry about. "Old enough."

She chuckled and he felt her fingers on his neck. "Wrong answer. How old are you?"

He rolled his eyes even though it was for no one's benefit. "Nineteen."

"Good." She reached over and turned the radio back up, resting her head on the back of the seat again, and Brad figured that was that. Maybe she'd hoped he was younger or maybe she decided she *needed* someone older. He'd never know. That was too bad, because he thought he might have taken her up on her offer.

When they got to her neighborhood, she told him the streets to turn down until he got to her apartment. "You wanna come in for a little bit?"

Maybe she wanted to play after all. "Yeah, sure."

Her apartment was on the second floor and she tripped once, giggling, so Brad held her arm to steady her. Maybe she was way too trashed to do anything. But when they got to her door, she pulled out her keys and she pulled him in by the hand. He started to look around once she had the light on so he could make conversation about something, but she opened her palm and slammed it into his chest, pushing him into the door. Before he could even catch up, her hands were in his hair, her tongue in his mouth. He couldn't quite tell what she'd been drinking, but it was strong. It wasn't beer or wine—it was something stronger. His cock started to perk up, but he tried to will it down. This woman was wasted, and he hadn't realized it at first. He couldn't fuck her right now, older woman or not.

She stopped kissing him, though, and took a couple of steps back. "Sorry, pretty aggressive." She grabbed his hand and led him toward the kitchen. "Can't help it, Bradley. I've had some pretty nasty thoughts about you." She turned on the kitchen light. "Want a drink?"

He was torn. If he had a drink, he wouldn't be able to go anywhere. He had work in the morning too, but it was late morning—ten. But it had been long, way too long, since he'd been inside a woman. Actually, that wasn't true. He'd had sex with girls. He'd never been with someone as old as Misti. He didn't think it would matter, but he was ready. He needed to get laid in the worst way. So he said, "Sure. What have you got?"

She turned around and gave him a wicked grin. "Well, if you promise not to tell your mom, I have beer and whiskey. Take your pick."

He could just imagine that conversation. "Yeah, mom, I fucked your coworker and drank some beer with her too." He grinned. He found it funny that she was more worried about his drinking than she was worried about having sex with her coworker's son. Of course, he supposed, underage drinking was illegal. Having sex with him wasn't. "Why the hell would I tell my mom?"

"I was hoping you'd say that, because I think me and you can have one hell of a party." She opened a cabinet and pulled out a bottle of whiskey. She opened another cabinet and set two glasses on the counter. "Would you grab a couple of ice cubes out of the freezer there?" He turned and opened the top door to the refrigerator, fetching out a handful of ice. When he reached her, she took his hand and held it over first one glass and tilted it and then the other, making sure she'd dropped all the ice in the glasses. Then she poured some whiskey over the ice. She handed one to him and kept one herself. It was merely a swallow. Brad took the glass and poured it down. No sense taking his time. Whiskey wasn't one of his favorite flavors, so getting it down was good enough.

She smiled and raised her eyebrows, then followed suit, slamming the liquor down.

Brad had barely set his glass back on the counter before she mauled him. As he tried to get his bearings, his first thought was to wonder why girls—young women *his* age— had never attacked him like that, but the thought was gone as his entire body responded to her assault. He was hard in seconds, something he might have found amusing because Misti was aggressive to the extreme. He probably should have been scared.

It happened too fast for him to be afraid, though. She had his cock out of his pants in short order, and before he knew it, she had him sitting in one of the chairs in the kitchen and was ready to jump on him. "Hold on a sec. You got a condom?"

"I'm on the pill. I can't get pregnant."

He felt like a fucking idiot and was surprised there was any rational thought left in his head. Still, he said, "That's not the only reason you use one."

She rolled her eyes. "Do you have one?"

"I might." He didn't remember the last time he'd actually needed one, but he was sure he had a couple in there. He'd wanted to be prepared in case Leah decided she was ready. He felt a moment of sadness which steeled his resolve, and he lifted his right cheek to pull out his wallet. Yep. Pay dirt. He barely had it out when Misti snatched it out of his fingers and ripped the package open. She maneuvered it over his cock and then slid him inside her before he could even register what was happening. He couldn't even remember her taking her jeans and panties off.

But, God, did she feel incredible. He knew he had to prolong climax as long as possible and he wasn't sure how, because he hadn't felt this good in a long time. His eyes were closed and he tried to focus on everything *except* the insane sensations below. He couldn't even tell if she was close. She leaned back and stuck two fingers between them and started rubbing herself. In no time, she was crying out, clenching against his dick, and then he knew it was safe to let himself go.

It felt like his brains were flying out of his cock. He realized his fingers were pressed into her back as he got his bearings again. His breathing started to slow. She grinned and sat up, and it sent a shiver clear through to his balls. "Rest up, big fella, because I'm not done with you."

He didn't know if he should run out of there, afraid for his life, or get down on his knees and say a prayer of thanks.

But he stayed.

CHAPTER SIX

THE GUYS IN the band were jealous when they found out Brad was boning an older woman who was hornier than hell. He felt more confident sexually than he ever had, and she gave him suggestions once in a while. She was sweet about it, but he could take a hint, and he felt like his time with her was making him a better lover.

He finally got his first tattoos that summer—he started with a half sleeve down his right arm. That was pretty expensive, so after that he just had some of his song lyrics tattooed on his left shoulder. Then he started banking his money, saving up for things for the band. His mom was nice enough to let him continue living with her. He knew why, though. It was a huge two-story, four-bedroom house that would have felt too empty. She didn't charge him rent, either, but Brad made sure he continued doing chores so he kind of earned his keep.

And he lined up a few gigs for the band. He wasn't able to schedule as many as he would have liked and all but one were out of town, but it gave them some practice in front of an audience, and the experience was invaluable. Playing onstage was so different from fucking around in his garage. Even when they'd played entire sets together, it was nothing like doing it live. They couldn't simply stop when something wasn't right. They had to keep going, push through the mistakes, recover, go on. And the energy was exhilarating. Brad didn't understand why Ethan felt the need to get stoned before going onstage. His friend was missing some of the best highs he could imagine. They also met some great bands to network with.

Brad felt like he was laying solid groundwork for the future. He imagined these bands would help his own band go further in the future. He'd already landed two gigs thanks to other bands. The band he felt the most solid connection to was a band out of Denver called Last Five Seconds. They were good guys with a hardcore sound, and Brad was surprised they hadn't made it already. All he could figure was that they just hadn't been heard by the right people.

Ethan didn't get to know any of the bands, though, even when they partied together, because the guy was taking his chemical dependency to new levels. Brad started to worry and considered talking to June about it, but he knew that would only make Ethan worse. He knew, because they'd been there before. The previous summer had been almost as bad, but when school started, Ethan managed to keep his partying confined to weekends only. Brad hoped having to attend college in the fall would have the same effect. In the meantime, he did his best to keep Ethan upright and away from the worst stuff. He now regretted the time last fall he and his friend had tried meth together, because it was something Ethan played with now and again. Brad never thought there would be a day he'd be glad to see his friend taking heroin, but it was better than meth and crack. Ethan seemed to prefer the drugs that made him mellow, anyway, and meth didn't work that way.

By August, he felt like he was completely over Leah. Part of him would always care about her, but he no longer felt sad. He was having the time of his life, because Misti only wanted him for sex. She didn't want a relationship. That opened the door to occasional other girls who just wanted a little fun with a guy who could sling an axe. He finally discovered the secret—sex, lots of it, was the cure for a broken heart. Did he feel a little empty? Yeah, but he was willing to pay the price. As one of Bullet's frontmen, the confidence he was gaining by becoming a master in the bedroom was priceless.

He still wasn't cocky, though. That wasn't his bag. It was a quiet confidence. He had no need to get in people's faces about how good he felt about himself. There was no need. But it was an attitude that drove him forward, and he saw results in his day-to-day life. More women approached him than ever had before, many of them older (but not to the extreme like Misti), and he got a large raise at work, where he was now employed full time. His newfound confidence and what he almost considered luck made him more determined than ever to make his band work. Bullet was going to make it big if it was the last thing he'd ever do.

Late August, Ethan and Zane left for school. Brad felt a little discouraged, but his friends had promised to return home when needed. Brad had gigs lined up in September, October, and November, and he'd even managed to land two during their Christmas break. The guys promised to practice at school, especially right before shows, and they'd try to come home occasionally to get together to practice and maybe even try on some new stuff. They'd find a way to make it work, and Brad hoped that maybe before next summer, they'd have a record contract, and then Ethan and Zane's families would see that they had a future in music.

Fall seemed to come quickly, faster than it ever had when he'd been in school, and—as promised—Zane and Ethan showed up for their gigs in spite of being in school. The nice thing was they were making a little cash, and Brad figured that had to be an incentive as well. He'd been watching other bands make money with merch tables, so he planned to invest in t-shirts (now that he'd made a logo), stickers, and other stuff, and he hoped they could record an EP in the spring. First, though, more amps. Living at home and working full-time made it easy to save up and buy things for the band. When he wasn't working, he was doing something band related. He was almost obsessed, but he was driven. He was determined to make it work. He was not going to be a fucking lube tech his entire life.

Girls weren't as important, either. Yeah, he was getting laid on a regular basis now, but he'd managed to keep his heart from getting snagged. His goal wasn't to be a heartbreaker either, so he tried to be upfront with girls, letting them know he wasn't ready for a relationship. Most of them seemed okay with it, and those who weren't, he didn't pursue at all, because he didn't want to hurt anyone. He'd been there himself and didn't want to do it to someone else.

He and Misti fizzled out sometime early October. She got back together with an old boyfriend and told Brad she was sorry for letting him down. He tried to assure her that he was okay, but she acted nervous that now he'd go tell his mother. Part of him felt relieved because it was often awkward. On occasion, though, she'd still buy him liquor if he wanted it, and that, he supposed, was a great payoff from the relationship.

He knew he'd gotten more out of it, though, and if he hadn't felt like it would make him look stupid, he would have profusely thanked Misti.

At Thanksgiving, Ethan and Zane hung out for several days before heading back to college. Ethan started talking about some girl he'd met at school, and Brad worried at first. He was angry that he felt that way, because part of him was anxious that a girl was going to take his best friend away from him, make his friend no longer interested in making music or even coming home. But the more he, Ethan, and Zane talked, the more he realized that this girl was just a friend…or at least Ethan played it off that way.

"Anyway, she keeps pestering me about seeing the band, so I'm gonna see if she wants to come home with us next weekend."

Zane said, "Dude, we're coming home next weekend? You know it's finals week after that, right?"

Ethan sneered. "Like you give a shit?"

Zane started laughing. "Right. But if I'm here practicing and partying with you guys, my parents are gonna know I'm not studying my ass off for finals."

"So? Do you really care?"

Zane shrugged. "No, but I feel like I should since they're spending money on it."

"You study enough while you're there. You're getting Cs, right?"

"Mostly."

Brad shook his head. "No problem if you guys want to wait till after finals. I hear college tests are a bitch."

Ethan smiled. "Like *I* give a shit. Yeah, so, my grandpa's paying for it. I told him I didn't want to go, but that if he was going to make me do it, fine. I'd do it. I'm showing up for classes, and I'm trying to study, but damned if it's gonna ruin a good weekend."

"Whatever. I'm here no matter what."

"So, like I was saying, I'm gonna see if Valerie wants to come home with us next weekend. I think you'd like her. She's a total metalhead, but she doesn't look like it at all. Well, in all fairness, she was able to pull it off when we went to a concert earlier this month. She's a nice girl, though. There aren't many of us there, if you catch my drift, so she's cool."

"You still want to practice then?"

"Yeah...she wants to see us play, so we *should*."

"Works for me." Brad had no idea that meeting Ethan's new friend would change the entire course of the rest of his life.

The first weekend of December arrived, and, with it, snow and cold. Brad was finally feeling like a real man, not just a kid trapped in a man's body. It had been a long, hard year, but he'd made the transition. He felt ready for anything. He wanted to take on the world. He knew he simply had to hold out for a few more months and then he and Bullet could make a real go of it. He knew living in this little burg wasn't helping. They needed to get out where there were more people. Sure, they could post a few YouTube videos, but there was nothing like a live audience. He knew that would be their key to success.

By the time Brad got off work that Friday late afternoon, he hadn't heard from Ethan. His friend had said he was going to call when he got home from school so they could arrange meeting that night. It had started snowing sometime around noon, though, so he wondered if maybe they'd decided to wait it out. He called Ethan's cell phone so he'd know if he should expect him or not.

Ethan answered after one ring. "Hey, dude. How's it going?"

"Hey, man. Fine."

"You know that friend I told you about?"

"Yeah. You guys come home?"

"Yeah. We're here, and she's here with us."

"Cool. So you wanna get together, do some practicing?"

"Hell, yeah."

"We have a couple shows later this month and next, so we have a lot of work to do. Nick should be free after six. You wanna plan for seven?"

"Sounds good."

Brad hung up. That gave him a couple hours to shower, eat some dinner, and do some much needed guitar maintenance. Tonight, Bullet would be performing for an audience of one, and he planned to treat it like a real show…so he had to be ready and at the top of his game.

CHAPTER SEVEN

BRAD HADN'T QUITE known what to expect when Ethan and his new friend arrived, but he hadn't expected *her*. She was outgoing and friendly, but there was something about her. She looked nothing like Leah, but she reminded him of her just the same. He couldn't quite figure out why, but that wasn't good. He was drawn to her from the second he laid eyes on her.

The only saving grace was that Ethan had talked of her only as a *friend*. He hadn't indicated any attraction whatsoever. In fact, Ethan had been bragging over Thanksgiving break about all the college pussy he'd been getting, so Brad was pretty sure this young woman was off the guy's radar.

They'd made their way through perfunctory greetings, but all of them headed to the garage, eager to play. They hadn't been able to practice as much over Thanksgiving break as they'd hoped, and now they could get in some solid time to prepare for their shows later in the month.

Their last practice session had sucked balls anyway, so Brad was hoping this one would help them hone and polish some songs.

The other guys were plugging in and setting up, something Brad had done an hour earlier, so after he'd shown Ethan's friend where she could sit to watch them play, he decided he needed to talk to her. Jesus Christ, was she cute. She had long brown hair and bluish-green eyes. She wasn't overly tall, but she was stacked. She seemed oblivious to how attractive she was, though, which drew Brad to her all the more. That was a definite Leah quality. There was something about this girl…*something*. It was inexplicable, but he wasn't going to question it. He hadn't felt this way about a girl *since* Leah, and it was a nice feeling, unlike the coldness he'd been growing accustomed to.

"Valerie, right? Ethan's told me so much about you. I feel like I already know you." She smiled, and then her eyes drifted toward his half-sleeve tattoo. He'd worn a sleeveless shirt after getting out of the shower, probably a stupid move since they'd be hanging out in the cool garage, but he liked showing off his tats whenever he could. He hadn't gotten them to hide them. He *wanted* people to look. So when he took Valerie's hand to shake it after she started nodding, he said, "Like the ink?"

Oh, that was even cuter. Her cheeks turned pink. She had no idea she had nothing to be embarrassed about. "Yeah."

God, he had to let go of her hand, but he didn't want to. He felt connected to her somehow. Yeah, it made no sense, and he could have kicked himself. He suspected it was because she was so much like Leah…only better.

*   *   *

They spent the next hour playing their hearts out for Val. Brad had warned her that neither he nor Ethan had good enough vocal chops, and maybe that was the next thing Brad should work on. For now, though, he hoped warning her would allow her to forgive their rough edges. In terms of music, he knew his guitar playing would rival anyone's.

Still, they'd played a mix of all their original songs as well as a lot of their favorite covers, and Brad could tell Valerie really was a metalhead when he caught her singing along, first to Judas Priest's "Heavy Duty/ Defenders of the Faith" (sung by Ethan) and next when he saw her mouthing the words to Marilyn Manson's "Coma White" (that he sang).

Brad treated Valerie like he would have any girl who'd be sitting in the front row. He wasn't stupid; he knew that sometimes it wasn't just the music when it came to females. Sometimes it was also sex appeal. He'd been working on that. In this young lady's case, there was even more to it than that, but she didn't have to know that. He was glad he'd been working on that since June—opening up to the audience, making eye contact. Ethan had somehow managed to do the exact opposite. He'd get onstage and look inward. Lots of people thought it was because Ethan was completely absorbed in his music, and Brad knew that was part of it. He knew his friend well, though, and he knew that wasn't all of it. Ethan was not a stage person. He wanted to share his music with the world, but he wasn't comfortable with people watching. It had taken Brad a while to figure it out. That was part of why Ethan would indulge before every single damn concert. The music was salvation for Ethan too, so he wished he could find a way to get his friend to slow down. At the rate he was going, he was gonna kill himself.

Tonight, though, Brad's thoughts were not with his best friend, who, amazingly, appeared to be quite sober. He was tense, but that was nothing new. No…Brad had taken it up a notch tonight. Everything he'd been practicing for months he was using full force on Ethan's friend, and it appeared to be working. He loved the look in her eyes. At first, she'd seemed embarrassed, pulling her lower lip into her mouth and holding it in with her teeth or blinking a few times and then looking down into her lap. But in that short time, he felt like they were making some kind of connection. He even winked at her once, confirming that they had shared some kind of moment, and she blushed again and smiled and then turned her attention to watching some of the other guys. Probably a good idea.

He noticed something else too. She kept looking over at Ethan, but his friend was off in his own little world. When he wasn't high on something, Ethan's next best defense against the overwhelming sensations he felt was drowning in his guitar. She was hoping to get his attention, maybe so she could pretend there wasn't something magnetic between her and Brad. And he realized that Valerie had some pretty strong feelings for Ethan…but he was pretty sure Ethan didn't feel the same way. He'd seen Ethan with girls, and he could tell that Ethan wasn't reciprocating whatever it was Valerie was feeling. In fact, Ethan had turned something off inside after he'd caught Heidi cheating on him for the last time. It was worse than what

Brad had done after Leah. It was like Ethan was putting a permanent lid on his heart. It was too bad for this girl he'd brought home from school. But Brad couldn't feel sorry for her, because that meant he was free to make a move.

They finished playing, close to an hour later, and Brad knew it was chilly in the garage because, in spite of the two space heaters they had blowing full blast, Valerie continued to hold her coat tightly around herself. He didn't feel a thing, though, and was probably on the verge of perspiring. Someone who'd never performed like they did would probably never understand, but he worked hard, and that exertion kept him plenty warm.

He and his three bandmates set their instruments (or drumsticks) down and looked at Val in anticipation. Brad wanted to know what she thought, but he knew all of them were eager to hear her opinion. His hope was that she'd be honest. They got plenty of praise from friends and girls who'd drooled over them, so an honest voice would be refreshing. Then again, the way she seemed to adore Ethan, she might not want to hurt his feelings. She might only say nice things too. He was hoping, though, that she'd know that anything constructive she had to say would be taken seriously.

Ethan grinned at her, finally his old self. "So, Val, what do you think?"

"Well..." Val had a concerned look on her face. Oh, fuck. He'd wanted honest but not painful. "I don't know how to tell you this, but—" He prepared himself for the worst. Well, maybe she'd have something to say that they could use to improve. He had to hope. But then she got a huge grin on her face, and Brad felt his spirits lift. "You guys are—*fucking fantastic!*" As if she hadn't meant to go that far, she covered her mouth, raising her eyebrows. That was cuter than hell. Maybe she didn't feel comfortable swearing in front of them, but he didn't understand why, considering they'd been singing curses all night long. She was Ethan's friend—surely, she knew he—and his friends—talked that way constantly.

They all started laughing, mostly from relief. Ethan grabbed Val, picking her up out of the chair and twirling her around. Oh, that feeling in Brad's chest wasn't good. He was already aching for this young woman, and he'd only met her a little over an hour ago. What the fuck was wrong with him? It was stupid, but he knew this much: he should *not* be feeling jealous about Ethan's friendship with her. She obviously had some strong feelings for his friend and Brad had to accept that.

Ethan stopped spinning her around, letting her stand. "You little shit. You had me fooled there for a second." Laughing, he asked, "Are you serious, though? Do you really like our sound?"

She had a twinkle in her eye, but Brad could tell she was being sincere. "Of course, I do. You guys will go so far if you keep playing like that. And you can play for *me* anytime."

Brad couldn't help letting out a howl. "Good. I told my mom and dad someone would like our stuff. My dad asked what mom said and before I could even answer, he said it was a sound even a mother couldn't love. Thanks for proving him wrong, Val."

Zane had already picked up his instrument again and played a mean bassline. "*We* like it, and that's all that counts." He grinned and put it down again, shoving his hands in the pockets of his jeans.

Brad was inspired. He knew a way to not only endear himself to this beautiful young woman, but he wanted to have some fun with her, and no one would be the wiser. He couldn't help the smile that spread over his face when he said, "Hey, Valerie. I saw you mouthing the words to all the covers. Would you like to sing one?"

The look on her face said it all. Part of her wanted to say no, but Brad could tell she was tempted to say yes. Still, she laughed, waving her hands in front of herself. "No, that's okay."

She simply needed a little encouragement. "I'm serious. You could give our vocal cords a rest."

Ethan got a huge grin on his face, draping an arm around her. "Besides, you said you'd always fantasized about being on stage."

She looked like she was starting to cave, but she continued to protest. "Well, I don't know. Both your voices are a lot better than mine."

And that's when Brad knew she was full of shit. He knew he and Ethan both needed work in the vocal department. Sure, they didn't suck, but the only way this girl could have a worse voice was if she was tone deaf. He doubted it. People who were tone deaf usually figured it out and stuck to singing out loud only when in a car by themselves. So he wanted to urge her one more time. He could tell she wanted to. "No excuse, Val. Come on." He was getting ready to get Nick and Zane on board too, but he couldn't stop looking at Val. She took them all in, though, as if to make sure everyone was okay with it.

It was simple, though. "Okay." Brad and Ethan high fived as though they'd won a championship game. Val added quickly, "But only one song."

He was cool with that. "Of course."

Zane leaned forward. He knew Val probably as well as Ethan, so it was good to have him on board. He asked, "What do you want us to play?"

She stood in thought for a few seconds and finally said, "No idea."

Brad didn't want to lose her now, just because she couldn't think of anything to sing. He slid his guitar strap over his head and asked, "How do you feel about Korn?"

"I like 'em."

"Name anything you could sing off one of their first four CDs." Ethan gave him a look. "What? I can play any one of 'em."

Ethan was staring him down. "*I* can't." He turned to Val, and she gave him all her attention. "Know 'Moon Baby' by Godsmack?"

"Yeah."

"Would you feel comfortable singing it?"

"I think so."

"You know the words?"

"Yep."

"You heard the woman."

It had happened so fast, Brad didn't realize what was going on until it was too late. Ethan had slid his guitar strap over his head, so Zane followed suit with his bass and Nick trotted the few steps back to his drum kit. Of all the songs they knew, Ethan knew damned good and well "Moon Baby" only needed one guitar. Sure, Brad could be a lame ass and echo, but no way. He knew Ethan liked to mix songs up and change them, and no way was Brad going to look like an amateur next to his friend. So he instead slid the mike out of the stand and offered it to Valerie like a present. Once she took it, he propped his guitar against the wall and sat in Val's now-empty chair.

It gave him an excuse to return the favor. This woman had been trading glances with him for the better part of an hour, and he'd enjoyed the hell out of it. He wanted to see her in action.

She was amazing. Brad wondered why she'd been so full of doubts and fears. She had a strong voice, loud and powerful yet sweet and smooth like an angel's. And once she started, there was no hesitation. She sang as though she'd been doing it her whole life.

Goddamn. That made her sexy in Brad's eyes. She was feeling the music, and when she would close her eyes at certain spots in the song, she never lost the strength. It got Brad to thinking, thinking about other possibilities, but those thoughts would stay tucked in the back of his mind a little while longer.

CHAPTER EIGHT

BRAD MIGHT HAVE been able to keep one set of thoughts at bay, but another—that of his growing attraction to Valerie—he wasn't able to deny. Ethan began playing the solo at the end of "Moon Baby," but he went off on his own musical tangent. Typical Ethan, but the guy usually managed to pull it off in a spectacular way.

Val slid the mike back into the stand and moved beside the chair Brad was sitting in to watch Ethan's mad solo. Brad couldn't resist. He wanted to find a way to acknowledge the insane attraction he was feeling, so when she glanced over at him, his smile was wide and he patted his knee, offering her his leg as a seat. God…if she took him up on it, he'd die. But she didn't. The look was all over her face—no way would she do something like that in front of Ethan.

Brad wasn't about to become a supreme asshole, though, so he stood up. "Seriously, go ahead and have a seat." He waved his hand toward the chair.

But she refused. "No, really, I'm good." Well, no way in hell was he gonna sit down again, so he stood next to her watching Ethan journey through a long but bad ass guitar solo. It was hard just standing next to her. He wanted to talk to her, ask her about what she liked and disliked, what her fears were, her hopes and dreams. He wanted to ask her the qualities of her ideal man, because he wanted to give it a shot.

What the hell was wrong with him?

Ethan finally finished, and it seemed an insane amount of time later. But everyone congratulated him just the same. He really was an incredible guitarist, and he always put off a cocky vibe. If Brad didn't know his friend as well as he did, he would have hated the guy, but deep down Brad knew Ethan was insecure and unsure. The arrogant act was just that—an act. And Ethan would often showboat as a way to gain a little bit of praise, because he was typically the guy who got none.

When they were done, they shut off the space heaters and went to the kitchen. Val managed to sit between Zane and Ethan, and Brad understood why. They were already her friends, and she was comfortable with them. It was okay. Brad knew he'd been coming on too strong, and it was time to back off. He got them all sodas out of the fridge and talked a little band talk but spent more time answering Val's questions. She wanted to know about their plans, yeah, but even more, she asked questions about their favorite instruments, who'd influenced them musically, things like that.

She asked, "What inspires the words you write?"

Ethan answered first. "Brad and I write the lyrics, and

so I know he's different. I usually pick a theme and just run with it. I think of my words as kinda in the Kurt Cobain vein, if that makes any sense. You listen and listen, and then it starts to make sense in a universal kind of way. I think Brad's are a lot more personal."

Val looked over at him. He wondered why she was so curious about the lyrics, but he didn't mind answering. "Yeah, they are. They usually center around something that is happening or has happened to me—they're usually emotional."

"Really?" Was she teasing him?

He smiled. God, he would have loved to be having this conversation alone with her, and then he wanted to kick himself. He was irrationally attracted to her. It made no sense whatsoever. Still…he was drawn to her. She was a flame and he had grown wings, a moth attracted to her, no matter the potential danger. "Really."

"I don't know if I'd admit that out loud."

"Why?"

Ethan started laughing. "'Cause you're a pussy, man…whining about some girl who broke your heart."

Brad took it in stride. He knew Ethan was teasing him, and it wasn't his friend's fault that he had some ridiculous attraction to the girl at the table he didn't want to look stupid in front of. "Fuck you."

"Not very metal, dude."

"Yeah. Fuck you anyway." They all started laughing, Val included. Brad thought she was the perfect addition to their group. They only stayed a few minutes longer, because Ethan hadn't seen his mom yet and was antsy, worried about her. Zane and Nick left when they did, leaving Brad by himself.

What really pissed him off was that he couldn't get to sleep that night. He finally got out of bed and went downstairs, turning on the computer in his mom's office. He went to Ethan's Facebook page, because he was pretty sure Val would have to be listed as one of his friends. She was. He couldn't believe he was acting like such a stalker, but he couldn't stop thinking about her. He wanted to know everything about her that he could. It wasn't simply because she reminded him of Leah. No, she reminded him of more than Leah. Sure, she was sweet and innocent and fresh faced like Leah, but the similarities ended there. Val seemed to have a bigger sense of humor. Add to that, she loved metal music. Leah hadn't liked it much at all. And Val wasn't some poseur who'd decided to pretend on a whim to like it to gain Ethan's affections. They'd talked enough for him to know. Well, that and she knew all the covers they did, and she sang all of "Moon Baby" from memory.

He almost got hard thinking about it again.

But he looked at her profile, and he figured he was able to view it because she was a friend of a friend. He considered clicking the *Add Friend* button and then figured he'd definitely look like a goddamn stalker. No, he hadn't even known her twelve hours yet. That shit could wait. But he wanted to know more about her. Sure enough, she had dozens of hardcore band pages that she followed. She had a brother named Danny. Her birthday was in August, and she was from a tiny Colorado town near the front range, a place called Winchester. Brad had never been there before. Then again, he hadn't been to too many places in

Colorado since his parents had split up.

He looked at a few of her pictures and then felt guilty and ashamed, like he was invading her privacy. He shook his head and shut the computer down, and then snuck a beer out of the fridge. He went upstairs and nursed the beer, thinking about Valerie until early morning.

Everyone arrived back at his house by two-thirty Saturday afternoon. Brad had managed to sleep till noon and felt better than he'd expected after not sleeping through most of the night. He was feeling less guilty about scoping out Val's profile, and he wasn't going to say a word about it. No one would ever know.

He'd been hoping he'd feel a little less drawn to her, but no such luck. That was okay, though, because they were just going to be practicing and playing. He'd be able to tend to music instead of her so much…or so he hoped.

They played for a couple of hours, taking breaks here and there, reworking things. More than once, Ethan asked Val, "You're not bored, are you?"

She'd shake her head and say, "No, not even. This is fascinating."

Brad couldn't tell if she was humoring Ethan or if, again, it was because she liked being with him and didn't care what he was doing. Brad didn't mind, because the longer he was around Val, the more he liked her.

What astonished Brad was how completely oblivious Ethan was to Val's obvious infatuation for the guy. He'd thought about it last night, but even so he felt like he'd have to talk to his friend alone sometime after the weekend, just to get Ethan's blessing before pursuing Valerie.

Then they played for a long stretch—one song that needed a lot of work. They hadn't practiced it much and they wanted it road worthy by the next month. Yeah, they could and did practice alone, but it wasn't the same as when they worked together. They decided then to take another break, and that's when Brad remembered the stash of goodies he'd asked Misti to buy for him earlier in the week. He wiped some sweat off his brow and walked across the garage. "Hey, guys, I can't believe I didn't show you this shit already." He moved a couple of boxes, opening one and producing a large bottle of rum. He saw Nick's eyes grow wide in anticipation, but Ethan wasn't impressed. That was okay. He knew his friend would still party, even if he didn't appreciate Brad's abilities. "And I've got two twelve-packs of Coke chillin' in the fridge." He walked back over to the group, lowering his voice. "Mom's working tonight…leaves around six-thirty, so we can get fuckin' wasted."

Ethan slid his guitar so it hung on his back, and Brad could almost see the guy's hackles rise. "Wait a minute. Do you even drink, Val?"

She acted demure. "Umm…" She smiled sweetly. "I can be your designated driver."

"Perfect."

Brad put the bottle back in its hiding place, rejoining the group. Ethan said, "Guys, there's something I've been meaning to tell you." He took a breath, and Brad was curious. "There's a reason why Val's our designated driver. She's fucking brilliant. And I hate to even admit it, but she figured out something none of us other numbnuts did. The name *Bullet*? Fucking cool, right?"

"Hell, yeah." Bullet was the name Brad wanted, the one he had pressed the guys to adopt.

"Yeah...and it's taken."

Brad was not amused. "So? I've never heard of 'em, so what?"

"Do you *really* want somebody's sloppy seconds?"

Brad laughed. "Fuck...not when you put it that way."

"Exactly. So...close your eyes and tell me...what do you think of *Fully Automatic*?"

Brad got quiet and let the words tumble around his head. Suddenly, the perfect band name was gone, gone in a flash. He saw Nick nod his head out of the corner of his eye, but he wasn't sold yet. He had to let it roll around for a few moments. *Bullet* had been perfect—bad ass, hardcore, dangerous, and in your face. *Fully Automatic* seemed to try to catch that vibe. It hadn't grown on him yet, but he could see the possibilities. "Yeah...that'll work."

"You don't sound convinced."

"I just need some time to try it on...know what I mean?"

"Yeah, that's cool, man."

Brad slapped him on the back. "Damn straight."

"So let's work out this next song." They started working on the next one on their list, going through the process that they had before. He and Ethan had both brought songs to the band, but the last couple they'd written entirely together—the process was organic and fluid, and Brad started wondering if he'd ever want to do it any other way again. The music was damn near perfect, and so it was time to start working on the lyrics. Zane and Nick were perfecting the percussion for the song, letting Ethan and Brad write the words. The two sat on lawn chairs and Val sat next to them, not saying a word.

"I can't help myself, baby, / The way you look at me. / You got me dead to rights, so damn helpless. / Why can't you just let me be?"

"Fuck, yeah," Ethan said, as Brad jotted the words down on a piece of paper.

"So I fall on my knees," Ethan offered.

"Down on my knees...how's that?"

Ethan said, "Yeah, yeah...that's good, and it rhymes with *me* too." Brad nodded, making more notes on the page. "Oh...this is better: 'I'm begging you please'."

"Yeah."

Val cleared her throat and sat up straight. "Um...guys...can I give you a suggestion?"

Ethan said, "Uh...sure." He didn't seem so sure to Brad, though.

Val took a deep breath, seeming to steel herself, but her voice was honey. "Your music is awesome. It's so original. Some of the words here, though...they're kind of..."

Fuck. Brad knew exactly what she was thinking. He might as well admit what he already knew. "Generic." He frowned while Val nodded her head. "Yeah, you're right." He looked at Ethan and then Val. "Any ideas?"

She twisted her mouth up, and he thought she was going to shrug and leave it at that, but then he saw her eyes light up. "Your words are a knife that twist with every breath."

Ethan smiled. "That's—"

Brad liked it. It was fresh, different. "Wow. Not perfect, but...I like the metaphor." He picked up the pencil again. "Do you care if I use it...even if we change it a bit?"

She grinned at him, and he loved that it was a smile just for him. "No…please." Ethan didn't really like it, but Brad knew he could get his friend to see the light. All of a sudden, it was like Val's suggestion had opened the flood gates. That one little phrase offered them untold possibilities, and Brad wanted to explore them. They ran with it, reworking the lyrics from scratch and creating a song filled with emotion, meaning, and layers. Brad was convinced it was the most powerful song—lyrically—that his band had ever written. It was a great way to celebrate the band's rebirth as Fully Automatic. Even Ethan was satisfied by the time they were done.

Brad's mom appeared in the garage wearing scrubs. She kissed Brad on the cheek and noticed Val. "I thought it was just the boys tonight."

"Oh, mom, this is Ethan and Zane's friend from college—Valerie Quinn."

"Nice to meet you, Valerie. I'm Barbara. Now, Brad, there's some leftover turkey and mashed potatoes in the fridge. I wouldn't complain if you all ate it. Just put the dishes in the dishwasher, please."

Ethan said, "Thanks, Mrs. P."

"I need to hurry. Apparently, there are already three women checked in who will probably give birth tonight during my shift. So don't worry if I'm home later than usual."

"I won't, mom."

"Have fun. Oh, and there are some DVDs in the living room if you want to watch a movie."

Brad's mother leaving was their cue to head out of the

garage and let the party begin. They'd worked hard and now it was time to have fun. Brad hoped he'd be able to spend a little more time getting to know Valerie before Ethan whisked her back off to college and out of his sight.

CHAPTER NINE

AFTER EATING DINNER, the five of them went in the living room to watch a horror movie. It was partially just background noise, because they continued to talk while it was playing. Brad decided it was time to get the party started and asked Nick to help. Brad fetched the Coke and rum, while Nick brought in five glasses filled with ice. Brad poured rum in four glasses, but before pouring any in the fifth, he made eye contact with Val and asked, "Sure you don't want just a little? Just enough to get a little buzz?"

Ethan, sitting next to Val on the couch, pried his eyes off the TV and said to her, "You don't have to if you don't want to."

She smiled at Ethan as though to humor him, but Brad couldn't help but notice that when her eyes returned to him, she seemed to be giving him a huge green light. "Sure…just a little, though. I'm the driver, remember?"

Brad laughed and said, "Okay." Then he poured a small amount in Val's glass, just so she wouldn't feel left out. It was barely a quarter of an inch, and if she even got a buzz off it, he'd be surprised. Then he topped them all off with Coke and slid the glasses so that each person had one in front of him...or her. "Bottoms up."

All the guys didn't hesitate, downing most of their drinks in the first try. Ethan looked irritated. "You shouldn't have put ice in 'em, Bradley. It's harder to drink."

His friend had no idea that oftentimes Brad did what he could to slow Ethan down, but he said, "I thought, since we were in the company of a lady, that we should show a little restraint." He looked over at Val.

"Yeah. Whatever. Top me off, pussy."

Brad handed the bottle to Ethan. "Do it yourself, cocksucker."

"Don't mind if I do."

The tension started to dissipate as they all turned their eyes toward the movie. Brad finally took a place on the couch on the other side of Val. How could he help it that it wasn't such a big couch, and his leg just so happened to touch hers?

God, he had it bad, and he needed to chill the fuck out. If he couldn't rein himself in, he'd scare her off for good.

The guys kept passing the bottle, but Val had only had a sip or two of her drink. Brad was going to give her a while and then offer her a straight Coke. She might have simply wanted to take her time, fearing an insane buzz, especially since she planned to drive, so he didn't want to push her.

Ethan kept saying things quietly to Val, causing her to giggle. Brad couldn't catch it all at first, but then he realized Ethan was making fun of the movie. Brad poured another shot and closed his eyes, letting it make its way to his belly.

He could see that Val and Ethan already had a pretty solid friendship, but he could tell just by looking at his friend that he had no romantic tendencies toward the girl. Brad would never say it, but he knew his friend well, and Ethan tended to prefer girls who put off a slutty vibe. Val was the exact opposite. She felt pure and sweet, nothing like the girls Ethan liked to date.

Maybe that was lucky for Brad.

He heard Ethan say, "Academy Award winning performance right there." Both Val and Nick, sitting on the floor in front of the coffee table, started laughing. That's when Brad realized he hadn't been paying any attention to the movie.

After the laughter died down, Ethan leaned forward and grabbed a Coke out of the soda box on the coffee table. He popped it open and turned to Val. "How about you trade me your drink for a straight Coke?" She smiled and handed him her glass, taking the can of Coke from him. Ethan slammed her drink down and said something else to Val, something Brad couldn't understand, and that's when he felt the first pangs of jealousy. He knew he had no right to feel anything for this girl, but he did, and he felt like Ethan was just leading her on. Surely, his friend knew Val was sick in love with him. How could he not see it?

Nick let out a long drunk giggle. "Oh, shit. This girl's gonna get killed."

Zane joined in. "Yeah...we saw her tits five minutes ago. Of course, she's gonna die."

Even though Brad hadn't been paying attention to the movie, he knew the formula of which they spoke. Val sat up and Brad loved the look on her face. "Why is it that they always make these girls so dumb? Why does she have to trip and act stupid? Instead of going back the way she came or following the trail, she's disappearing deeper into the woods where she's going to die."

That simply made Nick laugh harder. "You have a problem with that?"

Zane said, "I don't, as long as I get to see her goodies."

Val was beginning to act genuinely upset. "Real girls aren't like that."

It was just a movie, and Brad wanted Val to enjoy herself. She was hating the movie, and so he wanted to pull her attention away from it. Well, that and he had other motives. He got closer to her and put his arm around her shoulders. Yeah, so maybe the rum was helping his boldness. He didn't care. It was now or never. "Know what, Val? You're cool. Ethan has class when it comes to women." So that wasn't exactly true. In this case it was, but he wasn't about to tell Val about his friend's track record.

Zane overheard, though, and had to add his two cents' worth. "Correction. Remember Mary...*the mouth*?"

"Oh, fuck, yeah!" Nick lost it, lying on the carpet and holding his stomach. He broke out into an unstoppable gale of laughter.

Ethan's eyes looked like those of a Rottweiler ready to bite. "Can we change the subject?"

Zane, however, couldn't help himself. "I kinda liked her mouth."

Brad was feeling too good to be pissed that they were fucking up his moves. He wasn't about to give up, though, and maybe he could take some heat off Ethan too. "I just wanted to say Val was cool. I didn't want to get you guys started talking about Ethan's old girlfriends."

Ethan slammed the rum in his glass and poured more. Zane just couldn't let it go. "I want a girlfriend like that."

"Shut the fuck up, man."

Zane returned his attention to his drink, and Brad decided to try another tactic. Everyone seemed ready to watch the movie again, so Brad dropped his voice so that no one else could jump on whatever it was he wanted to tell Val next. "I'm glad you and Ethan are friends."

Finally. She looked over at him. At first, she simply looked like her sweet self, but then he saw something in her face change. That's when he knew the attraction was mutual. It *wasn't* just him. If he'd thought he could get away with it, he would have lowered his lips to hers right there and started kissing her, but he knew that couldn't happen. Besides, a girl like Val might not be able to handle a guy coming on that strongly, and he didn't want to scare her off.

Nick started laughing again and yelling something else at the TV, but Brad tried to tune him out. Now that he had Val's attention, he wasn't going to let her off the hook so easily. He made sure his voice was quiet enough so no one else would hear. "So…are you and Ethan dating or not? Are you boyfriend and girlfriend? He won't say dick about it, and I can't tell." Granted, he hadn't outright asked his friend, but he could tell by looking at Ethan how his friend felt about Val. He wanted to know if Ethan was stringing her along, though, and the only way to do that was to ask her.

He felt even more encouraged when she spoke.

"I...uh...don't think he considers us that." That's when he knew he had a solid chance. What was killing him was that he knew Val was as attracted to him as he was to her, but she felt some kind of weird loyalty to his best friend. He'd thought maybe if...but no. She had eyes for Ethan. So when she stood up, he let her go. "I...um...need a glass of water. Can I get anyone anything?"

No one answered, but Brad shook his head. God, that was disappointing. Maybe he *had* been coming on strong, but he'd always been so good at reading signals. She *was* interested—he was certain of that. So why was she running?

He sat there for a few moments, feeling empty. He must have been losing his touch. And he felt like this was his only chance with this girl. His *only* chance. When she and Ethan would leave tonight, Brad might never see her again.

So he took in a deep breath. He looked around the room. All the guys were enrapt in the stupid movie, and they were well on their way to getting wasted. He stood up, and no one noticed. He was going to talk to Val. He had no idea what he was going to say, but this was his one shot, and he wasn't going to fuck it up by just letting it slip through his fingers. If she told him to fuck off or showed no signs of any interest whatsoever, he'd let it go, but there was something there—he was sure of it—and he'd be a fool to not at least try.

He headed toward the kitchen, not sure what he was going to say, and when he got to the doorway, he paused. Val was standing in front of the refrigerator and had just turned around. Their eyes locked, and that was when he knew for certain. He could see it in her eyes. It wasn't just his imagination running wild. There *was* something there between them, something inexplicable. Yet it was strong. They looked at each other for several long moments until Brad felt like he had his bearings again and forced himself to walk over to her.

It was as if his instincts had taken over. He was slow, methodical, and he didn't stop until he was almost touching her. Their eyes were locked, and her breathing was deeper than it should have been. There it was—he could *feel* it, whatever *it* was, and he wasn't regretting his decision. He decided at that point to continue following his gut—unlike the rational part of his brain, his gut hadn't let him down yet when it came to this girl.

He wanted to pull her into his arms, recite the lyrics of his sweetest love song to her, taste her lips, but it felt too soon. He lowered his head, though, getting closer. She closed her eyes and tilted her head. At first, he thought maybe that was her way of spurning him, but that didn't make sense. She was still there, still close, and so he realized maybe she wanted him to kiss her there.

It was too soon, though, and he knew it. She might have had a strong attraction to Brad—he *knew* she did, because he felt it too—but her heart was still with Ethan, no matter how ridiculous that was. He'd be just a statistic if he tried moving in now when he'd barely known her for a day. He brought his face closer, though, and breathed in her scent, envisioned himself kissing her there. She seemed to tense up but she continued to stand there, and then...then she put her hands on his neck, pushing her fingers into his hair. It felt so possessive, so needy, and he forced himself to maintain his cool. He was not going to blow this.

Instead of wrapping his arms around her and shoving his tongue down her throat, he held himself back and lowered his lips to her ear. He was going to say one thing and one thing only. "I know you're into Ethan, and as long as you are, nothing's gonna happen between us. But I want you to know I'll wait."

After what seemed like forever—because he knew she was processing it, thinking it, feeling it—she loosened her fingers in his hair where they'd been clinging for dear life. And that was his cue. He backed away, their eyes still locked, and once he got to the doorway, he turned and left.

As he took one slow step after another heading back to the living room, he let it sink in. That had been an out-of-this-world experience, unlike anything he'd ever lived through before. It was like they'd been talking without words. He knew what she'd been feeling—that she loved Ethan and couldn't explain whatever was drawing her to Brad, but she couldn't *not* acknowledge it, weird or not—and he could tell she knew what he'd been feeling too. He'd never felt that way with another living soul before, and it was going to be hard to let her go. He knew, though, that he must. She wasn't his.

He made his way back to the living room, feeling like he was in a daze—confused, unsure, wanting something he knew he could probably never have. Zane and Nick were where they'd been when he'd left, but Ethan was nowhere to be found. Brad shook his head and sat back down, pouring himself a swig of rum. He could use a shot. Not long after he poured it, though, Ethan came back in the living room. He must have gone to the bathroom, but that would have meant one thing—he'd walked past the kitchen. What had he seen?

Brad wasn't going to say a word. And maybe the fact that Ethan hadn't said anything, either earlier when Brad was in the kitchen or now, meant that he was cool with Brad making a move.

But so much for that.

Ethan said, "Come on, Zane. We gotta hit the road."

"What?"

"Time to go."

"We just started watching the movie, man."

Brad saw Ethan's jaw clench. *Fuck.* So he'd have to talk to him sometime next week with the girl out of the picture. Ethan didn't have the hots for this girl, so what was the problem? Had Brad stolen some of her admiration? Was that it? But now wasn't the time to ask, not while Ethan was acting pissy.

Valerie came back in the room holding a glass of cold water. She too looked disoriented.

Nick told Ethan, "The movie's not over yet. You guys need to stay." Ethan shook his head but said nothing.

Zane tried again. "There's still plenty of booze."

Val said, "What's going on?"

"We're leaving now."

"Really?" Ethan nodded again but said nothing.

Zane wasn't done, though. "Man, we could stay here all night. We could even crash on the floor. Brad's mom won't be home till morning, and she'll be ready for bed when she gets here. Don't bail now."

Ethan's voice was cool. "We're leaving in the morning,

Zane, so unless you have another ride back to school…"

Zane shrugged. "Fine. What time you comin' by my house?"

"Ten. And if you're smart, you'll make sure you're not hung over."

Nick, in just a few short minutes, had passed out on the floor, probably having overconsumed. Zane said, "See you in the morning."

Brad said, "Take care, man. See you next weekend."

Ethan nodded, but he was not happy. "Yeah." He looked at Valerie but wasn't wasting any time moving toward the door. "Let's go." Val slipped on her coat and purse that were setting on the bench by the front door. Val said *goodbye*, but Ethan left without another word.

That told Brad what he needed to know. Ethan had no designs on the girl, but it didn't stop the guy from feeling possessive about her. They would definitely have to have a talk…and soon.

CHAPTER TEN

BRAD HAD IT bad. Over the next week, he'd even considered visiting Misti and begging for a little sympathy sex, but he couldn't bring himself to do it. It was going to take time to get over this girl.

Meanwhile, he bided his time. He was going to talk to Ethan. If he could figure out exactly what his friend was thinking, he could maybe get a green light, and if he had that, then maybe he could pursue Valerie for real. Right now it was just some weird attraction, but he'd like to act on it and see how it played out.

So he spent the next week working and trying not to think about her.

But it was damn hard.

He tried to write a new song too and just couldn't. He and Nick got together one night and even Nick could tell something was bothering Brad, but he wasn't going to say a word. He was perfectly content letting the drummer think he was under the weather.

He knew Ethan was going to be home on Friday. They'd said a couple of things to each other on Facebook, but Ethan said he was busy with finals week. Brad *did* notice that Valerie posted on Ethan's wall a "big thank you for the awesome Christmas present!" Brad used that as an excuse to send a friend request...and he was quite relieved when, the next day, Valerie accepted it.

God, he was pathetic, but he didn't know how to resolve it. He knew it was so bad because she reminded him so much of Leah. If she had been Leah, he already would have asked her out, and it would have been over with, whether she'd accepted or rejected him. The problem was Valerie had done neither and really couldn't at the moment, not with where her mind and heart were. She'd given him what she could, and that was...nothing, really, but Brad felt like there was so much unspoken between them.

So it took everything he had to not beat down Ethan's door Friday night. Instead, he gave his friend a little space and time, but by Saturday afternoon, he couldn't stand it anymore. In fact, it was pissing him off that Ethan hadn't even called. Knowing Ethan, the guy was still holding a grudge.

He called him, though, and asked, "McDonald's or Subway?"

"You buyin'?"

"Hell, yeah. I work, but you're a poor college student, remember?"

Ethan laughed. "Then I guess I can drive."

That offer oftentimes made Brad nervous, because he never knew when his friend would be indulging and, thus, impaired behind the wheel. He had to trust him, though. That's what friends did. So he waited patiently for Ethan to show up, and he kept running through his head all the things he wanted to say...even though he figured it would all fall to shit once they engaged in real conversation. With Ethan, he never knew how things would turn out. His friend was a wildcard, and Brad was nervous that their talk wouldn't end well. But there was no way he could hold it in, no way he couldn't *not* say something.

Ethan's black truck pulled up in front of Brad's house on time, a good sign. Ethan was never on time if he'd been drinking or doing something worse. Being punctual meant his friend was probably sober for the time being, and that meant the conversation would be fruitful. It wouldn't even be worth the time if Ethan wasn't fully in the present.

So Brad walked out the door, careful not to slam it as his mom was sleeping late. She usually got home around seven thirty in the morning if she left her shift at the hospital on time. She'd gotten home even later than that on occasion, and she'd usually stay up for an hour or so reading until she'd wound down enough to sleep. She was often in bed by ten or eleven, and Brad knew he had to be quiet until four or five. During the week, it wasn't a problem, because he was out of the house before his mom even got home. The weekends were harder, though, and he'd just learned to practice without any amps if his mom had worked the night before.

Ethan's engine was purring, steam pouring out of the muffler pipes, underscoring how the weather had turned cold. The sky was gray and Brad knew they'd get snow sometime that day. As he opened the passenger door to

Ethan's truck, he noticed his friend looked normal. The music was cranked, an Amon Amarth tune, and the heater was blowing out warm air. Ethan nodded, half smiling, as Brad climbed in.

After Ethan shifted the truck into gear and pulled back out onto the street, he reached over and turned the music down. "How you doin'?"

"Fine. Glad school's out for a while?"

"Hell, yeah. It's kicking my ass."

"I can't believe you're even doing it." Brad shook his head. "Still blows my mind."

Ethan ran his right hand through his reddish-brown hair. "Halfway done, man, and then fuck it. I'm never looking back."

Brad didn't say anything. Part of him hoped it was true, because Ethan was an important part of his band. More than that, though, Ethan was like a brother. The guy was more a brother to Brad than his real-life flesh-and-blood brother, and he hadn't realized how much Ethan had meant to him until he was miles away and never around. As fucked up as the guy was, he was more important to Brad than anyone else in the whole world. He and Ethan came from similar and yet very different worlds, but they understood and appreciated each other because of and in spite of their differences, and Brad had been struggling with his friend's absence.

He'd never tell Ethan that. He knew his friend and knew Ethan would give him shit about it if he ever said a word, so that—like so many other things between them—would be an unspoken fact.

And, because of that, part of Brad actually hoped Ethan

wouldn't piss on the once-in-a-lifetime opportunity his grandfather had offered him. A guy like Ethan would never go to college by his own choice, but Ethan was no dumb ass. Brad knew that if his friend would apply himself, he'd do pretty well in school. Hell, he could take advantage of the music program any school had to offer and learn shit none of them ever dreamed of. He knew, though, that Ethan was simply biding his time, doing enough to get by, just like he had all through high school.

Part of him didn't blame Ethan. Brad knew he himself would have been at a crossroads. He understood the value of education, but college held nothing for him. He didn't want to be a lawyer, doctor, scientist, teacher…he knew exactly what he wanted to be, and damned if he was going to find himself tens of thousands of dollars in debt when more school wouldn't help him progress to that goal. Both his mom and dad tried to get him to do it. His mother, after all, was a nurse, and she had had three years' schooling to become an RN. His dad had a two-year degree—something vague that Brad could never remember—but the man said it had helped him more than once land a job. Now his dad was a line supervisor in a government office, miserable as far as Brad could tell, and fuck it all if he was going to wind up like that. He'd rather be miserable in the struggle to be what he wanted to be.

So, for Brad, that meant no college, no marriage, no kids, not till he'd made his way in the world. He couldn't be tied down. He saw what it had done to his dad. His father had only said it once, heavily under the influence of alcohol, but it had stuck with Brad. His father had felt trapped by his marriage, his bills, his kids, and even though he said he'd accepted it and was happy the way things turned out (in spite of the divorce), Brad knew better. He could see it in the man's eyes. His fire had been extinguished.

Brad would *not* be that way. So while Ethan told him about the brutality known as finals week, Brad also tossed around thoughts in the back of his mind. Yes, he would make it or die trying.

They were halfway through the meal, and the conversation had dwindled. That was when Brad knew it was time to broach the subject that had really been on his mind. He rarely pulled his punches with Ethan, and he didn't plan to now, but he did know he'd need to handle the topic delicately.

"I've been meaning to ask you. What's going on between you and your friend Valerie?"

Ethan paused, then finished chewing his fry. He looked Brad in the eyes and said, "Why?"

No sense lying about it. "Bros before hos, man. I like her. But…" He took a sip of his Coke. Goddamn. He hadn't expected this to be so hard. What a fucking pussy he was turning out to be. It pissed him off that some girls had that effect on him. It was a problem he needed to find a way to fix. He decided to come at it from another angle. "I got the idea from what both of you said that you're just friends. I want to make sure before I make a move."

What the fuck was Ethan thinking? Brad could usually read his friend like a newspaper headline, but he was closed off today. Ethan ate another fry and then shrugged his shoulders. "I like her. She's a nice girl. But, you know.

She's, uh, *too* nice."

Which was exactly one of the things that tripped Brad's trigger. He had a thing for the sweet girls. He'd never been able to figure that one out. Maybe because they were less likely to cheat? He didn't know and wasn't going to question it. Analyzing the fuck out of it wouldn't change it, so why bother? Leah had been the first super sweet girl he'd dated, even though he'd admired many from afar, and—until the end when she'd broken his heart—she'd surpassed his expectations. "So it's cool then?"

"Yeah, but I gotta tell ya, man. For some reason, I think she really likes me."

"It's 'cause you're a suave motherfucker."

Ethan started laughing and set his drink down. "Yeah. That must be it."

One week left before Ethan had to return. The four guys had gotten together a few times, working on perfecting the songs they had, as well as writing three strong songs and playing two gigs Brad had lined up. The audience response was incredible, and it led Brad to believe, more than ever, that this was his destiny. He was glad to see his friends were starting to believe too, because then he felt like they had a fighting chance. It helped to play to a crowd bigger than fifty people, and not just any people—these guys were enthusiastic, headbanging, moshing, intense, hardcore metalheads.

After that show, the four of them went to a party. They'd have to figure out a way to get back home afterward, and what made it trickier was that they weren't even in their hometown, so Brad decided to go ahead and drink a little, but he'd go easy. That way, when the party was over, he'd be able to get them home safely. Yeah, it was Ethan's truck, but Brad was usually the designated driver, simply because he had more willpower than anyone else. He got one beer and planned to nurse it all night. He'd save outrageous partying for when he didn't have to drive.

Ethan, Zane, and Nick were celebrating. They deserved to. It was the first time Brad had felt like the four of them had been a cohesive unit. They'd moved and played together on that stage tonight. Instead of moving like arms and legs on different dolls, they were coordinated, like the limbs of the same person. Each sensed what the other was going to do. They were in the groove and just felt—yeah, they fucking *felt*—where the band was going, what was happening, and it was exhilarating. If Brad could have bottled that shit, he knew he'd be a billionaire.

Instead, he felt like a million bucks that night, and he didn't think anything could change that. As if to slap him in the face and remind him that he didn't have complete control of his destiny, the universe threw a wrench in the works. Ethan, partying hard as he often did, got his hands on something. The guy was fucked up and not in a good way. A lot of times, even if Ethan was a belligerent drunk, they could work around him, manage his moods, and he'd do just fine. This time, though, had nothing to do with how he was treating other people. He was fucked up beyond belief.

When Brad and Nick found him, he was lying in a corner, his eyes glazed over. He could barely talk. Brad squatted and tried talking to his friend, but to no avail. He looked up at Nick. "Do you know what he took?"

"No idea."

Brad snapped his fingers in front of Ethan's face. He wasn't even thinking when he did it, had just been wanting to get some kind of response from his friend. But Ethan seemed to barely register it. He looked back at Nick. "Go find Zane."

Nick nodded. Brad wasn't thinking it in the conscious part of his brain, but buried somewhere, he knew. Every time something good happened, something bad happened to balance it out. It was fucked up, but that had seemed to be the path his life had taken consistently. Why would it change now? He'd always known that he *would* have been the kid who'd gotten the BB gun at Christmas and, unlike the movie *A Christmas Story*, Brad really would have shot his eye out. That was the way his life worked.

Now, though, Brad was trying to figure out what they needed to do. Home was half an hour away, give or take (and the roads were good enough right now to make that kind of time), but he knew there was a good hospital here if they needed it. He just didn't know how to get there.

He remembered what had happened last year, right after Halloween. He'd thought Ethan had OD'd, and he and Heidi had rushed him to the hospital. Ethan had gotten in huge trouble and then later had laid into Brad, telling him he hadn't OD'd. He was "just really wasted" and his friend could have spared him a lot of trouble by simply taking him home.

So when Nick and Zane joined him back at the Ethan's truck where Brad had Ethan lying in the front passenger seat, he said, "Here's the deal. We're heading home. If his breathing changes or something weird happens, you tell me."

"Define *weird*." Nick didn't look as though he liked the plan.

"If we get home and things are the same, I have my mom look at him." Zane's expression was a mixture of pissed off and confused, but he didn't say anything. "My mom's a nurse, remember?"

Zane nodded. "Then what the fuck are we waiting for?"

There was one problem Brad hadn't thought of—he had the trailer hooked to Ethan's truck, and so the truck wouldn't haul ass like it usually did. Secondly, he didn't feel comfortable cranking the music like he normally would have, because he wanted them to be able to hear Ethan—if he was breathing or choking or gasping or if he wound up talking. The problem was playing no music made Brad even more nervous, and the ride home was tense and seemed to last forever.

They made it, though, and Ethan was no worse for the wear. He got to his house and cursed because he'd forgotten his mom was working that night. So he called her and asked if he brought Ethan by if she could take a look at him. She told him it was his lucky night because they were slow. They had three recovering moms and one nowhere near needing to push. There were two other nurses on duty, besides, so she could take a break. When she asked why, Brad said he'd be there in a bit. Stupid as it was, he unhooked the trailer, not wanting to imagine how he'd maneuver the fucker in the hospital parking lot, and then he asked if Nick and Zane wanted to come with or have him drop them off at home.

Both guys said they'd come along, so they jumped back in the truck and flew to the hospital. Brad texted his mom when they got there, and in less than five minutes, she was outside. "What's going on, boys?"

"Ethan took something. We don't know what. But we want to make sure he didn't OD."

His mom cocked an eyebrow at him, and he knew what she was thinking—why hadn't they taken him straight to the ER? But then she answered her own question. She'd been a teen once. She knew. And then he could see the next question in her eyes, which was wondering what they'd been doing. But she was cool. And she was prepared. She had a little flashlight, and she lifted one of Ethan's lids and shined the light. Brad couldn't tell if she was shining it directly in his eyes or beside them, because he wanted to give her some space. He, Nick, and Zane huddled around on the side of the truck, and Brad didn't even notice the cold. He knew part of it was because he'd had that beer, but he thought part of it was fear for his friend. He felt the cold *now*, though, now that he'd processed the thought, and he considered getting his jacket from the driver's side of the truck and decided against it.

His mom had the stethoscope on and was listening to Ethan's heart. Then she picked up his wrist and Brad thought she was measuring his pulse. Finally, she said, "Ethan. Ethan, talk to me. It's Barb, Ethan. I need you to talk to me." Her voice was firm but not harsh, and she kept talking to him, saying his name.

Ethan fluttered his eyes and stirred. He muttered something. Brad couldn't hear it, but his mom responded. He missed that too, but Nick was visibly relieved, gesturing to him and Zane. His mom said, "Ethan, I need to know what you took."

"Don't know."

"What do you mean you don't know? You were there, weren't you?" Oh, she was using the mom voice on Ethan, and Brad knew fully well that his mother had the same effect on his friend that she did on him.

Ethan's eyes widened, and he seemed to try to sit up, but then his head fell back on the chair and his eyes closed. Brad couldn't take it anymore and walked deeper into the parking lot. His fear was that maybe his friend had ruined his brain or maybe his mom couldn't help him. Should he have stopped him? He knew he wouldn't have been able to. In February he and Ethan had come to blows over something Ethan wanted to take, and finally Brad had to simply throw his hands in the air. Nor would Ethan listen to reason. Ethan was an adult (even if in the loosest sense of the word), and Brad could no more control him than he could the sun.

That said, should he have taken his friend to the nearest hospital rather than bringing Ethan home for his mother to check him out? Probably, but it was too late to fix it now. And he knew Ethan would have killed him once he was awake and aware.

A few minutes later, he heard his mom's voice in the distance. "Brad. Bradley Payne! Come here."

Oh. That was serious if she was calling him *Bradley*. He hustled back to the passenger side of the truck. Nick and Zane were still close, but they were standing back some, talking quietly to each other. Brad's mom said, "Okay, here's the deal. I can't get out of him what he took, but I think he's going to be okay. You are *not* going to take him home, not because I want to keep it a secret from June, because I think we need to let her know what's happened tonight. Call her if you need to, to let her know he's spending the night sleeping it off. You are going to place him in the recliner in the living room. He needs to be mostly sitting up so he doesn't choke on his own vomit. And I would appreciate it if you got up every couple of hours to check on him until I get home."

Brad nodded. He felt like his mom had saved everything. He nodded again, feeling pathetic but relieved. And he planned on staying up all fucking night until he was sure his best friend was okay.

CHAPTER ELEVEN

BY MARCH, TWO revelations had given Brad some perspective on his crush—and that was what it was: a crush. An irrational one at that.

Brad realized first that he'd met Valerie at a point in his life where he was primed for that kind of reaction. He hadn't been in a real relationship for months, and he'd been hanging with skanky girls and banging an older woman, so when he met sweet Val, a young lady who reminded him of his Leah, he'd found her irresistible. A little time gave him perspective and helped the crush die a quiet death.

He'd also gotten a few tidbits here and there, mostly through what was *not* said—well, that and Facebook. Putting the pieces together, Brad was pretty sure Val and Ethan had become involved *somehow*. How, exactly, he wasn't sure, but he had the idea something was going on.

But then, one of the weekends Ethan and Zane came home for a show, Ethan showed Brad lots of new song lyrics he was writing music for. They were unlike anything

Ethan had ever written before, full of depth, wonder, and beauty, and when Brad asked more questions, he discovered why. Those words hadn't been written by Ethan; they'd been written by Valerie, and Ethan had taken to calling her his *muse*. Reading those words gave Brad the same feelings he'd had when he'd been around her, but he didn't feel like he could approach her, whether he was her Facebook friend or not. She didn't know him (in spite of the promise he'd made her in the passion of the moment), so she probably wouldn't appreciate if he became overly friendly, whether or not he'd read her lyrics.

But maybe he could change that. Ethan and Zane had almost missed one of their shows in February, and Brad had decided maybe he needed to slow down on gigs until the summer when Ethan would be nearby and easier to control. If Ethan decided to not show, Brad could move on. They could take a couple songs out of a set and they could just use one guitar for other songs, but he couldn't move forward without a bassist. Zane had always been trustworthy, but when he had to rely on Ethan to give him a ride, all bets were off, and Ethan seemed to be moving toward another bad phase.

So, between Ethan's instability and Brad's desire to see Valerie again to find out if his feelings for her were insignificant, he booked a show at The Cave which was close to Ethan and Zane, and there would be no excuse for Ethan not showing up. If his friend couldn't be bothered to make it to a goddamned show, Brad would bring the show to him.

The whole thing with Valerie, though—it pissed Brad off more than he wanted to admit. He wasn't mad at

Valerie. The girl herself had never hidden that she was smitten with Ethan. Ethan, though, had given Brad the go ahead, had said he wasn't interested in Val. Ethan was fucked in the head sometimes, though, and Brad thought he knew why. He was sure his friend just couldn't resist being adored anymore and had given in to her worship.

Well, it was probably better that way. Brad hadn't stood a chance, no matter how drawn to her he felt.

Zane called a few days before the show and told Brad that Valerie was going to watch the show. He wanted to warn Brad and Nick, because Zane and Val were still friends, but she was no longer on speaking terms with Ethan. Brad asked why.

"Man, I don't know what the hell's wrong with Ethan. They were actually dating for a while, and I was like, *it's about time*. But Ethan started fucking around on her. Made no sense. And I think it was a complete slap in the face because she'd been writing all those lyrics for him."

"Yeah, I know."

"She's a really sweet girl."

Brad didn't disagree, but he was afraid of what his voice might betray if he told Zane what he really thought about her. "But she's coming to the show anyway?"

"Well, yeah. Val and me are good friends, and if you wrote a bunch of words to some rockin' songs, wouldn't you want to see them performed live?"

"Yeah, I guess I would." Brad wasn't going to complain. He wanted to see her again, see if he still had those same crazy strong feelings for her. No way would he say that to Zane, though. As it was, he was kicking himself for saying anything to Ethan to begin with. The more he thought about it, the more convinced he was that he had practically pushed his friend into her arms. Ethan hadn't thought twice about the girl before Christmas break. Brad knew that much based on their conversation. But when he found out Brad was interested and the guy admitted that he knew Valerie was carrying a torch for him…well, he just couldn't resist trying her out. But, like Brad had suspected, she wasn't enough to keep Ethan. Ethan liked his girls with a harder edge, and Valerie just didn't have that. Yeah, she loved their music, but she wasn't dark and tormented or skanky beyond belief. Those were the kinds of girls Ethan liked—the ones just like his demented ass or the ones who could fuck him twenty different ways on the first date alone. Brad suspected the second trend would get even worse as they got older, because they'd be able to find more and more women willing to do weird stuff. Right now, the young girls weren't too experienced, so they weren't as eager to try things as those who'd been around the block once or twice.

So, once more, Valerie was heavy on his mind as the day of their gig approached. He hoped that his feelings would be diminished, that he would see her and realize he'd just experienced some weird, inexplicable infatuation before and now things had returned to normal.

He was afraid, though, that he would find that nothing had changed.

Nick's dad let him and Brad borrow his truck, and they packed up the back with Nick's drum kit, amps, and two of Brad's guitars, plus all the little things they needed. They usually used Ethan's truck with the trailer but that would, of course, have involved Ethan. Brad knew he needed to find another solution to how they toured. For now, though, they'd manage.

He hadn't wanted to, but he felt himself growing excited as they got closer and closer. He was feeling like a kid at Christmas, anticipating something that he had great hopes for but that would probably let him down, much like the gifts under the tree often did. No matter how great the presents were, they'd rarely been able to live up to his way-too-high expectations. As his mind dwelled on Valerie, he tried to keep reminding himself of that.

But he couldn't. He was jazzed beyond belief. When they got to The Cave, he was pleasantly surprised to see his other two band members there already. Ethan and Zane helped Brad and Nick unload the truck and get all their gear set up offstage in preparation for their turn. They would be the second band to play that night. The first had already set up.

Brad had never played with either of the bands that were there that night, but he always made sure to introduce himself to other band members when he could. No one stayed a stranger around Brad for long, and most times he considered the people he met on the road allies. They all had the same goal, the same dreams. Once in a while, he'd meet people who were perfectly content only playing locally, who wanted to play and be heard and nothing more, but most of the people he met wanted big recognition—just like he did. He wanted to be heard; he wanted people to love his music. The money? Not as important, except in the regard that earning enough money as a band would mean he could spend more time focusing solely on the music instead of working for someone else for minimum wage. But to pour his heart into his art…he didn't do it only for himself. His art was meant to be appreciated by others as well.

So, as was his usual custom, he made his way around the backstage area first, introducing himself to the first person he could, and it went from there. He knew that pissed Ethan off; he wasn't sure why. The only thing he could figure was that Ethan thought they were better than most of the other people they played with, and so he was above mingling with the riffraff. He'd never asked Ethan and wouldn't because he didn't want to know. He hoped Ethan would come around eventually. Zane and Nick had no problems socializing with other bands, but they didn't go out of their way like Brad did, and he was okay with that. He knew he was unusual in that regard. Nick even bordered on shy, so Brad could understand why he had a bit of a harder time, but Ethan was flat out aloof sometimes, and he was worried about what kind of reputation that would give his band. Maybe that was why he himself went overboard on the flip side, to make sure other bands knew they were approachable. If his band was perceived as not only great sounding but easy to get along with, it could pave the way to being invited to more (and bigger) shows. He wanted to be thought of when those opportunities came up.

And so he spent a good half hour pressing palms, chewing the fat with other bands, getting to know the guys in them. The last band of the night had a big merchandise table, and Brad started asking questions. He knew Fully Automatic was missing out on opportunities to make money by not selling merchandise. He'd seen lots of great tables over the past year too—not only t-shirts, but buttons, bumper stickers, and—of course—CDs. The CDs would have to wait until they could afford to buy some studio time, but he wanted to know if having a merch table would be worth it. If they could make more money, they would be able to spend more time honing their craft. There was no denying it.

The guy he was talking to said, "Let me take you out to our table to talk to Shane. We all man it sometimes, but he's the guy doing it tonight. He can show you how it's done."

They walked out front and Brad was introduced to Shane. He asked, "What's the most important thing you can tell me about having a merch table?"

Shane took a second, giving it some thought. Then he said, "Well, sometimes it's to give your stuff away. I know. Sounds like the worst thing to do, but trust me. You have some beautiful chick walk past your table without giving you a second thought, give her a shirt. And it's not to score. But if she's walking around wearing your shirt, tits out to here, your band name stretched across her rack, she'll get noticed, and so will your name. Ask her to wear it during the concert. Free publicity, dude, and that's worth every penny."

Brad was dubious but didn't say anything. A couple of people approached the table, and one wanted to buy a shirt. Shane offered a discount if the guy bought two. While they were negotiating, Brad was scanning faces. The place wasn't packed yet, and the house lights wouldn't be turned off until the show, so he could see the people in the crowd.

And that's when he noticed *her*. Except she looked a little different. She was sitting at a table next to a girl with short blonde hair, talking and looking excited and happy. If that was Valerie (and he still wasn't completely sure), she'd teased her hair a little. Her eye makeup was heavy and dark, something she hadn't done last fall, and she was wearing a black tank top. Without taking his eyes off her, he leaned toward Shane. "Be back in a few."

He stood, and he knew he had to put on a game face. One thing he'd learned in his few short years was that chicks dug confidence. He knew that was why Ethan got away with so much shit. Brad didn't intend to push his luck, because he knew you could go from confident to cocky in short order, but he did want to communicate through his body language that there was no hesitation. He knew what he wanted, and he wasn't afraid to go after it.

As he got closer, he knew it definitely *was* Valerie, but she'd metaled out. She looked...*hot*. She'd been sweet and innocent before, something that had attracted Brad from the get go, but now she was dressed like a metalhead and she was gorgeous. Oh, fuck, he had it bad. Just seeing her confirmed it. But he needed to test the waters, because maybe what he'd felt last December had been a fluke. Physical attraction was one thing, but it wasn't *everything*, and it wasn't the basis of what he'd felt. No, instead...instead, there was something else, something intangible between them.

Or at least that's how he remembered it. He needed to find out if it was for real.

So he took a deep breath and imagined testosterone coursing through his veins, and then he made his way to the table where Valerie and her friend sat. Oh, hell, yeah. Jesus. She was wearing spiked wristbands too. She'd tripped some trigger last time they'd been together, but this time, he knew exactly what alarms were going off in his head. She was sexy and he was turned on. Another deep breath. He had this.

He slid into the chair next to her. She sensed him, because she turned, and he noticed her friend looking at him as Val turned her head. As soon as her eyes met his, he saw the recognition in hers and she smiled. He said, "Hi, beautiful." Fuck. The reaction he got was more than he'd hoped for. She was happy to see him and...she was checking him out. He saw her eyes scour his lips, his chin, his hair. That was nice. And he'd been worried.

She propped her chin in her hands, resting her elbows on the table. That was so cute and flirty. Yeah, much more than he'd dreamed of. Her reaction alone was worth the trip here, even if the whole damn crowd hated his band. But she wasn't done bowling him over. "Well, hello back, gorgeous." Goddamn. He had to maintain his cool, but he was feeling his blood surge harder than it had in a long time. What was it about this girl? She turned her head slightly back and to the side to indicate the girl next to her, but she held that flirty pose while she spoke. "Um...this is my roommate, Jennifer Manders."

It was easy to stand and reach over, so he did. He held his hand out as though to shake hers. "Jennifer." The young blonde extended her hand to his and he leaned over, bringing it up to his lips. Val's roommate was thrilled—he could tell—but he wondered what Val herself thought. He was hoping to score more points.

It was definitely working. Val said, "How debonair."

Yeah, and that told him it was time to push his luck, and he sat down. He lowered his voice so her roommate wouldn't be able to hear it easily. "*You*...I'll kiss elsewhere." Fuck, yes. It was working, and so much better than he'd ever dreamed. He could see it on her face. And she probably had no idea all the places he'd love to kiss on her. He took a breath and smiled, then raised his voice, because what he was going to say next, he didn't care if her roommate heard. He already knew the answer, but he wanted to hear her response anyway. "So...you here to watch us play, or is this just a coincidence?"

She had a devilish grin on her face. "I came to watch *you*."

Fucking God. He couldn't believe it. She was messing with him—he knew that much. Still, that she was going to the trouble to inflate his ego and flirt with him at the same time...well, that told him everything he needed to know, and he was going to keep the ball rolling. "You're here just for me?"

"Yep. Just for you." He winked at her then, as if to communicate to her that he knew she was playing but he appreciated it just the same.

Time to leave while he was ahead and she was eating out of the palm of his hand. "Gotta go. I'm hanging at another band's merch table to see how it's done." Without thinking it through, on impulse, he kissed her on the cheek. Then he stood. "See you after the show?"

"Maybe." Oh, that little shit. God, now she was teasing him. Now he'd have to get out of there before he popped a boner.

He raised his eyebrows, wanting to keep the flirting tone in his voice. He pointed at her and said, "You better be here." Then he turned to leave.

He wasn't sure, because it was so loud in the joint already, but as he walked away, he thought he could hear her roommate say, "Oh, my God. Who *was* that?" If her friend was impressed by Brad, it could only help him out, right?

He joined Shane at the merch table again and took mental notes the entire time he was there. Brad caught that the guy was really good at upselling, something Brad didn't know he'd be good at. He'd always believed in the power of his music. He believed that if it was good enough, that was all he'd need. He wouldn't have to sell bumper stickers and other bullshit. Yeah, that was true, sure, but he also knew sometimes fans would *want* merchandise—he knew he spent money on band merchandise. Why wouldn't his fans want merch too? Besides, if it helped move his band forward by providing them with a little extra cash, why wouldn't he? Now that they were one-hundred percent solid on their name (and he'd been redesigning their logo), why not do it? It couldn't hurt, unless for some reason they spent more on merchandise than they made. But that would be stupid. They would know how much they'd have to charge to make a profit, and they'd make sure they would. He didn't know that he'd follow Shane's advice of giving pretty girls a t-shirt for free, but he'd have to try it once or twice before ruling out the idea.

When the first band started playing, Brad bought a t-shirt from Shane as a way of saying thanks for letting him sit with him and learn. Their band was good too, so he'd wear it. He considered joining Valerie and her friend to watch the first band and decided against it. He didn't want to seem like an eager puppy dog. Yeah, there continued to be some weird inexplicable spark between them that he could no better explain than he could the properties of a black hole, but he *was* smart enough to know that, no matter what she said or how she acted toward him, Valerie now had a bit of history with Ethan, and he didn't know if that would trump whatever moves he made. From this point forward, he knew he had to be cautious…and prepare to give that girl a hell of a show.

CHAPTER TWELVE

HE COULDN'T HAVE played a better show if he'd planned it. Really, though, Brad went into every show planning to give it his all, and this one had been no different. Each audience deserved the best show it could get, the best show they'd paid for, and Brad intended to deliver. Still, there were some nights where things just didn't click—where they'd felt sluggish, or out of sync, or like anything that could have gone wrong had. Tonight, though, it was like magic.

In spite of the fact that he was there for the whole crowd, Valerie was at the forefront of his mind, and after the fourth song of their set, he pulled off his Black Label Society t-shirt and threw it to the side of the stage. He'd been hot and sweaty anyway, but if she was watching, he wanted to show himself off. He had some new ink anyway, and it was going to waste hiding under the shirt.

Midway into the fifth song, he noticed Val and her friend at the foot of the stage. He knew she had to be more invested than other audience members, because several of the songs had her words as the lyrics. Ever since that night in his garage where they'd written their first song as a group effort that began with Val's constructive criticism, he'd tried harder with his words. He'd always felt that the words were secondary to the music, because that was the kind of music lover he was. If he loved the music, he loved the song. Yeah, he'd listen to and (maybe) appreciate the words later, but if he didn't love the music—if the tune didn't speak to him—he'd never hear the words. The lyrics would never stand a chance. Since Val had hopped on board with her word wizardry, he'd taken a step back and rethought his ideas about lyrics. He'd since paid more attention to the lines he wrote and the words he chose. He wanted them to mean something, and if he could even come close to the brilliance of some of Val's lyrics, he'd have it made. He'd even retooled the words of a couple of his older songs, hoping to make them fresher, more original.

He hoped she would notice.

God, he also hoped he wasn't making her uncomfortable, but seeing her there, he could hardly take his eyes off her. She was beautiful. She was loving the show too, headbanging, throwing the horns in the air, rocking out. Her friend liked the music too, but Brad could tell Valerie loved it. What made him feel better was that, even though she was watching the whole band, Ethan included, she kept her eyes mostly on him too.

Yeah, he had a chance. A good chance.

So, by the second to last song, he was more self-assured than ever, and he was prepared to venture past the point of no return. When the applause from the previous song died down, Brad said into the mike, "I'm dedicating this song to the cute brunette standing near the edge of the stage." He made sure he caught Val's eye before he added, "You know who you are." At this point, he wasn't going to look over at Ethan, because his friend knew how Brad felt about Val, and Brad was no dummy. He knew something had happened between Ethan and Val, but he was hoping that whatever it had been was over. It was time to move in. "This song is called 'Want You'." It was a song he'd written the week after he'd met her, before he and Ethan had had their little talk. It had also been his first attempt at trying to write something with more meaning, more substance...more like the way Val wrote. He started feeling nervous as he played the chords on his guitar, because he wondered what she'd think. He was especially nervous because he'd written the damn song *about* her.

"A chance encounter,
Two strangers meet.
A hidden smile, a secret glance.
You're in my sights,
Won't take defeat,
No second thought, no second chance

"Want you, baby, be mine tonight.
I need you more than words can say.
I'll make you my queen, make you my whore,
But I know I can't have you anyway."

He was pretty sure that the chorus had freaked her out a little bit, especially with the word *whore*, but she didn't know the song was about her, right? Or did she?

He moved forward. He didn't have much of a choice. So he made sure his voice was strong as he began the second verse.

"As I gaze upon you,
Sparks ignite.
The smoldering becomes a burning flame.
Do you feel the same?
I think you might.
A blazing desire that can't be tamed."

He kept his voice steady, his guitar keeping him anchored and focused as he sang the song. He'd been working on it for months and could have sung it in his sleep, so he simply had to make sure his voice was solid and calm, his fingers sure, his gaze off her so he could ensure a stellar performance of the song. He could feel the eyes of the audience on him, and as he looked up, aside from being blinded by the bright lights flooding the stage, he could see cell phones swaying from side to side in the audience. *Holy fuck.* That was cool.

More than that, it was powerful.

And that told him what he needed to know. It wasn't just a lust song; it was a *falling for someone* song. It was hardcore. The girls got the message, so surely Val had too…if it had sunk in with her that he'd dedicated it to her for a reason.

When the song was over, the crowd went wild. For that reason alone, he was glad their next song was the last. It was a song called "Bullet Through My Soul," a song they had always played last. It was heavy and loud and energetic, a great way to end a show. Even though the band name was no longer *Bullet*, he was sure this song would be their go-to song forever. It was Ethan's song, but the whole band had worked on the music together, and it wasn't just heavy sound-wise. The words were weighed with meaning, and most people only heard the superficial message, that love hurt. It had layers of meaning, though—love for two people, love from parents, love from an audience—and Ethan had poured his heart into the song. It was one that his friend had said he would never be able to sing, though, so Brad sang it for him. When the words came out of his mouth at the end of every show, he could almost feel Ethan's pain but doubted any of their listeners had any idea how deeply scarred his friend was. Still, Brad was convinced that if their band made it, Ethan could let go of his past.

When their set was over, Brad was doubly glad he'd decided to do the show here. The audience was unbelievable. He knew the crowd was mostly full of college kids, but he knew they would always be a good chunk of his audience. He didn't know that he'd ever experienced a show that infused with energy and a sense of power. It was incredible, and he knew he'd feel high all night.

After the applause died down and they'd thanked the audience, they started taking their stuff off stage. The drum kit always took the longest, and all the guys had to work on it. But Brad hardly noticed that night, because he was dreaming about his future. He knew it would just keep getting better and better. *This is what it feels like*, he'd thought.

The last band started setting up, and Ethan, Zane, and Nick went backstage and started slamming some drinks. Brad excused himself, not that they noticed, and found Val and her friend out front. They'd moved away from the front of the stage, but they weren't too far off and they were easy to find. The last band was awesome, and Brad couldn't quite place their sound but would say they leaned heavily toward melodic death metal. It wasn't his usual flavor of metal, but they were good and he could understand why they had such a huge following.

Still…he didn't want to rock out anymore. He had designs on the young lady beside him. In between songs, he cupped his hands and said in her ear, "You guys wanna come hang with us backstage?"

The girls liked the idea and followed him backstage into a smallish room where Fully Automatic and the first band were hanging with a few people. They could hear the music, but it was quieter and they didn't have to shout at one another. There was a sign on the door that said, "KEEP DOOR CLOSED DURING SHOWS. RESPECT YOUR FELOW PERFORMERS." Brad saw that someone had taken a Sharpie to the sign and added another *l* to spell *fellow* properly. He knew that he and his group didn't need to be told by a sign or otherwise. They all worked hard for their moment under the spotlights and damned if they'd fuck it up for their brothers onstage. So both the sign and its correction were unnecessary. If they had to be loud, they'd go outside.

As soon as he and the girls entered the room, Zane made a beeline for the blonde with Val. Brad heard just enough of their conversation to gather that they'd been involved before...and it sounded like Zane was trying to reignite something. Brad asked Val, "What did you think of the show?"

She smiled. "Oh, wow. It was incredible, Brad. You guys were so good in your garage but here, with a huge audience? You were amazing."

It felt nice to hear her say that. "We've been working hard. I hope it shows."

"It definitely does." And while he could tell there was still that magnetic draw they had to each other, he could also tell she was distracted by Ethan. His friend was off in the corner chatting with a girl, and while Val tried to be respectful and not look, he could tell she was also thinking about his friend...the guy who didn't deserve her. So they talked for a few minutes about individual songs and her impressions of them, but he didn't have her undivided attention. Still, he tried. He didn't want to compete, though, and so he was considering going out to watch the band again. Just as he had made that decision, Ethan looked over at him. When he saw he had Brad's attention, he cocked his head toward the door and pointed his thumb, and Brad knew what that meant. No better time than the present. He looked at Valerie and said, "We're gonna go party at Zane's in a minute. Much as I wanna stay and headbang, 'cause this band's awesome, Ethan's in a hurry to get out of here." He knew now that he had a snowball's chance in hell, but he had to try. "So...you'll come by after?"

Her smile was shy and sweet...and *that* was for him alone. "Yeah."

"Promise?"

"Yes. I said *yes*."

"Just making sure."

Brad and Zane exchanged looks and Zane said something to Jennifer, then laid a hell of a kiss on the girl before she and Val left the room. At this rate, it was gonna be a long fucking night.

CHAPTER THIRTEEN

HE HAD ONE shot. He knew that. So while the rest of the guys started drinking in Zane and Ethan's room, Brad asked them to point him in the direction of the shower. No way was he going to subject Val to his sweaty self. He wanted to be ready for her when she showed.

More time passed than should have, though, and he started to doubt she was coming. He cracked open his bottle of rum and Ethan said, "Why don't we play quarters?" Ethan looked at the girl sitting beside him, and Brad knew then that his friend was wanting to loosen her up a little. Hell, they could all stand a little loosening up. He knew he could. He'd been a little nervous at first, and now as the minutes ticked on, he was starting to feel down. He was afraid he was probably going to be stood up. So he took a long swig.

Yeah, why would Val want him when she was pining over his good-looking friend? Well, seeing Ethan whisper into the ear of the girl beside him told Brad why Val should want him instead, but she wasn't having any of it. For some reason, she was drawn to Ethan, much like a comet to the sun, and she was going to be lucky if she didn't get burned. He took another drink.

Zane said, "Give me some." Brad handed him the bottle. At least they could get drunk together. Zane took a swig.

"I have some vodka around here somewhere. And I need to find a glass for quarters."

Ethan was kissing the girl beside him, and Nick had slumped onto the floor. The gorgeous girl he'd brought was shaking his arm, trying to get his attention. Brad took another swig. This was beginning to feel like a lot of the other band parties they'd had in the past, and it didn't exactly make him thrilled.

And then there was a knock on the door. He tried not to get too excited. He made an attempt to look relaxed. Zane was walking to the door and whispered loudly, "Hide the bottle under the desk."

Brad was confused at first but then realized his friends lived in a dorm room. Not only were they all underage drinkers, but he imagined they'd get in even bigger trouble if they were drinking on campus. Brad screwed the cap back on the rum and tucked it under the desk, turning his chair so his leg could also block the bottle from view should anyone walk in the room.

It made his night to see Val walk in the door, followed by her roommate who paused in the doorway to kiss Zane. He picked up the bottle of rum and hugged Val when she walked into the room. Her hair smelled nice—sweet smelling, like coconut, and he tried to emblazon in his mind how she felt up against him, because he didn't know the next time he'd get to hold her. If he had his way, it would be the first of many, but he still wasn't too sure.

He wrapped his arm over her shoulder and led her inside the room. "We're getting ready to play some quarters. I know you don't drink, but will you hang with me?"

"Yeah."

They set up the game. They all sat on the floor between the two beds in a tight circle. Brad almost put his arm around Val's shoulder again, but he didn't want to make her feel uncomfortable. They started playing quarters—well, at least three couples did. Nick's date wound up resting her head on his chest and dozing off. Brad wanted to try to keep Val's mind off Ethan, so he tried to keep her engaged in conversation. He started by asking her about her classes, but she didn't have much to say about them, and he saw her eyes continuing to drift over to his friend. She never made eye contact with him, but Brad could tell her attention was there. He moved the conversation to the show then, and she became more engaged then, enough that he felt like he could get away with putting his arm around her again. She didn't seem to mind. They moved on to talking about the band itself, and while everyone was there playing quarters, it was as though there were three different games going on, simply because couples were only communicating amongst themselves. He knew why Val didn't want to talk to Ethan, but that didn't explain why no one else was talking. It was like they were all intent upon getting hammered.

No, he looked around the room and knew what everyone else had in mind. It was weighing on his mind too, but he didn't know how Val felt. He looked over and saw the discomfort on her face. If she'd been any other girl, he would have offered her a drink of his rum. Instead, he asked, "Wanna get out of here?"

She nodded without hesitation, so Brad stood and held his hand out to her. She took it and stood. It was then that he could feel just how much he'd had to drink, and when he looked at the bottle, he knew too. Yeah, Zane had helped, but the bottle only had an inch of liquid left. Holy shit. His head was light and he felt swimmy.

It didn't change the gravity of the situation, however. The other couples in the room (save sleeping Nick and his date) were no longer interested in the game, and he didn't want to make Val uncomfortable…not that he would feel exactly at ease in the midst of that either, but having had plenty to drink (that was now hitting him with full force), he could have managed. Val, though—he wasn't going to do that to her.

Once in the hallway, he took a deep breath and got his bearings. He had no idea what time it was, and he felt a little disoriented. That aside, he felt quite happy that he was now alone with Val, even if it really wasn't a big deal. It made him feel braver, though. He slipped his arm around her waist and asked, "Where are we going?"

"Let's go to my room."

He couldn't help but smile. That wasn't a bad sign. They started walking. "So…that shithead Ethan's not even writing his own lyrics anymore? That right?"

Val nodded and glanced at him but she looked shy. "Yeah…a lot of those words were mine." Then she slid her arm under his and wrapped her arm around him at the waistband too. Inside, he thought, *Score!* But he knew he had to keep his cool.

So, back to the subject at hand. "Goddamn, girl. Pretty impressive. That one song—'Metal Forever.' You write that?"

"Yeah...and 'Coming Down,' 'Intended Punishment,' and 'Fates Aligned.' Also, the basis for 'Scythe' was one of my poems too."

He'd thought Ethan had written "Coming Down," because the words felt like something Ethan might have come up with. It was similar to some of his previous work. All that knowledge did was impress Brad further. "No shit." They were quiet for a little while as Brad wrapped his mind around the fact that Val was like a fringe member of Fully Automatic, considering she was writing most of their words. He was only half kidding when he said, "Maybe we need to hire you as our full-time songwriter."

She laughed. "I just like writing."

"I'm not fuckin' with you, Val. You're writing shit the likes of which we've never seen." She leaned her head into him. Oh, fuck. She had no idea what that did to him. He forced air into his lungs as they reached the stairs and started walking. Again, he could feel just how fucked up he was. He had to focus, but he couldn't help it. When she did that, it made him feel protective of her, and that response made him think of something else. "Zane told me about some fight you got into. Your ex-roommate just tried to beat hell out of you?"

"Something like that."

They reached Val's room and she unlocked the door and turned on the light. Brad stepped in, closing the door behind him. He couldn't lose his momentum at this point. He slid his thumb over her forehead. "I'm glad she didn't leave any scars on that pretty little head of yours."

"Yeah. And I wouldn't want to have to sue her ass." For some reason, in his drunken state, her words set him off. He started laughing and couldn't stop. Val led him in the room and then walked back to the door, locking it. "Come on in." Brad had to sit down. The room was starting to spin, thanks to his gales of laughter, and he moved over to the nearest bed to sit down. "No, not there. The other bed."

He stood up, wondering why she wanted him in a specific bed. It didn't matter. He couldn't drop the ball now. He walked over to the other bed and sat down. "Oh…you gonna come curl up with me?"

"I think I need to put you to bed."

That hit him hard, and he could feel his blood starting to speed through his veins. Was that an invitation? "I'd like that. Want me to tell you where to start?"

She started walking over, a smile on her face that he couldn't quite interpret. "Oh, Brad. You are such a bad, bad boy."

"You like bad boys?"

"I like *you*."

That's what he needed to hear. It meant he had a chance. "Did you know I turned twenty in March?"

"Yeah? So now you're an older bad boy?"

She walked over to the bed, and he held out his hands. She took them, and that was when he knew tonight was his lucky night. "I think you're probably the best birthday present I've had." She sat down next to him and he touched her cheek, then kissed her. It was an innocent kiss, no tongue yet, simply testing the waters. But he was beyond fucked up, and he knew there was no way in hell, not the way he was feeling, not right now anyway. He opened his eyes, happy that at least Val hadn't spurned him. Anything else could wait until he was more in control. "I'm way fuckin' drunker than I thought. I need to rest my head. The room is spinning."

Brad's world grew black as his head sunk into the pillow.

It didn't feel like much time had passed when Brad started to stir, hearing raised voices, but what pulled him completely out of his slumber was Ethan's hands digging into his shoulders while the guy shouted in his face. "Wake up, you motherfucker." Brad forced his eyes open while his friend wrapped a fist around Brad's t-shirt, trying to pull him out of the bed. "Did you fuck her?"

He was having a hell of a time getting his bearings. He was completely disoriented. "What the hell are you talking about? Where am I?" It all came rushing into his head...the night before, sitting on Valerie's bed, then nothing. He couldn't remember anything after that—and it was gonna piss him off if something happened and he didn't remember. But he didn't think so. Still...he had to be sure. "Valerie...Did I? Did we...?" Fuck. It was driving him crazy. He couldn't remember anything past the time when he was flirting with Val on the bed, and he was pretty sure he had only been sleeping, but he couldn't be sure. His shoes were off but his clothes were on, and Val was wearing a t-shirt and pajama pants, so he thought it was safe to assume nothing had happened between them. He was glad, because he'd be pissed if they *had* done something and he couldn't remember it.

Jesus. Ethan was blitzed out of his mind. The alcohol on the guy's breath was fresh and heavy. Brad wondered if he'd slept at all. The only reason Brad knew it was early morning was because of the sunlight shining through the curtains on the window. But he knew that much—it *was* morning.

Val had been tugging on Ethan's shirt, trying to get him to let go of Brad. As Brad began to awaken, he realized his friend was seriously considering beating the shit out of him. He probably should have been scared—but he wasn't. Val yelled at Ethan, "What are you doing?"

Ethan let go of Brad and turned to Val, putting his hands on her shoulders. "You mean…you invited him here? Did he force himself on you?"

"Force himself on me? Whatever gave you that idea? Brad is a gentleman."

Brad was starting to awaken more and he sat up, taking in a deep breath. He was beginning to find the scene hilarious but said nothing as Ethan continued his rant. "Gentleman? Then he seduced you."

Val sounded angry. "Get out."

"He did. *You* did."

"Get the hell out of here, Ethan. I've had it with you."

"But Valerie…"

Val was pushing against Ethan's chest, and Brad sensed that he might have to help her. He didn't want to fight his friend, but he knew he'd have to consider getting a little physical with him to get him out of the room. Val persevered, though. "For your information, we did not have sex. But if we had, I can assure you that we both would have been willing."

Ethan sounded hurt. "You mean…you would have slept with my best friend?"

Her words had just sunk in with Brad as well, and he couldn't ignore the implication. "Really?"

"And not with me?"

"You asshole. After the way you've treated me, you think I'd *want* to sleep with you? You never even *tried*, Ethan Richards. And neither did Brad. But that's unimportant. Nothing happened. Now, if you wouldn't mind, I'd really like to get some sleep. Good night, Ethan."

This time, when Val pushed against Ethan, he let her guide him out the door to the hallway. She'd no sooner gotten the door closed, though, that he was opening it again. Brad heard his friend ask, "You sure you didn't sleep with him and just forgot?"

"Positive." Val slammed the door and locked it, walking back in the room with an exasperated look on her face. She might have been tired, but she looked gorgeous to Brad, and he could have kicked himself for not taking advantage of the situation the night before. No wonder she'd called him a *gentleman*. He'd been too far gone to try a goddamned thing.

He had to know. "What happened exactly?"

"You don't remember?"

"It's fuzzy."

"You fell asleep."

"What were we doing?"

She smiled. "We were just joking around, and you passed out on my bed."

He knew, though. He wasn't positive, but he was sure they'd been in the same bed. That again gave him hope. "But…you slept here…in this bed…*with* me, right?"

She nodded. "Yeah. This is my bed. That bed over there belongs to my roommate. I didn't think it'd be cool if I crashed on her bed, just in case she came back needing it."

That sounded right. He seemed to remember her being close to him all night long, but he'd been too wasted to do a damn thing about it. "I lost a golden opportunity. I need to quit drinking so much."

"Maybe. Now…I don't know about you, but I'm exhausted, and you need your rest too. Do you mind sleeping for a little longer?"

He'd love more sleep, no question, and he might have felt hung over, but he was also a realist. "No way in hell will I be able to sleep if you cuddle up next to me like you did last night."

The look on her face was priceless. She looked helpless and lost. "Oh…"

He didn't want to miss this opportunity. For the first time ever, Val had seemed like she wasn't worried about Ethan or how she felt about the guy. For once, she seemed to think only about Brad, and he was going to blow it if he came on too strong. Truth be told, he felt like shit anyway. "No. You know what? You said I was a gentleman, so I guess I'll do my best to keep being a gentleman."

"You sure?"

"Shit, Val…it's *your* bed. I'm not kickin' you out of it just 'cause I'm a—what'd you call me last night? I might be a bad boy, but I can keep my dogs down."

"I didn't say *that*."

He laughed. "No, but I *do* remember you calling me a bad boy. And you seemed to like that."

She smiled and sat on the bed. "So is it okay if I lie here too? I'll roll over so my back is to you."

He couldn't help but sigh. God, what he wouldn't love to do with her right next to him. But he'd promised. "Do what you gotta do. I'll…just roll over too." He lay on his side, facing her roommate's empty bed, while Val lay next to him, her back barely touching his, and she faced the wall. Not only was it uncomfortable and he felt like he was hanging on the edge of the bed (besides the fact that he had a killer fucking headache), he hated not holding her, even if nothing happened. They'd managed to sleep next to each other all night long and not do anything, so why not now?

He rolled over and said, "I can't get comfortable. I promise…no funny business." At first, he wasn't sure if she was awake until she turned her head. "But are you okay if I face this way? Isn't that what we did last night?"

She turned her head back to face the wall and said, "Yeah."

"Do you mind if we do it again? I don't think I'll be able to get to sleep the other way, and I've got a headache. I just want to sleep it off."

"Yeah, that's fine."

Good. Facing the same way felt more natural, because they didn't feel like they were at cross purposes. They curved the same way, so they took advantage of the space instead of fighting against it. He rested his right arm between their bodies and closed his eyes. Not a minute later, he felt Val's hand on his arm, pulling it over her body. He was glad he felt like shit or he would have gotten way too excited before she said, "That's not an invitation."

He smiled but tried to keep it out of his voice. It was nice anyway. "Is it okay to close the gap?"

"I guess that would be okay."

So he moved right up next to her and focused on his headache...because if he didn't, feeling her soft body up against his, her sweet-smelling hair flooding his nostrils, he was gonna pop a boner—and then she'd kick his ass out for sure.

No, he was simply going to try to enjoy the moment and pray he could fall back asleep.

CHAPTER FOURTEEN

A FEW HOURS later, Brad sensed that Valerie got out of bed, but he fell back to sleep. If it hadn't been hours later, he would have worried and thought maybe he'd made her too uncomfortable and she had given up, but he knew they'd been out for a while.

He woke up again later when he heard the door to her room close. She wasn't being loud, but he'd awakened anyway. He heard her chair slide on the floor as she sat down, and he imagined her sitting there staring at him, and it freaked him out. So he opened his eyes and smiled when he saw her back was to him. She pulled a drawer on her desk open and started putting makeup on. He could only imagine what her face looked like, framed by the white towel wrapping her hair. He couldn't tell what she was wearing—only that it was pink, not the black Godsmack t-shirt she'd been wearing the night before—but he couldn't stop watching her, thinking about her. He let out a breath. He didn't know the last time he'd wanted someone so badly, if he ever had.

Several minutes later, she pulled the towel off her head and set it on the side of the desk, then started running a comb through her hair. God. This was bad. He could have watched her for hours, just pining away for her, enjoying the way she moved, wanting to touch her, tell her. She started to stand, and that was when he knew the jig was up, so he sat up in bed and said, "Morning."

"Did you sleep okay?"

"Yeah. Thanks." Aw, fuck. She was wearing a pink robe that ended at her knees. It was held closed by a little fabric belt that she'd tied in a bow. God, that would be so easy to undo and find out what she wasn't wearing under there after her shower. *Focus, Payne. Focus, man.* He hoped the look on his face wasn't as lustful as the thoughts in his head. Back to practical conversation to take his mind off her body. "Did I make it hard for you to sleep?"

"Nope. I slept fine."

He had to get out of there, or she would be in trouble. And he wouldn't make a good first impression anyway. His mouth was dry—that was thanks to the rum—and he knew he could stand a hot shower. He ran his hands over his face and then looked for his shoes on the side of the bed where he lay. They weren't there, so he peeked on the other side and found them.

As he put them on, his brain was at work on a master plan. He too would clean up and then he was going to return and tell Val exactly what he'd been thinking. Well, no, he couldn't do that, because he would scare her for sure. But he wasn't ready to give up yet. Just because his body hadn't cooperated the night before was no reason to throw in the towel. So, once his shoes were on, he stood and said, "If you can just point me in the right direction, I think I can find Ethan's place. I need to see what the guys are up to—I'm not sure when we're hitting the road."

She led him to the door and pointed down the hall. "Go through that door to the stairs. When you get to the ground floor, go out the door. Then there's a long hallway. Follow it all the way to the end. There you'll see a door just like this one. Those are the stairs to Ethan's dorm. He's on the second floor."

"Yeah…I remembered that much." He wasn't ready to go—not yet. "Hey…thanks."

"For what?"

He smiled and shook his head. He was grateful he'd found his balls, but he wasn't going to give away what was floating around in his head. "For everything." He started walking down the hall, turning around before she closed the door. "I'll be back in a while."

"Okay." That was all he needed to hear.

He made his way back to Ethan's room—between her directions and his memory, it wasn't too difficult. He knocked on the door. Nothing. He knocked again and thought he heard motion so he stood and waited. He might have to return to Val's room sooner than he'd hoped. He shook his head. No way was he gonna hit on the girl without showering and brushing his teeth.

Zane answered the door, looking disheveled and in pain. Brad knew why. Yeah, Brad had had way too much to drink and had been hurting because of it, but Zane had mixed rum and vodka, a killer fucking combination. Zane looked exhausted too. He'd be glad he didn't have to travel today. When Zane saw it was Brad at the door, he stood back to let his friend in. "Where you been?"

"Over at Val's."

Zane raised his eyebrows. "You fuckin' with me?"

Brad grinned on one side of his face. "Nothing happened."

Zane tilted his head back toward Ethan's bed where Ethan lay, sprawled out and alone. Brad wondered what had happened to the girl with the blowjob mouth who'd been hanging with his friend the night before. "You'll have a hell of a time convincing him of that."

The smile on Brad's face faded. "You think I give a fuck what he thinks?"

Zane raised his eyebrows and sat on the edge of the bed, avoiding Jennifer's feet. "You know he and Val dated for a while, right?"

"We're not goin' there, man. You have no fuckin' idea."

"What?"

Brad shook his head. He really *didn't* want to go there. He'd have to, though, or Zane would think he was a scuzzball. He sighed. "I was interested in Valerie the weekend you guys came home and brought her with you...*and* I asked Ethan if he would care if I pursued her. And guess what? He said *no*."

Brad watched the realization wash over Zane's face. Yeah, the bassist knew—when he really thought about it—that it made perfect sense. Valerie wasn't Ethan's type—not even close. Zane had known Brad for a while but hadn't been close friends with him, so he might not have known that Val was the kind of girl Brad was attracted to. It made no sense, really. With the tattoos and the hair, the whole music lifestyle Brad was pursuing, the last kind of girls he should be pursuing was nice girls. The dads of the girls Brad had dated never said anything, but it was obvious they hated him. Hell, part of him believed that was why Leah's dad had moved their family to Lakewood.

He knew that wasn't true, and he'd started to sense Leah wouldn't have wanted him forever anyway. That was okay. What he felt for Val...well, it felt different somehow. And he knew she felt something too.

Zane shook his head. "Sorry. I didn't know."

"It's cool, man." He looked around. Nick and the girl he'd been with weren't where they'd been the night before. In fact, they weren't in the room, near as Brad could tell.

"Nick with that girl?"

"I think so. He was wasted, dude."

"Yeah, I know." He told his friend he needed to shower, so Zane showed him where everything was and lay down next to Jennifer again, pulling her into an embrace. Brad was glad he'd learned from shows that he always needed an extra change of clothes, so he'd brought one for last night and one for today. He didn't want Val thinking he was a grungy rock star who didn't give a shit about hygiene. He planned on finally making that move...and he wanted nothing stopping him. Nothing.

He walked back to Val's room a while later, feeling more confident. He was clean and felt a lot better than he had earlier. He hadn't been able to stop thinking about holding her all night long.

When Val answered the door, she looked surprised to see him. He was glad she didn't look upset. She invited him in and he told her about the state of his Fully Automatic bandmates who were in bad shape overall. He told her they would stay there a while longer, and she invited him to hang out with her.

That was when it was time to make his move. He let the confident feeling surge through his veins, and he stepped closer to her, close enough to touch her. "That's not the main reason why I came back here, though." He waited a few seconds to let his words register with her and then he said, "We have a little unfinished business."

She seemed so innocent in that moment. "We do?"

Yes, innocent maybe, but not unwilling. He leaned over and took her face in his hands, lifting her lips to his. He kissed her, as gently as he could allow himself to, but, goddamn, it was difficult. He'd been imagining this moment for months now, and he wanted her badly. Way too badly. Fuck. He should have jerked off in the shower, because controlling himself was going to be harder than usual. Would losing his load have helped? He didn't know, but he had to stop thinking about that right now.

It was hard, though, because she tasted so sweet, and her response was just as he'd imagined. She parted her lips and took him in. Yeah, she was willing and eager, and all that did was fuel his fire. She was feeling it too, that weird attraction between them igniting into something bigger than he'd expected, something he knew he'd be lucky to control. Still…he kept his breathing (and his cock) under control for the meantime and ended the kiss. Oh, fuck. And she placed her hands on his pecs as though to steady herself. It took her a few seconds to open her eyes, as though she'd been transported. When he had her full attention, he said,

"Unfinished, right?"

She gave him a tiny smile, sweet and naïve, and seemed to give the tiniest of nods. Well, she wasn't pushing him away. In fact, she seemed breathless and expectant. He wasn't going to disappoint her, so he kissed her again, and he would have sworn it was magic. Okay, so he never would have said something like that to one of his friends. Ethan would have called him a *pussy* if he'd even known Brad had been thinking something like that. But it was, though—it was more than just a kiss. It felt like they deepened their connection in that moment, like he could see inside her soul and, yes, she was pure and light and everything he could ever want.

He knew her response was a sign to move forward, so he wrapped his hands around her waist and pulled her close. Fuckin' A. She smelled so goddamn good and felt so right up next to him. She moved her hands onto his neck and then slid them up into his hair, driving him insane. Jesus…he wanted to fuck her right there, but he knew a girl like Val would need finesse. And he wanted to give that to her. He wanted her to know she wasn't just a cheap lay for him. Still, he wanted to move the proceedings forward, so he slid his hands down to her ass, using it as an excuse to press her harder into his body.

And her fingers in his hair. Shit. She was driving him fucking crazy.

Her breathing got deeper, so he knew he was on the right track. He couldn't hold it back anymore and just let the blood flow straight to his cock…like he'd be able to stop it anyway. He moved his lips to her neck and not only did she let out a sigh, he could have sworn he heard a moan. Fuck, yeah. He didn't know that a girl had ever done that before they'd actually engaged in the real deal. He moved a hand up underneath her shirt, feeling the bare skin above her jeans, and he heard her breathing quicken again.

It was then, though, that she took a hand out of his hair and placed it firmly on his chest. No. Fuck, no. If he was reading her right, she was putting on the brakes.

"Brad…please stop."

He opened his eyes and looked in hers. "Stop?"

"Yeah."

Why was she changing her mind? Was that really what she wanted? He had to try one more time. He kissed her again. Yeah, there were those sparks. Could she deny them? "Stop *that?*"

She blinked. "Yes."

"You don't seem so sure…" He pressed his forehead on hers and bore into her eyes with his. He wanted to understand. "What's wrong?"

She moved both hands to his chest. She wasn't pressing against him as if to push him away, but they seemed to ground her. "I…It's not you, Brad. Oh, God, it's not you. I swear. I want you bad."

That's what he'd thought. "So why not? If you're worried about birth control…" He wasn't going to be irresponsible. She had to know that.

She hesitated. "No. I'm…um… I'm a…"

"Virgin?" He knew it even before she nodded her head. "Oh." He nodded too as if to process the information. "Oh. Yeah. Uh…your first time should be…special, right? At least, for girls. I didn't give much of a shit." He didn't know how to do that for her, not right now, anyway. He was nearly out of his mind with desire, and she was pulling the plug. He needed a bathtub of ice water to jump in. She giggled and, in spite of his feelings of desperation, he found it endearing. But then it dawned on him. Fuck. He had to know. As much as it was gonna hurt, he needed to know. Her eyes all but said it, but he needed to confirm it. "That's not it, though. It's Ethan, isn't it? You still care about him." She didn't say a word. She didn't need to. It was written all over her face. And thank the fucking saints, because he felt his hard on wilt. He sighed. "And...I already told you, as you'll recall, nothing between you and me as long as he's in the picture." He let go of Valerie and walked across the room. He sucked in another deep breath and then turned to look at her. He wasn't sure where to go from here, but as long as she was pining for Ethan, he wasn't going to press his luck. No fucking way. He wasn't going to be rebound guy. That said, he cared about Valerie and didn't want her to feel bad, especially after being honest with him. Next best thing. "So...how about we go grab a bite to eat? I'm starving."

"Uh, I..."

"On me."

She blinked and then nodded. "Okay." Any other girl, he would have been pissed, but that look on her face. He knew he was gonna have a hell of a time getting over her. A hell of a time.

CHAPTER FIFTEEN

IT SEEMED LIKE no matter how small the town, there was always a McDonald's. Well, it was a college town, so it didn't surprise him. That was good. McDonald's was cheap, and he could get a lot of food for a little. He wasn't hurting for money, but he was tight with it. He was saving it up for all things band and music related, and food wasn't one of those things, so he was tight. Still, he wasn't going to let Val know that. As they approached the register, he told her to get whatever she wanted.

He was going to have to sublimate his sexual urges with food, so he ordered a shitload. Then, when Val ordered, she got a sandwich, hash browns, and coffee. "That's it?"

She grinned. "Well, I'm not a growing boy like you are."

He smiled back and handed the cashier a twenty. "You're gonna waste away to nothing."

She rolled her eyes. "Yeah, right."

In just a few minutes, they took their tray of food and stopped to grab napkins before sitting down. Brad stirred cream in his coffee and Val asked, "So…what do you do besides play in your band? Where do you work?"

"I work for one of those places that changes oil. Pretty much sucks. Course, anything that doesn't have anything to do with music sucks, as far as I'm concerned." He took a bite of his sandwich. He decided it wouldn't hurt to tell her. "But I'm saving up so I can actually make something of my life."

"What are your plans?"

"I'm pretty sure you have the idea. I don't have any crazy notions, like we have to move to New York or L.A. or Seattle, but we need to amass a fan base. Nothing happens nowadays without fans, and we won't get fans by sitting around on our asses. That's part of why I booked that show here—the sooner Ethan and Zane realize college isn't their future, the sooner we can get on with our lives. They need to feel the need in their blood."

She seemed a little dismayed. He couldn't figure out why, but he took another bite of his sandwich. He'd let her explain herself…or not. "So what are you thinking?"

"I dunno. Colorado Springs, Denver, some of the big college towns. But that would involve moving to one of those places. I'm thinking Denver. It's huge. I bet we could have shows booked all the time." He took another bite, and they got quiet for a little bit. Val was dunking her hash brown patty in ketchup, but she wasn't talking. He wondered what she might be thinking. And he suspected he might have an inkling. Still, he wasn't going to push her into talking if she wasn't ready. He took a sip of orange juice and then said, "So, that's what I'm saving up for. I'm sure my mom will be thrilled for me to move out."

"You think so?"

"Actually, no. I'm her youngest kid and she's divorced, so she really doesn't want me to leave. But I've been trying to prepare her for it." She sipped her coffee. She was holding something close. He wanted to know what it was. "So what about you, Val? What big plans do you have for the future?"

She took a deep breath and tried to smile. I have no idea what I want to be when I grow up."

He laughed. "Okay…I'll ask you what my douchebag counselor asked me my junior year in high school." He closed his eyes and conjured that old fart earning a paycheck for being fucking lame and tried to do his best imitation. The guy had a raspy, folksy, high-pitched voice and a wrinkly face. He'd worn glasses that always slipped to the bottom of his nose, and when he talked, it looked like he'd just taken a big whiff of shit. So Brad tried channeling the man's aura when he spoke. "What are your interests, Mr. Payne? What do you find yourself doing when you lose track of time?"

Val laughed. At least his humor wasn't wasted on her. "Those seem to be reasonable questions."

"Yeah, they were, even though he was reading them off a card while looking out the window watching the cheerleaders practice on the front lawn. And when I told him my answer, he told me to *be realistic*."

"You seem to be talented with your impersonations too."

"Yeah, but seriously…what interests you, Val? There's gotta be something, right?"

She seemed to give it some thought. He knew what he

wanted to tell her, but he would rather she say it. So he sat in silence, sipping at his coffee again, waiting for her to talk. "Well, isn't that why I'm taking all these classes, these varied classes, to help me figure out what I like?"

"Maybe...so have you found something?"

"That's the problem. Everything seems fun...for a while."

Come on, Val. Say it. "You like writing?"

"I guess."

"Because that shit you wrote for us was phenomenal."

"I thought you were just saying that."

He smiled. "Because I was drunk? I'll let you in on a little secret. I'm brutally honest when I'm drunk. Scary honest." He didn't know that that was completely true, but he had thought her lyrics were brilliant. His shit was kindergarten words strung together compared to the talent in her pinky finger. She was thinking about it. Good. He wanted her to come to it on her own. She took another sip of her coffee, and that's when he realized she wasn't going to say a word. He was going to have to suggest it to her. He knew he was on the right track, because Ethan had said it one time, that Val had told him she'd dreamed being a lead vocalist. "You ever think about being in a band?"

And there...that was when he saw her eyes light up. They were filled with doubt too, but he could see the spark. *Yeah.* He knew where she lived. But then she shrugged and tried to look neutral. "Nah." She took another drink of her coffee.

She was lying to herself. She was going to be the good girl and go to college, just like her parents, friends, and teachers thought she should, and she was going to ignore the siren call, the cry from her soul, telling her what she really wanted to do. He'd felt it too. He knew it and chose to follow it, and that's why he'd seen it in her. And after what little he'd heard her sing, he knew she could be a great vocalist. Still...it would have to wait until she decided to embrace it. He'd planted the seed and now she'd have to water and nurture it. He just hoped he could be there to see it grow into fruition.

He'd make sure he was.

Ethan and Zane came home from school in May, and Brad had plenty to show off. He'd managed to not only book them a fuckload of shows, but he'd also purchased an old church van that would become their touring van. They'd have to continue renting a trailer, but they could take a smaller one and have plenty of room to spare. The van had needed a few repairs, and his friends at work were able to help him with them. He hadn't had to spend a fortune on the van, and he knew the minor problems had been why.

He was relieved to hear that Ethan and Zane had the school experience out of their system. Zane said maybe someday he'd go back, but he wanted to give the band an honest try. Ethan? He'd only done it to say in his grandfather's good graces. The old bastard was the only male figure in Ethan's life who seemed to give a shit, and Ethan didn't want to fuck that away. Too bad the guy didn't live close enough to keep his friend on the straight and narrow.

Now that the band was on track and his friends home for good, Brad decided to not let Val slip through his fingers so easily. Sure, he was going to give her the time and space she needed, but she was going to have to tell him to back the fuck off if she didn't want him to be part of her life. She was too special to him to just let go. He worried too that he would be "out of sight, out of mind," and he didn't want that to happen. He knew that Val and Ethan remained on the outs, even though she was still hung up on him, so there would be no connection there. He'd have to do that himself. So he sent her a text now and then to see how she was doing. She hardly ever got on Facebook or he would have connected that way, but she always responded to texts. He asked her to get on Facebook, though, so she could like the page he'd set up for Fully Automatic. He'd made it look as professional as possible, adding pictures and a couple of MP3s, and he made sure it looked good when he invited her. They only had about thirty-three likes at the time, because it seemed secondary to actually playing for live audiences. He had simply wanted to give audiences a place to look for more info after shows.

Val *did* like the page, though, and it wasn't long after he'd asked her.

He had also managed to set up gigs near her, one in her hometown, and he couldn't wait to tell her about those. Instead of telling her, though, he set up events on Facebook and decided to invite her to two—the one in her hometown and one in Colorado Springs the night before.

And then he waited.

In the meantime, they started messaging some, and he decided that he really liked her as a friend. Even if nothing further ever happened between the two of them, he wanted to continue their friendship. She started sharing poems and songs she was writing, and he encouraged her. She really was a hell of a writer.

One night she sent him a song/ poem that he wanted to read so much more into but thought better of it:

> I need something I shouldn't have.
> It's wrong, the way I crave
> But I can't stay away.
> Please tell me it's okay.
>
> You're the flame that I'm drawn to
> Every single time
> I can't stay away
> But I know you're not mine.
> Need to go away,
> Need to run and hide,
> But I keep getting drawn to you
> Time after time after time.
>
> Why is it I always need something bad for me?
> I want something I shouldn't have.
> It's wrong the way I cave
> To you but you feel like mine.
> Please make me feel like I can stay.

He wasn't stupid. He knew the poem was about Ethan. So he told her the truth—that, like everything she wrote, it was good stuff. But then she sent him one that, if he wasn't mistaken, was about him, and he felt his heart swell (hell, he felt his dick swell) when he read it.

FULLY AUTOMATIC

What is it about you
That makes me weak in the knees?
You're the only one on this earth
Never needs to say please.

But you know my weakness,
Know where I hide my soul.
Yet you kept me safe
And you made me whole.
You made me whole.

CHORUS:
But you're the rainbow I can't touch,
The forbidden fruit I want so much.
Just one taste, one night together
Would help me endure the rest of forever.

You said that you'd wait for me
But you didn't know what that entailed.
You didn't know my heart was diseased.
In all things love I have failed.

But you seem to see right through me.
You know my heart's desires.
I don't think I ever fooled you
When you set my soul on fire.
You set my soul on fire.

BRIDGE:
You will be my heaven and hell,
My promise so far away.

Can I wait until that day?

He felt like she'd taken his breath away. He would have thought that song was about Ethan too except for one thing, one line: "You said that you'd wait for me." He was pretty sure Ethan had never made a promise like that to Val. His line, if he had one, would have been, "I'll run from you every chance I get." Once the emotions calmed, he composed (and recomposed) his response. He didn't want to sound like a fucking idiot, and he definitely didn't want to call her out. She was sharing words that were personal and intimate, and no way was he going to destroy that trust. He finally wound up messaging her: *These fucking rock, Val. Where the hell do you come up with this stuff?*

After several minutes, she messaged back: *All in my sick little head.*

Brad: *lol* Then, after several minutes, he messaged her again. He was not going to just let her talent slip through his fingers, any more than he wanted her out of his life. He messaged her again. *How would you feel if I took your lyrics and turned them into a song? I could write a kick ass tune for that.* He was thinking, "Just like Ethan did," but there was no way he was going to remind her of that.

She responded: *Write away!*

And so he copied and pasted the song into Word and printed it out, then grabbed his guitar and sat on his bed. He had a tune in his head that he had to work out, and he hoped the music would speak to Valerie as much as her words had spoken to him.

And he worked on it for a solid week, making it perfect. He hadn't said a word during band practices, either. He wanted to know what Val thought before he had the guys learn it. When he was one-hundred percent satisfied, he recorded an unplugged version of it on his acoustic guitar and then he emailed it to her. He wanted to know what she thought. She was most important. If she didn't like it, he'd start over. It wasn't as heavy as most songs he wrote, because he felt like the words warranted something a little lighter. He was hoping he could get Val to sing it, so he wanted to write something that he thought would be in her range as well as something that would show off her voice.

He was nervous and edgy for hours. Had she opened the email? Had she listened to it? Did she like it or had she hated it and didn't know how to tell him? Several hours later, though, he received a text from her that made all the waiting worth it. *Holy crap! This is sooooo good! I can't wait to hear it plugged in. Your voice has never sounded better.*

The last sentence—wow. She didn't know what that did for him. He almost told her he wanted to hear her sing it, but he didn't want to make her feel uncomfortable. He'd hear her sing it soon enough. He could wait. So he texted her back saying, *Thanks. The guys will learn it fast. We'll play it at our shows near you, so you better be there.* She texted him back an *Of course* with a smiley emoticon. She clicked *Yes* to attending both the shows in Colorado Springs and Winchester, and Brad found himself counting the days.

Fortunately, the guys did learn the song quickly. He told them Val had written the lyrics, and he saw Ethan's face glower, but the guy said nothing. And he damn well better not. Brad had been up front from the get go with Ethan about how he felt about Val, so the guy had no right. None. And yet he'd moved in on her anyway. He loved his friend, but Ethan knew as well as Brad did that he didn't care about Val. Not like Brad did, anyway.

The day came for the Colorado Springs show. Brad wasn't familiar with either Colorado Springs or the venue, so they left extra early. Colorado Springs was on the other side of the slope, and he wanted to make sure he could find the place okay. He'd reserved a motel room for them too, and they could check in as early as three, so that's when he wanted to arrive. Then they could find the venue. They could grab a bite to eat and hang before the show, but he didn't want to be late or fuck anything up.

He just hoped Valerie would be there as promised.

CHAPTER SIXTEEN

BRAD HAD WORRIED for nothing. Every place they had to go, including the motel and the venue, were easy to find. After they knew where to go and how long it would take to get there, they found a Pizza Hut and decided to try to relax. They had a couple of hours before they could set up, so they had plenty of time.

He was more excited to see Valerie—and to see what she thought of her song—than he was for the concert, and that was saying something. He'd always felt more alive on stage than he did most of the time.

Fully Automatic was first on the ticket that night, so they'd set up and be ready long before the show started. He couldn't wait to see the inside of the place. They'd never played a show on this side of the Continental Divide before, but Brad was convinced it was where they needed to be if they wanted to grow their band's audience, and no one could tell him otherwise.

In the van on the way back to the venue, Ethan took

something. Brad wasn't sure what it was, but his friend had insisted on riding in the back, and he got really quiet. But he knew Ethan often liked to get high or drink before going onstage. It strengthened him. As long as his friend could control it, Brad didn't have a problem with it. And, after the last time Ethan had overdone it, Brad worried more about it. Still...until Ethan overindulged again, Brad felt like he couldn't say anything.

They got to the venue and, before they knew it, they were mingling with the other bands and getting ready to set up. Brad also took a peek at merch tables. Now that he had the van, his next goal was getting merch made to sell. He'd been talking about it for a while. Now it was time.

He hadn't been this excited for a show in a long time. Yeah, he was pumped to be playing in a bigger venue, but he was really looking forward to seeing Valerie again. He wasn't going to look around for her and potentially be disappointed, though, because he knew she might have decided to only go to the Winchester show and skip this one. But when they were doing sound checks, Brad happened to spot her in the crowd anyway. He'd have to talk to her for a few minutes before the show started; otherwise, he'd be staring at her through the whole show. If he talked with her, he hoped he'd be able to focus on the show itself. It wasn't a huge venue, so he wouldn't have a hard time finding her. He saw that she was with a couple, and he hoped that meant she didn't have a date wandering around somewhere as well.

He was tuning his guitar center stage. Ethan had already disappeared somewhere, and Zane was tweaking his bass. Two girls stood right in front of the stage trying to get his attention. He looked at them and smiled, and one of the girls started giggling. The other one mouthed, "I love you." He tried not to laugh but smiled again. He supposed, if he reached the goal he was aiming for, that he'd have to get used to that.

God, he hoped he'd get used to it. He'd had girls flirt with him, sure, but he'd never been hit on hardcore. It happened to Ethan all the time. But then, when Brad thought about it, it had to do with the kind of girls Ethan liked too. Brad tended to like girls who were a little more demure. They weren't forward. He supposed, though, that he'd be exposed to all manner of women as their band got more popular. He liked the looks those girls were giving him, but it would take him a while to adjust.

Zane walked over, his bass draped over his body, and chin nodded at the girls. He smiled and then said toward Brad's ear, "They're cute, huh?"

Brad chuckled. "Yeah."

"Which one?"

"What?"

"After the show—which one?"

It sunk in with Brad what Zane was saying. A kind of one-for-you-and-one-for-me offer. Brad smiled again and said, "I kinda have my eyes on someone else."

Zane raised his eyebrows. "Yeah?"

He nodded. "Yeah."

That was all he was going to say, but Zane asked, "Happen to be someone I know?"

He wasn't going to lie. "Yeah."

Zane nodded his head and didn't say another word. "Lemme know if you change your mind." He walked closer to the end of the stage, and Brad decided now was the perfect time to seek that *someone else* out. Except he couldn't see her out there where she'd been before. He decided to go out to the crowd and look anyway, so he walked off the stage and Ethan passed him to head outside. His friend seemed to be halfway coherent in spite of the fact that he was blitzed. That was good, because show time wasn't far off.

When he started looking out over the crowd bathed in shadow, he thought he could see Val back where he'd seen her before. The crowd was getting thicker as it got closer to performance time, and Brad was glad for that. He wanted to play for lots of people. Val was talking to her two friends—still no other guy hanging around, and he was grateful for that—and she was animated and smiling.

He got close and she noticed him. Damn, she was a sight for sore eyes. He hugged her and then asked, "How are you, sweetheart?" He left an arm around her shoulders. She was going to have to tell him to go to hell if she wanted him to stop pursuing her. She didn't shrug him off, though.

"Great. So good to see you."

"How's your break so far?"

"Okay." She smiled at him. "Better now." He raised his eyebrows—oh, God, he hoped she meant that. "Oh, Brad, this is my old friend from high school Jill and her husband Chad." The guy named Chad put out his hand and Brad shook it. "This is my very good friend, Brad Payne."

Goddamn. "*Very* good friend? I feel privileged. Nice to meet you folks." He looked back to Valerie. "I gotta get backstage. See you later?"

"You bet."

It took everything he had to not pull her into another embrace. He hadn't been able to stop thinking about the kiss he'd given her in her dorm room the last time he'd seen her. He had a show to perform, though, and he was going to be the bad ass rock star he wanted her to fall in love with.

And when they took the stage, it felt like magic. They were *on* that night, really on. They hit all the right notes, melded together, and the audience became a part of that. It was an incredible feeling. They were playing more of their newer songs, and he wished he knew what Valerie thought. She knew a couple of the songs that he'd sent her audio files of, and he caught her singing along to them. It simply confirmed that he should do something he'd been tempted to anyway.

So, five songs in, Brad didn't cue his band to start the next song. Instead, he grabbed the mike. "Colorado Springs, you've been great so far. Thanks for welcoming us here." He pulled the mike off the stand and stepped closer to the edge of the stage. The bright lights had been shining straight into his eyes so he couldn't see the audience. They'd just been a huge black abyss, and usually that was comforting. Now, though, he wanted to see faces…and he hoped he wasn't about to make a huge ass of himself. "I want to do something a little different right now. A friend of mine is here in the audience. She's written a lot of the words you've heard tonight." His eyes locked on Valerie, close to the foot of the stage, and he saw recognition wash over her face. Yes, he was talking about her. "Anyway, this is a song we wrote together, and I'd really like to have her sing it with me." He smiled at her. She looked reluctant and shocked and even shy...but he saw something else too. He saw temptation. Yes, she wanted to do it. So he pointed a finger at her and then crooked it toward himself, inviting her up on stage.

She'd heard the tune, and he knew she knew the words. He knew Val well enough already to know she was already intimately familiar with the song. But then she started shaking her head frantically, and he even saw her mouth the word *no*. He would have let it go right there, but he knew better. He could see that part of her really wanted to do it—she was just a little unsure of herself. She needed time in front of an audience was all, and what better place than here? He smiled at the audience, his co-conspirators, and then looked Val in the eye. "See, Val? Everyone wants to hear you. You can't let them down now." If she turned him down at this point, he'd let it go...but he'd offer her another chance in private. Because no matter what Valerie *said*, he knew she wanted to. He knew she loved music, felt it in her soul. He could see it in her. He'd known it that night in his garage when she'd sung Godsmack's song like she'd been born to.

She shook her head, smiling, and then he saw her try to look angry, but it wasn't working. The guy named Chad helped her up, and Brad held out his hand to help lift her onstage. Once she was standing, he picked the mike back up and said, "Please give Valerie a big hand."

He hugged her and she said in his ear, "You could have at least warned me. I'm gonna kill you."

"Gotta catch me first."

He caught Ethan's eye as he let her go, and his friend

was pissed. Well, that was too damn bad. It wasn't Brad's fault he'd been a shithead to Val. She was still his friend and, he hoped, maybe more later, but as a friend, he was making this offer. He placed the mike back in the stand and yelled, "Let's turn this shit up." While the audience was agreeing with hoots, hollers, fist pumping, and devil's horns, he turned to Val. "I'll sing the first verse, you do the second, and maybe we could harmonize on the bridge?"

She was nervous, but she was also game. Brad was glad he'd done it. "What about the choruses?"

"Same deal. That okay?"

"Yeah, sure. Why not?"

He gave Nick a sign with a look in his eyes and a nod of his head to cue them for the next song. They started playing then, and he wondered what Val thought about the song plugged in. She'd only heard the one he'd sent her on his acoustic guitar, so he knew she'd know the tune, but it was heavier. Plus, he'd start off, giving her time to feel the song. If she seemed unsure when it was time for her to sing, he'd accompany her, but just like he'd suspected—she had it.

He knew it would freak her out (and it would likely have the same effect on him) if he looked her in the eyes. Hell, he didn't know if he could do it looking at her. It was a song he was pretty damn sure she'd written about him, and he hoped having her sing it was enough for her to figure out that he knew. And so, as he sang the first verse, he had to hold his shit together. As he wound it down to the chorus, he was feeling confident again, and he peeked over at her.

Then, when it was her turn to sing, he allowed himself

to half look. She was gripping the microphone and looking out at the audience, her knuckles turning white. Her voice was a little unsteady at first, but one line in and she pushed herself through the nerves. Her voice was soft but strong as she sang the words he knew were for him: "You said that you'd wait for me." Yeah, he'd said that, and he was beginning to believe it had been worth the wait. Val was a spectacular young woman full of life and emotion, and he wanted to get to know her better—not just texting and messaging, not just exchanging lyrics.

When she got to the chorus, he decided to sing harmony to her melody, and he got close to her so he could share the mike. That was a *wow* moment. He hadn't expected their voices to sound so good together, but they did. It felt like a sign. And when he got to the guitar solo, he didn't look at—*couldn't* look at—her. He hoped she thought the song was deserving of the emotion-laden solo he had given it.

When it ended, he looked at her and joined her back at the mike for the chorus one last time. God…that was incredible. There was something there between them, something he didn't think would ever disappear. And, at this point, he didn't give a shit if the whole world could see it. He threw his guitar pick out to the audience and placed his hand on the back of Val's neck. He kissed her on the cheek and then said, "Thanks for being a good sport."

She grinned, but he could see it. She was glad she had. Then she hurried offstage, sliding off the front. So, she'd enjoyed it but was more than happy to be done. The cheers were winding down, and Brad said into the mike, "Wasn't she great?" And the audience was already giving their roars and cheers, but he added anyway, "Let's give her a huge hand." He looked down at her again. "Thanks, Val."

She disappeared into the abyss again as the lights flooded his vision, but he already knew...she too had the sting of the lights in her eyes, and it would be hard for her to forget them anytime soon.

CHAPTER SEVENTEEN

THEY'D LOADED THE van and trailer back up with all their equipment, and Brad could hear the next band warming up. He hoped the audience was as on fire for them as they'd been for Fully Automatic. It usually worked that way—if the first band could get a momentum going, it would continue through the night...unless the second band completely sucked.

But when they were done, Brad sought out Val again. When he found her, she was alone. The first band hadn't started playing yet, were just checking things out, so he knew he had about three minutes. Once they started playing, he wouldn't be able to talk at all. "Hey," he said, taking the opportunity to hold Val in his arms again, hugging her. "Still want to kill me?"

She smiled. "Yeah. A little."

"They loved you."

"They loved *us*."

He shook his head. "Nope. I know better." She rolled

her eyes, but it wasn't subject for debate. She knew it and so did he, and he'd find a better time and place to discuss the future with her. For now, though, he wanted her to relish the feelings she'd had onstage. "So...wanna party with us after?"

"Maybe. I came with Jill and Chad, though. Is it okay if they come along?"

"Of course. The more, the merrier, right?" It was time to ask the more important question. "You coming to tomorrow night's show too?"

"I wanted to but...oh, yeah. Never mind."

"What?"

"Well, I didn't think I was gonna have money for tickets, but I forgot Chad and Jill paid for their own."

"So? Text me when you get there, and I'll get you in the back door."

"Actually, it's a bar, so should I even be there?"

"Who cares? If you're with me, they can't say shit. You're part of the band."

"Oh, no. You're not getting me to sing again."

Brad smirked, searching her eyes. "You trying to tell me you didn't like that?"

"No, I did. But I don't want to get too used to it."

"Why not?"

She didn't answer, because her friends Jill and Chad returned to her side. She used their presence as an excuse to avoid his question. "Hey, guys. Brad wanted to know if we want to party with them after the concert."

Chad said, "Probably not. Sorry. I have to work in the morning."

"Not a problem." Brad felt his heart sink, but he wasn't

going to push her. He never had and wasn't going to now. She would come to him when she was ready. "You'll be partying tomorrow night too, right?"

"If you have to ask, you don't know me very well."

She rolled her eyes. "And you'll be in my hometown tomorrow night."

He smiled. "Yeah." Zane, Nick, and even Ethan joined the four of them to enjoy the other two bands. Brad got brave at one point and draped his arm around Val's shoulder. He was relieved when she let him and even reciprocated the gesture.

After the show, the crowd started shuffling out, one body at a time. It had been a great show and most folks were reluctant to let it go. Brad and the entire band walked out with Val and her friends, and she hugged each guy in the band, even Ethan, wishing them a good night and telling them she'd enjoyed the show. Chad shook all the guys' hands too. He said to Brad, "You guys are kick ass. I hope to see you on a label someday."

"That's the plan." Brad turned to tell Val goodbye one more time and saw her in Ethan's arms. His friend not only held her close to his body, he was kissing her hard on the mouth…and Val was letting him.

What a fucking idiot Brad had been. Yeah, sure, there might have been something between him and Val, but Ethan had a hell of a pull on the girl. From what Brad knew, Ethan had shit all over her multiple times, and she just came back for more.

Well, no, that wasn't fair. He also knew Ethan was a charming son of a bitch, and Val didn't exactly look like she was reciprocating. She wasn't pushing him away, though, and that too was telling. So, after they left, Brad pulled Zane aside before they headed to the van. "That offer still stand?"

"What—the twins?"

Brad chuckled. They weren't exactly twins, but... "Yeah."

Zane whipped his phone out of his pocket. "Just one text away."

"Do it."

Zane gave him a look but started thumbing his phone.

Ethan asked, "We leaving?"

"Hold on a minute."

"What's up?" Ethan asked.

Zane said, "Chick patrol."

"We scorin' tonight?"

"Fuck, yeah."

"Well, hold on. C'mon, Nick. You were eyein' that one blonde girl, right?"

"Which one?" Nick laughed as the two of them headed toward the receding crowd.

"Should we wait by the van?"

Zane said, "Yeah, let me tell 'em." He tapped out a text while they walked out the back door. A few minutes later, Ethan and Nick arrived at the van, girls in tow, but Zane and Brad were still waiting.

Inside, Brad was seething. His friend—his *brother*, for fuck's sake—could kiss Valerie, rob Brad of her undying love, and then without another thought pick up another girl. Brad was going to do the same thing, but that was because he'd once again been rejected. If Val had chosen him, he wouldn't even *look* at another girl.

It was like a knife in his heart.

And so, when the Asian girl with the beautiful black hair sat in the passenger seat of the van and smiled at him, he smiled back and said, "Hang on," putting the van in gear and cranking the music to drown out his thoughts.

Why did he always manage to get a girl in the bathroom? Things had been hot and steamy in the hotel room all four guys had crammed into. As usual, the girls Ethan and Nick had chosen knew no shame, but the girls Zane and Brad were with had a little more modesty and self-respect. Zane asked for the keys to the van, and Brad handed them over. Shortly after, his girl (a girl who went by the name of Ginger) pulled him up off the chair where they'd been making out and led him into the bathroom.

It was a moment of truth. Brad started to back out, because he felt bad. He cared about Valerie, wanted to be with *her*, and instead he had this beautiful girl in front of him pulling his zipper down. She would be nothing but a one-night stand, and Brad had never done that before, not even with his mother's older friend Misti. To not know this girl's last name and engage in intimate relations…well, that was Ethan's thing, not his. Still, she was kissing his neck, and she'd already gotten in his pants and was stroking his cock. *Whoa.* Okay, so there was no way he could stop it now. Jesus.

"Tell me you got a condom, big boy."

The way she breathed the words made his cock swell more. Holy shit. So, yeah, he could do this, but he hoped he could get Val out of his head for the few minutes they'd be physically entwined. "Uh, yeah," he said and reached around for his wallet. It wasn't long before the damn thing was hugging his dick, and he was pounding into her like there was no tomorrow.

She was a screamer. From the second he entered her, she started screeching and carrying on, moaning and groaning and crying his name. He suspected much of it was for show, but he didn't care. It did something for him anyway, and he just kept driving into her. He probably should have worried more about her and if she was getting what she needed, but he was too focused on numbing his mind with sex.

Her howling became more intense. Had she come or not? He couldn't tell. He sometimes had a hard time telling anyway, but it was even more difficult this time and with this girl. He'd have thought she was coming when he slammed into her the first time. But that was it—he couldn't hold it back anymore. He could feel it in his balls as his brain exploded. He'd made some kind of sounds too—he wasn't sure what. He was completely out of it by that point.

As he regained his senses, he tried to get his breathing under control. She was smiling, her head resting against the wall of the bathroom. He wasn't sure, though, so he asked her, "Was that okay for you?"

She giggled. "Okay? That was incredible."

And, with that, his thoughts returned to Valerie, and he felt guilty.

He shouldn't, though. If she had her choice, she'd choose Ethan every time over him. He was starting to realize that. So he shouldn't feel guilty about taking care of himself.

And yet, even while he drove the girls home early the next morning, he couldn't shake the feeling that he'd betrayed Val.

CHAPTER EIGHTEEN

THE NEXT AFTERNOON, Fully Automatic was back on the road, heading toward Winchester. Brad was feeling a little better about the night before. The guilt was gone, replaced by the realization that he had to learn to look out for number one.

This show was the same as the night before, even down to the bands. So they got to the venue—a biker bar called Bad Boys—and set up. A while before show time, he got a text from Val saying she was almost there. He texted her back, telling her to come to the back of the building.

He was leaning against the wall, trying to look casual, trying not to be upset with her. First and foremost, they were friends, and she'd never promised him a thing. In fact, he was the fool who kept trying to win her over. The sooner he realized it was a losing battle, the sooner he could get on with his life and be happy.

She rounded the corner, and he stuck his phone in his back pocket. Fuck. He'd never seen her dressed like that.

It wasn't fair. How was he supposed to get her out of his head when she looked like that? He'd been smiling, but he was pretty sure he looked ravenous now. He caught his breath and let out a long whistle to let her know he appreciated what he saw. A short black leather skirt and red t-shirt, and they highlighted every asset she had. She grinned at him as he said, "I do believe this is the first time I've seen your legs, young lady." He stood up, ready to lead her inside the building. "Sure I can't talk you into singing with me again tonight? You kicked ass doing it on the fly last night."

She was giving it some thought. He wasn't going to push her, but he hoped she'd give in to her passion. After several long seconds, she said, "Yeah, okay."

"Good. Now I can take *Worrying that Valerie's gonna kill me* off my list. Seriously, you won't have to worry about being underage in there then, because you're part of us." He started walking, showing her inside. "Maybe we could have you do *two* songs. Maybe you should sing 'Metal Forever.' I fucking love that song."

"Oh, no. I'm not stepping on Ethan's toes."

They started walking through the hallway, and he lowered his voice. He was a little pissed that she didn't feel like she could sing it. "*You* wrote the goddamned song, Val. It should be your choice."

She stopped walking and after a few seconds, he turned to face her. "I wrote it for *him*. He sings it. End of story."

He smiled. Sometimes she was exasperating, but he could appreciate where she was coming from. "Fine. But you're cool with a duet again?" She nodded, but he decided to try going one step further. "Or would you rather sing it solo this time?"

"What would *you* rather do?"

"I asked you."

She was quiet for a few moments, but then she said, "As tempting as it is, Brad, the audience is here to see Fully Automatic, not Fully Automatic and some unknown named Valerie Quinn. I would be cheating your audience if I sang it solo."

"That's cool."

They started walking toward the stage and Val said, "Besides, we sound good together."

Yeah, he thought they could do a lot of good things together, but no way was he gonna say that. Val would have to realize it herself.

They made it to the stage where Zane was helping Nick set up his drum kit and Ethan was messing around with his guitar. He saw Valerie give Ethan a hopeful look, but his friend never looked up. Brad looked at Zane and Nick and asked, "Got this?"

"Almost done."

When he turned around, he saw Val looking out over the bar. It was about the same size as the venue the night before, but it was closed to packed already. He draped an arm over Val's shoulders. "Sure I can't talk you into singing one more song?" He knew she was going to turn him down again, but he had to give it a shot.

"Yes, I'm sure. So, where do I hang until then? Can I join the audience?"

"Maybe you could, but I'm not sure how we'd get you back up here in a smooth fashion. You wanna just hang out over there by the side of the stage, kinda out of the way? Maybe we could get a chair out of one of the rooms in back."

"I guess that would be okay." She started looking around the stage.

"Let me see if I can find a chair somewhere." He went backstage to look for one, but it hadn't escaped his notice that Val made a beeline for Ethan as he walked down the stairs.

Payne, you are a fucking idiot if you think she sees you as anything more than a distraction.

Yeah, he *knew* that—and yet he felt helpless to resist her.

When he returned with a chair, he was relieved to see Val was talking with Zane and Nick. When he got the chair in place, off stage but with a decent view of what would be happening onstage, he showed it to Val.

Not long after, they were performing once again, and Brad forced himself to keep his eyes forward, on the crowd. Yeah, he was tempted to look over at Val, but he didn't want to set himself up for disappointment, because she'd probably be watching Ethan the whole time. When it was time to ask her to join him for the duet, it was as magical as the night before, except it seemed even smoother. It was like they'd been singing together for months. And, like the night before, Val got a lot of audience attention—cheers, applause, and general appreciation—and he hoped it would fuel her fire.

When their show was over, he asked her if she was going to party with them after the concert was over. "I promised, didn't I?" Yeah, she had, but he wanted to make sure.

It didn't take them long to get the equipment loaded

into the van and trailer, but before they went back inside to watch the next band play, Brad wanted to show the van off to Val. She was teasing him about it, comparing it to a tour bus, and he said, "Gotta start somewhere. At least, tucked in all the right places, we can fit all of us *and* any extra shit we need to tote that won't fit in the trailer. When we get more of our own amps and shit, the little trailer won't cut it anymore. For now, though, it works."

"Where'd you get it?"

"I bought it from a church that was upgrading to a newer model. If you look closely, you can see the old lettering I had to peel off."

"Very cool." She looked like she was impressed. He hoped so. He wanted to show her that anything was possible if she set her mind to it. Sure, his life was pretty much shit right now, but it didn't feel that way. Every time he got onstage, it felt like he was doing the right thing.

They went back inside to enjoy the other two bands. He noticed that Val was trying to be subtle, but she was looking for Ethan nonetheless. She seemed to finally relax and let it go, but Brad knew what his friend was doing. He'd already started the party somewhere around the venue—it might have been backstage in one of the rooms back there or outside somewhere, but knowing Ethan, he had booze, drugs, and women in tow, and he was already having a good time. He wanted to shake Val and ask what the appeal of his friend was. Sure, the guy was disarmingly good looking, and Brad also knew he was charming as hell. He'd seen his friend talk himself out of trouble more times than not to realize he had an unnerving way of captivating people in his gaze. But he knew that Ethan had hurt Val more than once, so why was it she seemed to be begging for more?

True to form, though, his friend showed up right before it was time to leave—he was backstage, surrounded by several hot women, and he saw Val's face drop. How was it Ethan had such a hold on her?

He couldn't dwell on it. It made no sense, but it was what it was, and all he could do would be to bide his time…if he could hang on that long. After Ethan had pissed all over her, he would have thought she'd have told him off, but she kept going back for more.

They got to the van and he unlocked it. He slid the side door open and said, "All you motherfuckers in back. Val is riding shotgun with me. You guys work out the details amongst yourselves back there."

He opened Val's door and helped her inside, then he got in on the driver's side. He told everyone to "Buckle up," refraining from adding *bitches* at the end. But he leaned over and whispered to Val, "There aren't enough seats for all of 'em. This should be fun." He started up the van and put it into reverse. It was a feat he'd gotten better at when the trailer was attached, but he had to pay attention. He saw in the rearview mirror that Ethan had solved the problem by placing one of the blonde twins on his lap. Once he was able to put the van back in drive, he glanced over at Val. He needed to distract her. "You like being onstage, don't you?"

"Well, yeah…"

"You should do it more often. You're good at it."

That was when the shenanigans in the back started getting vocal—giggling, whispering, and—for all Brad knew—possible foreplay. He didn't want to hear that shit and he knew Val didn't need to either, so he cranked the music on the stereo—some kick ass Betraying the Martyrs—to drown it all out. Then he headed back to the motel, wondering if both he and Val would wind up miserable this night.

CHAPTER NINETEEN

BRAD PULLED UP to the motel, almost embarrassed. He didn't care about anyone else in the van, but he *did* care what Val thought. He opened her door while Nick opened the side one from the inside and all the passengers made their way out. Val got out and he closed her door. He nodded his head toward the building. "Yeah, I know it's not the greatest accommodations and, yeah, we're all sharing just one room, but we're starving musicians, right?"

"I didn't say a word. I'm impressed as hell at the van."

He smiled and touched her chin with his fist. "I knew there was a reason I liked you." It was a nice thing for her to say. He knew they were staying in a pit, but it was nice of her to not call him on it.

Everyone else was already in the room by the time Val and Brad joined them. Nick and Zane were pulling one bottle after another out of the top dresser drawer. Val looked at Brad, a shocked look on her face. "Where do you guys get all that?"

Brad wiggled his eyebrows up and down and simply said, "Connections."

He closed the door and waved Valerie inside. Everyone sat in a circle, some on the edge of one of the beds, a couple on chairs, Ethan on the floor with his blonde twins. Brad invited Val to sit on the edge of the bed closest to the door, and he sat next to her. He felt bad that Val had to see Ethan at his sleazy worst, but maybe that was the wakeup call she needed. Brad was a good guy and he cared. He hoped she would see that.

Ethan pulled a joint out of his pocket and wasted no time lighting it and sucking the smoke down. Then he handed it to twin number one on his left. He took three other joints out of his pocket (where the fuck had he scored all the weed?) and handed them and the lighter to Nick. Nick took over lighting and passing. Zane started uncapping the liquor and passing it around too. Brad was going to wait for the rum and a puff or two. The other guys could have the shit that tasted like lighter fluid.

A joint made it to Brad first, and he sucked it down hard. He'd never been a cigarette smoker, but he liked pot. He'd forgotten how much he liked it until he took a hit. It tasted good, smelled good, and going down, it was smooth. He held the smoke in his lungs and let it out slowly, his eyes closed. Then he just needed to relax and let it hit him. He handed it to Val. He was a little surprised that she took it, because she had a horrified look on her face. She started to hand it to the girl on her right. Brad got close to Val and whispered, "Come on, Val. Just try it."

He could tell she was considering it, but she shook her head and handed it to the girl next to her.

He nodded. He wished she'd give it a try. She looked so tense, so on edge, and he knew the pot would help her let go of it all. Still, he respected her decision. Then he could feel it. "Fuck. That's nice." He closed his eyes, letting the feeling overtake him. He'd tried harder stuff in the past and had decided none of it was for him, especially after seeing what it did to Ethan. Weed, though…he loved it and had no problems with it. He didn't do it often, either, because he could see how it could easily make him a lazy slacker ass, but once in a while? It was a rare treat.

Val was totally uncomfortable. She said, "I'm gonna get some water. Do you know where the vending machines are?"

He didn't know if she was going for the water or just to get away. He didn't want her to go. "Don't waste your money. There are glasses on the counter over there, and I'll go get some ice since none of these douchebags bothered."

She was agreeable to it, so he found the ice bucket and stepped out of the room, pulling the bar of the top lock open to keep the door from closing and locking. The night was warm, but he could barely feel it. He felt like everything was clear, but he was so mellow, and he was okay with whatever would or wouldn't happen tonight. He just wanted Valerie to have a good time.

He found the ice machine at the end of their building and pressed a button that sent a shower of chunky ice into the bucket. Then he found his way back to the room. There was a little talk about music and the show, but Brad crooked his arms and half lay back on the bed. Val sat next to him, nursing her cup of ice water. Brad didn't feel like talking; he just wanted to enjoy the sensation of floating, and when he had another chance to toke and drink some rum, he took them.

It wasn't long that his bandmates started getting handsy with their "dates." It was nothing unusual, but Brad was waking up to the fact that he'd invited Val and she was looking more and more uneasy as the evening progressed. She was looking over at Ethan again—big mistake. His blonde twins were facing each other on either side of him, and they started kissing each other. Oh, God, no. No matter what kind of epiphany Brad had wanted Val to experience, he didn't want her heart to be broken. So he touched her arm and said, "Why don't we go sit in the van and talk?"

She said nothing but nodded, and Brad stood and grabbed her hand. *Fuck*. There—it hit him, full on. Jesus…he was feeling fuckin' fine. He hoped Val didn't see the two girls touching each other's breasts as they made their way out of the room. Zane was running toward second base, his hand under his girl's t-shirt, moving upward.

When they got outside and he closed the door, he could see the relief in Val's facial features, even in the semi-dark near the doorway. He led the way to the van. There was a big streetlight in the motel parking lot, but it wasn't much help when Brad had to guide his key into the lock. He felt like his eyes were squinted closed, and he didn't care. He tried several times and couldn't get the fucking key in the lock. He started laughing, thinking about how he'd suck if he scored tonight. If he couldn't get the key in a lock, how the hell would he be able to guide his wasted dick inside this beautiful young lady? And the more he thought about it, the more he laughed. Oh, God...that felt good. He felt for the slit in the lock and managed to maneuver the key inside.

He finally got the door open and helped Val up. He got inside too, but after a few seconds realized it wasn't going to work. He hadn't felt the heat earlier, but it was like a jungle in the van. They wouldn't want to sit in there if it was uncomfortable. "We need to open the windows." He got out and moved to the driver's side and turned the van on so he could roll all the windows down. Val got comfortable in the passenger seat. No way. He didn't plan to stay up front in those bucket seats. He wanted to get as close to her as she'd let him, and he was feeling a little more in control now. He looked over at her and said, "Let's sit back there where there's more leg room."

She nodded and that was his cue to get his ass over to the passenger side and help her back out. She opened her door, but he put his hands on her waist and helped her slide out of the seat back to the ground. Fuck...that skirt was killer. He took a deep breath.

He pointed to the very back seat, because it had a little more wiggle room than the middle one. He wanted to make it as comfortable as possible for her. He sat next to her, and his thoughts went back to the key again, and he lost it. He couldn't stop laughing that time, and he hoped Val couldn't figure out what his intentions were. He had to decide to just enjoy her company, no matter what ultimately happened. She started laughing with him, and that only made him laugh harder.

At last, he was able to get himself together, before tears started streaming down his cheeks. He looked over at her.

It was mostly dark in the van, but he could see her enough. Goddamn, she was beautiful, and she seemed to grow more beautiful every time he saw her. He wanted her, wanted her badly, and he didn't know that he'd ever wanted any other woman as much as he did her. He didn't want to rush her, didn't want to pressure her, but he wanted her to know that she was special. She was worth more than he could ever afford, but he damn well knew Ethan didn't deserve her. She didn't seem to know or appreciate that, though. And he felt bad now for putting her in such an awkward situation with his friend. He should've known Ethan would be an ass. He shouldn't have subjected Val to that, and deep in the back of his mind, he wondered if he'd done that on purpose to show Val that Ethan wasn't the guy for her. He knew he felt bad that she'd seen it, but had he done it deliberately?

He felt guilty about it, whether he'd done it intentionally or not. He looked in her eyes and stroked her cheek with the back of his fingers. "Sorry about earlier. I guess we put you in an uncomfortable position. I didn't know you didn't smoke pot."

"I was accused of being prude in high school more than once."

Why was she acting like her behavior had been bad? It was he who should feel bad about what had transpired. And still...she had no idea. He moved his hand to her thigh. He couldn't resist that bare leg anymore. "Oh, I don't think you're prude, Val. You just haven't met your drug of choice, and you definitely haven't met the right guy."

She raised her eyebrows, and a half smile turned her lips

up. She didn't touch his hand. Goddamn. *Down, boy. Down.* There was a flirtatious twinkle in her eye. "Meaning you're the wrong guy?"

He smiled, feeling ravenous. His only response was truth. Was he the right guy for Val? Probably not, but she hadn't even given him a chance. "Yeah, I'm sure I'm the wrong guy, but I can feel like the right one if you let me try." There was something in her eyes then…and that's when he knew he had a chance. It might barely be a snowball's chance in hell, but he was going to seize the opportunity. He gently squeezed her thigh and said, "Did I tell you already how much I like this skirt?"

She took a deep breath, and he could see it—desire. Yeah, she felt the same way he did. He could feel his body listening to his emotions, and his blood took a nosedive. *No.* It wasn't time yet. But it was there—the chance, the spark, the go ahead. Her smile was slight when she replied, "Your eyes did."

Time to move. As much as he liked touching her leg, it was time to go forward. He placed his hand on the back of her neck and brought her lips to his. And that kiss— fucking magic. Not like their kisses before. This one felt deeper, like it meant more. He explored her mouth with his tongue, wanting to know how far forward he could go. She responded too. Her tongue danced with his, and her hand moved to his chest. He could have kissed her for hours, but he felt the need to move forward. He moved his lips to her neck, and he heard her inhale a sharp breath, signaling him that he was on the right track.

"Come on up here." He placed his hands under her arms to help her straddle him on his lap, and she wasn't prim and proper about it. She didn't leave a gap between them, instead pressing up against him, and then he couldn't hold himself back anymore. His cock responded to her nearness, swelling against his jeans. And he was happy to let it.

She thrust her fingers into his hair, and he started kissing her again. Her lips, her mouth tasted so sweet, but he wanted to taste her all over. He wanted to bring her to ecstasy, erase Ethan out of her brain for good. He wanted to touch her over her entire body, press up against her, be inside her. It hadn't been so long ago that they'd been in an embrace, and she'd told him she was a virgin. He wondered if she still was, and he thought she might be. If so, he'd probably have to wait to bury himself inside her, but he could do that. If he was hers, he could wait a very long time.

She was breathing harder, and he could feel how hot it was in the van, but he didn't know if it was the air or the friction between them. She shifted against him, and he nearly groaned at the sensation. Holy fuck. He hadn't been this aroused in a long time. And then he thought he was gonna fuckin' lose it when she moved her hands from his hair and trailed them down his chest to the bottom of his shirt. For a second, he got excited, thinking maybe she was going to undo his zipper. God, he was tingling and on fire from head to toe, and it didn't matter where she touched right now. It all felt fucking incredible.

She started pulling up his shirt. A damn good sign. They hadn't gone this far before. She was serious. God, he loved this girl.

Whoa. *Loved her?*

Yeah, he thought so. In this moment, definitely, but he was starting to think it was more than just a heat-of-the-moment thing. He could hear a song forming in his head, a hard, driving beat with a sweet melody. That was Valerie to him, and he let it sing to him as he leaned forward to help her get his shirt off.

He hadn't thought it was possible, but his cock got even harder. He shoved his fingers in her hair and brought her mouth to his again. He couldn't get enough of her. He slowly pulled his fingers down the length of her hair and then down her back until he reached the bottom of her shirt. Her fingers had been dancing on his chest, and he thought maybe she would let him take her shirt off too. It was worth a shot. If nothing else, she'd appreciate the opportunity to cool down a little. It was the true test, though. If she didn't let him take her shirt off, they wouldn't go any further tonight. He had to know, even if they spent hours taking their time the rest of the night.

Holy shit. When he started pulling up on her shirt, she moved back and lifted her arms. Hot damn. Oh, God, could he make it? He set her shirt on top of his on the seat and brought her mouth to his to start kissing her again. He knew he'd have to move slowly. He didn't want to freak her out, didn't want to move too fast. He would take his time, go as slowly as she needed, but she'd just made his night.

He moved his hands to the small of her back and started feeling her skin from the top of her skirt to the bottom of her bra strap. He wanted to ease into things, and he could tell she appreciated it. She needed to be warmed up each step of the way, and he could do that. Her fingers on his chest were driving him crazy, especially when she'd drag them down his torso, because his cock would get harder again, aching for her to touch him there.

She shifted against him again, almost grinding into him. And then he thought they could just dry fuck tonight if she was comfortable with that. He didn't care. It was just nice being with her, feeling her, tasting her, spending time with her and only her. He started kissing her neck again, and this time, she let out a long sigh, encouraging him to go further. So he kissed lower, trailing his tongue along the top of her breasts, just above her bra. He moved his fingers up to the bra at her back so he could unclasp it. He was pretty sure, based on their previous conversations, that she'd never had a guy kiss her breasts, and he wanted to warm her up more. He knew he could make her feel good that way.

He was hardly aware of the sound of a girl giggling just outside the van, but it all came crashing down when the side door to the van slid open. The dome light came on then, shining its harsh beams on them, and Nick and the brown haired girl he brought along with him crawled into the van.

Val gasped. Nick said, "Oh. Don't let us stop you." Then he slid the door closed. The light was off again, and Brad hoped Val would be okay with having them up there. "We're just gonna take the seat up here. Proceed."

Val was tense now, but Brad hoped he could pull her back into the mood. In his mind, he thought, *Goddammit, Nick*. He kissed her neck, moving up to her ear, and whispered, "You okay?"

"Define *okay*."

He chuckled. Nick and his girl were being noisy, so

making Val feel comfortable with them there was going to be difficult. "We can keep going."

Val started pawing at the seat next to them, searching for her shirt. "I really should go."

"Oh, Valerie," he said, whispering. This was his last shot, and so he had to tell her exactly what he was thinking. He ran his fingers through her hair again and said, "I could make you feel like you were born to fly. I want to do that. I want to show you what you were made for." He kissed her neck again. If she could just get back in the mood...

But, even though she'd paused for a moment, she was feeling for her shirt again. "Brad, I'm sorry. I can't." She found her tee and slid it back over her head. Then she got off his lap and felt around for her shoes. While she did that, he grabbed his t-shirt and put it on. She was heading to the door, and he scrambled to get up. His hard on was gone, but it was replaced by a dull ache in his balls. Fuck. He'd have to kill Nick later...especially since, as he followed Val out of the van, he noticed that Nick was getting some.

The air outside the van was cool, and it made Brad notice the front of his jeans were damp. Oh, God, he couldn't dwell on that. He'd had her turned on, and they'd been so close. Well, one last shot. He pulled Val close to him in an embrace. "Did they make you uncomfortable? I know that was weird. I can get us a room, just you and me..."

"I can't, Brad. I just can't." She looked down, avoiding his eyes. "I think I'll just go home."

He brought her closer, holding her head to his chest. Goddamn, he was hurting, but he had to give Valerie credit for sticking to her guns. She had a hell of a lot more willpower than he did. "No, that's cool. I respect your decision...probably more than you'll ever know. Doesn't mean I didn't wish you wouldn't change your mind." He sighed. "How far do you live from here?"

"Not too far. Probably less than a mile."

"I'll walk you home." He put an arm around her shoulders so they could begin the walk. Maybe it would help. "You okay?"

She smiled, wrapped her arm around his lower back, hitching her thumb in his belt loop. Then she leaned against him. "Yeah, I think so."

Maybe he still had a chance...sometime down the road. Whatever the case, his feelings for this girl ran deep. "You are amazing."

She giggled, and they started walking. Brad knew it was gonna be a long damn night.

CHAPTER TWENTY

BRAD AND VAL took longer than half an hour to make it to her house, a nice leisurely stroll in the cool early summer air. She even let him kiss her good night before she went in her house. It assured him he continued to have a chance.

The walk back to the hotel, though, was something different entirely. He was fucking pissed—not only at Nick for the cock block of a lifetime, but he was pissed at Ethan for making Valerie feel like shit. He was gonna give it to them both with both barrels.

By the time he got there, though, he was tired and, even though his balls ached to their core, he was feeling calmer. He walked in the hotel room, and everyone was passed out. Ethan was in one of the beds with a blonde on both sides. Zane and his girl were in the other bed, and there was no sign of Nick. Still in the van maybe. He grabbed a pillow that had slid onto the floor and sat in one of the chairs, setting the pillow on the table and resting his head on it. Before he knew it, it was morning. He felt like hell, so he got in the shower. The guys (and the girls surrounding them) were sleeping, so he got dressed and decided to walk around town in search of a cup of coffee.

He slammed the door on his way out.

Immature, yeah, but he wanted their asses out of bed by the time he returned.

He felt a little better. His head stopped throbbing, and he felt a little calmer about the situation with him and Valerie. But he'd also been hatching a plot—not only would it keep her more fully in his life, but it would also help her realize the dream she'd been denying herself.

He found a café on Main Street and drank a few cups of coffee. He wrote some notes on his phone—that song, that tune that had been floating around in his head the night before. He had to get it down before it was lost for good, because it signified something special in his life. When his head was clear and his mood improved, he paid for the coffee, left a nice tip, and then walked back to the motel.

Sometime after ten o'clock, Brad unlocked the door to the motel room he and his bandmates (and their dates for the previous evening) had shared. He was dying to get home to his own bed and real sleep. Before then, though, they had some business to finish. He nearly started shouting, finding them all in various states of slumber—including Nick, who'd found his way back to the room. The drummer was curled up on the bed next to Zane, his mouth wide open and snoring. He was also tempted to kick their asses. It was a little too early to start doing the whole sex, drugs, and rock and roll thing. They weren't established enough at the rock and roll part to go nuts yet.

Instead, he stayed under control and cool and said, his voice loud, commanding, but not overbearing, "Guys, time to get up. We gotta check out and then hit the road." He had to shake Ethan's shoulder once to get him to stir, but one of the blondes sat straight up and then freaked out when she realized her tits were hanging out uncovered. She woke her sister, and both women made their way to the bathroom.

Zane was moving his head back and forth and started opening and closing his mouth as though there were a bad taste in it. Then he opened his eyes and saw Nick curled up next to him. He sat up, his date waking at the same time. He said, "Nick, get your ass up."

Brad was moving Ethan's shoulder back and forth. The guy was dead to the world. He heard Zane behind him say, "What? Your girlfriend didn't want to cuddle with you so now you're hitting on me?"

"Whatever."

"Yeah, whatever." Zane cleared his throat. "Fag."

"*Fag?* You're the one who was cuddling *me*. Just 'cause I curled up next to you."

"Kiss my ass."

"Yeah, you play tough. I felt your dick getting all hard with me next to you."

"Get the fuck out of here."

Nick started giggling, and then grabbed his head. "Oh, fuck. Laughter—not good."

"That'll teach you to hit on your friend, butt munch."

"Fuck you."

Brad would have laughed if he hadn't been so angry. "Come on, Ethan. Get your ass up." Finally, his friend registered Brad's voice, and he sat up. In the meantime, Brad heard the girl with Zane mutter something, and then she rustled around a bit and left.

"What?"

"We gotta go. We need to get back home. I have to work in the morning."

"Work shmirk. I don't know why you bother. If you wanna have a band, you need to fully commit."

That was it. "Are you fucking kidding me, Ethan? You have the balls to go there? Did you know we wouldn't even have that goddamn van or be able to rent that trailer if not for my job?"

Ethan shrugged but said nothing. The blonde twins emerged from the bathroom. They giggled and tiptoed over to Ethan. Both kissed him on the cheek. "Call us next time you're in town."

"I don't have your number."

"Yeah, you do. We added ourselves to your contacts list on your phone."

They blew kisses and one of them shook her ass on the way out the door. Once they'd shut it, Zane said, "How the fuck do you do that, man?"

"Do what?"

"Score such prime meat."

Ethan shrugged. "I dunno."

"They're cute."

"Monique and Dominique. They had a unique technique."

Nick started laughing again and then he grabbed his head once more. "Ow."

Brad sighed. "Guys, we have a lot to talk about."

"Sure, dad. What's on your mind?" Ethan draped his legs over the edge of the bed and grabbed the crumpled pack of cigarettes on the nightstand next to the phone.

"Don't *you* start that bullshit right now, Ethan. Actually, no. Since you did, we'll start with you."

Ethan scowled. "What the fuck did I do exactly?"

"What *didn't* you do?" Ethan glared at him, challenging him. Brad took that as a cue to chill, so he took a deep breath and made sure his voice was calm and even when he finally spoke. "Dude, what the hell are you doing to Valerie?"

"What? *Valerie?*" Ethan lit a cigarette and slammed the lighter on the nightstand.

"Yeah, Valerie. Didn't you kiss her when we were in Colorado Springs?"

Ethan rolled his eyes. "Maybe." He took a drag off his cigarette. "So?"

"So…she cares about you."

"And?"

"And she thinks you feel the same way. That was an asshole move, bringing those two girls to the party when Val was expecting to spend time with you."

Ethan stood. "Don't even fuckin' start with me, Bradley. I saw you more than happy to pull her out of here. Why the hell should I even try when you're with her?"

Brad stood as well. "Are you *that* goddamn stupid?"

"What's that supposed to mean?"

"Guys, help me out here. Who does Valerie really have eyes for?"

Zane said, "Fuck that. I'm not getting in the middle of this bullshit."

Brad nodded. "Fair enough. Maybe you need to ask her yourself."

"Tell me the truth, *brother*. Did you fuck her last night?"

Oh, God...he'd wanted to. He hadn't ever wanted anything so badly in his life. Nick could attest to the fact that he hadn't—if he could even remember anything. Of course, he could also let them know that Brad and Val had been doing a little more than talking. But that led him to topic number two. "No. But I wish we had. She needed someone to make her feel better. And, by the way, Nick, thanks a lot."

"What the hell did I do?"

"Biggest cock block in history, man."

Nick's jaw dropped as he seemed to remember the past night's events. "Oh, shit. Sorry, dude."

Brad's shrug was halfhearted. "Too late now."

"I thought it would be okay. We do shit like that all the time."

"Yeah, but...Valerie's different. She's not a groupie."

Ethan crushed his cigarette out in the glass ashtray on the nightstand. "And that's where your problem is, assholes. You think of Val like a friend, rather than just another chick."

Brad felt his blood pressure rising again, but he caught Zane's look, so he knew it wasn't just himself thinking Ethan was way out of line. That was good, because he was going to need back up for the final thing he was going to say—a proposition of sorts, and if he had to, he was going to make both Ethan and Nick feel guiltier to get them to agree to his terms. He wanted to instead beat the shit out of his friend, but he also knew it was Ethan's dark, drug-fueled side, and he'd let it slide…for now.

"Go clean up, animals. There's something else we need to talk about."

"Spit it out."

"Fuck, no. Go clean up. Then we'll talk." Brad went outside for a few minutes of fresh air. It was almost hot outside, but for now, the warm sun felt nice on his arms. He looked down and saw the half sleeve of tattoo from the hem of his t-shirt sleeve down to his elbow. He loved that mishmash of tats, and they made him feel like an honest-to-God rock star. He knew better, though. It was time to take it seriously, time to take it to the next level, and he thought maybe his proposal would help them.

After close to ten minutes, he walked back in the room. Zane had taken a shower and was wearing a new pair of jeans. Ethan was smoking another cigarette, and Brad couldn't tell if he'd done shit, but he looked more awake. Nick appeared to have, at least, scrubbed his face and made an attempt. Brad could tell that the guy was feeling last night's overindulgence. He was glad he himself had found coffee, because it was helping him deal better.

"All right, guys. Ready to hear me out?"

Ethan growled, "If you're done nagging like a bitch."

Ethan was getting under his skin today, and he'd get nowhere if he let him. So he took a deep breath and pretended his friend hadn't said anything. "I have a question first. What'd you guys think of Val when she sang with us?"

Zane didn't hesitate. "She's got a great voice. And the guys seem to really like her."

Guys? "What guys?"

"The guys in the audience. They dig her. She looks hot with a mike in her hand."

Brad felt a little green monster rear its ugly head in his gut, and he had to fight it. Maybe that was true, but that wasn't what Brad was thinking...or wanting. "Yeah, but singing...what do you think?"

"She kicks ass."

Nick said, "Yeah, she really does. She wrote the song you guys sang, right?" Brad nodded. "I think that's why she put so much emotion into it. She has solid pipes, man." He tilted his head. "What are you thinking?"

Ethan had been unusually quiet, and Brad didn't want to show his cards until he knew what his brother thought. "Ethan?"

His friend scowled again—something that was becoming a frequent occurrence—and then lit another cigarette. "If you're thinking what I think you are..."

"Just answer the goddamned question."

"What was it?"

"What did you think of Val onstage?"

Ethan took a long draw on the cigarette in his hand and seemed to consider it. "She was good, I guess."

Well...for him to admit it, even if in a noncommittal way, said something to Brad. "Guys, I'm thinking she might be just what we need to move to the next level." He let that sink in for a few moments. They didn't quite know what to think, but he could see them processing it. Time to drive forward. "You guys know she's a phenomenal songwriter. Her words blow ours to utter shame, and if you deny it, you're fucking liars."

They all nodded, *including* Ethan, and that was telling,

because out of the two of them, Ethan was the better songwriter. The guy had deep wells of pain to draw from, and when he focused on the pain and driving it through the pen onto paper and into his music, he was brilliant. More often than not, though, Ethan preferred to drown the pain in booze and drugs, squandering any writing talent he had.

"But she's a great singer too. For not practicing at all, she was amazing. And you can tell she's into it. I think once she got over being nervous, she could take us to the next level." Ethan blew out a cloud of smoke, ready to protest, but Brad interrupted. "No, think about it. Ethan, you and me, man…we're doing double duty. Wouldn't it be nice to just focus on your axe, concentrate on perfecting your skills? Instead, we're so busy singing too that our attention's divided. Rhythm, lead, it doesn't matter. I know *I* personally could get a thousand times better if I wasn't worried about singing too—and keeping the audience excited and engaged."

Zane said, "So…do we try her out or what?"

"Well—yes and no. I mean…we already tried her out, right? And she passed with flying colors."

Ethan said, "I don't know about *flying colors*."

"Still—she kicked ass, right?" There was general consensus around the room. "As far as a trial period, don't you think now's the time to talk to her first? What if she thinks we're fucking stupid? What if she says no?" That's where Brad felt confident—he didn't think she would. He'd seen the draw of the stage, the way the siren call of metal had pulled Val in, and he would be shocked if she turned them down. Either that, or he would have underestimated Val's future plan for herself. But he was damn sure she would jump on the offer. "So—what do you say?"

They didn't know it at the time, but their group affirmation to Brad's proposal would change all of their lives forever.

CHAPTER TWENTY-ONE

BRAD DROVE TO Val's house, the trailer attached to his van and all the gear and equipment already tucked and stowed away. He hoped he was remembering the route (and the house) correctly from the night before. It had been dark, and he'd been in an overly emotional state, so he didn't know if his memories were impaired.

At least the hard part was over. He was certain Val would be an easy sell. He didn't think he'd misread her—not one bit. She might take a little convincing, but he had no doubts in his mind that she wanted to do it.

He couldn't figure out what Ethan's problem was, though. As they were loading up the van, his friend had said, "Yeah…this is just an elaborate excuse to get into her pants." That wasn't it. Not at all. Would he love to get into her pants? Hell, yeah, and he wouldn't deny it, but asking her to sing for them wasn't just a complicated ruse to deflower her. Instead, it was the natural end result of what Brad had seen in her eyes, that despite all her protests, she dreamed about the stage. And she really was a hell of a writer. They'd be fucking idiots to let her go without even trying to extend some kind of offer.

He *cared* about Valerie, and that was part of what had driven him to ask. He hoped that, unlike Ethan, she could see that. And that was why he was going to go to her house alone. He didn't need Ethan fucking it up before she'd even had a chance to hear him out.

But as he got closer there, he thought he'd need all his friends to help convince her to do it. His goal instead would be to get her to come to the pizza joint where the guys were already hanging out.

So he pulled up to the modest two-story unassuming house painted white. The yard was immaculate, with a matching white picket fence out front—pretty cliché, and yet it didn't surprise Brad at all. He hadn't paid much attention to the fence or the color of the house the night before in the dark, but in the stark light of day, he couldn't help but notice it.

He made his way up the walk and wondered who would answer the door. He'd already had a few experiences with adults not caring for the way he looked. Leah's dad had hated the fact that he didn't have short hair, and now he had visible tattoos as well. He didn't care what most older people thought, but he found himself nervous about what Val's parents might think.

He took a deep breath before he rang the doorbell. He had to get his shit under control. He wouldn't do well at all if he looked like a fumbling, nervous idiot. He took another breath and punched the button. Better to just get it over with.

Several seconds passed and he started wondering if anyone was home. But he thought he'd heard something inside. Finally, the inner wooden door swung open, and it was answered by a teenage boy, probably only two or three years younger than Brad. He had light brown hair that was long enough to touch his collar, but Brad noticed that the kid had the same eyes and lips as Val. He had to be her brother. The kid looked distracted and maybe even a little irritated, and Brad quickly saw why. He had a PlayStation controller in his hand. Brad had interrupted his game. Maybe he was the only one home, or he'd been waiting for someone else.

And why the fuck was Brad worried about that shit?

Another breath. "Is Val home?"

"Yeah." The kid pushed the screen door open, and Brad grabbed it, following the kid inside. He didn't exactly invite Brad in, but Brad took his cue. He walked inside the house and paused at the foot of some stairs in the hallway. He yelled, "Val, the door!"

It wasn't long before Val was at the top of the stairs, and her little brother had disappeared. She looked as beautiful as ever, but she looked almost bashful, and he guessed it was because she was feeling a little funny about the previous night's proceedings. He didn't want her to feel guilty for telling him no. He'd gotten over it. So he smiled back at her, letting her know *no hard feelings* as she descended the stairs.

Once there, she walked around him. "Come in," she said, inviting him into the living room. They both sat on the sofa and she asked, "So…what's up?"

He reminded himself of his new goal—to just get her to

come talk to the guys. Together, the four of them could convince her. As awkward as he could tell she felt, she wouldn't agree to it with him by himself. She also needed to know the whole band had agreed on it. "Me and the guys wanted to talk to you about something before we blow town."

"What?"

"We're gonna eat a late lunch before we go. The guys are already at a pizza place downtown. Can you join us for a few minutes?"

He thought he could see some hesitation, but she agreed. "Sure." She stood. "I need to let my mom and dad know, though." She walked out of the living room, and he followed her back down the hall. She turned and yelled down some stairs that led to a basement. "Hey, mom, is it okay if I go hang with my band friends for a while before they leave?"

He could hear her mother, but she only appeared at the foot of the stairs when she was done talking. "Where are you going to be?" Crazy—he could see the resemblance with her mother too. Her mother's hair was lighter, almost blonde, but she had the same cheeks Valerie did—he could see Valerie in her smile.

"Napoli, I think."

"Oh, is this Ethan?"

Like he needed the confirmation that Val talked about Ethan constantly, but he was nothing. Still, he wasn't going to let it make him a rude bastard. The woman was walking up the stairs toward them when he said, "No, I'm Brad Payne, Mrs. Quinn." Her mother was already walking up the stairs, so he held his hand out to her as she got near him.

"Nice to meet you," she said, shaking his hand. Then she looked at Val. "I'm sure that's fine, hon. What time do you think you'll be home?"

"I should have her home in two hours or less."

"Have fun, kids." Well, *that* had been easy.

It didn't take long to get to the restaurant. Brad had played music on the way there so they could chill. He wasn't ready to make the sales pitch. They walked into the semi-dark restaurant. As his eyes adjusted, Brad spotted the guys at a table not far in. A hostess had started approaching, but Brad pointed to the table and said, "We're with them."

Once they got there, Zane said, "We ordered one pepperoni and one with everything and a couple pitchers—one Pepsi, one Dr. Pepper. Is that okay?"

Brad said, "That's fine." The guys, all wanting to appear cool or masculine or who knew what, all sat with a chair between them, so there was no way Brad could sit next to Val without making a big deal out of it and making someone else move. So he sat between Nick and Zane.

Val then sat between Zane and Ethan and asked the waitress to bring her a glass of water.

Brad poured soda in one of the empty glasses. "Okay, guys. Who wants to tell her?"

Ethan sat up. "I will." Brad tried not to sigh aloud. He was going to trust his friend, but if the guy fucked it up, he'd have a lot to answer for. That was what Brad got for not keeping total control, but he knew he had to trust his bandmates. Ethan looked sincere, though, even if he'd looked irritable earlier. Maybe he *could* convince Val. "All four of us have talked about this seriously, and we want you to sing for the band." Val raised her eyebrows, but Ethan was moving in for the kill. "You probably already know Brad's lined up a bunch of shows this summer, and we want you to go with us."

She was quiet. Really quiet. For a long time. Brad could almost see the gears turning, though. She was giving it real thought. Finally, she said, "So...what would I do? Just sing?"

"Yeah...sing."

"But then what would you and Brad do?"

Ethan shrugged. "We could sing on occasion and even do a duet or two, but we could focus more on honing our guitar skills. I mean...we're good, but we wanna be great. And we need a frontman—er, *woman*—who can really interact with the crowd. That's harder to do when you have a guitar strapped to you. We need someone to stir them up, make them energetic, and I know you could do that."

Goddamn. Ethan was doing it, and he wasn't doing a half-assed job. He needed some backup, though. Brad added, "And face it, Val. We can't hold a candle to your voice. The crowds ate it up both nights. They really like you."

He could see it, the doubt in her eyes. She wanted to believe what they were saying but was afraid to. "Yeah, but what if that's only because it's something different?"

Ethan was losing his patience. "Would you stop that already? Give us a good reason why you can't."

She deflated like a balloon. "Oh...I can give you more than one."

Zane asked, "Like what?"

"My job."

Ethan looked incredulous. "You have a job?"

"What? Like that's so unexpected? Yeah…I babysit two girls Monday through Friday from now through the first week of August."

"So? Give 'em your two-week notice."

"I can't do that. It was a difficult decision for them to hire me as it was." The waitress set a glass of water in front of Val. She tried to be as invisible as possible, vanishing as quickly as she'd appeared. "Besides…that's the easy problem."

"So tell us."

"I don't think my parents will let me."

"Fuck your parents. You're a grown woman."

Brad could see Val's figurative feathers ruffle at Ethan's suggestion, and whatever good will he'd won he was flushing down the toilet. Brad didn't want to lose her just because Ethan had decided at the last minute to be crude, crass, and cruel. He leaned in closer and said, "You could ask." He wanted Valerie in the band for so many reasons, and not for the reasons Ethan assumed. He wanted it for her—for the hope and desire he'd seen in her eyes. He knew too that she'd be good for them. It was a win-win, as far as he was concerned.

"Okay. So let's say for some strange reason my parents have been replaced by pod people and say *yes*. Then what? I already told you I'm not going to ditch my job, and I'm sure you'd need to practice with me, and I doubt all your shows are Saturdays only, and—" She was doubting, still looking for easy reasons to say no. He had to make her think of the possibilities, rather than the negatives.

"Whoa, Val," Brad said, reaching across the table to grab Val's hands. He needed her to focus on him and just *believe*. He looked in her eyes, hoping they said more than his words could. "Why don't you ask your parents? If they say *yes* and you want to do it, then we can figure out the rest. One step at a time."

It sunk in. Her eyes scanned his, as though she were looking for all the answers inside them. And she did—he could see the trust between them, and that's when he knew she was taking it seriously. And that meant she had a fighting chance.

The food came and she didn't eat; instead, she asked about their upcoming shows, and he could see her getting more and more excited. Yeah, the idea of being in a band and performing live was enticing to her. She was letting it sink in.

So when they were done eating, Brad asked, "You want us to talk to your parents with you? Let them know we're legit?"

Val smiled. "No. Trust me. It's better if I do it myself."

Brad nodded. "That's cool."

"I promise I'll text you later and let you know." Brad nodded at her until she said, "But don't get your hopes up."

Then he frowned and hoped she could see it in his eyes: *Believe.*

CHAPTER TWENTY-TWO

THE TRIP HOME was long, hot, and tiring, and he swore he'd never heard guys bitch as much as his three bandmates did that day. He didn't feel much sympathy, though, because they'd done it to themselves, partying way too hard. He hoped they'd take it as a lesson and learn to do things in moderation. He finally told them all to shut up and stop whining and said two of them could lie down on the seats in the back and one could recline in the passenger seat up front. Then he turned up the music (not too loud so as to disturb their delicate conditions) and drove.

As Val had suggested, he tried not to get his hopes up, but it was difficult. No matter how he felt about Val as a maturing woman, he cared about this same woman who was becoming his close friend. He cared about her hopes and dreams for the future. She made him smile and laugh, and every time he saw her, he felt better—about everything. If they could make music together—and become successful—he would be happy, even if their relationship (if he could call it that) never progressed.

They hadn't heard a word from Val all afternoon, and she said she'd text with the answer. The longer it went that he hadn't heard from her made him more and more apprehensive. The longer it took, the more he believed that the news wouldn't be good when she *did* contact him.

They got home and unloaded. Brad would take the trailer back to the rental place the next day when they were open. He visited with his mom for a while until she had to go to work, and then he made some dinner. He was feeling anxious but didn't feel like he could give anything real focus until he knew, so he plinked on his guitar for a while until his phone made a buzz on the nightstand.

He saw Val's name.

He took a deep breath and picked up the phone to read the text on screen. *If u guys r serious, I'll b ur singer!*

He couldn't text back. News like that deserved a phone call. When she answered her phone, he said, "Fuck, yeah! I'm glad you agreed, Val."

"It was an easy decision. The hard part was convincing my parents to let me do it."

"I'm glad you did. I'll email you the show dates tomorrow morning, and you can let me know how that fits in your schedule. Then I'll email you all the songs we've recorded so you can learn them. I can do a couple rough cuts of the newer ones that we haven't recorded."

"Shouldn't we practice together?"

"Yeah, but...look over the schedule first, and then maybe we can figure out some times."

"Okay."

"Seriously...glad you decided to do this."

"Me, too."

He felt renewed vigor and spent the rest of the night sending Val everything she'd need. He sent her their schedule first, dates and locations, and asked her to let him know if all those dates would work for her. Then he emailed her a file with attachments of all their song lyrics, Ethan's included. He was glad he'd made his friend give him copies of those when the guy was still writing. He'd wanted to make sure he learned the words himself, just in case Ethan ever crapped out. So he had the files, and it was simply a matter of attaching them to an email. He apologized for not having electronic music sheets to go with them.

But then he sent a few more emails to her, the next ones containing sound recordings of all the songs they'd ever made. Some were crappy and rough and others were of higher quality. None of them were mixed and mastered—they were all live recordings of some type, so he hoped Val was okay with it. He wanted her to memorize the notes, not appreciate the beauty of the songs—she already loved the songs, so the music files were educational only.

He went to bed that night feeling more hopeful than he had in a while.

When he checked his email the next morning, she hadn't responded, so he wondered if he'd maybe sent them to the wrong email address. He hadn't heard from her by lunch, so during his break at work, he sent her a text, asking if she'd gotten the emails. She texted back, letting him know she'd check her email when she got home from work that night.

And, that night, he did have an email from her. She was

concerned about their one Thursday night concert in Denver and she also said she'd be going back to school late August and so she probably couldn't do any dates after that.

Brad was hoping that maybe once she got a taste, she'd want to work her school schedule around the band too. He believed she would, but he wasn't going to say a thing about it—not yet, anyway. She did say she thought all the other dates were "doable," and she said she'd start working on learning the songs right away.

He was glad to read that, because her first show was in a week. They could modify their set list if they had to in order to accommodate songs she felt comfortable singing, but he hoped she could learn most of the songs and feel good enough about them to perform live. He knew she'd do fine once she learned the songs, because he'd seen her perform. In fact, he'd seen her perform songs she *wasn't* confident about yet was able to pull off, so knowing the songs really well would make her just about perfect, he thought.

Val sent the occasional text, updating him on her progress. She also sent texts here and there, voicing small concerns, and he'd text her back, trying to reassure her. One of the last ones she sent, she asked if they would pick her up on the way to the concerts or if she needed to invest in a vehicle. She also said she didn't know exactly where any of the places were or how to get there. She was starting to panic, it sounded like.

So, instead of texting her back yet again, he called her up on Saturday. He would be better able to gauge her state of mind by the tone of her voice instead of a dry text or email.

"Are you as worried as your emails sound?"

She laughed. "No. Actually, I'm really starting to get into this." Good. He was glad to hear it. "Who's your tattoo artist?"

He smiled. "Seriously?"

"I wish. No…my parents would kill me."

He tried not to sound lascivious, but he couldn't help himself. "If you got one on your ass, they'd never know." He'd love to see that.

"Yeah…right."

Time to change the subject back to business. "So…the Thursday night show in July. It's not till eight that night, and I could maybe make sure we're one of the later bands. What time do you get off work?"

"It depends…but usually between four and six. I could let them know what's happening to see if they could let me go earlier that day."

"It doesn't take long to set up. How long from Winchester to Denver?"

"If you're not driving through rush hour, two and a half to three hours. Downtown?"

"Not sure. Not a problem, though, because if you got done at work by five and it took three hours *and* we played a little later, we'd be okay. Pushing it and not able to set up a merch table, but it would be doable."

"You know what would be easier? You guys just do that show without me."

"Fuck no, Val. If you're part of the band now, you're part of the band. If you can't make it, we don't do the show."

"But no pressure."

He laughed. "The other dates work, though?"

"Yep."

"How are you feeling about the songs?"

She gave him a hard on then, choosing to sing a song he'd written over a year ago, a song called "Take You Down." Her voice sounded sweet and hot, and then when she got to the chorus, she did a kind of growl, kind of an imitation of how Brad had sung the song, and he wanted to jump through the phone and lay one on her. God, it was sexy as hell, and he couldn't wait to see her take over the stage.

He didn't want her to feel self-conscious, though, so he instead just said, "Nice."

"Thanks. So...I'm learning the songs, but I'd feel a lot better rehearsing with you guys a little before we play our first show. Could we maybe Skype some night next week?"

"What are you doing Friday?"

"Working." *Duh.*

Well, yeah, but "After that..."

"Nothing."

"So why can't we do a rehearsal Friday night? Maybe even Saturday?"

"Where?"

He gave it some thought. "Good question. My garage is always free. Would you be able to drive here?"

"I don't know. My parents might not have a car they'd want me to borrow for that long a trip. I'm hoping to save enough for a car this summer, but until then..."

"You're off work around five?"

"Ish..."

"Five-ish. Nice. Maybe I could pick you up and bring you back here. It might be kinda late. We might not feel like rehearsing that night, but maybe Saturday late morning, early afternoon, before we hit the road to go to Denver. Would that work for you?"

"Yeah. I think so."

"Then plan on it. I think you'll start feeling one-hundred percent better once you've had some time to practice with us. You know as well as I do that there's a huge difference between singing with a recording and doing it live."

"Yeah. Just knowing we'll be practicing together is good. I feel better already."

"All right. See you Friday."

The days flew. Knowing he'd see Valerie again soon made him feel light and happy and free. He felt silly thinking it, but it was true. He told the guys they'd be practicing before the show so Val felt comfortable performing. Brad told them he'd be picking Val up Friday, and Zane offered to go with him to keep him company. He said he was getting keyed up for the show, and he hoped hanging with Brad would help calm his nerves.

That was cool with Brad. He got the feeling Val would still feel awkward if it was just the two of them. Their close encounter had really freaked her out. So maybe it was better that Ethan volunteered to let Val stay at his house...unless, of course, she hated that idea. She might. She wasn't happy with Ethan. If she didn't want to stay at his house, she could stay at Brad's.

He and Zane had a good trip going to Winchester. Brad had asked for the afternoon off from work so they could get her early evening. They didn't talk much, instead enjoying playing a lot of music and jamming out. When they got to Val's house, both guys walked to the door, and Val threw the door open within seconds. She'd been eager to be picked up. Brad took her suitcase from her and carried it to his car. "What the hell do you have in here? Bricks?"

She giggled. "I was afraid of needing something and not having it, so I probably *did* overpack it."

He grinned at her. "I'm pretty sure you did, but I think that's okay. Us guys never take enough shit, so maybe it'll balance out." He put her suitcase in the trunk and then held the door for her. Zane offered to sit in the back so she could sit shotgun, but she said the back was fine. Then she could "kind of" sit next to both of them.

Once they were on the road, Brad said, "Taco Bell on our way through Colorado Springs." He looked back at Val. "No arguing. My treat. I'm fuckin' starving."

They talked some about what had happened with their week. Brad could tell that, in spite of her complaints, Val liked caring for the little girls she babysat. He couldn't even pretend to like his job, but he had a couple of funny stories to share. And Zane told them about his fight with his dad's lawnmower the past week.

They went to Taco Bell, used the facilities, and got two bags of food before returning to the road.

After they finished eating, Zane shut off the CD player and turned in the seat. "So, Val, can you give me a sample of what you've learned so far?"

Brad glanced at her through the rearview mirror but said nothing. He thought her cheeks turned a little pink. "It would be easier with the music."

Zane smiled. "Ah." He started tapping out a beat on

the dash and then scatting a baseline. After a few measures, he started imitating the guitar, and Brad knew he was performing the intro to one of Ethan's songs, "Not My Time." That was all it took, though, because Val recognized the tune and started singing. Zane kept tapping out the rhythm, and both he and Brad sang backup. After finishing that one, they sang several other songs, and it helped pass the time. It didn't hurt that Brad was hauling ass. He was tired of driving and, while he enjoyed her company, he wanted to actually *see* her.

At one point, Val asked, "Where will I be sleeping tonight?"

Brad answered, "Oh, yeah. Ethan said, since you'd stayed at his house before and you knew his mom pretty well already, you could sleep on his couch."

She sounded pretty irritated when she replied, "It wouldn't be imposing on his busy social life, would it?" Not that he blamed her. He'd seen how Ethan had treated her.

Zane couldn't resist the opening, though. "You know about that?"

No. Bad move. Val likely wouldn't take that retort with good humor, so he stepped in before she could respond. "He's just fuckin' with you, Val. Ethan really did mean it as a nice gesture. But if you're not comfortable there, you're always welcome at my place. I know my mom wouldn't have a problem with it." And neither would he. He knew he couldn't push the girl, but a little suggestion might not hurt. And maybe then they could take the next natural step in their *relationship*—or whatever it was.

"I suppose Ethan's place is fine. I like his mom."

Brad wasn't going to let Val know June wasn't going to be there. She'd find out herself, and if that made her change the mind and decide to stay with Brad, well, then so be it. He wouldn't be upset in the least.

It turned out they all stayed there. It was pretty late when they arrived, and Ethan flat out said he wasn't in the mood to rehearse. Besides, he said, Nick told him he was busy but that he'd be free Saturday morning. So Ethan set several bottles of booze, a six-pack of beer, and tortilla chips and salsa on the coffee table and told everyone to drink up. They watched a movie, and Val fell asleep.

Brad had been sitting next to her on the couch. Her head was resting against the back of the couch, her mouth slightly open, and she breathed rhythmically. Aw. The poor girl was tired. He wanted to pull her head down to his shoulder but knew that would probably wake her up instead of help her sleep. Instead, Brad nudged Ethan's boot with his foot. Ethan looked over at him. "Why the fuck you playin' footsie with me, man?"

"You got a sheet and pillow for the girl?"

Brad was glad Ethan didn't give him a smart ass answer. Instead, he got up and walked upstairs. He brought back a pillow and sheet, just as Brad had requested. Brad got up off the couch. Val's shoes were little slide-on sandals, so he pulled them off her feet without disturbing her. Then he put the pillow on the end of the couch nearest her head and eased her torso down until her head rested on the pillow. Next, he lifted her feet up onto the couch and covered her with the sheet. Then he sat on the floor, resting his back against the couch. Zane was already on the floor, a couch pillow under his head, and he occasionally sat up slightly so he could take a drink of the beer in his hand.

At some point, Zane fell asleep and Ethan said he was going to his bedroom to crash. Brad moved to the chair. It was uncomfortable, but he didn't want to sleep on the floor like Zane was. He could have easily gone home—it was ten minutes away—but he wanted to be near Valerie, and he didn't give a shit how crappy his rest would be. He didn't think it would affect his performance the following night.

He hadn't realized just how tired he was, and he actually slept okay. He woke up once to find his arm asleep, so he adjusted position and fell back into a peaceful slumber. And then he slept like a baby, his dreams filled with visions of Val.

CHAPTER TWENTY-THREE

BRAD AWOKE THE next morning to the sounds of two women chattering on and on about home decorating. It was insipid and obnoxious, and it wasn't long before he figured out it was the television. But he was tired, so he tried drifting back to sleep.

It wasn't happening, though, no matter how much he wanted to. After five minutes of listening to the two stupid women, he couldn't stand it anymore. He kept his eyes closed but spoke in a falsetto voice, trying to sound as giggly and irritating as the overly cheery women on the television did. "Oh, my God! Doesn't this lamp have so much potential?" He tried to be deadpan, but he couldn't stop the smile from spreading across his face.

"I thought you were sleeping."

He opened his eyes. He couldn't remove the sarcasm from his voice, but it didn't matter. She knew he was full of shit anyway. "Who can sleep through this riveting programming?"

She started giggling. "What else was I supposed to do while you guys were getting your beauty rest?"

He sat up, stretching his neck. It was stiff from how he'd slept the night before. "You trying to tell me this is the only shit you could find?"

She stood and placed the remote in his hand. "I just wanted something to do while I waited for you guys. I want to practice."

He paused a moment. "Val, you'll be fine. We'll have a goddamn blast and make a little cash while we're at it. It's cool."

She smiled and he could see in her eyes that she believed him. "When can we start?"

Brad stood and walked over to Zane, his body splayed on the floor. "First, we gotta get these lazy motherfuckers up." He nudged his friend with the tip of his boot. "Hey, man…we got a vocalist here itching to try us out."

Zane muttered and stirred while Brad walked across the room to the bottom of the stairs. He hollered. "Ethan! Get your ass out of bed!"

"I'm up."

"Hurry up. Val's chomping at the bit here."

"Gimme five minutes to shower."

Brad made his way back to the living room and refrained from winking at Val. "Did you hear all that?" When she nodded, he asked, "Feel better?"

She smiled and nodded and he could see the stress in her eyebrows, but she was trying to be brave. "Once Ethan's done making himself pretty, we'll get the hell out of here and go to my place. We can have a bite of breakfast and we can shower too. Shit. Zane!"

Zane stirred again. "Yeah?"

"You still gotta pack and get your bass, don't you?"

"Yeah."

"Why don't you have Ethan take you and that way Val and I can head to my place? I'll make some breakfast."

"Like what?"

"Biscuits and gravy sound okay?"

Zane sat up. "Yeah. That'll work." He yawned. "You gonna get Nick too?"

"Yeah, I can." He looked at Val. "Let's go. See you guys in a bit." He pulled his phone out of his back pocket and pulled up Nick's number.

"Want us to bring the booze too?"

Brad chuckled. "You still have some?"

"No fuckin' idea. We can always get more."

Brad looked at Val. "Got your luggage?"

"Oh, yeah." She'd been following him to the door but then turned back around. Her luggage was on the side of the sofa near the wall, and she picked it and her purse up and walked toward him. He'd pressed his phone so it was dialing Nick's number.

Nick picked it up after several rings, sounding groggy. "Dude, we're gonna be practicing in the next hour and then we'll be leaving sometime this afternoon. When can you be to my place?"

One thing Brad would say—Nick partied hard. The guy partied his ass off, harder than anyone he knew. Unlike Ethan, however, Nick maintained focus. When it came to the band and band matters, most of the time, Nick was all business. Once or twice, he had dropped the ball, but it just didn't happen that often. Overall, Nick was a pretty steady guy, and Brad appreciated it. So when Nick said, "I'll be there in less than an hour," Brad knew he meant it.

"Don't forget your stuff for the road, 'cause when we're done rehearsing, we'll be heading out."

"Consider it done. See ya."

Brad held the door for Valerie as she stepped out. Zane said, "See you soon. Better be the best goddamn biscuits and gravy I've ever had."

Brad smiled. "I can pour vodka into the gravy if that'll help." He closed the door but before it closed, he heard Zane coughing, and he figured it was because the idea of liquor in gravy sounded disgusting. Good. His biscuits and gravy might not be the best, but it would be a solid, hot meal to counter all the alcohol in his friend's gut, and that was all Zane should have been worrying about.

Once they got to Brad's house, he asked if Val wanted to shower, and then she told him she already had. So she asked if he wanted her to do something while he took his shower. Oh, he had lots of ideas, but the poor young woman was so nervous, he didn't know if hitting on her as hard as he'd wanted would calm her down or wind her up more. He asked if she could cook the sausage, and she said she could. So while he showered and packed an overnight bag, Val worked in the kitchen downstairs. By the time he joined her, the sausage was done, so he turned the heat off. He grabbed some cans of biscuits out of the fridge while the oven preheated and they talked for a while. He was making the gravy as the biscuits finished baking when Nick showed up. It wasn't five minutes later that Ethan and Zane arrived, and they all ate like horses.

All except Valerie.

Brad asked why she wasn't eating. "I'm too keyed up to eat. I'd just throw it all up."

"Why don't you try?"

"No, I really can't. Water's all I can handle right now."

Brad worried. She'd need to eat something or she'd have no energy, not under the hot lights. Her nerves alone would burn up what reserves she'd have. "Come on, Val. Just a little something."

She took a deep breath. "I'll eat later...maybe after we rehearse."

He started to nod. Then he said, "Do you maybe want something different to eat?"

"No, thanks, though."

Damn. He hoped the guys would hurry. They were having fun, though, and they were used to performing. They all still got anxious too, but it was old hat now. They'd done it enough that it wasn't scary. He remembered that feeling, though. He'd never forget it. It was intense. He said, "Guys, let's hurry, okay? Val's wanting to try us out."

Instead of giving her grief or making her feel bad about it, they nodded and focused on eating. Apparently, Brad wasn't the only one who remembered the first show. Unlike the guys, however, Val hadn't even had the pleasure of extended practices. It was going to *all* be new. He was glad the guys seemed to appreciate that, because they were respectful...and quick. Val got up and cleaned the skillet, pan, and spatulas while the guys finished up their food. They all loaded their dishes in the dishwasher and then headed out to the garage to play.

The first couple of songs were shaky. The music was

okay, but Val was feeling lost. Brad approached her. "Relax. You got this." She nodded and gulped, and he knew she wasn't feeling it. She was starting to worry.

Another problem, though, was that Ethan and Nick were in some kind of pissing contest. Ethan started it by saying something snotty to Nick, and Nick was bristling and glaring. It was continuing through the music, but because Brad hadn't heard any of the words the guys had initially exchanged, he couldn't stop it. He couldn't prevent it from escalating because he didn't know what had started it. Well, he could, but then they'd probably be pissed at him. He hoped they'd both chill out and just focus on the music.

After about an hour of the muted undertones of irritation, Ethan hit a sharp note, getting everyone's attention. Then he turned around and yelled. "Goddammit. What the fuck are you doing, Nick?"

Brad saw what their arguing was doing to Val. It was taking her nervousness and turning it into full-blown worry. The guys would work through it, but Val was going to freeze up if they didn't reassure her—that and she was going to wear herself out for a simple rehearsal. So he walked over to her and placed his hand on her shoulder. "You're doing a great job, Val, but don't sing at top capacity. You need to save your voice for tonight. No need to impress us. Just do what you gotta do to feel comfortable, and drink lots of water." She nodded, picking her water bottle up off the floor and downing a few gulps.

Then Brad turned to Ethan and Nick. Ethan stood at the drum kit, close enough that he could grab Nick by the collar if he'd wanted to. "You're fucking up the song, Nick."

Brad turned and said, "Shut the fuck up, guys. Work through it. Val wants to go through the set twice, and we're never gonna get it done if you keep this shit up." Ethan wasn't budging, though. He was over at the drum kit hovering, and Nick was standing too, puffing out his chest. Nick might have been a quiet guy, but he wasn't backing down from Ethan's challenge.

Neither guy was backing down. Both wanted to save face. Ethan was a hothead and he got himself into trouble with his mouth all the time. It was something Brad was used to. Hell, he knew the guys were used to it too, but Ethan was pushing Nick's buttons. It was typical Ethan, but the good news was his friend was sober right now, so even though he was being ruled by testosterone, he wasn't being fueled by senseless chemicals. He might listen to reason. So Brad walked over to Ethan and put his hand on his friend's shoulder while looking him in the eye. Ethan continued staring at Nick for a few moments before backing up. He didn't look at Brad—wouldn't, in fact, but he was backing down, and that was all Brad wanted. If the guy needed to make a huge display so as to not look weak, so be it. As long as they didn't go to blows, he didn't care how it resolved itself.

Still...Val was beside herself, and their antics weren't helping. As Ethan backed away, Brad said, "This practice isn't for you guys. It's for Val. Let's give her what she needs."

Brad had to give Ethan credit. For the remainder of the set, he kept his mouth shut. Brad could tell he was getting pissed at what he perceived Nick was doing with the percussion. He couldn't hear anything different, but he knew once in a while Nick liked to try new things, and he was okay with it. That was how they would evolve, and Nick was a damn good drummer. The guy had unbelievable stamina and, as far as rhythm went, he was creative and liked to try different techniques to see if they'd make a song better.

When they were done going through the set once, Brad could tell his entire band was frustrated as hell. Tensions were high. Val looked like she was ready to cry. Brad could see it written all over her face—she was regretting joining the band and was feeling overwhelming doubt. "Break time."

Zane said, "Didn't you want to go through this once or twice?"

"First off, we hardly ate any breakfast. I'm starving. And Val needs to eat something. But we need some time to relax. If you all want to go do your own thing, I'm cool with that, but we need to focus, and we need to get our heads on straight. When we come back here, we need to be ready to work together. If we can't do it here, how can we do it tonight?" Everyone seemed to mutter a general consensus. "If we want to go to lunch together, I'll buy."

The guys agreed, and Ethan even stuck out his hand to Nick. Nick shook and Brad breathed a sigh of relief inside. He knew it was normal, but they didn't need to be doing their primal shit during Val's first rehearsal. They needed to wait until she'd settled in a little bit. But they must have worked it all out, because they all enjoyed lunch and had fun together, laughing and joking as though nothing had happened earlier in the morning.

Val even ate a small salad. Brad wasn't going to

pressure her. He was just glad she'd eaten *something*. And when they returned to rehearse the second time, it was much better. Ethan had taken something and so he wasn't as edgy. Brad didn't think that was a good way to do it, but he was glad his friend wasn't as aggressive. He could see relief in Val's eyes after they finished the set. He didn't care how the guys felt—if she needed another run through the set one more time, they were gonna do it, no matter what personal pain the guys felt because of it.

He approached her, wanting to know. "How do you feel now?"

She smiled. "Much better."

"Good to go?"

She nodded. "Yeah, I think so,"

Brad raised his voice. "Okay, guys, let's break for ten minutes. Have a quick drink. Ethan, if you need to smoke, now's the time to do it. In five, we'll start packing everything up." In the meantime, Brad went outside to hook the trailer up to the van. He was glad that they continued getting along as they loaded up their equipment, gear, and personal stuff.

Before they left, Brad asked Val, "Are you wanting to wear that for the concert?"

"Are there places to change before the show at the venue?"

"Sometimes there are and other times there aren't. I haven't been to this place before, so I'm not sure. You might want to change now, just to be sure."

When she stepped out of the bathroom wearing her outfit, he thought he was going to have a heart attack. She was wearing skin-tight black leather pants with black leather boots that went up to her knees. The t-shirt, though...that's what made the outfit. It was red and snug and there were holes ripped in it, showing off little glimpses of skin here and there, and on sweet little Valerie, it looked super hot. It was difficult keeping himself focused and his jaw closed.

Maybe they could spend some time together after the show tonight. The other guys, as usual, would be looking to score, and maybe he and Val could find an out-of-the-way place to hang out for a while. With her being a virgin, he didn't intend to put on any pressure, but he'd sure love to kiss her more and hold her close.

Nick's voice pulled him out of his thoughts. "Val, you look great."

Zane's comment made Brad feel a little monster well up inside his chest. "God, you look hot." But the guy was right.

And he had a little something to say about it too. He couldn't help the sly smirk that crossed his face when he said, "Nice...I like the skin."

And then Ethan. Goddamn Ethan. Why couldn't the guy stop toying with Val's heart? "We gonna have to beat the guys off with a stick?"

Val, however, didn't seem impressed. They made their way to the van, placing their personal items inside as well, and Ethan started to get in the passenger seat. Apparently, his friend hadn't learned from last weekend that shotgun was now Val's seat...and he'd just have to get used to it. "No way, man. Val's sitting there. From now on, that seat belongs to our muse." Yeah, so he was pissed, but he'd get over it.

The trip was long, and once they made it to the eastern slope of Colorado, the weather was warmer, so they opened all the windows and felt like they were getting a beating. They joked and laughed some, because Brad was trying to make Val relax, and he thought putting a smile on her face might work. When that didn't seem to help, he turned up the music, and they'd all sing for a while. Then he realized that was a stupid idea, because he wanted her to rest her voice.

He turned the music down again and heard Nick talking to Zane. Ethan was sleeping, his head resting on the back of the seat. Nick was a funny guy, so he hoped maybe he could make Val laugh. And he was obviously telling one of his stories. When he looked in the rearview mirror, he saw Zane's eyebrows raised, and he had a huge grin on his face.

"Seriously, dude, I don't know why she wanted *me*. She was all like *Teach me, teacher*. Well, shit. She's goin' down on me, what the fuck else am I gonna say? 'Oh, no, really, sweetheart. I think you should try a banana instead'." At that point, Zane started laughing. Brad looked in the rearview mirror again, and Nick was selling it. He was mimicking grave sincerity in his eyes first, and then he was pretending to be a girl peeling a banana and giving said banana a blowjob. He smiled too but then decided he'd better gauge Valerie's sense of humor.

She looked distracted. She wasn't offended, but he started to think she wasn't even listening.

Nick continued. "And fuck me. I thought she was gonna eat me like a big turkey leg. She looked like she was gonna fuckin' tear into my meat like I was her last meal. So I screamed like a seven-year-old girl."

Zane busted a gut at that point. He wasn't able to catch his breath. When he stopped laughing, he said, "I would have paid to see that shit."

"Anyway, man, she made short work of me."

"I'll bet she did."

"That's not what I meant, cocksucker." Zane broke out into peals of laughter again. "I jizzed harder than I ever have. Seriously—I think it was the initial fear that made it so fucking intense." Zane was still chuckling when Nick said, "I was looking down on her. She'd been chewing this big wad of gum, and I guess she forgot about it. I was looking down and saw that this big fucking hunk of pink gum was stuck in her hair. I guess she didn't feel it, but I knew she was gonna freak if she couldn't get it out. And I was spent, man, but I had to tell her. So I said, 'Hey...there's some gum in your hair.' And she looked up at me, all smiling and shit. I think she must have watched a porn movie or two, you know, 'cause she looked like she wanted to slap her face with my dick and squirt my jizz all over it. And she goes, 'Oh, honey, haven't you seen *There's Something about Mary*? Cum is good for your hair'." Zane started laughing again. "What the fuck was I supposed to say to that? So I just smiled."

"Goddamn, why can't I find chicks like that?"

Valerie turned her head at Zane's statement. Brad was pretty sure it was because Zane had been dating her roommate for a while, and Val didn't like that he was asking for a stupid slutty girl when he had had the opportunity to date a girl who was sweet and innocent like Val. So...as entertaining as he was finding the conversation, he figured he'd better turn the music on for Val's peace of mind and hope she wouldn't sing. If he had to, he'd pop in an As I Lay Dying CD or Suicide Silence or something like that that Val would find it hard to sing to. That would be the ace up his sleeve if he needed to play it.

When they got to Colorado Springs, Brad stopped at Burger King. "Let's grab a bite to eat."

As they piled out of the van, Val said, "I'm too nervous. I can't."

Brad lowered his head at her. "You sure that's it? I can buy."

"Yeah. I have plenty of money. I just…can't do it. I'm way too nervous and my stomach's upset."

"I know, Val, but you gotta eat." She shook her head. "Val…if you don't, you're not gonna have the energy you need. Eat *something*."

She sighed but got a chicken sandwich meal and ate half of the food before she couldn't eat anymore. Ethan seemed somewhat lucid and ordered a full meal. That was a good sign. He was messing around on his phone, and halfway through dinner said, "Bradley, did you know if you went up 285, we could have saved at least an hour of driving time?"

Brad blinked twice. "Yeah, I guess you're right. I wasn't even thinking about it, since we came this way last weekend."

"You'll probably save gas money that way too."

"I'll remember that next time."

Over an hour later, they had reached their destination, and they were unpacking the van and trailer and setting up the stage. Val still looked nervous, but having tasks to do seemed to help keep her calm. If she'd been a little older,

Brad might have suggested taking a small drink to calm her nerves. When she didn't have anything to do, she'd shake her hands as though trying to wake them up. Once or twice, he rubbed her shoulders, trying to help her relax.

They were set up and the guys were doing sound checks and tuning guitars. Val was offstage, and Brad figured it was because she wasn't ready to be watched yet. He'd glance offstage once in a while and catch her pacing or muttering to herself, and he thought she was going over the songs, reassuring herself that she knew the words. He was certain that once she started going, she'd be fine, but until then, she was going to be anxious. It was a fear of the unknown, of not knowing if the audience would accept her and love her. Brad knew they would, but Valerie would take a little more convincing.

Ethan walked offstage wearing his guitar. He approached Val. Brad couldn't tell what he was saying—he was too far away—but the mood Val was in, the guy was probably going to get it with both barrels.

From where Brad stood, he could tell that whatever Ethan was saying, Val was listening. He was glad. Maybe she needed to hear a pep talk from Ethan.

He changed his mind when Ethan slid his guitar so it hung on his back, and he pulled Val close to kiss her hard and passionately. Brad felt his jaw go slack, his eyelids lower...

and his heart sink.

It sunk because Val wasn't pushing Ethan away. She didn't even try. Ethan's lips let go of hers and then she wound her fingers into his hair, pulling his mouth back to hers.

Fuck.

So much for spending time alone with her. Now Brad felt like his nerves were in a bundle. And there wasn't a goddamn thing he could do about it.

They stopped kissing again and shared a few more intimate words, and then Ethan turned, pulling his guitar back around, swaggering back onstage. Val only had eyes for Ethan then, and they were glued to the guy…until they looked at Brad.

She looked—guilty, maybe? Or maybe more like a frightened rabbit? Brad took a deep breath. He knew he didn't look angry, but maybe he looked hurt or betrayed. There wasn't a damn thing he could do about that.

Val got a shocked look on her face and freaked out, bolting for the outside door.

She was losing her dinner, but Brad felt like he'd lost his heart.

CHAPTER TWENTY-FOUR

THE FIRST SONG was a little shaky, mainly due to vocals. Val's nervousness could be heard in her voice, a little high-pitched and thin, but as she continued, she gained confidence. By the end of the song, her voice was strong, and by the time they were on the third one, she sounded like a pro. Midway through the set, she was moving around and stirring up the audience. Just as Brad had always known, she was a natural.

He was so proud of her and loved watching her. And the stage was where he always felt like he should be, but inside…inside his heart was breaking.

Still, he was happy for Val, because that night, he watched her blossom. She'd been a shy little bud on a vine, and with the shower of the bright lights and adoration of the crowd, he watched her open up and grow right before his eyes.

He tried not to let it bother him. Val was still his friend, and he knew they would always be close. There was just something between them, something intangible and hard to explain. They clicked. They appreciated and understood each other.

But, God, he was pissed at Ethan. What the hell was wrong with his friend? It was almost as if the guy didn't want Val to be happy…like he wanted her to suffer. Or maybe he was feeling miffed because, instead of the constant adoration Val used to shower on him, now she was giving him eye daggers.

He pushed all the shit out of his head and focused on the music. Music had never let him down. It had always been there for him, in good times and bad, and he could always focus his emotions through it. So he muted his brain and homed in on his guitar and the audience and let the bad stuff go.

After the show, though, there was no way to ignore those feelings. But he knew what he had to do, and that was to figure out how to give up on the idea of Val—for now, at least. In spite of whatever there was between him and the girl, Ethan had a greater pull on her. It was like the guy was a black hole, and anything nearby got sucked into his pull. Whatever Val's feelings for Brad, they were no match for the gravitational draw of Ethan. He didn't stand a chance. And he was tired of throwing his heart out there to be shredded by this girl whom he had grown to love. He couldn't let it happen anymore.

He considered being completely honest with her, telling her that he'd grown to care for her deeply over the past few months. Something about writing together—whether online or in person—had done that to him. But no. She'd think he was a fool because she obviously didn't feel the same way. And he didn't want to appear weak in her eyes either. The only thing he had going for himself was who he already was and what he let her see. If she didn't love him back, there was no way he could show her that part of him.

And maybe it was irrational and stupid. Maybe he'd grown to care about her so much because she reminded him of Leah, his true first love. He knew now that he was over Leah, but he wondered if it was because he'd turned those attentions onto Val. He had no way of knowing for sure.

In the meantime, though, he had to play it cool. So they loaded up the van and trailer and watched the other acts. Then, at the end of the evening, they got in the van in search of a cheap motel. Until he could sort through his emotions, he had to act like everything was normal. So he sat in the driver's seat and Val in the passenger seat, and he asked, "So…what did you think of your first show?"

She was quiet for a few moments as she let his words sink in. She was still in a bit of a trance, it appeared, and he didn't know if that was from performing or from Ethan laying one on her. She looked ahead at the traffic in front of them and said, "Wow. It was amazing."

Brad nodded. "And what did I tell you? You were great."

"I can barely remember the first part of the show, though. It's like I was in a daze."

He couldn't help but smile, because he remembered what his first show had felt like. He hadn't been as nervous as Val (of course, he'd had a beer before going onstage), but he remembered feeling out of it, yet in awe and completely jazzed. There really was nothing like being under the lights.

"It's not over yet. After I pay for the hotel and keep some for gas, I'll divide what's left among us. You'll get your first paycheck."

"Oh, yeah. I hadn't thought of that."

He grinned. "Don't hold your breath. It's really not much."

"Doesn't matter. I'll get paid for doing *that*. That's awesome."

"We need to start running a merch table regularly too. That'll bring in money too."

"Oh." He glanced over and could tell she was thinking about it. It was all sinking in. It was just too new. So he simply listened to the radio and drove down the road to an area where he knew there were lots of motels, and it was just a matter of picking the one that looked least offensive while not costing too much.

When he found one that seemed to fit the bill (that also had a lit-up old-fashioned *Vacancy* sign), he pulled in. Val got out with him, and while he wasn't sure why, he wasn't going to complain. Still…he didn't want to spend a lot of time with her, not yet. He needed the raw feeling to dissipate. He wasn't going to tell her she couldn't come with him, though.

He approached the desk, and the clerk looked up from the book she was reading. The gal wasn't much older than they were. Brad said, "Do you have any rooms with two double beds?"

"Yeah."

"I need one of those please."

Val said, "I need to get my own room."

He looked over at her. "That'll double the cost, Val.

We'll make sure you have your own bed."

The clerk looked up from the computer screen and said, "We can get you a cot. Then you'll have three beds."

Brad nodded and looked over at Val. *She* had to be comfortable with it. Hell, he could sleep on one of the back seats in the van for all he cared, but he liked the idea of a shower. Val took a deep breath and looked at him, her eyes pleading. "I promised my dad, Brad. *My dad.*"

He sighed. He wasn't going to argue it. He understood where she was coming from. "All right." Maybe, too, that would keep Ethan's hands off her.

"But I'll pay for it. I don't want to cut into our earnings."

"Fuck that." He glanced at the smiling clerk, realizing he'd dropped an F-bomb. "Oh, sorry." He looked back to Val. "No way. You keep doing what you did tonight, you'll be earning that goddamned room." He looked back at the clerk. "I guess two rooms. One a double, the other a single. Any way you can get them close to each other?"

The clerk tapped on the old computer. "Yeah. Next door."

Brad pulled out his wallet and driver's license. The clerk did more tapping and then handed them keys. Old-fashioned metal keys. Val didn't know motels did real keys anymore. He handed her the one for the single, and they walked back out to the van. He had a big grin on his face. "At least if we're next to each other, there's less chance of neighbors complaining about a noisy party."

She had a deadpan look on her face. "That's what *you* think."

They got back in the van, and Brad moved the van so he

could park it closer to where their rooms were. When they grabbed their luggage, Brad asked, "Are you gonna hang with us for a while?"

"Yeah. Just give me a minute."

Brad didn't necessarily feel up to continuing to wear a happy face, but he thought it would be noticeable if he didn't at least try. Besides, one of the other guys would have invited her if he hadn't. In less than ten minutes, they were all in the guys' room, and Zane had wasted no time setting out the three bottles he'd packed.

Zane passed the bottles around, but Val waved her hand to indicate she didn't want any, instead drinking the bottled water she'd brought with her.

Ethan sat across from her and kept his hands to himself, but he said, "Val, Brad and I were okay on vocals, but you blow us out of the water. You're exactly what we needed." Brad hoped Ethan was sincere and meant it. He hoped the guy wasn't just flattering her, although Ethan had used his charm in that way on other girls in the past. Brad knew his emotions were clouding his judgment, so he kept his mouth shut. He hoped Ethan wasn't working some angle.

Zane took a swig from his vodka bottle and said, "Yeah, and you keep wearing shit like that, our fan base'll grow a lot faster."

Val laughed but didn't say anything. Brad could tell she didn't like the thought, but she simply said, "I hope it grows because we're a kick ass band."

Nick said, "Of course, it will. And we just got better tonight."

"Seriously," Zane said, taking another drink, "we'll get even better as we go. We already sounded great tonight.

Can you imagine what a month or two together will do?"

Ethan was mellowing out. Brad could tell he'd taken something, but he hadn't seen him do it. He'd probably done it when he'd gone to take a piss before Val had arrived. Or it was his earlier indulgence just lasting a long time. But he got quiet.

Brad took a long swig. He wanted to drown out some of the stronger emotions he was feeling, but he couldn't drink too much, because then he might not be able to hold his tongue. It was a fine line he had to walk. But he drank as much as he thought he could handle, and he wound up tuning them out part of the time. He was doing a lot of soul searching when he should have been celebrating a huge success. At one point, Valerie asked, "Everything okay?"

Fuck. He forced a smile on his face. "Yeah. Just a little tired, I guess."

"Yeah. Me too. I should probably head to bed."

She did seem tired too and left shortly after. Brad was surprised the guys didn't demand they scope for girls, but they seemed to be enjoying each other's company. They wound up finding a movie on the television, and Brad used it as an excuse to drift off, just lying on top of the bed in his clothes with his shoes off.

So he'd managed to avoid having to think about it, but he woke up the next morning and lay in bed for a good hour, mulling it all over. He didn't feel a bit better about it, and the longer he lay there, the more he thought he needed to get a few things off his chest with Val. He needed to be honest with her and let her know where he was coming from. He needed to try to just let her know what she was doing to him. He felt brave now, but facing her…would he be able to say what he needed to?

He needed coffee and breakfast. But, first, a shower. He took a lukewarm one, because it was already feeling overly warm in the room. The air conditioner in the room didn't seem to work very well. He supposed that was okay, because he was hoping to hit the road by noon. He had to work the next day, and he wanted to get home with a little time to relax.

After he showered and changed into clean clothes, he wrote a note for the guys. They wouldn't want breakfast with the hangovers they were bound to have acquired, but if they woke up, he wanted them to know he'd be back soon. Then he put the room key, his phone, and his wallet into his back pockets and stepped outside. At first, he thought he'd go eat breakfast and then see if Val was up and available to talk, but then he decided to text her. No better time than the present. *U up?*

It wasn't a minute later that she responded. *Yep.*

He couldn't resist. He knocked on her door. Seconds later, she opened the door a crack and peeked out. "Gimme a second. I need to get dressed."

He grinned. "I could help you with that." Well, *that* was fuckin' stupid. *She* obviously *wouldn't* like that.

But she smiled back. "I'm sure you could."

He leaned against the wall of the motel. The sun was already beating down, but it felt good on his skin. He closed his eyes and relaxed until he heard her door open again a few minutes later. "So what's up?"

She looked as sweet as ever, and seeing her in simple, faded, snug blue jeans and a Black Tide t-shirt made him feel dopey. She had no idea what she did to him. But he needed to talk with her, and he definitely had to get his shit together when it came to the girl. He had to stop thinking of her as anything other than a friend, and the sooner he did that, the better. So he tried to sound casual, tried to sound like just a friend…which was what they were, and friends commiserated. "Jesus…those guys are trashed. They're gonna be fun on the drive home. I need to get some breakfast and coffee and just wanted to know if you want to come with."

"Sure." She slid some sandals on. Then she grabbed her purse, throwing her room key and phone inside, and took a ponytail scrunchie off the dresser. As they stepped out the door, she pulled her hair up and away from her face.

When they got in the van, he decided to cruise down one of the main drags until he saw a restaurant that looked halfway appealing. But he couldn't talk. Not yet. The time wasn't right. The music was blaring, and that was okay. It would help him focus.

It wasn't too long that he found a diner that screamed pancakes and greasy eggs. He imagined they had a pot of coffee on all day, and that was the kind of place where he wanted to be right now. He parked but didn't shut off the engine. He turned the music down and looked at Val. "This okay?" If it wasn't appealing to her, he'd keep driving.

"Yeah. It's fine."

The waitress was efficient. Brad imagined she'd been doing the same job at the same diner for a good decade. She wasn't rude, but she wasn't polite either—just matter of fact. He didn't care, though, because she was fast. They had their menus and had barely scanned them when she brought the coffee they'd requested. Then she took their orders and whisked their menus away. Brad poured cream in the coffee and put a spoonful of sugar in and stirred it, trying to think of how to start the conversation.

But Val wasn't a fucking idiot. He needed to give her credit for that. She was stirring cream in her coffee too when she said, "Um…about last night…"

And then he felt bad. He must have been doing a shitty job at hiding his feelings, and he didn't want her to feel guilty. He knew as well as anyone that people couldn't logically decide who they wanted to fall in love with. Val was human just like he was, and the fact that she knew it had bothered him made him feel like a shitheel. He looked up from his coffee and shook his head. "No…Val, we don't need to do this." He could be happy having her as just a friend. He didn't want to cause her pain by making her talk about it—Ethan inflicted enough on her as it was.

She lowered her voice, but her eyes didn't waver. "I'd like to."

Goddamn. He had to give her credit. That was classy. Okay…so he'd find a way to say what she needed to hear. He couldn't look at her, though. Just couldn't. He stared into the cup of brown liquid and thought hard. What should he say? How should he say it? Honesty. Even if he couldn't say anything important, he knew he couldn't lie to Val, not about something so close to his heart. So he let out another breath and finally forced his lips to move. "I knew what I was up against." He looked at her. *This* was gonna hurt. "I *know* where your heart is, and I chose to take that chance anyway." He inhaled sharply. He couldn't help what he was feeling, and shit…he was going to try to find a way to bury it, but for now...for now, he was raw and exposed, and he had to get it out. "I told you...I'm a patient man." And that was fucking stupid—because it was turning out to be true.

She was quiet for a bit. He could hear the other noises in the restaurant, aside from his own steady breaths in and out of his lungs. He could hear spoons clinking against coffee cups. He could hear some stupid elevator tune blaring out of a staticky speaker somewhere overhead. He heard the two old guys behind him talking about a baseball game. He could hear the cooks laughing in the kitchen and then one of them ringing an old-fashioned bell and yelling, "Order up." And, meantime, his life was passing by, and, for the moment, it felt meaningless.

Val finally spoke, and her voice was so quiet, he had to strain to hear. "Still...whether I'd expected what you saw or not...I'm sure you didn't appreciate seeing that."

She had that right, but he felt like it was better that he *had* seen it, because then she couldn't deny it or pretend it hadn't happened. He had to hold down the emotion. He was going to come across as angry or more hurt than he wanted her to know, so he had to rein it in before he spoke. He couldn't look at her again, so he took a sip of his coffee and let his eyes follow the cup back to the table. "Doesn't matter. It was a good reminder."

She reached across the table and touched his hand. "Hey..." He looked up and didn't pull his hand back, but it stung. He knew she'd made her choice; she wasn't denying it. "You are...one of the best men I know."

What the hell was that supposed to mean? That made him feel even more like shit, because if he really was all that to her, why did she run to Ethan? Yeah, Brad would have done anything for the guy, loved him like a brother, but he'd be a fucking liar—and so would she—if he'd said Ethan was an upstanding citizen. He couldn't think of what to say and could have kissed the crusty waitress when she rescued him seconds later with their food. How she carried it all—syrup, two plates, and a pot of coffee to refill their cups, he'd never know—but he was grateful to have the distraction. Talking to Valerie about her irrational infatuation of Ethan had proved to be fruitless and painful, and damned if he'd ever make that mistake again.

He'd rather have a flaming hot fork shoved in his chest. He suspected it wouldn't hurt as badly.

CHAPTER TWENTY-FIVE

AS THOUGH TO add insult to injury, Val decided she needed to talk to Brad *about* Ethan on the ride back to the motel. It was as if she were trying to find new ways to torment him. "So what's Ethan taking, Brad? Do you know?"

Oh, God. Why? But he cared about both Ethan and Valerie. If she was kind, she'd let it drop. "Hmm...what?"

No such luck. "Come on, Brad. I'm not stupid. What's Ethan been on lately?"

She was going to make him talk about it. Maybe he could discourage her. So he shook his head and said, "You really don't wanna know."

"Yeah, actually, I really *do*."

God, she was being stubborn. He pulled the van into the motel parking lot. After he parked and shut off the engine, he turned to face Valerie. "I'm not positive, but I'm pretty sure he's taking Vike."

"Vike?"

"Vicodin."

"How do you know?"

He was irritated that he even had to have this conversation, but he figured it would only be fair to be honest. "I don't, Val. But I have my reasons for why I think that."

He grabbed the door handle, planning to could get out of the van, but Val grabbed his arm. "Wait. Just tell me. Why?"

He inhaled and looked out the window. How much did he want to tell her? How much would be enough to satisfy her? But, goddammit, he couldn't bring himself to be dishonest with her. He doubted he'd ever be able to. He looked back at her, ready to tell her whatever she needed so she could let it go. "A couple years ago, his mom had some in the medicine cabinet…leftovers from something, and she never used the rest of 'em. So we both took one before going to a party. Well…we wound up not going to the party. We were wasted. It was…hard to describe. Pretty peaceful feeling. I didn't want to do anything, just lay there, vegging, watching whatever stupid movie we were watching on TV. And then I just wanted to sleep. But Ethan…over the next year, he'd take one now and then until the whole goddamn bottle was gone."

"So if it's gone now, how's he getting more?"

If they'd been having this conversation yesterday, he might have smiled. Today, though, it simply rubbed him the wrong way. If Val wanted to be involved with Ethan, her naiveté was going to get her in trouble. "How does anyone get illegal drugs? You think it's that hard? All you need is the right amount of cash and a connection."

"So…what should we do about it?"

Oh, hell, no. She was *not* going to make Ethan even more his responsibility than the guy already was. She was *not* going to use his misguided affection for her to do her bidding for a guy who couldn't give two shits about her. He let the air out of his lungs. "What do you think we can do about it, Val?" He wasn't about to tell her of the times Ethan had scared the shit out of him. He wasn't going to tell her about the times he'd lectured Ethan (or been lectured *by* Ethan for trying to stop him from doing the shit he did). She was a relative newcomer to the Ethan's-a-drug-addict scene, and Brad was about out of patience. "We can't do shit. He has to decide he wants to stop. You try to make him stop, he'll just do it more. You stand back. That's what you do. You…" He squinted his eyes and kept himself from gritting his teeth. "You go on loving him and be there when you need to." He pulled his keys out of the ignition and opened the door so he could end the conversation. "Just like I always have."

He got out and waited in front of the van. Val sat in the passenger seat for a long time, staring at him through the windshield as if she couldn't believe he'd walked away from her. Finally, he walked over to her door and asked, "Are you coming?"

She let out a breath and rolled her eyes. She opened the door and stepped out. She was pissed at him. *Good.* Maybe she'd quit asking questions. What the fuck did she expect? She asked, barely concealing her anger, "When are we leaving?"

He shrugged. "Let me see if I can get the sleeping princesses up. I'd like to leave by noon."

"I'll be ready."

He nodded and walked to his door. This day couldn't end soon enough.

After a few weeks, Brad was able to let it all go. He forgave Valerie in his heart—he never told her aloud that he'd been angry and upset with her. She didn't need to know it. She'd never intentionally meant to hurt him, and it wasn't like Brad hadn't known the girl was head over heels crazy for his best friend. Brad didn't think Val had been a cock tease, either. He'd initiated every encounter the two of them had ever had—she'd just been an easy victim. So he was able to let it go and ease back into a *just friends* relationship.

They had shows every weekend, and he was able to enjoy watching Valerie get better and better. She grew more confident, and as she grew more sure of herself, she ventured forth, trying new things. It was exciting. In addition to that, she was freeing him up to become a better guitarist. He could honestly credit her as the reason his playing was improving by leaps and bounds.

They were trying to write more songs too, but they didn't have much time. They did it some through email like they had over the spring. Brad was glad for that too, because it was a natural place for their friendship to go. It was based around music anyway—if it hadn't been for the music, they probably would never have met, and they certainly wouldn't have had much in common.

He didn't think anything was going on between Val and Ethan, in spite of the kiss he'd seen them share in June, but he wasn't going to ask, and he didn't want to know.

One night in August they had a show in a rural town in eastern Colorado—a fantastic kick ass show, one of the best they'd done that summer. It had been such a great show that they were partying hard. There were quite a few people with them, people from another band and some fans. They were loud and also lucky that no one was complaining about the noise. Brad had been waiting for a few minutes to use the bathroom. When it was finally free, he walked in...and felt sorry for whatever person would have to clean it the next day. He'd have to sneak a large tip in the room before they left—but after the guys were out of the room for good so one of them didn't pocket it, thinking some dumb ass had forgotten his money and *finder's keepers* (he could just hear Nick sing-songing it).

When he left the bathroom, he spent some time talking to the guitarist of the other band. He was a solid guy, and he hoped to play with him again sometime. When the guy's girlfriend joined them and they'd been introduced to each other, Brad decided he was ready for another beer. He walked to the mini fridge in the room and then realized he hadn't seen Val and Ethan before. *Oh, fuck.* That probably meant it was finally happening.

Part of him didn't want to know, didn't *need* to know. But that wasn't true. He *did* want to know. They were both his friends, and he didn't want to be the last to find out. Still...what the fuck kind of creep would he be if he went to her room to find out?

He wasn't sure how he justified leaving his room where the party was, but he had to get some fresh air. He promised himself he would not go to her room, wouldn't do all the things he wanted to deep down. No—he would get a few breaths of fresh air and then return to the party. Maybe the chick with black hair and ass like there was no tomorrow would take a walk with him. He needed a distraction.

When he stepped outside, though, Val was right in front of the door, her back to it, and Ethan was facing her. She was holding his hand and talking to him, her voice raised and desperate. "That's bullshit, Ethan. I thought you *loved* this…and if you're not giving it your all, if you're not fully here, then you'll never reach your full potential. You're not just letting yourself down. You're letting us all down."

Ethan grabbed Val's arm and growled at her. At first, Brad had thought they were having some kind of a lover's spat and he was going to turn right back around and go back to the party, but then he realized that wasn't it at all. "Listen, Val, I know you think you know me, but you don't. I do this shit to survive, and I'm here, all right? The day I don't perform, the day I don't show, that's the fucking day you can tell me I've let you down. Till then…"—he let go of Val's arm and started backing away—"not another goddamned word about it."

Brad walked past Val and put his hand on Ethan's shoulder. He knew how volatile his friend could be sometimes, and the guy was probably scaring the shit out of Val. He kept his voice low and calm. "Everything okay here?"

"Yeah. I was just leaving."

She was just as angry as Ethan. "Yeah. So was I." Ethan walked back into the party, and Val stormed away, letting herself in her own room, leaving Brad outside by himself.

He stood there for a good minute. If he were smart, he'd go back to the party himself and not worry about it. But he couldn't. He knew Val and knew this summer had been hard on her, as much as she'd loved it. She was having to stretch and grow…and grow up. She wasn't used to being surrounded by seediness.

So he went back into the party and did what he'd planned to do before he walked outside. He found the beer…and he took two bottles. Then he left the room again, but not without seeing Ethan getting cozy with the black-haired girl Brad had considered earlier.

He gritted his teeth but let it go. He walked down to Val's room and rapped on the door. After a few seconds, she opened it and said, "What?"

Oh, that was really nice—taking out her anger with Ethan on him. Still, it just kind of underscored what he felt he needed to say to her. "Can I come in?" She stood back, holding the door open for him. He sat at a chair next to the desk in the room, and she sat on the edge of the bed near him. He asked, "Want a beer?" He handed her a bottle, but in typical Val fashion, she shook her head, vehement. So he placed it on the desk and twisted open the cap of the other one. He looked her squarely in the eyes and made sure his voice was cool. "I know you want to help Ethan, Val, but what you're doing now…he'll just blow you off completely. He needs to realize on his own what he's doing." She rolled her eyes. She was blowing him off. "I mean it, Val. Don't push him. Trust me. Doing that is a bad idea. I don't think he'll overdose on it. I've never seen him go overboard." Well…that might not have been entirely true. He knew for sure Ethan had gotten into some bad shit before, but he didn't think he'd OD'd. A hospital could have confirmed it. Just because Brad thought Ethan might have, he didn't know for certain, and he didn't want to upset Valerie with possibilities.

"But can he become addicted?"

"He probably already is."

"And you just let him?"

"What the fuck is that supposed to mean? I *let* him? Like I'm his mom, or I have any control over what he does?" For some reason, her accusation set him off. She was *letting* Ethan as well, if that was what she insisted on calling it. "I have my own shit to deal with, Val. I'm not the fucking cops. That would be like me asking you why *you* just let him."

He saw the anger and frustration in her eyes dissipate, and then she looked almost sorry. She nodded her head. "Fair enough. But what can we do, Brad? We can't just let him keep doing this."

"What the hell are we *supposed* to do?"

"I guess there's nothing. I just feel so helpless…and lame not doing anything."

"How do you think *I* feel? I'm his best friend, and you were right about one thing. I used to encourage a lot of that shit. Hell, we used to do a lot of shit together. First time I tried meth and coke were with Ethan."

Her eyes almost popped out of her head. "You've tried meth?"

He shrugged. "Yeah."

"Are you crazy?"

"Probably. Yeah…we did stupid shit, Val. Just…I knew when to stop. And…apparently Ethan doesn't.

And…at least he's *not* hooked on something like meth. So, we gotta be here for him. We need to catch him when he falls, because he will. He'll fall. And that's when he'll decide he needs to do something different."

"So what's the difference between you and him? Why could you stop and he can't?"

"I don't know. Maybe he has a more addictive personality than I do. Hell, I don't know. Seriously, Val. The man's been through hell. You have no idea. And this is one of the things he does to cope." If Val only knew half the shit Ethan had been through and seen throughout his whole life, she'd go a lot easier on the guy. Part of Brad continued to want to protect her from that, though, but he doubted that he'd be able to.

He saw her processing it. She was trying—he'd give her credit there. She asked, "Offer on the beer still stand?"

He raised his eyebrows. "You serious?"

"I know…stupid."

He laughed. "Nah. If you're gonna drink, this is better than a lot of other things." He twisted off the cap and handed it to her. She took a sip and winced and he smiled. Sweet innocent Val. And since he was already here talking with her, it was time to lay it all out on the table. "There's something else we should probably talk about." She squinted her eyes, but it didn't matter. It needed to be said and sooner rather than later. He'd had a couple of months and had some perspective, and this was the first time they'd been alone in a long time. He took a deep breath. "You and me. I want you to know I respect the hell out of you, Val. Now that you're in the band, it's hands off. I don't want to lose you for Fully Automatic. You're exactly what we needed. No way am I gonna fuck that up. So…I just wanted to assure you, in case you had any worries, that I'll keep my hands to myself."

She was quiet for the better part of a minute, absorbing his words. Then she said, "I respect you too, Brad, and I trust your decisions for the direction of the band."

He stuck out his hand. "Shake on it?"

She grinned. "Deal."

The next step would be convincing Valerie to stick with the band after school started…but he'd save that conversation for another day. Instead, he wanted to share a beer with his friend, now that they were also sharing an understanding.

CHAPTER TWENTY-SIX

BETWEEN HIS JOB and Fully Automatic shows (and their small merch table they'd finally started), Brad had a little extra cash, and he was ready for fresh ink. So he went to the guy downtown he'd always gone to. The guy had some new original designs, and Brad found a couple that spoke to him, so over the course of a couple of weeks had a couple of new tattoos painted on his right forearm and the right side of his chest. He knew getting a tattoo on his forearm was flagging himself. The more tattoos he got, the less likely he'd be able in the future to get a "real" job.

That was another way he would keep himself driven.

He had a schedule for himself, aside from his forty-hour-a-week oil-and-lube job. One of his goals was to book at least three new future shows a week. Another goal was to write a new song every two to three weeks—music only. He wasn't going to touch lyrics again, unless for some reason he felt driven to, because it came so naturally to Val, and she was way better at it than he'd ever dreamed of being. There was no sense even trying. He also made a point of working out twice a week, because otherwise he tended to focus on music to the exclusion of all else.

He had a plan, though, a big one, now that August was half over. He simply had to convince the guys to help him out. So he invited them over one Monday night, tempting them with his mom's killer spaghetti. And then he managed to get them on board. Now they just had the monumental task of convincing Val.

Brad and the guys drove to Winchester to pick Val up for what was to be their last show with her. She'd told them all the reasons why she couldn't do it while she was in school. It was too far away and playing shows with them would take her away from valuable study time. Brad had sensed, though, that she was trying to convince herself more than them. And he and the guys had a plan.

She'd settled in her seat and they were heading toward Colorado Springs, their ultimate destination the Denver Metro area. Brad had been cranking a hard and heavy song, but he started thinking maybe there was no better time than the present. At some point, her going back to college would be talked about anyway—he knew it was on the back of everyone's minds, including hers—so why not just get it over with? If she declined their offer, the rest of the drive might be a little somber, but Brad was pretty sure he knew her heart.

Yeah, he knew what made Val tick. How, he didn't know. He just did.

He turned the music down and glanced over at her. "Val, we wanted to broach a pretty serious subject with you, and now's as a good a time as any." He looked toward the back of the van. "Right, guys?"

There was a general consensus and then she said, "Okay."

She was acting nervous, like they were going to deliver bad news to her. He couldn't help it—he was grinning from ear to ear. Well, good. If she was feeling anxious, then maybe when she heard what they really wanted to talk about, she'd give it some serious thought. "We've been talking, Val, and we're not ready for this to be over. Not by a long shot. You know we've already got dates clear through November, and I'm still booking shows out past that. We don't want to lose you, Val. You've become one of us, and we can't see doing this without you anymore." That was his best pitch. He hoped it was enough.

She nodded. "Yeah, but I've got college soon."

"Yes, that's what you've said. So you've decided on a major then?"

"Well, no."

"You've narrowed it down, though, right?"

He could hear the amused sound in her voice. "No..."

"So why can't school wait *until* you know?"

Ah... That made her stop and think a little. "Okay, so let's say I wait. But then I have to get my parents on board. More than that, though, my job's ended. What do I do then? How do I support myself? It's not like we're rolling in the dough."

"But what if we were playing four or five nights a week?"

"Yeah...I can see how that might add up. But you'd have to spend it all on gas, though, wouldn't you?"

"Not if we moved to where the shit is."

She paused again. She was considering it. "Are you thinking we should all move somewhere and play all the time?"

He smiled again. "Yeah...that's what we're thinking. We mostly play around Denver, so why not find a place that fits all of us? I keep booking shows, and I could do more if we lived there and didn't have to drive all over the place. Instead of figuring out if it fits around work and if we could make it to a show on time, I would just have to make sure we had the time free. There are lots of shows we could do, and Denver's a huge place. And that wouldn't mean we couldn't do shows somewhere else, but it would make the ones there a lot easier to get to." She nodded, listening. "We have a better chance of building a big audience, maybe even of getting picked up by a label someday in the future, if we're playing more shows." She looked like she was building up to a major objection, so he asked, "Would it help if all us guys talked to your mom and dad, let them know you're safe with us?"

She looked over at him and then back at the guys. Brad could see them in the review mirror. They were all smiles. She nodded then looked at Brad. "Yeah, I think that's a good idea."

Yeah. He couldn't have asked for more. And the rest of the night they let themselves dream. Now that the members of Fully Automatic had fully committed to one another, the show that night was beyond great. It was one of the best shows they'd ever performed up to that point.

And that was why it would have been a damn shame to just let it end.

*   *   *

That Sunday, the boys of Fully Automatic got up earlier than any of them had in ages to begin the long drive to Winchester. They had to get there before one in the afternoon. Valerie had told her parents they all wanted to talk to them (she told Brad she hadn't told them *what*), and her mother had suggested inviting them to their Sunday barbecue. It was to be Val's last Sunday at home, because she would be leaving for college at the end of the week, ready for classes a week from Monday.

Time was, obviously, of the essence.

Brad had lectured them the night before about "looking presentable." He got a few grumbles, most of them from Ethan, Mr. Bad Attitude, but even he saw the importance of looking as normal and "respectable" as possible. They weren't going to win Val's parents over by being the epitome of dissention and rebellion, no matter what their actual heavy metal message might have been.

Much as he hated the idea of it all, he'd promised Valerie and would do whatever it took. He pulled his hair back into a ponytail and was going to wear a t-shirt for the ride, but before they got to Val's house, he was going to change into a white, long-sleeved button-down shirt. Jesus. When he saw himself in the mirror, he almost *did* look respectable. All he needed was a tie. He also got rid of all jewelry. From everything Val had told him (and from meeting her mother and brother earlier that summer, even though it was only for a few minutes), her family was ultra conservative, and looking buttoned down was a good thing. None of his tattoos were showing, although if anyone tried too hard, they could see some of them through the fabric.

But his job here was not to appear to be someone he was not; instead, it was to show her parents respect and put their minds at ease.

Ethan and Zane wore their typical attire—t-shirt, jeans, and sneakers—but they were low key. They didn't look too far out, and neither had hair that was too long or lots of tattoos. They looked almost like college kids…which they *had* been up until a couple of months earlier. Nick dressed the same as the other guys, but he had short hair and he didn't even have any tattoos peeking out from under his sleeves. He had one small one on his upper right arm that was only seen when he wore sleeveless shirts. Brad examined them before leaving and declared that they'd done a great job.

It was a tense drive, only because Brad knew what was at stake. When they finally got to Winchester, Brad pulled into the parking lot of the first supermarket he spotted and took off his t-shirt, replacing it with the office-type shirt. "Why you gotta go and do that?" Ethan asked.

"You know why."

"Yeah. Just seems unnecessary."

"I have lots more tattoos than you, man. I don't want to be the problem." Then he started walking to the front doors of the store.

"Where you goin'?" Zane asked.

"Trust me." In minutes, he returned with a bouquet of flowers for Val's mom and a few moments later, they were walking up the concrete to Val's front door.

She opened the door and damn if she didn't look as cute as could be. She was wearing a light white cotton sleeveless dress, her hair pulled away from her face but hanging down her back. She grinned when she saw them and said, "Hey, guys! Follow me."

She led them through the living room and kitchen toward the back door, and Zane said, "Nice place."

"Thanks. I've lived here all my life."

They stepped out onto a patio. There was a picnic table there covered with an umbrella, and there was already a huge spread—iced tea and lemonade, baked beans, coleslaw, potato salad, corn on the cob, condiments, and paper plates and utensils. Brad could see her father barbecuing over at a grill farther away, and her little brother was sitting at the picnic table texting someone. Val's mom, though, smiled warmly and walked to the other side of the table where they stood. "Welcome. We're so glad to have you here."

Brad handed the bouquet of flowers to Val's mother. "Mrs. Quinn, we wanted to thank you for inviting us over…and for letting us borrow the vocal skills of your talented daughter."

Her mother smiled, and he could again see the resemblance. She said, "Oh, you're certainly welcome."

Val said, "Mom, Danny, you've already met Brad, but the rest of the guys are Ethan, Zane, and Nick." She pointed at each of the guys as she said their names. Her mom smiled at them, and Danny looked up from his phone.

Her mother said, "I'd better get these in water. Valerie, could you introduce them to your father?"

Her dad had turned off the grill and was walking toward the picnic table, a platter full of steaks in his hand. When he made it over, he put the platter on the table and Val said,

"Dad, these are the guys." She introduced her father to each of them, and they shook hands as she introduced each one. Her mom came back out then and they sat down to eat. It was civil, with the food going around, a couple of dishes at a time, and everyone was either buttering corn, cutting into a steak, or taking a first bite when Val said, "Well, I guess I need to just tell you what we're thinking." Both her mother and father nodded. She continued, "We've had so much fun and done so well this summer as a band, that we feel like we were just getting started. So…we've talked about it, and we'd like to give it a hardcore try. Not just play on the weekends, you know, but really give it a solid effort. We think if we move to the Denver area, we can give it an honest shot."

Wow. Val wasn't wasting any time, instead just going for the jugular. Well, he supposed, that was one way of doing it—get it over with and see what would happen. Her mother put her fork down and said, "You're not planning to go back to college this fall?"

Brad wanted to help, but now was not the time. He didn't know her parents well enough to know what to say or how to say it. He'd help when the time was right. He just had to support Val in silence for the time being.

The girl was prepared. She'd finally allowed her passion to take over, and she was ready to fight for what she wanted. "Mom, I've thought long and hard about this. I'm wasting your money. I have no idea what I want to do with my life, and so I don't have any solid ideas about a major. I thought after a year of attending school, I'd know, but I'm no closer to a decision now than I was a year ago. And I *want* to do this. It might not be for a lifetime, but I want to do it now. It's like those kids who travel around the world for a year or two before going to school. I went to school for a year, and now I'm going to try something different. I need to figure out who I am and what I want."

Val's mother nodded her head. Her father, though, had been listening intently but not saying a word. He looked from Val to Ethan, then down the line, to Nick, Zane, and his eyes landed on Brad's. If he'd been a young guy vying for Val's affections, he would have been taking up a challenge. But that wasn't it. This was a father who loved his daughter and cared for her well-being. His eyes gave nothing away. "Let me tell you my concern here. I want to know what your intentions with my daughter are." He continued eyeing the rest of the band again, staring them down, challenging them all.

Brad had prepared for this, though. All he knew about Val and what she'd said about her family had given him an idea of how he should handle the situation. Honesty—always the best policy. He respected her parents because he thought Val was a hell of a young woman. He made sure he looked and sounded calm when he answered. "Mr. Quinn, Valerie and I actually already had a conversation about that earlier this summer. And I'll be honest with you, even though it probably won't help my case at all. Valerie and I got a little friendly, but when we invited her to sing for the band, I told her that would be a line that we wouldn't cross. Relationships and work don't work, so there's no way I'm going to ruin my band just because I find her attractive. I want to assure you, sir, that we respect your daughter and value her contribution, and we have and will continue to treat her as one of us." He thought a little humor might lighten the conversation, so he threw in, "With one exception. We'll use different bathrooms."

Her mother giggled, but her dad's face didn't even crack. He seemed to relax a little, though, so that was something. He had a stern look on his face when he said, "Just so we're on the same page, there will be no hanky-panky, and one of you so much as *touches* my daughter without her consent, I will gladly go to prison for the rest of my life for murder." Yeah…Brad had no intentions of pissing off her dad. He might have been a confident young man, but this guy was pretty intimidating. No wonder Val was still a virgin. Any potential suitors were likely still trying to coax their balls back out of hiding.

Brad had no words. He'd already assured her father that he'd keep his hands off. He looked over at Val and could see she was getting ready to say something. When she did, her voice was quiet. "So you're saying I can do this, dad?"

Her dad said, "You're an adult, Valerie. I can't really tell you what to do anymore. All I can do is give you my advice. I know you've already made up your mind, but I need to tell you that I don't think this is a good idea. Now is the time for you to work on getting a degree and figuring out what you want to do with your life. You said that much yourself. And I don't know that traipsing around the state singing your loud metal music is going to help in that department."

She smiled. "So you're saying I can go?"

Her father smiled back at her, and that was the first time that day he seemed human. "Yes, Valerie, you can go. But know you always have a place to come home to."

The remainder of the meal was light-hearted and fun.

Not only did her brother have lots of questions for the band and their plans, but even her mother and father relaxed and seemed to be happy for their daughter. Val promised to take care of withdrawing from school so there would be no more charges to her parents, and then the conversation moved to deciding what they would all do next—as a band.

CHAPTER TWENTY-SEVEN

BRAD'S LIFE CHANGED completely in a matter of two short weeks. He gave his notice at work, because he was ready to start his new life—the one he'd been waiting for since graduation over a year ago. They weren't going to make it, weren't going to get anywhere in this little town out in the middle of nowhere. Yeah, he loved his mom, loved his dad, and some of the friends he'd leave behind. He'd miss his town too, but his future wasn't here, and it certainly wasn't going to be changing oil in cars for forty hours a week.

His future was out there—and he was gonna grab it.

His band was sounding professional, and that was partly due to all the playing together they'd done over the past three months. And he knew that you could sound fine in your garage, but put yourself under some pressure—under the lights and the scrutiny of a crowd. You'd learn to play well fast—or you'd give up. They'd survived in that crucible, and now it was time to take it up a notch.

His boss offered to give him a couple of extra days off when Brad said he had things he needed to do. He texted Valerie and asked if she wanted to go with him to Denver to check for places to rent. She asked who else was coming. *Just me.* He hoped she didn't ask more. He knew the guys wouldn't give two shits about where they lived. He had to keep Val happy. The guys didn't much want to go look either, but the three of them managed to pledge several hundred dollars for deposits.

Brad had a lot of money he'd set aside too, but he'd try to keep it even and fair. They found a couple of dives and Valerie was thoroughly unimpressed, so he planned to come back the next week. The first time was probably good, because then Valerie would understand that places there were expensive. They couldn't afford to be too choosy. He let her know how much money all the guys had, and he said he could pitch in more if he needed to. She had money too and was happy to pitch in.

The second time, she settled for one of the places they'd looked at the week before. Really, it could have been much worse. It was a two-bedroom place, but if they went bigger, Brad was afraid they wouldn't be able to afford monthly rent. Valerie agreed. Fortunately, the place was furnished, so they wouldn't have to buy beds, a couch, or a kitchen table. They signed the lease and paid the deposit, with the agreement that the apartment would be available in a week. Brad sent a text to the guys letting them know they got a two-bedroom place, and they'd figure out a way to make it work. The good news, and Brad said as much to Val, was that he didn't plan on them being there much—the place was central to most of the places where they'd be playing, and he hoped to keep them working so much that they would only sleep and eat at their apartment.

They took care of utility deposits too, and that's when Brad and Val had to rely exclusively on their own money.

On the way back, they talked about all the things they thought they'd need. Val took notes on her phone. Brad thought of either sleeping bags or cots, since there were only two beds and a couch. Brad could see the worry etched in Val's face and hoped he was able to alleviate it. When he dropped her off, he told her the next time he showed up would be with all the guys, and they'd be ready to begin their big adventure. She promised to be packed and ready to go.

Brad and the guys actually moved their stuff up the day before, and Brad texted her, letting her know with four guys there, the place seemed smaller. *Bring only necessities, Val*, he texted her.

The hardest thing he had to do was agree to let Ethan pick Val up when his friend asked to. That meant Ethan was showing interest in her again, and he'd likely break her heart...*again.* But Brad had to stop worrying about it. Val was a big girl and she seemed unable to let Ethan go for whatever reason. He couldn't let it bother him anymore. He had to let it go. His band was most important...and maybe that meant he needed to let Val and Ethan do whatever it was they were gonna do—and he had to just step back and stay out of the way.

That didn't mean it felt good, though. When Ethan left late the next morning to pick her up, Brad decided he needed to stay busy—and get the ball rolling. He had a list of things they needed as a group of people living on their own for the first time—stupid things like waste baskets, towels, sheets, a broom and dustpan, a vacuum, cleaning supplies. And food and dishes. They'd need to eat. God. He was tearing through his money, even when he was doing a lot of shopping at thrift stores. It wasn't going to last much longer.

He kept reminding himself they had three gigs that week alone, and now that the music was his sole focus, he could make sure they worked even harder, got more exposure. But they picked up everything they needed and got things put away before Ethan and Val arrived. At that point, Brad pulled out his laptop and reviewed the gigs coming up for the next several months. It was concerning. As much as he hated it, he was going to have to get a job here. There was no way they'd make it on gigs alone, and there was no fuckin' way he was going to give up now. They hadn't had a chance to even try.

He was sitting at the kitchen table, and Nick and Zane were in the living room talking when Ethan and Val arrived. Both had their arms full and set her things just inside the door. "One more trip—Bradley, you want to help?" Brad nodded. Ethan looked at Val. "We got this."

"You sure?"

"Yeah."

Brad followed him out into the hall. No, it hadn't escaped his notice that Val was flushed when she came in, and it wasn't just because the ride had been hot—the day had been mostly cloudy and cool. Ethan, on the other hand, was as smooth as usual. God, he wanted to ask. He did. But part of him didn't want to know. At first, he thought maybe that's why Ethan asked him to help; instead, it was just that Brad was right there.

They got to the truck, and Ethan handed Brad a box and he grabbed the other. Brad wanted to tell him he could have gotten it all by himself, but he didn't want to be a dick. "How was the trip?"

Ethan shrugged, leading the way back to the apartment. "Fine. Traffic was thick here and there, but no big deal. Drove through a little rain."

God, Brad ached to ask about Val, but he was going to keep his mouth shut.

When they got back to the apartment, he expected to see Val talking with Zane and Nick, but instead she was looking around the apartment, a disheartened look on her face. *Oh, shit.* She was already regretting the move, and she hadn't been there five minutes. What the fuck had Ethan said to her on the drive?

"First things first—we need to put Val's stuff in the small bedroom." Brad grabbed one of the suitcases along with the box he was already carrying and placed them in the corner of the bedroom. Ethan and Val were right behind him with the rest of her things. As they walked back out of the room, he felt compelled to put his arm around her shoulders to comfort her—but he wasn't going to. No...he could sense that something huge had happened between her and Ethan that day, and he wasn't going to interfere, as much as his protective side wanted to hold her close.

Once in the kitchen, Brad said, "We need to get our living arrangements sorted out." He started walking to the living room, because Nick and Zane were already there. There was only a couch and a chair, though, so he grabbed a couple of chairs from the kitchen.

He saw Val's sad visage again as he walked back to the living room, and he couldn't ignore it anymore.

"What's wrong, Val?"

She sighed. "I know we checked out this place before, and it was all we could afford, but am I the only one who thinks it's depressing here?"

He smiled. Yeah, he'd read her right—partially. He still wanted to know what had happened with her and Ethan, but he was just gonna have to wonder. He wasn't going to ask. Back to the matter at hand—yes, the place was small and it was dingy, but it was the nicest they could afford and he hoped they would make the best of it. "Yeah…it's not the greatest. But it'll be what we make it, right? Besides, we don't want to spend much time here anyway. We want to be out playing gigs all the time. Am I right?"

She smiled back and nodded. "Yeah, I know. I'll get over it."

Brad addressed the group at that point. "I don't know how much practice we'll be able to get in, guys, at least plugged in. We'll have to check with our neighbors…"

"We don't have to crank it."

"It just gonna be harder to write new stuff, but we'll manage. The big bedroom's on the corner of the building, so if we're gonna plug in and practice, I think that's where we need to." Everyone nodded in agreement. "Now…living arrangements. I really think Val should have the little bedroom, the one with the twin bed." He felt the need to say it explicitly, even though he'd already put all her belongings in there.

"That doesn't seem fair, Brad. There's one of me and four of you. I can sleep on the couch, and you guys can share the rooms."

"Bullshit. I promised your dad we'd keep our hands off."

"That doesn't mean I need my own bedroom."

"It does in *my* mind. You need a place where you can feel safe, where you can have some privacy. You won't have to worry about one of us walking in while you're changing clothes or staring at you while you're sleeping."

She giggled. "Should I have had to worry about that before?"

He was serious, though, and even though he smiled, he hoped his message got through to all the guys...especially Ethan. If Val consented to the guy's advances, that was one thing, but she needed to have her own space, and he was going to assure it. "Now...as to the other bedroom, we're not gonna fight over it. Us guys are gonna share. We bought two cots today at an army surplus store for cheap, and when we're not using them, we can store them in the closet over there. Not the best plan, but it works."

Ethan asked, "So we're just gonna use the big bedroom for our gear?"

"No. One of us will sleep on that bed, one on the couch, two on the cots in the living room. We're gonna get a calendar, and each one of us will get the bedroom the same amount of days every month on a rotating basis."

Nick said, "I don't give a shit where I sleep, man."

Zane elbowed him. "Yeah, but if you have a girl wants to get friendly with you..."

Nick was deadpan when he replied. "I don't give a shit where I fuck, man."

Zane started laughing. "No, but *she* might."

God, these guys were going to make Val regret the move. Back to business. "We'll arrange the details tomorrow, and I think we need to schedule chores too. Don't give me that look, Ethan. You know goddamned well that if we don't map out who has to take out the trash, we'll live like pigs, and Val will get stuck cleaning up, just because she actually gives a shit. Right?"

She smiled at him. Okay, so that made it all worth it. Ethan was pissed, but he had to know Brad was right. "Fine. Whatever. But don't expect me to wash dishes every day."

"No one's gonna expect that. So…there's a dresser and a closet in each room. Let's figure out who needs what. Val, if you have extra space in your room for clothes, would you mind sharing?"

"No problem. I'll unpack my clothes first."

"Okay, so guys…whoever winds up using the extra space in Val's room—make sure you only put shit in there you can live without for an hour or two."

So…they'd tackled several problems that day, some big ones even, and they had other issues to work through. For now, though, they had lots of setting up to do, and Val insisted that they clean the place before calling it a night. They'd have lots more time to take care of other items on Brad's list—including getting another fucking job.

The rest of the night, though, he was going to get them pumped about their future, and then he was gonna have a couple of beers—because he had no idea when he'd be able to find someone around here to buy alcohol for them like the people he'd known back home.

CHAPTER TWENTY-EIGHT

BRAD AWOKE THE next morning to the sound of a spoon scraping a bowl. He shifted and then realized he wasn't in his bed. He fluttered his eyes, trying to get his bearings. Oh, yeah…his new home in a tiny apartment in Denver, sleeping in a cot.

Aside from the occasional discomfort around the middle of the cot when he'd shifted too quickly, it wasn't bad and he'd slept pretty well. He thought it was partly due to exhaustion and the beer.

He rolled on his side and tried to go back to sleep.

After several minutes, he rolled on his other side, but it wasn't happening. He was thinking too much about the next few hours, the entire day, the next week—and so much was depending upon him.

So much for sleep.

As he sat up, he realized he'd slept well definitely due to the beer. He wasn't hung over, not by a long shot, but his mouth was dry. Zane was on the other cot in the living room, Ethan on the couch, and both were completely out. He was wearing his jeans but no shirt. He found yesterday's t-shirt on the foot of the bed and grabbed it, sliding it on. Then he got up and went to the kitchen. He would put the cot and bedding away after he had some water and a few cups of coffee.

He was glad he'd had the presence of mind to prep the coffee pot the night before. He got the coffee brewing by pushing one button and then poured a glass of water, guzzling half the glass. Then he sat at the table.

He couldn't sit and wait. He got up and folded up the cot and the bedding, tucking them into the closet in the living room. By the time he got back to the kitchen, the coffee was ready. He poured himself a cup and then sat at the table again, trying to decide what he should do first. He'd grab his phone in a few minutes and go through the list he'd been making in the Notes app. First, though, he was going to enjoy his first cup of coffee in his new place.

He'd been wondering if it had been Valerie or Nick he'd heard in the kitchen, but he'd already deduced it was Val. Nick didn't get up this early in the morning. He wondered why she was up so early.

He was halfway through that first cup when she came out of her room into the kitchen. She was dressed and ready for the day. He asked, "What's up?"

"I'm going to spend the day looking for a job."

"Already?" And he thought *he* was feeling desperate.

"A good idea, don't you think?"

He smiled. Yes, it was a great idea, and he *had* been thinking about it. "I was gonna wait for a day or two, but I really can't put it off when you're so motivated."

She shrugged. "I need a head start. I don't have much experience. So what are *you* doing up so early?"

He hadn't checked the time. He didn't know it was *that* early. "Can't sleep. Too much on my mind."

He heard Ethan make a hacking noise from where he lay on the couch. There was no full-blown wall between the kitchen area and the dining room, so they could see him from the table. He muttered, "Kinda hard to sleep with your goddamn blow dryer making noise."

Ethan's lack of gratitude—*especially* for this girl who obviously worshipped the ground the asshole walked on—rubbed Brad the wrong way. "Shut the fuck up, Ethan. She's doing this whole band a solid."

Ethan grumbled into his pillow, but he made sure that time they couldn't hear what he said. Good thing, because Brad wasn't in the mood. Val forced a smile. "Well, I guess I better get started."

"Hold on." He stood up and pulled out his wallet. He'd had keys made the day before and had forgotten to give Val and Ethan theirs. He took out one for Val. "Here's your key to the apartment. Good luck."

She took it and put it in her pocket. She told him *thanks* and then left.

Brad hadn't been kidding—if Val was going to look for work, he couldn't very well just sit on his ass. So he finished the cup of coffee and made his way into the shower.

He didn't plan to search for work all day, but he drove around the neighborhood. He was going to look for work he knew. He found several lube and oil shops and filled out applications, whether or not they said they were hiring. By mid-afternoon, though, he was done, and when he got home, he was halfway glad the guys were still sleeping. It allowed him time to do his computer things. The one splurge he'd wanted was internet access, and they'd gotten it. It was the one thing he felt like he couldn't live without. He didn't need an Xbox or a television, but to book their shows, he needed a computer. It had turned out to be his greatest networking tool. He could do it with his phone, but it was a pain in the ass. He'd set up a Facebook and Twitter account for the band, but he hardly did anything with them. They had some fans and followers, but nothing worth going nuts over yet. He'd post a snippet of a song once in a while or someone would post a video from a show for them, but it wasn't a lot. His own page, though, he used to network. He was friends with a lot of guys in bands, and they all stayed connected. When there was a show, they'd spread the word like wildfire. Fully Automatic already had a reputation as being reliable, and it worked in his favor. If a band dropped out of a gig six weeks before show time, people would contact Brad, and if Brad said they could make it, they would. In spite of Ethan's occasional teetering, they'd never let another band or an audience down yet, and Brad didn't plan to start.

So…he didn't have many problems booking shows, but he needed his computer to do most of the work. It was the one thing he'd purchased since their move that could have been viewed as an indulgence—but it really wasn't.

Later that afternoon, he started getting concerned about Valerie. He considered calling her, but he wasn't ready to start freaking out. The guys finally awakened one at a time, and Brad let them know that they had more things to work through, but he wanted to make Valerie comfortable and pampered when she got back. Ethan bristled a little (and all Brad could figure was it was because it hadn't been *his* idea), but he said nothing. "I'm gonna start dinner. Who wants to help?"

Nick said, "I can. I had to cook a meal or two at home."

Brad hoped his look at Zane and Ethan was pointed. "That means it's your turn next." Ethan rolled his eyes but said nothing. Brad was expecting him to start pushing back, but he hadn't. Not a word. He had to give Ethan credit— in spite of the huge chip on his friend's shoulder, the guy was keeping it together. He was taking Brad's direction too, even when it pissed him off. Brad had to give him huge kudos for that.

And he made a promise to himself so he'd quit worrying—if Val wasn't back by the time they were ready to eat, he'd call her cell. Until then, he was going to chill.

It turned out to be a good thing that he hadn't called her, because she showed up a few minutes before the food was finished. She said a quick *hi* and then went to her room. She looked exhausted and her face was flushed. When she returned, she was wearing a t-shirt and her shoes were off. She poured herself a glass of water and asked, "Do you guys know where the nearest laundromat is?"

Nick couldn't resist the opening and turned from where he stood at the stove. "You need one already? Damn...you're worse than any of the other girls I know."

Brad, used to his witty retorts, told Valerie, "We'll have to look it up. Maybe we could pick a day for laundry."

"Another thing I didn't think of."

"You look tired. Sit down and relax. We'll be eating in a little bit."

She nodded, sitting at the table, propping her chin in her hand. "It smells good. What are you making?"

Nick, completely deadpan, answered her. "Something exquisite that will make you feel like you're home again…an exotic taste with just a hint of delicate cheese that will transport you to another world."

Brad couldn't help but smile. "Hamburger Helper."

Val laughed. "Well, I'm not complaining. It sounds lovely, Nick."

Nick bowed. "Anything for the lady."

"And we're having a salad and baked potatoes with it. These guys eat like there's no tomorrow, so I figured we needed to make a lot."

Nick started waving around the large spoon in his hand. "Don't expect this every night. Brad's a slave driver. I can't work with him anymore."

While Brad started getting out the bottles of salad dressing out of the fridge, Ethan walked in the kitchen from the big bedroom where he and Zane had been working on a song. "Val. You look beat. What the hell were you out doing all day?"

"I was looking for work."

"Doing what? Singing not enough for you?"

"Oh, it's plenty, but I want to make sure we can pay our bills." He nodded and then started rubbing her shoulders. Brad busied himself with dinner tasks, because Ethan's actions were pissing him off. Why couldn't the guy go on the prowl for his usual make and model?

Who was he kidding? It was inevitable. He knew it in his gut.

In spite of his fear that there was a budding relationship between the two people who were likely his best friends on the planet, the meal that night was exactly what they needed. After their disheartening first day and night in their tiny, dingy apartment, the second had given them hope. They talked about what each did for the day and then focused on what would be happening at the end of the week and then beyond—the hopes and dreams that had brought them here in the first place. Brad looked around the table and, for the first time in a long time, felt like he was surrounded by family.

CHAPTER TWENTY-NINE

AFTER DINNER, VAL bowed out, but not after offering to clean up the kitchen, enlisting Zane and Ethan's help. She'd had a long day and just wanted a shower and to go to bed. They'd been having such a good time that Brad was disappointed, but he understood. She'd been hiking around the neighborhood looking for work all day, a process that could be both physically and mentally tiring.

Much as he hated missing her company, Brad knew this was the perfect opportunity to discuss other arrangements he and the males of the house needed to make. Whether or not they wanted to have women over, they would all enjoy an occasional night sleeping in the double bed, and it wouldn't be fair to be haphazard about it. He wanted to stop any potential arguments before they would start.

As they settled in the living room, Nick asked, "What movie we gonna watch?"

"We'll figure that out soon enough, but first…something we need to get out of the way." Brad held out a small pocket calendar, one the size of a checkbook with a picture of a dog on the front. It was a two-year calendar, and they were more than halfway through the first year of the calendar, but that was why Brad had found it so cheap at the dollar store. He held it up for the guys to see and said, "We need to create a schedule for the other bedroom."

Ethan said, "What do you mean exactly?"

"I mean we'll rotate. Every fourth day will be your turn in there. I don't give a shit what you do in there, but on your night, it's yours, no one else's. That means, too, that we'll be rotating what night we get the couch."

Zane said, "Maybe to make it easy we could have the couch the night after we have the bedroom."

"Good idea."

Nick's eyes lit up. "So…we can bring chicks over on the night we have the room?"

Brad nodded. "That's the idea. I think you can go three days without, right?"

"Fuck that. I just won't do it *here* on my off nights." He put a serious look on his face, one of the ones that usually indicated he was half joking. "I just have to start lining up some dates." Nick whipped out his phone, pulling up his contacts list.

Zane asked, "You trying to find Angelica?"

Brad shook his head. He'd often wondered if Angelica really existed. She was a mysterious girl who happened to take care of Nick at more than one of their concerts, but she was nowhere to be found when it was time to party. But he knew Nick and knew the guy had incredible luck when it came to the ladies. He figured he must have had some great pick-up lines. The guy was never hurting for a girl.

Nick didn't miss a beat. "Hell, yeah. She gives good head."

Ethan laughed. "What makes you think she'll wanna fuck your scrawny ass again?"

"They all want Nick again once they've tasted him the first time."

Back to business, Brad said, "Okay. You're fourth." It was probably only fair, considering Nick had had the bedroom the night before anyway, but he wasn't going to say anything. It had just worked out that way.

Ethan asked, "So who's tonight?"

"Me, I guess."

Nick said, "That's cool, though, right?"

"What?"

"Guests."

Zane piped in. "Fuck, yeah. I thought that was the whole point. If we can't invite our girlfriends, why bother setting up a schedule or even having the room to ourselves?"

Nick said, "You don't need a girl to take care of your needs."

"Maybe *you* don't."

Nick confirmed that he was okay with Brad's schedule. "Yeah, I'll go last. That'll give me time to put it to good use."

They all heard a cabinet door close in the kitchen and looked toward the sound. Val was getting a glass out, wearing a robe with a towel wrapped around her head. Brad had no way of knowing how much she'd heard, but he knew for a girl that none of it could have been savory. She moved to the sink and started pouring water into the glass, not looking at the guys.

Brad knew she'd overheard them, though. There was no way she couldn't have. "Sorry you had to hear that, Val."

She walked into the living room. "Please, don't be. We're gonna have to get used to living together, and just 'cause I'm a prude doesn't mean the rest of you have to be."

Nick rolled his eyes but half laughed. Zane said, "Hey…what's fair is fair. You can have guys over too if you want."

Well, in a fair world, Zane was right, and Brad wouldn't say a word, but he'd die if Val started traipsing guys into her room whenever she felt like it. And, if she did it frequently, he knew it wouldn't be long before the guys started complaining that it wasn't fair that she had her own room. He suspected, though, that Val wouldn't even dream of it. To the best of his knowledge, she was still a virgin. But the other guys didn't necessarily know that, and he wasn't going to be the one to tell them.

She smiled and blew him off. "I'm gonna go do a little writing and then hit the hay. I'm tired."

Ethan asked, "Sure you don't wanna hang? Bradley here was gonna put a DVD in his laptop. Movie night."

"Thanks, but you guys can resume your conversation."

"We're done. Don't go."

"Thanks, really. I'm just tired."

After she left, Brad said, "Okay, so how's this sound? Me, then Zane, Ethan, and Nick. And we'll rotate that way from now on. And I like Zane's idea, that you have the couch the night after you have the bedroom." The guys nodded. "And I know you guys are gonna accuse me of being a hard ass, but it needs saying—cots and bedding in the closet after you get up. This place is way too small to leave that shit out all day."

"Bradley, why the fuck you feel the need to be a dictator all the time?" Ethan put the emphasis on the first syllable, indicating in no uncertain terms that he thought Brad was a *dick*.

"Man, don't give me grief. We gotta have ground rules. Otherwise, we'll wind up wanting to kill each other."

He looked at Brad through half-lowered lids. "Too late."

Brad had just about had it. Zane said, "Come on, guys. Ethan, Brad's right. This is the democratic way of doing things. It's only fair."

Ethan rolled his eyes. "Yeah, I guess so."

He didn't apologize, but at least he chilled out. Brad would settle for that. "Anything else we need to cover?"

Zane said, "I think we're good."

Nick said, "Movie time!" Brad got out his laptop and slid it over to Nick. Nick had a movie collection online and had a compilation of bad horror movies he liked to share. Brad got the last six-pack of beer out of the fridge and settled on the floor.

They started watching the movie—dumb by any standard, but Nick made it funny. The guy had so many zingers, it was hard not to enjoy the movie.

And that was why it didn't escape Brad's notice that Ethan left for a while. He realized Ethan might have just been using the restroom, but he had a feeling it was something else, something involving Valerie. And he bit his tongue and tried to shut off the part of his brain that still wanted her…because she wasn't his and never would be, and the sooner he admitted that to himself, the sooner he could let her go.

By the end of their first week, Brad was feeling better about his whole life. He managed to get an interview, followed up with a job. He fucking hated changing oil and lubing cars, but it would help pay the bills until they could make serious bank with the band. If they could get a good following, they could record a quality EP instead of the shitty one they'd done during a practice session—but that was a far-off dream. For now, he lived for the shows.

And the two shows they played that weekend were incredible. They got better and better as a band, every time they played together. Brad knew it was just a matter of time before they broke big. He had to be ready—and have them all prepared—for that moment.

They were all chilling out Sunday afternoon. It had been a long week, but he could tell by the general mood that they all felt good about it.

They ate hamburgers and fries around the kitchen table, celebrating their first week. They were settling into a routine, getting used to working and living with each other, and they weren't killing each other.

He had an idea for a song, and he needed a strong bass line to go with it, so he asked Zane to help him work it out. They went to the big bedroom and started working out a cool chorus. Nick asked to borrow the laptop to pick out some movies for later.

After a while, he and Zane got tired, wanting to return to it the next day, and Nick said he'd picked out three great movies for the afternoon. One was actually a comedy on purpose. So the three of them sat around the silly little laptop, and, after a while, Brad dozed off in the chair. His belly was full and he knew, starting the next day, he was going to have to start playing responsible adult again. For now, though, he wanted to chill.

He woke up sometime during the second movie, and as the day grew later, he, Nick, and Zane started talking about dinner. "Where's Ethan and Val?" Zane asked.

Even though Brad had been sleeping, he was under the impression that they were gone. At a couple of points during the afternoon, the front door had opened and closed more than once. He shrugged and considered texting his friend, but somehow he knew. He got up, trying to look nonchalant, but he wanted to beat the shit out of something. Instead, he wandered to the bathroom under the guise of using the facilities, but he glanced down the hall and confirmed what he already knew—Val's bedroom door was open. She wasn't there.

The other bedroom door was open. Ethan was nowhere to be found.

They were together. He didn't know what they were doing or when they'd be back, but he knew they were together.

That called for a bottle of liquor. They had one or two somewhere. As long as he didn't get drunk, he'd be okay, but he needed something to drown it out. And, as he took a swig, only pretending to watch the movie, he wondered when the wounds would start to scab over so he could get on with his life.

CHAPTER THIRTY

BRAD'S PHONE ALARM woke him up bright and early Monday morning. He rolled off the couch and made some coffee. Then he headed to the bathroom. Sure as shit, Val's bedroom door was ajar. Of course, there was only one cot being used in the living room too, but seeing that Val wasn't there simply confirmed his deepest fear. Not only were she and Ethan together, but there was only one reason why they'd spend the night somewhere else.

Unless...

He knew how Ethan was. There was a chance that Ethan had overdone it on something illegal, and Val was keeping him safe.

He had his doubts, though. They hadn't been living in their new city long enough for Ethan to establish new connections—or had they? Ethan was resourceful and, if he were desperate, he could have tracked down whatever it was he needed. He had a hard time believing Valerie would handle an OD on her own, though.

Brad was torn. As much as he wanted to believe Val and Ethan were friends only, he hated the idea of Ethan hurting himself with drugs…and yet, in the darkest part of his heart, he halfway hoped that was what had happened. It was better than the alternative, the option the rational part of his mind suspected was the truth.

But he wouldn't know and had to pretend like he didn't care or even know, because he had to go to work.

He was glad to have the distraction of a new job. Yes, he'd worked in a similar place before, but every business had its own way of doing things. That, and he had to get to know new people. Fortunately, the guys he worked with seemed down to earth and simple, guys he could relate to. For the most part, he was able to keep his mind off his problem.

The one drawback of the job was no girls. He could have used a distraction. Sure, plenty of girls and women got their cars serviced, but they didn't have any females working with them. It's not that women couldn't do the work, but obviously none had applied or been hired at this particular job. He'd always thought the right woman in this kind of job could be downright sexy, but most women wouldn't even consider getting themselves greasy and gritty, and he really didn't blame them.

The job wasn't bad. He hadn't told his employer about his main goal in Denver, because he didn't think it would ever interfere. The business closed at six. Most of the earliest shows he'd ever played started at seven, and the rest of the band could always set up without him if they had to. If he ever had to do a day show on a weekend, he'd ask for time off, but he wanted to settle into the job first. He needed to prove himself first before making requests or demands. And if this job was anything like his old one, turnover would be high. If Brad stuck it out, he'd be a veteran on the job before he knew it, and oftentimes employers would treat employees with loyalty better. Whether he liked the work itself or not didn't matter. If he could get along with his fellow employees and keep his boss happy, he could make sure the rent was paid and continue pursuing his dream.

Another plus was this job paid better than the one back home, and he had to guess it was because of the local cost of living. Groceries didn't seem to cost more and gas was cheaper, but rent was higher, and he wouldn't know about utilities until their first bills started trickling in. He wanted to be prepared.

When the day was over and he started driving home, it washed over him again. He was grateful he was in his little piece of shit car. He had few associations of it with Valerie and his mind was there anyway, but there was nothing tangible in the car to slap him in the face. He'd had Zane drive it behind him in the van when they came to Denver, and now he was glad. The car got better gas mileage and was easier to navigate. That kept the van reserved for shows only.

He managed to stay calm until he started walking up the stairs to their apartment. He had no idea what to expect. He stood in the hall for a few moments, focusing on his breathing. He had to put on a happy face. No, a neutral face would do, but he couldn't let anyone know that whatever was going on between Valerie and Ethan bothered him. If he hadn't been so fucking stupid—playing a chivalrous gentleman, both with Val and her dad—all bets would be off, but he'd pretty much told her he was cooling things off between them. He supposed then that it was only natural for Val to cozy up to Ethan. He was pretty sure, though, that Ethan had made a move, because neither of them had seemed interested in each other over the summer. Yeah, Val had bitched about the drugs (and, he supposed, that was a sign she cared), but nothing else had happened.

When he finally forced himself to enter the apartment, his nose was assaulted with the smells of dinner. It smelled good. Then he saw Val in the kitchen at the stove, working away. He could hear the guys in the big bedroom playing something new too, so that made him happy. They weren't screwing around—they were starting to see that they had to work hard to get to where they wanted to go.

Part of him wanted to go straight into the shower, but there were several reasons why he couldn't. The first would be that it would make him obvious. Brad wasn't antisocial, for starters, but he also had the problem of needing clean clothes he'd have to get out of the big bedroom. So he mustered up as cheerful a face as he could manage and said, "Smells great."

Val turned from the stove, smiling. She looked radiant but tired. "It's really nothing."

"I'm sure it's fine." He started moving toward the hallway.

"New job start today?"

"Yeah. Overalls give it away?"

She laughed. "The powers of deduction."

He smiled and walked toward the bedroom. It was too

painful. He walked in the door, and Ethan and Zane were sitting on the edge of the bed, hunched over a sheet of paper, both with their instruments resting in their laps. Nick was sitting in front of a tom and a snare with two sticks, probably just to give them a beat, but without the entire set up, he couldn't envision the magic percussion Nick could give something. He knew already that they were going to have to push the bed against the wall to set up the entire kit. There was no room for it at the moment.

For now, he was just going to grab a t-shirt and jeans. He had a couple of pairs of coveralls from the company, but he was going to have to do laundry every three days. There was no way to keep them from getting too filthy. So he figured he'd have to do laundry twice a week. As he walked to the dresser, Zane and Ethan deep in discussion, Nick looked up at him and said in a high-pitched voice, "Honey, I'm home."

The other guys looked up. Zane asked, "First day, right?"

"Yeah." He walked over to the dresser and opened up his drawer to grab underwear and socks. Then he made his way to the closet. He had folded his t-shirts and jeans into boxes so they didn't have to fight over space. He pulled out one of each and headed toward the door.

"That bad?" Nick asked.

Brad shrugged. Yeah, Ethan's silence was telling. *Something* had happened the night before, and considering the guy didn't look any worse for the wear, Brad concluded it wasn't drug-related. "I wasn't holding my guitar, so yeah." And he headed for the shower, ready to wash the day off himself.

He had to act normally too, so as he stood under the warm water in the shower, he tried to shove it all down deep. He had, whether he'd wanted to or not, become their leader, and, as such, he needed to let his angst go. He himself had done it and expertly so. He'd told Valerie—and then assured her father later—that nothing would happen between them. What else had he expected when he'd basically let her go?

So he got out and toweled off, dressing and then throwing his dirty clothes in the box in the closet where he kept his soiled laundry till he could wash it. The guys had already left the bedroom. He forced himself again to take a deep breath and let it all go. Out there, at the kitchen table, were his four best friends, and they were his band, his family. No matter what happened, they were his life, and he had to find a way to get past this. He had to.

After dinner (which wasn't anything to write home about but edible—and he'd never say that to Val), he wasn't as convinced that anything had happened between her and Ethan. They hardly even looked at each other. And that night at bedtime, they weren't together. Brad started to doubt his earlier suspicions. Yeah, they'd been gone for a night together, but he was starting to think maybe they hadn't consummated anything. They were acting too *normal* around each other. True, Val no longer acted permanently pissed at Ethan, but she hadn't acted that way in a while.

It was like *old times*—if he could say they had them yet. They were all laughing and joking and having a good time. Val said she had an interview the next day, and everyone asked about Brad's job. Then they talked about the three shows planned for the weekend, and they all got pumped. The guys started talking about writing new material again.

The next day, in fact, the three other guys put something together. Brad was glad they were being productive, and it felt different, making it even better. When they were done playing it (raw and unpolished, but Brad could hear the potential), Ethan looked at Val and asked, "Think you can pen some words to it pretty quickly?"

"How quickly?"

"By our next show?"

"Well...probably...but getting it down is another story. We'll need to practice it together some like we always do."

He was glad to see some drive, but what game was Ethan playing? Every once in a while, the guy felt the need to upstage Brad. It was some deep-seated desire in his friend, one he'd never understood. He got why Ethan could so often be self-centered and even cruel, but the need to one up his best friend in the world never made any sense. Still, he didn't need this to be a source of contention between them. It wasn't important enough. So, after considering it for a few moments, he said, "I need some time too...unless you're wanting me out of this one, man."

Yeah, and there it was—the flare, the challenge. Either Ethan was pissed that he hadn't gotten the rise out of Brad he'd wanted or he knew Brad wasn't responding on purpose, and that was making him doubly desirous of pushing him. But then his features softened as though it was no big deal, and he said, "Nah. I'm just excited to play this one."

Brad hoped that was all it was. He wanted his friend to know he wasn't blowing him off, and he hoped Ethan was sincere. "Me too. It's fuckin' awesome. Good stuff. Maybe we could shoot for next weekend."

And, maybe by then, everything would feel right again, because the only time it did anymore was when he was onstage. That was the only time everything in his world was perfect.

CHAPTER THIRTY-ONE

BURY HIMSELF IN the music—that's what Brad had always done when things in real life weren't going the way they were supposed to. And that's what he'd do now. Unlike back at home, he had to drive longer to get to and from work and the traffic took some getting used to, so those things took away from the time he could sink into music. Fortunately, he could spend the drive thinking. That was sometimes also a downfall, though, and today had turned out that way.

He needed time. He didn't understand why not having Val was bothering him more *now* than it had all summer long.

That wasn't true. He knew why when he admitted it to himself. It was because she was now fully on Ethan's radar, and Brad didn't know if Ethan cared enough about her to treat her right. Still, it was what Val wanted, and he needed to stay out of it.

He was going to try. He wasn't going to look for

significant glances between Ethan and Val or try to determine anything. It was better if he didn't know. If they would both go off somewhere, he'd try not to think about it. He had to let it all go and just give the music his undivided attention.

So that night, while he was trying to drift off to sleep in spite of the guys watching yet another horror movie on his laptop with the sound turned halfway down, he didn't force himself to sit up when he heard…what sounded like a woman having an orgasm.

It could've been across the hall, right? It might not have even been what he thought it was. And, the next morning, he tried to convince himself it was something on the movie the guys were watching the night before. He wouldn't ask, because he didn't want to know. It didn't help that Ethan wasn't in Val's room the next morning, leaving Brad full of more doubt.

God, this was bad, and he had to find a way to let it go. He was making himself miserable.

What made it worse was he wasn't able to book many more shows per week than he had living farther away. One or two more, maybe, but not like he'd wanted. One plus was they were finally running a decent merch table, and he made the rest of the band run it. No one complained about it, but it was the one thing he didn't want to be responsible for. He put Zane in charge of purchasing t-shirts and other items. The guy had found a company that would make them bulk buttons, but they were going to wait to buy them. Nick, their artist, was designing a better logo for them, so they didn't want to buy all the buttons they'd have to purchase to make it a good deal if it wasn't with their final logo. Zane had also had bumper stickers and smaller stickers made, but the bumper stickers weren't selling for shit and the little stickers they'd just decided to give away. Zane thought they might want to make a poster too, but they were still discussing that one. Val was going to sit at their table for the first time that weekend, and then all of them would have done it at least once. But he told them it was their responsibility, their baby, and they swore they wouldn't let him down.

It was important, though, because Brad had to deal with the money and contract issues. He was the one finishing things up, but more than that, he was also networking. He was the one befriending new bands and introducing himself to the people who made things happen. He was a naturally friendly guy, and he was convinced that was why they had regular shows. Not every band could claim that.

It was a magical night that night, the kind of crowd and show Brad wished they could always play. He could feel the energy in the air, and—looking at his bandmates—he could tell they were feeling it too. By the time they took the stage, they were pumped, and the first part of the show was incredible. By the end, though, Ethan had dissolved into a puddle. He was on something, probably *too much* of something, and he wasn't fully with them, wasn't even aware how fucked up his playing was. If the audience would have noticed, Brad would have shooed him offstage. As it was, the audience was loving them and didn't seem to be aware of Ethan's continual fuck ups. Brad hoped his playing was covering up some of the worst ones. It made sense, though, because a lot of people didn't know their songs really well, so it would be apparent to the band but not the new folks listening.

When their set was over, they needed to clear the stage for the next band, a group of guys Fully Automatic had played with before, a band called Last Five Seconds. They were a few years older than Brad's band, but they were solid and hardcore. Brad loved their music and was looking forward to watching their show.

First, though, he needed to talk to Ethan. So they said their *thank you*s to the audience and relished the applause for a little bit, and then Zane, Nick, and Val started packing up. Brad walked Ethan offstage, though, and hoped his bandmates would understand why he wasn't there for a few minutes. "Ethan, what the fuck are you taking, man?" His friend raised his eyebrows and started to talk, but Brad suspected it was going to be bullshit right off the bat. "Never mind. Here's the rule. Fine if you gotta take something before a show. I get that. But take a *little*. If you gotta get blitzed, save it for after the show."

Ethan scowled. "The show was fine."

"The hell it was. You were fucking up left and right, hitting wrong notes and chords…when you bothered to hit them at all. Val had a hell of a time up there tonight, and that was thanks to you. You pull that shit again, I'm turning down your goddamn amps." Ethan just stared at him and blinked through his long lashes. God, yes, the guy was hammered out of his mind. Then he shrugged as if to concede that Brad was right. "Go find a place to sit this shit out and be ready to go when the show's over. We'll pack up." Ethan nodded and turned, stumbling off toward the crowd. Well, that wasn't exactly what Brad had had in mind, but he hadn't told his friend he had to sleep it off in the van.

He and the other three decided to watch the show together right at the foot of the stage. He was glad, because he really liked these guys. Midway through the show, he was regretting it, though, because—if he wasn't mistaken—their guitarist, a guy who went by the stage name Jet, was making eyes at Val the entire time. What the hell?

He wondered if Val was even picking up on it, so he looked over at her. Yeah, she was. She smiled at Brad, but he could tell Jet had her under his spell. Chicks dug the guy. But Val? God, between Ethan and now Jet, he'd never have a chance. And seeing the way she looked at this guy made him start doubting she and Ethan were together, because they were definitely flirting through eye contact.

Last Five Seconds finished their set and there was one more band that would play, but Brad was starting to worry about Ethan. He hadn't seen him since he'd told him to go chill somewhere, and now he was starting to feel concerned. Chances were Ethan had found some girl to fuck around with for a while, but he had to know, because he had a bad feeling.

He looked around inside the venue and couldn't see him. It was cursory and he'd have the others help if he had to check again, but he wanted to look quickly first. Then he checked the men's restroom—nothing. He was going to check the van last and then have the band assist if Ethan wasn't there. But Ethan was sitting on a step outside, not far from the band exit area. Brad walked over to him, wanting to make sure it *was* him. There were lights outside but it was hard to see. As he got closer, he could tell it was Ethan, and he knelt over. "Ethan, how's it goin', man?"

Ethan looked up at him, and the way his head wobbled, it looked like his neck was unable to support it. His eyes were glassy—Ethan was fucked up. Goddammit. "Did you take something else?" Ethan stared at him as though his brain wasn't even processing his friend's question. "Stay right here. I'll be back."

Brad was sure Ethan wasn't going anywhere, but this time he was scared. Ethan was fucked up beyond belief. He needed to find his friends and have them help decide what their next move was—did they rush their friend to the ER?

He walked backstage. He saw Nick first and said, "We're leaving now." Nick excused himself from the girl he was with and said, "I've got other plans. I'll find my own way home."

Brad nodded. "Okay. Show tomorrow night." He wasn't even going to worry Nick with whatever was going on with Ethan. The guy was going to get lucky tonight, and he didn't want to interfere.

So he made his way out front, hoping to find his other two band members. He spotted Zane talking to two girls. He was glad his friend was tall, because he was easier to spot. He caught his eye and Zane asked, "What's up?"

He didn't want to make a big scene, but he wanted out of there. He got close. "Meet me by the exit in a minute. Ethan's messed up and we gotta get him out of here." He could tell Zane wasn't happy about it either. The guy was making serious headway with these girls, but he wasn't doing as well as Nick. He didn't blame the guy for taking an extra minute to give them his number.

Then he saw Val close by and she was talking with Jet.

Yep, had he nailed that or what? Well, he was probably going to seem like a major dick to her too, but it couldn't be helped. He walked over and said, "Val, we gotta go."

"Yeah?"

"Yeah." He couldn't pretend like he hadn't noticed. "Hey, Jet. How's it goin', man? Great show, by the way."

"Thanks. You too. Nice addition to your band."

In spite of his overwhelming emotions—with Ethan and with Val—Brad couldn't help but smile at her. "Yeah. We thought so too."

Jet said, "By the way, I really like my shirt on you."

Brad looked at Val and, for the first time that night, realized she was wearing a Last Five Seconds shirt that she'd altered. "Cool. Didn't even notice." Well, that wasn't *entirely* true—he'd noticed the ripped-up shirt; he just hadn't noticed it was a Last Five Seconds shirt. To Jet, he said, "See you around." Val waved at him, flirting without words, but followed Brad, and as they got to the exit, Zane joined them.

Zane asked, "What's going on?"

Brad answered. "Ethan. What else?" He pulled the keys out of his pocket and handed them to Zane. "Can you open the van? I'll be right there." He started walking toward Ethan. Val followed. Jesus, the guy was fucked up. "Wrap your arm around my neck, buddy." Ethan didn't respond. Brad wrapped his arms around Ethan and pulled him up, and Val wrapped Ethan's arm around Brad and then got on the other side to help Brad lead him. He wasn't completely out of it. Brad had at first thought he was going to have to drag Ethan, but his friend was moving his feet. He was grateful for that.

By the time they got to the van, Ethan was mumbling, and it took a moment, but Brad realized what he was saying. "Back off, Val," he said, and she didn't appreciate it much until she saw Ethan lean over and vomit. It wasn't pretty.

Ethan said, "Thanks, man." Brad was glad to hear his friend was coherent. He threw up again. Then, when he was done, Brad helped him up in the van, and he passed out on the long middle seat. But, a good sign—he'd mostly pulled himself inside. Brad slid the door closed behind Ethan.

Brad needed their input. His voice was low when he said, "I don't know if I should take him to the ER or not."

Val's voice was accusatory. "What'd he take, Brad?"

"No fuckin' idea."

"Why the hell does he do this?"

Brad looked at her. They'd had this conversation before, and he wasn't going to explain in detail all the ways Ethan was fucked in the head. Zane asked, "Nick coming?"

"Nope. He's got a ride."

"Yeah, I bet he's got a helluva ride. Lucky motherfucker."

Brad wanted their assessment. He wasn't the guy to ask. "So do we take him to the hospital or not?"

Val asked, "How's he doing?"

"Better than before."

"Can I talk to him?"

"I guess." Brad looked at Zane then Val. "Good luck."

Val slid the door open again and got in. She knelt beside him on the floor and placed her hand on his forehead. It was painful for Brad to watch. Whether or not anything had transpired between the two, it was pretty obvious that Val worshipped the guy. Brad turned to face Zane—he wasn't going to look, and he hoped he couldn't overhear either. He kept his voice low, because he didn't want Ethan overhearing their conversation. "What do *you* think?"

Zane was no dummy. His voice was also barely above a whisper. "I have no idea what he took. With Ethan, you never know."

"No, I didn't figure. I mean do you think we should take him to the ER?"

"Oh, shit. I don't know. It's not like he's never done this before. What are you thinking?"

"Fuck." Brad ran his fingers through his hair. "I don't know. That's the problem. It's like last time—I'm afraid if I take him and he really doesn't need to be seen, then he'll be pissed at me, but if I should take him…shit. I don't know."

"What about this? As long as he seems clear, you know, like he seems now? Where he can talk a little and stuff, focus his eyes. Then maybe we don't worry about it? Maybe he's okay, you know. But, like, if he loses it, if he goes unconscious or anything, then he has no choice and we drag his ass there. I'll support you, man."

Brad nodded. "Okay. That seems fair."

Val joined them back outside the van. She seemed less worried than she had before but more upset. So, Ethan had managed to put her mind at ease as far as his health, but he'd obviously said something to make her feel bad. Brad wasn't completely surprised. She said, "He doesn't want us to take him anywhere. He says he's fine and just wants to go home."

"All right." Brad was surprised that Val rode shotgun, but she did. She shouldn't have bothered, though, because she was constantly watching Ethan to make sure he was okay. Zane was sitting in the back seat on his phone, and Brad imagined he was sexting one of the hot girls he'd been dragged away from, again thanks to Ethan.

When they got home, both Brad and Zane helped Ethan to their apartment. He was walking some and his eyes were open most of the way, but he was feeling no pain. Val opened doors for them along the way.

He and Zane continued leading Ethan and Brad said, "I'm gonna put him on the couch so we can keep an eye on him."

Val walked beside them. "Then I'm sleeping out here too."

"You can have my cot."

"No. I'm not taking your bed. I'll just sleep in the chair."

"Val, don't be ridiculous. The cot's better than the chair."

She just smiled and left the room while Brad and Zane helped Ethan lie down. Brad pulled his friend's sneakers off and asked Zane to grab Ethan's sheet out of the closet. He asked Ethan, "You feel okay, man?"

Ethan nodded and mumbled an affirmative. Brad and Zane went to the kitchen and both grabbed cans of Pepsi out of the fridge. Val walked past them into the living room and sat on the couch next to Ethan. Brad told Zane, "I'm going to sleep out here tonight and keep an eye on him. Anything fishy happens, I'm taking him."

"I'll stay out here too. If you need my help, just say the word."

"I just wonder when he's going to outgrow this shit."

Zane shrugged. "He might be one of those guys who never does."

Brad didn't know what to say. He had to believe Ethan would get his shit together, but Zane was right. What if he never did? What if this was going to become a lifelong pattern?

Val came back in the kitchen and grabbed a glass out of the cabinet, pouring a glass of water. Brad asked, "He still seem okay?"

"He said he wanted something to drink. That's a good sign, right?"

By the time Brad and Zane made it to the living room and set up cots, Ethan was snoring, and Val had already staked a claim on the chair. Her arms were crossed in front of her chest as if challenging one of them to wake her up and ask her to move. Ethan seemed to be breathing fine. Brad did get him to roll over on his side, though. He'd heard one too many stories of guys choking on their vomit in their sleep, and, by God, Ethan wasn't going to die on his watch.

But he was just goddamned sick and tired of *having* to watch in the first place.

CHAPTER THIRTY-TWO

BRAD WOKE UP the next morning to the sound of coffee brewing. He sat up, feeling a little panicked and out of sorts. He had checked on Ethan mid-morning but hadn't awakened since. Neither Val nor Ethan were in the living room, so he got up to see what was going on. He grabbed his jeans off the floor beside the cot and slipped them on, followed by his t-shirt.

He rolled his neck. He felt stiff. Coffee sounded perfect, but, more than that, he wanted to know how Ethan was doing. As he walked into the kitchen, he saw Valerie but no Ethan. "How's he doing?"

"He said he's okay."

Things weren't usually stiff between them, but it felt a little tense. She stood in front of the cupboard and pulled down two cups, filling them up with coffee. She grabbed the creamer and sugar and set them on the table and then set a cup of coffee for him on the table. "Thanks."

"Everything okay with you?" He was about to ask the

same thing, but she no doubt sensed that he was still wondering what—if anything—was going on between her and Ethan. Still, he didn't plan to say a word. He simply nodded. "You don't seem too sure."

"It's cool, Val. It is."

She stirred her coffee. "I just...worry about you too. I know you're doing a lot for all of us, and I appreciate it."

He forced a smile because he knew she was expecting one. "Thanks." She grabbed his hand, squeezing it. He heard the bathroom door open and she let go. He wasn't an idiot. He knew exactly what that meant and why she did it.

Ethan came into the kitchen seconds later. It looked like he'd just taken a shower. "Man, did I get fucked up last night."

Yeah, and it sounded like he was proud of it. Brad couldn't help the "Jesus" that rushed out of his mouth.

Val asked, "How are you?"

He walked over to the cabinet to pull out a mug and poured himself some coffee. "I told you I'm fine. Not one-hundred percent, but I'm fine."

"We were worried about you. What did you take?"

"Stop, Val. Christ. You're not my mom."

Brad saw that Ethan's words bit her. She sucked in a quick breath, and her eyes flashed with anger. When she looked at Brad, he studied her. Surely she remembered the conversation they'd had over the summer. As much as he wished he could bitch slap Ethan into thinking about his health and his future, he couldn't. Stupid or not, Ethan was living his life and was doing exactly what he wanted to do. Until he decided to change, nothing any of them did or said would make a difference.

He couldn't take it right now. Whether or not there was anything between his two friends, he felt like he didn't belong there at that moment. So he got up and used the excuse that he needed to take a shower. Really, he just needed some serious time alone.

Brad was glad to see Ethan was lucid for the show that night. He hoped maybe Ethan would stop partying so hard and try to enjoy the performance.

But Val was trying something new that night. He had no idea what had inspired it, but she was singing differently. She was doing some breathy hot thing with her voice, and he was pissed because it was a turn on.

He found out later that he wasn't the only one who thought her vocal antics were sexy as hell. They were in the van on the way back to the apartment and Nick said, "What the hell was that you were doing with your voice tonight, Val? Holy shit."

Zane added, "Yeah. That was some cool shit."

Yeah, Brad liked it too but he didn't want her doing it all the time. "It *was*. But just make sure the audience can hear you."

Zane disagreed. "They could."

"Was I too quiet?"

He had to explain. "Maybe a little too breathy." He couldn't tell her it would be hard for him to listen to it, and not because he wouldn't be able to hear it. It wasn't bad, though, and he knew he wasn't coming from the right place. "But I liked it. It needs a little work, but keep doing it."

It had been a long week and Brad just wanted some rest. One of the bands they played with gave them a twelve-pack of beer, and they planned to drink a few while watching movies in the living room. Instead of watching movies, though, they talked about the concert. Brad was glad his bandmates could feel it too—something was changing with them, changing for the better, and they were growing and improving every time they got onstage. It was like hyper practice, and Brad was starting to believe that there was nothing better for their skills than playing live. He was convinced of it, because they'd never grown like this before, not when they were practicing in his mom's garage.

He'd had enough beer to relax after being keyed up. It was his night in the bedroom and he was grateful. The cots weren't bad, but they made him appreciate the feel of a real bed. Even the couch couldn't compare. What was funny was Brad knew the bed had seen better days. But it didn't matter.

He was having a hard time drifting off. Sleep was elusive, and he was sure it was because the progress Fully Automatic was making helped him hope for the future. He could almost feel it.

He rolled to his other side, trying to clear his thoughts...

And then he heard it.

The unmistakable sounds of a woman having an orgasm.

Not just *a* woman.

Val.

Oh, God, no. His worst fears confirmed and in what a shitty way. His mind was struggling with it, trying to help him find a way to deny it. Maybe she was masturbating, right? *That* would be hot.

But he knew. It was something he'd known in the back of his mind for a while. He knew it was Ethan with Valerie, and he was trying not to imagine them fucking. It was hard, though, as her cries lingered, and he squeezed his eyes tighter, bending the pillow to cover his exposed ear, trying to block out her sounds of passion, trying not to hate the man who was a brother to him.

Now there was no question as to if Valerie was a virgin anymore. If Ethan hadn't been diving deeper into some heavy shit, Brad might be okay with it.

All right. Not completely. But Brad did want Val to be happy. He could at least learn to live with it.

And, as though the universe wanted to make sure he wasn't in denial, he heard them talking after. They weren't loud, but he could tell it was Ethan and Val. There was no question. He considered covering his ears with his pillow again, but then they were quiet. And if the adrenaline would leave his body, he could try to go to sleep.

But, moments later, she started orgasming again. Jesus Christ.

If he'd thought sleep was difficult to attain before, he'd had no idea. And, suddenly, the bed just didn't feel as comfortable anymore.

The next morning, Brad poured water into the coffee pot, trying to force himself awake. He'd hardly slept the night before. His stomach had been in a knot. He wasn't even sure how he'd managed to fall asleep, but he was grateful that they'd grown quiet after the second time.

He stretched and turned around, leaning against the

counter, and he saw three guys sleeping in the living room instead of two. What the fuck was Ethan doing sleeping out here? Had Val kicked his ass out afterward?

No…that didn't seem like something she'd do. More likely, Ethan had felt uncomfortable and selfish (nothing new) and left her room. Fucked her and left her. Brad nodded, gritting his teeth again and pouring a cup of coffee before heading into the shower. He had a song brewing inside him he'd have to write, a song no one but himself would ever see.

Since he didn't have to work that day, he started writing his song in the bedroom on his acoustic guitar. He heard Val leave for work, and he felt relieved that he hadn't had to look her in the eyes. He couldn't right now—just couldn't. She'd be able to tell and, if she was happy, he didn't want to ruin it for her.

He wanted her to be happy. He was going to do his best to make sure she was.

So, later that afternoon, he just couldn't help himself. Ethan had treated Val like shit in the past, and by God, it wasn't going to happen again. If he'd deflowered the girl, then he was going to treat her like his girlfriend and not just another whore. If Brad had had the money, he would have just joined a gym and pumped iron until he couldn't move or beaten a bag until he fell down. But he couldn't. All he had was his guitar and his mind. And so he spent the entire morning thinking…thinking about how he was going to say to Ethan what he had to say.

He did get out of the house to take a walk to clear his mind and, when he got back, decided to talk to Ethan soon. If nothing else, maybe he could talk some sense into his self-destructive friend. When he got back, Ethan was sitting on the chair in the living room. He'd been up for a while by the looks of it. Nick was back in the bedroom pounding on the drums, and Zane was in the kitchen eating breakfast. Ethan was dressed but he didn't seem fully alert. Brad stopped in front of his friend. "Hey, man...let me know when you're awake. We need to talk."

Ethan looked up, squinting one of his eyes as though Brad were the sun. His mouth curled on one side, but Brad couldn't read him. "Say what you gotta say now. I *am* awake."

Brad inhaled. Yeah, his thoughts were organized enough. He nodded, took a slow breath, and swallowed. "What's goin' on with you and Val?"

Ethan let out a breath and shook his head. "I knew it. I *knew* I should've talked to you first. Val said there was nothing going on between you two."

That almost winded him. *Nothing?* There was *nothing* between them? He wasn't sure how the hell to respond to that. Val was a liar if she'd said there was nothing...there was definitely *something*, even though they'd both chosen to sublimate it. But Brad also knew his friend Ethan a little too well and suspected his friend might be exaggerating what Valerie said. Maybe Valerie had told him their agreement...that stupid hands-off policy Brad himself had put into place, and Ethan had simplified it. Yeah...that sounded right. Val had always seemed open and honest with Brad, so he could believe that a little better. Either that or she was fooling herself. That too was a possibility. So he took another breath before answering his friend. "For the good of the band, we decided not to go there.

You knew that."

Ethan shrugged. "I know that's what you told her dad."

Brad kept his voice level even though he could feel anger starting to simmer in his chest. "I meant it." He took another deep breath. "But you didn't answer my question. You and Val…"

Ethan raised an eyebrow. "What about it?" He let out a breath and closed his eyes. "Yeah, okay. So…we're kinda together."

"What do you mean *kinda*? Either you are or you aren't. I'm sure Val doesn't feel so half-hearted about it."

"Exactly how would *you* know that, Bradley?"

Brad sucked in another deep breath, trying to keep calm. Ethan usually called him *Bradley* when he wanted to poke at him, and he knew this was one of those times. Ethan was implying that, just because Brad had never made love to Valerie, he didn't know what she wanted…but Brad suspected he knew more about what Val wanted and needed than his drugged-out friend did. He thought he might know a lot more about the way Val thought than maybe even she did. "Ask her yourself if you don't believe me." Ethan rolled his eyes. Brad decided to try a different approach and sat on the sofa so he was seated diagonally next to Ethan. "She really cares about you, man." Why, he couldn't understand. "Try to be good to her."

He saw Ethan bristle. "I have been." His eyelids lowered.

"Then be *better*." Ethan looked up at him again. "Quit takin' the shit. She worries about that."

Ethan's voice was low. "She's not my mom. Neither are you. I didn't ask what she wanted. I didn't ask for her to want me."

"Doesn't matter. You're committed now. You have more than just yourself to think about."

Ethan stood. Yeah...Brad was getting under his skin. *Good.* Maybe that was what he needed to wake up. "I didn't ask to watch out for someone else. She's a big girl. She makes her own decisions."

"Jesus, man. *Think* about what you're saying." He stood up. Ethan seemed to think he could intimidate Brad by hovering over him, but Brad was taller. He didn't even need to puff his chest out like Ethan. He just stood up.

"I have. She knows me. She knows what I'm like. I've never hidden that from her. She takes me as I am or not. I don't give a shit."

Brad couldn't keep it out of his voice anymore. It was all he could do to not jab Ethan in the chest with his finger. All that emotion he'd been bottling up inside... "You don't deserve her."

"Fuck that. I make her happy."

Brad fought to not punch his friend in the face, even though Ethan had it coming. "Does she *look* happy to you?"

Ethan smirked. "You *heard* her yourself."

Oh...fuck that. It took everything in Brad to not just beat the shit out of his friend. Not only was Ethan being a certified asshole to the woman who'd fallen prey to his charms, but he was rubbing his best friend's nose in it. Ethan had to know Brad cared for Val...a lot. So to throw that out there... Still, he wanted Valerie to be happy, and that was what he was going to focus on—not the red rage and jealousy threatening to overtake him. "Ethan, you're a mess. You know it and I know it. You wanna *make* her happy? Get your shit together, man."

Ethan got close to Brad, raising his shoulders to give the appearance that he was almost as tall as his friend. Brad felt a primal urge inside himself, the part of him that would have survived pre-civilization, and it wanted him to give in, to just get physical with his friend, beat some sense into him—or at least to beat him into submission. Out of the corner of his eye, Brad saw Zane walk in from the kitchen. Apparently, even their friend sensed what was in the air.

But then the front door opened…to none other than Val. Brad didn't want to back down from the challenge, but at the same time, he didn't want to upset Val. He couldn't quite pull his eyes away from Ethan's, wasn't going to, because he knew his friend would view that as a sign of weakness, no matter why he'd looked away. When she closed the door and started to approach them, though, they both backed down. Nothing would happen now. She said, "What's going on?"

Brad took a small step back and looked at Val. He cleared his throat and hoped he could pull off the lie. He knew she'd know anyway, but he had to say it just the same…out of respect to both her and Ethan. "Nothing. Just a little misunderstanding."

Ethan had an angry look on his face, but he wasn't going to contradict Brad. "Yeah."

Brad inhaled, trying to shift gears. "How was work?"

Val shrugged her shoulders, but her eyes looked concerned. "Nothing exciting."

Brad nodded and forced a smile. He too had to do what he'd just lectured Ethan about. He couldn't make Val happy either if he was constantly poking at Ethan and making him mad. Val certainly wouldn't be thrilled to know about their argument. So…he'd have to just keep his mouth shut. "Well…you're home now. Take a load off."

He saw the look that crossed Val's face as she looked at Ethan. The girl loved the guy—for better or worse. Yeah…it would be best for Brad to just go finish writing another song and keep his goddamned mouth shut. She loved his friend, and there wasn't a damn thing he'd be able to do about it. Not now, at any rate.

But he was going to have to find a way to get over it. Val had made her choice…and he was going to have to find a way to live with it.

CHAPTER THIRTY-THREE

IN THEORY, BRAD was making peace with the Val-Ethan thing. But the next time he heard her having another orgasm, he couldn't take it anymore. When he slept in the living room, he'd taken to playing movies on the computer until he fell asleep; it also helped drown out any potential noise. In the bedroom, though, it was a crap shoot. He'd been able to sleep the following night he'd been in there, but his next night after that, Ethan was giving it to her good, and he just couldn't lie there and listen to their lovemaking.

Val should have been his girl.

He shouldn't have waited, shouldn't have been patient. From the second he'd seen her, he should have acknowledged whatever it was between them and acted on it. He should have made it his mission to wipe Ethan out of her mind.

Part of him knew it wouldn't have worked, but he couldn't stop kicking himself for not having tried.

Damned if he was going to lie there listening. He was tempted to lie on Ethan's bed in the living room. That too would force his friend to think about staying with Val all night instead of sneaking out of there like an uncaring bastard.

He got up and put on a fresh pair of jeans and t-shirt, then found his boots beside the bed. He wasn't sure where he was going to go, but he couldn't stay in the apartment. He grabbed his black leather jacket out of the closet, because the evenings were starting to cool off, and then he tucked his wallet, phone, and keys into the pockets. He turned off the bedroom light and opened the door as quietly as possible, trying not to make a sound as he crossed the kitchen linoleum. When he got out the apartment door, he walked normally down the hall, the fear of waking up or alerting his roommates no longer a worry.

He wasn't sure what he was going to do or where he would wind up, but he figured if he was gone for a few hours, they'd be asleep if nothing else. He got in his car and drove around for a while and then decided he knew what he wanted. He didn't know if he was too young for it or not, so he pulled out his phone.

Yeah…there was a BYOB stripper joint a few miles south of his location and the only requirement was that he be over eighteen. He needed some entertainment, something that would take his mind off his emotions, and having some nude girls dancing in front of him for a while might do the trick. Just driving there, thinking about it, having a goal in mind made him feel better.

He had to show his ID at the door to verify his age. He was glad it wasn't a bar or he would have been fucked. He was also glad he had more cash than he'd thought he would need.

At first, he'd thought it was perfect. Dozens of hot women were grinding and dancing right in front of him. He hadn't completely known what to expect, having heard on occasion about how the women at these kinds of places weren't actually attractive, but the women here were damned sexy.

Unfortunately, the ladies—even the drop dead gorgeous ones—just weren't doing it for him. They weren't Val and his pain was too fresh. It had been an excellent thought, but it wasn't doing a thing to pull him out of his funk. He could even imagine one of these hot girls doing anything nasty to him, because he couldn't get Valerie out of his head.

One of the women—a girl introduced to the audience as Sugar—looked like Val, except she was probably a few years older. She was a little short but cute with long, dark brown hair. She didn't smile but Brad suspected that if she had, her cheeks would have looked like Val's when she would. Val's smile lit up her entire face.

That thought just made Brad pissed because he couldn't even stop thinking about her here. She consumed his thoughts.

And here was this gorgeous angel, ready to peel clothing off at any given moment. She was dancing to some hip hop tune Brad had no chance of recognizing. More than once the girl looked him straight in the eyes. She was probably wondering why he didn't move closer and give her a dollar bill or two.

He glanced down to check the hour on his phone. It

was probably about time that he could leave and go home to peace and quiet. But he was first going to allow himself to try to enjoy one or two more acts. He tried to clear his mind and focus on the woman onstage.

The girl who called herself Sugar ground herself next to the pole, thrusting and pumping, and if Brad hadn't felt like shit, he would have thought it was one of the hottest things he'd ever seen. The woman had long, straight dark hair and green eyes. She was stacked. Brad couldn't tell if her tits were real or fake, and he didn't care. Either way, they were a work of art. She was thin but curvy and, goddamn, did she know how to move. She was sexy and she earned every bill thrown on the stage at her. And, even though Brad knew all the men at the base of the stage gripping their drinks were under her spell, something didn't look quite right to Brad. He couldn't figure out why. But then he realized it was probably his own shitty mood overshadowing what he thought he saw.

Sugar left the stage, making way for "Sexy Sapphire," and Brad took another sip of his water. He was considering going home and seeing if they had anything else to drink somewhere in the apartment or if someone had hidden some weed somewhere. He needed to become numb. He didn't want to feel anymore, not tonight anyway. He was done, and he couldn't let himself continue feeling the way he had been. He had to get over this shit.

He was glad he was sitting farther back, because he didn't have any of the incidental conversation, with either the dancers or the guys. He'd never been to a strip club before, so he didn't know enough to know if conversation was normal or not, but he didn't want to chance it. If he'd been hanging with friends, it would have been one thing, but talking about sex or a hot chick with a complete stranger when all he was trying to do was ward off an erection might be weird.

Ten more minutes, and he was going to leave, and just as he had that thought, a girl sat next to him. Brad could sense she was trying to get his attention, so he turned his head to look at her. The woman was dressed in ripped jeans and a tank top covered with a jean jacket. She had tall black boots on that were, Brad could admit, sexy, but he was not in the mood. It took a few seconds, but then he realized the woman sitting next to him was Sugar, the stripper who'd gotten his attention onstage earlier. When he made eye contact, she said, "Hey."

She was young. Onstage, she'd looked older, but up close, he could tell her real age was closer to teens than thirties. If she was older than Brad, he would have been surprised. She looked him over and gave him a flirtatious smile. He said, "I know you have to work, but you might as well know I'm not in the mood tonight. Those guys over there?" he said, tilting his head toward the guys at the bottom of the stage. "They're the ones you should be talking to."

"I'm off the clock. Why? Did you *want* a lap dance?"

He shook his head. "No. Thanks."

"Really, I'm off the clock. I just thought you might want to talk."

Brad smiled and pried his eyes away from the stage. "Talk?"

"Yeah. You look…kinda sad. I thought maybe you wanted to talk about it." He didn't say anything, instead taking another swig of his water. Yeah, he bet that looked really cool too. He probably looked like a kid.

"You're not gonna get anything from me."

"I said I'm not working. I just thought maybe you and me could go grab a cup of coffee. I don't know why that has to seem sinister."

Brad couldn't help himself. He started laughing. He downed the rest of the water. "Fine. We'll go have a cup of coffee."

"Great idea. You've already seen the best act of the night anyway."

He smirked. "Where are we going, Sugar?"

She eyed him. "Well, first things first. Don't call me *Sugar.*"

"What should I call you?"

"My real name's Joanne. Call me Jo. What's your name?"

"Brad." He stood. "Let's get out of here."

Brad had already figured out she was using him so she could get a ride home, and, for some reason, he was okay with it. He wound up buying the coffee too…and then a piece of pie for her on top of that. She could afford a few calories. He didn't mind. She was gorgeous and she was making him smile.

Yeah, he suspected she made more in a night than his band usually did, but she'd worked hard for it, and—unlike his dreams for the band—she probably didn't want to spend her whole life stripping. He figured she wanted to save up and get out.

She offered Brad a bite of the pie, and he grinned but

shook his head at her. He sipped at the coffee. It was good. He was glad he'd taken her up on her suggestion. After she took the last bite of the pie, she said, "So...do you only go to strip clubs when you're depressed as hell?"

He smiled. "*Depressed?* Did I *look* depressed?"

"Uh, *yeah*. Totally. You didn't smile until I started talking to you." He wanted to deny it, but he knew it was true. She took a sip of her coffee and winked. "Guys like you make it hard for me to do my job."

Okay, yeah. He was smiling more than he had in a week. "How so?"

She huffed as though she couldn't believe him. "We know we're doing a good job when guys can't take their eyes off us or they get this look in their eyes. And sometimes—now I *know* this is gonna seem weird to you—but they, like, *smile*. We can tell we're appreciated. Shit. If my boss had walked in and seen your face, I would have gotten my ass reamed."

"Seriously?"

"No, not really. But if all the guys around you and in front of me had looked like that, I bet I would have been in trouble."

"I'd say *sorry*, but the reason I went was so *you* could cheer me up."

She raised an eyebrow. "*That's* not my job." He shrugged and took another sip of coffee. She was losing her amusement factor really fast and was pushing at becoming annoying. She gasped and said, "Oh, no. Depressed man has returned." He shook his head. "So...why don't you tell me what's got you down? Talking can help."

"No, thanks."

"Seriously. You're probably thinking I'm just the stupid whore who gets up on the stage and strips and then tries to find a guy who I can talk out of money, but that's not it. I asked if you wanted to hang, because I'm not feeling so happy either. I guess I'm just better at putting on a happy face."

"Yeah?"

"Yeah. See, I got this boyfriend..." The waitress stopped by their table and filled up their cups, asking if they needed anything else, but they told her no.

"A boyfriend..."

"Oh, yeah. He's usually a great guy. Sweet, gorgeous, treats me right, but...sometimes he's not."

"I take it right now, he's not?"

"Yeah. In fact, he's a real asshole right now. Part of the problem is..." She looked around. "Well, I've said too much already."

Brad couldn't figure out this girl's angle. He continued to feel like she was trying to work him out of money. She was going to be sorely disappointed to find out that he was worried if he was going to be able to pay the rent, let alone give her any money to show him a good time. He didn't know that he was in the mood for sex anyway.

He almost laughed out loud at the thought. Of *course*, he would be in the mood for sex. He never hadn't been, no matter what his prevailing mood—sad, angry, happy. Sex could enhance a good mood or change a bad one. And this girl? Very hot. But he didn't think he trusted her. So he sipped his coffee. He wasn't going to encourage her either way.

"Let's just say when he's a bad boyfriend, he's very bad, and that makes me want to spend time with someone else." Brad nodded. She raised an eyebrow. "Not just drinking coffee and eating pie." She lowered her voice, and Brad didn't know if she'd done it on purpose, but the quality of her words turned husky. "It makes me want to be naughty with someone else."

He nearly spat his coffee out, but he managed to keep his cool. Holy fuck. He'd been getting ready to find a way to usher her back out to the car and get her home, and now it was all he could do to not get a massive hard on. He couldn't help the look on his face, and he knew it was a mixture of incredulity, intrigue, and hunger. He hadn't had a good fuck in a long time, and now, considering the possibility that this girl was really offering, he could think of little else. That she'd said she had a boyfriend didn't even cross his mind. He still didn't know that he trusted her, though, so he raised his eyebrows and said, "Yeah?"

"Yeah…but, first, you need to tell me what's got you down. I already know it's a girl, all right. Just tell me more. I want to know. I want to know you feel like I do."

"Feel like you do?"

"Yeah, like we're kindred spirits or something."

Her words then felt genuine, as though she wanted a reason to care about him. He paused, but then he said, "Yeah, it's a girl." He stared into his coffee cup.

"I already knew that. What's the problem? What's she done to make you glum?"

"Nothing, really."

"BS."

"No, really. She…" Brad shook his head. He was

going to sound pathetic, but why did he care? This woman didn't know him. What she thought about him wouldn't change his life. "She's been in love with my best friend forever, and they just hooked up."

"But...?"

"But there's been something between her and me, has been from the first time we met. And it's not like I didn't let her know how I feel."

"Oh. Ouch."

"Yeah."

He could feel the side of her left foot—still in its boot—rubbing against the inside of his lower leg and then she put her right foot on the other side, trapping his leg in between hers. "Let's get out of here." He looked at her. "Maybe forget our problems for a while." He raised his eyebrows.

He was tempted, but no fucking way was he taking a girl back to his place, whether he had the bedroom for the night or not. That was Nick's thing. It seemed stupid, but he didn't want Valerie to know. He shrugged. "Can't go to my place."

"Why not?"

"I have four roommates. It's a little crowded."

She nodded and then he saw her expression change. "And the girl and best friend are two of them?" All he could do was move his head up and down in affirmation. "Well...we could go back to my place, but you can't spend the night."

He agreed in two seconds flat...because he had nothing to lose.

CHAPTER THIRTY-FOUR

JO, ALSO KNOWN as Sugar, barely got the key out of the lock before she and Brad started tugging at their clothes once they were inside the door. She'd managed to get them both worked up on the drive to her apartment. She'd started by nibbling on his ear, and he'd pulled her into a kiss at a red light, but then she started snaking her fingers up his jeans, teasing him through the denim, running her fingernail up the zipper, creating a vibration that made his dick hard as a rock. Then she squeezed his thigh.

He was already wondering if he could make it when she unzipped her own jeans and said, "Not fair that you're hard and I'm not." She stuck a hand down her pants and started playing with herself, panting and moaning. "Oh, I can't wait to feel you inside me."

His sentiments exactly. She'd given him vague directions, and if she didn't pay attention, he was just gonna pull over and fuck her brains out. At the next stoplight, he asked, "Which way?"

"Mmm." She rolled her head to one side and opened her eye. "Straight ahead one more block, and then turn left."

Left? Fuck. It would have been nice if she'd warned him earlier. He was in the right-hand lane. Well, traffic wasn't too heavy. He could make his way over there once the light turned green. Stressing about that managed to help him stay under control, but when he parked, she was all over him again. So by the time they'd gotten to their destination, he thought he was going to explode.

Inside her apartment, they both got unzipped, and he found it all the more exciting that he was going to fuck her with those goddamned boots on. He slid his finger inside her tiny panties, and she was slick with need. He was going to make sure she got off first, because he knew he wasn't going to last for long once he started. She was breathing hard. "Feel good?"

"Oh, God." She started moaning, then screaming, and Brad thought he was gonna blow. She was fucking crazy. Then she said, "God, I need you inside me."

He stuck his tongue back in her mouth while fumbling in his back pocket for his wallet. He felt around for a condom, his hands meeting behind her back, and he found one, dropping the wallet to the floor. He got it on just in time, because she was tugging on the side of his jeans, pulling them down farther, and then when he had the condom on, she started digging her nails in his neck. He lifted her up and turned around so that her back was against the door, using the wall to hold her in place, and then he drove himself into her. She started moaning again, and he kept telling himself to hold off, hold off, don't blow it yet.

She bit his shoulder—*hard*—and that was it. He couldn't contain it anymore. He could feel it clear to his balls and it felt so fucking good. It was like his whole body was shoving itself through his cock and he was gonna die…but it was gonna be a good fucking death. He even heard himself groan. *What the fuck?* He'd never done that before. He figured that was what happened when he went way too long without the company of a woman.

He wasn't going to let that happen again.

Yeah, he could take care of himself, had for years, but there was nothing like being inside a woman, especially a beautiful one who smelled like cinnamon and kept demanding him in between breaths to *fuck her good*.

Well, he felt like a complete asshole, but he had to ask. "You were able to finish, weren't you?"

She giggled. "I was on my third one. I was plenty done, stud, but don't think *you* are. We're just taking a short break, and then I'm gonna ride the fuck out of you." She grabbed his cock—*holy shit,* that was a shock to his system—and peeled the rubber off his dick.

He let out a chuckle. He didn't think he had another one in him. "I think I need to rest a minute." He tucked himself back in and zipped up. He turned around and got a good look around her apartment. It was small—smaller than his, even—and so it felt busy. The kitchen and living room were the same room, but the space was tiny. It didn't feel cluttered or crowded, but it looked like it would take him hours to look at everything crammed in the place. It was neat too—just packed. There were floor to ceiling bookshelves all along one wall in the living room, and she had fabric draped on all the furniture, little knick knacks on all the shelves and books too. Candles, doilies, pictures—not an inch of space went unutilized. It felt like a mall at Christmas. He picked his wallet up off the floor and walked toward the chair. "Mind if I sit down?" He made a mental note that he needed to get a wallet chain. Not only were they bad ass, but it'd keep the damn wallet attached to his jeans in moments of weakness like the one he'd just experienced.

She shook her head. "Go ahead. Can I get you something to drink?"

Much as he'd love a beer right now, he didn't dare. She didn't want him staying the night, and a beer would ensure fatigue. It was so late anyway, but he was grateful for one thing—he felt better than he had in weeks. "I'd love a glass of water."

He heard her giggle. "Oh, I like that. You took me seriously."

He rested his head on the back of the chair and stretched his legs. "About what?"

"Well, you're avoiding whiskey dick. I appreciate that." Brad started laughing and he heard her pouring water from the tap into the glass. "You want ice?"

"Up to you."

She walked over to the chair and handed him the water. Her jeans were still unzipped but she'd pulled them back up. God...he hadn't even had a chance to touch her breasts. How the fuck had she managed to get him so worked up when an hour ago he'd been convinced he wanted nothing to do with her? Amazing.

She had a drink too, but hers looked a little stronger than water. She set it on the coffee table and then sat on the couch and opened a wooden box that rested on top of a square piece of red velvet. She pulled out a joint and lighter and was holding a flame to the spliff before he even realized what she was doing. God, that looked good, and she leaned over toward the chair, holding the joint toward him. "Honey, you want me to leave tonight, I don't dare get high."

She shrugged. "Suit yourself." She took another puff and then said, "Just tell me when you're ready to go again."

He chuckled again. Jesus, she was gonna eat him alive—and he liked the idea. She was crazy, good crazy, and he couldn't believe he'd been trying to turn her down earlier. She was winding up being the best accidental thing that had happened to him in a long time.

But then, as she pinched off the end of the joint into the amber-colored ashtray next to the box and leaned her head against the back of the couch, he started wondering again what *she* was getting out of all this. He drew in another deep breath and hoped he could trust his instincts. This girl seemed harmless, though maybe a little lonely.

After another minute or two, she got up and turned on her stereo. She was playing some weird Middle Eastern music, something exotic, and then she walked around the apartment with her lighter. He hadn't noticed all the candles in the busyness of the room until she lit them all up one by one—he'd seen a few, but he had no idea she'd had dozens. Then she turned off the light. She tossed the lighter onto the coffee table and stood in front of Brad's chair, her hand extended. He took it and stood, shaking his head. "I don't think I'm ready yet."

She smiled. "I didn't think so, but I want us to move to

the bedroom anyway."

He nodded and took her hand but didn't use her to help him up. He stood and that was when he could tell she really had worn him out. Still...he wasn't going to turn her down. As soon as he was ready, he was going to take her up on her offer for a second go.

He hadn't even taken his jacket off yet, so he did and threw it on the chair, then followed her to her bedroom.

It too felt busy. The woman owned a lot of shit, but it felt exotic somehow, and everything, big or little, had a place. Maybe that was what was making Brad feel weird about it. There was no room for anything else, and each item in her house had to have a specific place, because there was no room for deviation. She just plain had a lot of stuff, but it was cool looking stuff. Her bed was the only place in the bedroom—aside from the floor—where it felt like there was room to move. "Why don't you sit down?" she asked.

He shrugged. "Okay."

"Better yet, lay down."

He smiled. He liked the sound of that, so he leaned over and untied his boots. Then he lay back on the bed, several pillows propping him up. Most of them appeared to be for decoration, just like most of her house. They were comfortable, though. Jo said, "I wanted to see you looking at me like you mean it."

"Mean what?"

"Well," she said, starting to do a swaying pelvic thrust in rhythm to the music coming from the other room, "back at the club, you acted like you wanted to be anywhere but where you were. I'm not used to men looking at me that way. I prefer them looking at me like no other women exist, even if it's only for a few minutes."

He wanted to ask her if she was going to expect payment from him later, but she'd promised she wasn't working. "I'm going to tell you something…Brad." He tried not to smile. She'd almost forgotten his name. "I love my boyfriend, but he's a domineering jerk sometimes. He's not always tender and gentle when I need him to be. Problem is he's my boss too. And I sometimes think maybe I'm not his only girlfriend, if you catch my drift." He nodded. Maybe the two of them had a lot more in common than he'd suspected. "So I don't want anything messy, but you are super cute and pretty damn hot, and I just need to forget my problems tonight. Got it?"

He nodded, now entranced. That had been the first time in a long time a girl had told him he was hot, so not only had she made him feel incredible, she was stroking his wounded ego too. She pulled the tank top over her head and swirled it a couple of times, then threw it to the floor in a flourish. She turned around, facing her closet, and stuck her ass out at him, running her hands up and down over it, and he started feeling twinges in his cock again. Oh, fuck, yeah. She wanted to see his eyes filled with lust, she was gonna get it.

She turned around and peeled her jeans down one side and then the other, down to where the boots hit her thighs. Goddamn, he wished she could leave those on, but to take her jeans off, she was going to have to take the boots off too. She unzipped them, one at a time, and the way she did it was sensual. The look on her face, the way she moved her mouth and tongue and the little noises she made were making it seem like one of the most erotic things Brad had ever seen. It was like foreplay.

And then she slid the jeans off too. They'd been snug but she somehow made them fall off her like silk. She did some sexy dance moves around the tiny area in her bedroom and then stuck her ass toward him again. She was wearing a thong, so her gorgeous ass was in full view. She had a decorative tramp stamp just over the string on her lower back that said *Bitch* with swirls underneath it. She ran her thumbs under the strings and pulled them down, teasing, then back up to her hips. Then she turned around, moving up to her tiny bra, and as she started pulling the straps down, that's when his cock came to full attention. The blood was pumping down there hard, engorging his cock and making him ready to fuck her again.

He knew she wasn't disappointed in his response this time.

She pulled the bra off and he thought he was going to lose his mind. He had no idea if they were fake, but they were big and beautiful, and he thought his jaw was going to hit the floor as she touched herself. But she moved back down to the barely there panties and teased them off too.

She then danced her way closer to the bed. Her eyes were dark. She knew the power she had over him, and he could tell she was most definitely pleased at his response this time. She pranced over to him, grabbed his chin, and gave him a look. He wasn't sure what she was thinking. "You like the boots, don't you?"

He couldn't contain his enthusiasm. "Hell, yeah."

She turned back around, making sure he could appreciate her ass, and then she sat on the end of the bed, sliding the boots back on. She then turned and got on the bed on all fours. Jesus Christ, he thought he might come just looking at her. "You and me—we're gonna get together again, stud, and I'm gonna be bossy, but tonight I just wanna make you forget about the bitch who broke your heart."

She straddled him and he started to protest. "She's not a bi—" But she covered his mouth with hers and he couldn't talk. Instead, he thought he was going to be buried alive under her kiss, and he didn't know how much more he could take. This woman was beautiful and she was his, even if for just a short time. And it dawned on him, as she began pulling at his jeans, that she had just made him a promise that they were going to have another night together. He wanted to make sure he'd survive this one first.

She pulled his cock out of his underwear and stroked him, eliciting another moan out of his mouth. Holy fuck, this woman. She giggled and then reached over to her nightstand, pulling out a condom. She had it unwrapped and on him in seconds, and he was glad, because that muted the feeling just enough that he thought he'd be able to enjoy the full gamut of sensations before he came this time.

She poised herself above his cock, those black boots stopping midway up her naked thighs. He could feel the rhythmic throbbing of his dick in time to his beating heart. Then she slid herself over him, and her pussy sucked him in. It was like she was continuing to dance, only this time with him inside her, and she threw her head back in ecstasy. When she looked back down on him, he placed his hands on her hips. He almost didn't feel like he could touch her, because it felt almost like he wasn't present, like he was watching it happen to someone else.

Oh, but no fuckin' way, because he felt so goddamned incredible. She reached down and, with each of her hands, grabbed his off her hips and placed them on her breasts. As he touched her at her bidding, she let out a long sigh. "God, you're so hot. I love your tattoos. They make you look so bad, so dangerous, and that's why I want to fuck the shit out of you." She slid her fingers down her stomach, another erotic move, and then touched herself until she moaned and started yelling like she was on fire. She was clenching against him, and that was when he couldn't take it anymore. His eyes clamped closed as an explosion of pleasure washed over him. She continued grinding against him, prolonging it just a little longer, as her orgasm wound down too. He wasn't sure what he'd done to deserve this sex goddess, but he felt like tonight had become his lucky night.

CHAPTER THIRTY-FIVE

AS SUMMER DRIFTED into fall, Brad and his friends fell into a routine. His job was fairly regular, whereas Val's schedule was all over the place, but her boss worked around the dates they played. They always had at least two shows a week, but sometimes as many as four, depending on what Brad had been able to book, and the merch table was starting to pay for itself as more and more people became fans.

Jo had sent him a couple of risqué texts since he'd seen her, but nothing else had happened between them. She was a great memory, and if he ever felt desperate again, he was going to go to her club. She'd helped him through a low spot, and, for that, he'd be forever grateful.

He was finally able to allow some distance between himself and Val, and he was able to think of her as just a good friend again. Jo was a huge part of that. He wasn't happy about her relationship with Ethan, but that was only because Ethan was continuing to be a selfish asshole. If the guy would make Val a priority and treat her like an angel, Brad would bless the relationship.

He started worrying about her, though. He was afraid she was going to fall prey to Ethan's bad habits.

He was waiting for the perfect opportunity to talk to her—alone. He wasn't going to say anything when anyone else was around. She seemed to be fine, but she was thinner, and he knew, if she was doing something like meth, that it could do that. He could see her indulging, considering she had a lot on her plate. She was working a lot and she walked to and from her job. She could have taken the bus but said it wasn't far enough to bother. When it got cold or snowy, she might, but for now she was walking. And she was working hard on the music, often singing for hours to get a song exactly the way she wanted it. She was spending a lot of her leftover free time with Ethan. She also did extra work around the house, in spite of Brad's best efforts to prevent it, but he was glad he'd set up all the schedules and lists he had when they'd first moved in, or she'd be doing nothing but cleaning.

Finally, one morning, all three guys were sleeping and Brad and Val were in the kitchen drinking coffee before both of them had to go to work. She was—she was lots thinner. She actually looked hotter than ever before, but he was worried that there was more to it. He had to be sure. He had to know everything was okay.

"Do you have a minute to talk before work?"

She seemed hesitant but nodded. "Sure."

"Please, Val...please tell me you're not indulging in any of the shit Ethan does regularly."

She got a confused look on her face. "What? Why

would you even ask that?"

"You've lost a lot of weight."

She shook her head. "That's not why."

"Something I should worry about?"

She paused, then said, "Oh, no. No. Hell, no. I'm just…not eating as much and I'm exercising a lot. I'm not starving, and I'm definitely not doing drugs."

"Okay. Good. Just…you really *are* our muse, Val. I…" He couldn't find the words, so he struggled, looking in the cup in front of him for answers.

"What?"

It didn't matter—he had to say it. "I feel the need to protect you."

She smiled. "From what?"

"Lots of things. I…just want you safe." That realization was when he knew he was completely over lusting for her and now loved her like a sister or another bandmate. And he felt that it was a good love, a necessary love—and much safer than the alternative.

"I *am* safe, right?" When he didn't answer immediately, she said, "Right?"

"Yeah, sure. You are. Just…" He wanted her to know that he was there for her, no matter what happened with her and Ethan. "Just remember you have a friend here, okay?"

She rested her hand on top of his, trying to reassure him. "I know that." And perfect timing. Ethan walked in the kitchen from the bedroom and sat at the table. He said nothing, but it was pretty obvious what he was thinking. As though Brad's temperature had raised two hundred degrees in a matter of seconds, Valerie pulled her hand off his and wrapped it back around her coffee mug. She looked at Ethan. "Hey, how'd you sleep?"

"For shit." Brad was glad to see Ethan was his usual self, a beaming ray of sunshine.

He said, "There's plenty of coffee if you want it."

"Nah. I *know* what I want."

He glanced over at Val. Jesus, what the hell was wrong with the guy? He understood—if Val was his girlfriend, *especially* the way she was looking lately, he'd want to fuck her all the time too. Unlike his friend, though, he wouldn't go around pissing on everything. Brad already knew Ethan had won the girl; he didn't have to continue to flaunt it or, worse, continue to challenge Brad. Brad had already stepped back. And until Ethan could see that, their relationship was going to be strained, and Brad was beginning to wonder if their friendship could even survive.

But, if Brad could believe his senses, that wasn't all that was going on. Ethan was challenging him, yes, but Brad was pretty sure he was on something. What the guy had in mind, he didn't know. "Think it through, man."

"Fuck off, Bradley."

He maintained his eyes locked on Ethan's. He was pretty sick of the guy's shit. Val asked, "Can we please stop?"

Fine. She continued to make the same choice. Of course, she would defend her boyfriend, even when he was out of line. Okay—she'd made her bed. She could go lie in it. "I gotta go to work anyway." He rinsed his coffee cup and set it next to the sink. "Nice talkin' with ya, Val."

Ethan, though? Ethan could suck his dick. He was pretty over his brother's shit. He pulled his jacket off the back of the chair where he'd been sitting and put it on, shoving his hands in his pockets to make sure he had everything he'd need for the day, and he left.

After he walked out the door, he was even more pissed that he'd let Ethan get the upper hand. He'd been so distracted and angry that he'd forgotten to make a lunch for himself to take to work. That meant he'd have to eat out today, because no way in hell was he going back to the apartment. Yes, Fully Automatic was starting to earn more money, but Brad had plans, and they didn't involve a daily Big Mac or Nachos Bell Grande. Well, once in a while wouldn't hurt, but it led him to realize that he had to stop investing so much emotion into Ethan. Brad could talk a good game, but it was hard to play it well when so much was at stake—his friendships, his band…hell, his whole fucking life. It was damned near impossible to be objective about any of it.

Brad was at work one afternoon when he got a phone call from Jo. He thought it was strange, because she'd only ever texted him. They were between cars—one of the other guys was getting ready to drive the next one into the garage—so he answered. "Hey, Jo, what's up?"

Her voice was low, almost a purr. "Brad?"

"Yeah."

"I have been thinking about you all afternoon, and I think you need to come over here right now."

He smiled. "I can't. I'm at work."

He could almost hear the pout in her voice. "Oh. Can't you just tell them you have an emergency?"

"I really can't." He looked up at the clock on the wall,

the one that constantly kept them on task, drove them to be quick and efficient with each car they worked on. "I get off at five-thirty. I could come by then."

She was silent for a few moments, and then she said, "Fine. I'm going to keep myself plenty wet until then, but I want *your tongue* to get me off, so don't waste any time."

He sucked in a breath. Holy shit. He swallowed. Okay, so it was going to be hard to think about anything else the rest of the day. He managed a chuckle. "I'll see you soon. Do what you gotta do, I guess."

"Oh, I will." He was glad he could do his job in his sleep by this point, because his mind was not on the job—it was in Jo's busy apartment, imagining everything they could do once his body got there.

When he got off work, he was afraid that, at first, he wouldn't remember how to get there. He'd call if he had to, but he did fine finding it.

He stepped out of the car and took a deep breath. He was looking forward to this more than he would have thought he would. As he made his way to her apartment, he could see her in his mind—her long dark hair, emerald eyes, shapely breasts, and her filthy mouth. That was probably what he was looking most forward to—he'd never had a girl talk to him during sex like she did. Even Misti, the older woman who'd helped him make the transition from awkward teen to more confident man, hadn't talked dirty like Jo did.

Jesus...he could feel himself heating up just thinking about it.

When he got to the door, he didn't even get a chance to knock, because she opened the door and pulled him in.

Brad hardly had a chance to register that she was wearing some kind of lingerie in red, complete with black garters and heels, before she had him slammed up against the wall, her tongue in his mouth and her hands all over his body. She cupped his package in her right hand and said, "Sorry, stud, but you have to wait. Me first." She stepped back, pulling his jacket off, and then she noticed his khaki overalls, grease-stained and more than a bit dirty. She grinned. "You really *did* come straight from work. What a good boy. Why don't we get you in the shower?" She pulled on the zipper and he helped her, but he was going to have to take his boots off to make it easier. His overalls pooled at his feet, and he bent over to loosen his laces. "I'm gonna go start the water. You better hurry up."

He didn't take long to get his boots off, and then he rushed to follow her into the bathroom. She already had the water pouring out of the faucet and turned the shower on, pulling the curtain closed. "It's a shame, really."

"What?" he asked, pulling his t-shirt over his head.

"You can't really appreciate the outfit I wore for you."

He grinned and wrapped his hands around her waist, pulling her close. "Oh, I appreciate it, and I'll be imagining it on you the entire time it's not." He kissed her then. "But we should probably get you *out* of it, unless you want me to shower by myself."

"No, I'll be there." She stepped back and pulled a strap down, and Brad figured he'd better take the opportunity to peel off the remainder of his clothes. He pulled his socks off while she unclipped the garters and pulled her hose off one at a time, and then he took his jeans off. He was pulling his shorts off by the time she was removing the lingerie.

She slapped him on the ass and then pulled the shower curtain aside. "Get in there."

He grinned again and got under the water—almost a little too hot—but he didn't plan to be there long. She might have thought he was dirty but the overalls protected him from most of the grime at the shop. It was his hands that always got the dirtiest, and he'd washed them before leaving. He didn't want to get the steering wheel filthy, so he always washed his hands before leaving work.

He grabbed the soap and started lathering up when she stepped in the tub and got close. He asked, "So, did I hear you right?"

She grinned. "What?"

"You said something about wanting my tongue to do all the work?"

Her smile grew wider. "Yeah, that's what I want."

"Then you tell me when you're ready."

"I was ready three or four hours ago when I called you."

He grabbed her ass and pulled her close again, pushing her into him. "I'm sorry, Jo. I can't just leave work whenever I feel like it."

"Then you better make it up to me."

"I will." He lifted her up, wrapping her legs around his torso, and he kissed down her neck and the top of her breast. "I don't know about you, but I'm pretty clean." He looked at her. "You happy?"

She smiled and nodded, a twinkle in her eye. He set her down and she turned around to shut the water off. She stepped out of the shower and grabbed his hand, leading him out. He had a hard on now; there was no way to stop it. But he was going to make her feel great first. She yanked a towel off a stainless steel rack and patted herself off, then bunched it up and held it to Brad's chest. He took it and patted himself off a little. It wasn't too chilly in her apartment, so he didn't care about getting completely dry. He tossed the towel back toward the rack, hooking it enough so he could let it go and the rest draped down off the front, but he already had her face in his hands and he was kissing her.

They took their time walking to the bedroom, spending more time kissing, but when they got to the bed, he said, "I also think you said something about staying wet until I got here."

"Oh, I'm very wet."

He grinned and ran his hand down her neck, past her collarbone, and to her breast. He cupped it in his hand and said, "I think I'm gonna have to check that out myself." He licked her nipple and she drew in a deep breath. He sucked it into his mouth and slid it through his teeth. He didn't want to hurt her but wanted her on the edge. She gasped, so he knew it was working. And then he slid his hand down her belly to her pussy where she had that tiny, trimmed patch of hair and worked his fingers down into the folds. Holy shit. "You weren't kidding."

"I told you." She was smiling. "It's been hell waiting for you all this time."

"Well, I keep my promises." He lay her down on the bed and wasn't going to waste any time. He kissed her once more and then kissed between her cleavage, down her belly, and then he lifted her legs and draped them over his shoulders. It had been a long time since he'd done this with a girl, and he hadn't done it enough that he felt like any kind of expert.

He ran two of his fingers down her slit, parting her, and then he flicked his tongue over her clit. "Mmm." God, as promised, she was wet and ready. He moved his tongue up and down against her, and she let him know vocally that he was right on track. He kept it up—a steady but slow speed—until the muscles in her thighs clenched and she got louder. "Oh, fuck!" she screamed and then started moaning loudly, writhing. He felt himself grow harder, but he tried to maintain his focus on her, continuing to move his tongue over her until she relaxed and let out a loud sigh. "Shit."

"You good?"

"Mmm. Thank you for making the wait totally worth it."

"Let me know when you're ready." He moved up the bed and started kissing her neck.

"Are you kidding? I'm ready now."

He sucked in a breath. "Just gotta find my jeans."

"Why?"

"I need a condom."

She reached over and opened the drawer on her nightstand. "Take your pick."

He glanced in. She had tons of them, a smorgasbord. He didn't even want to think of why. Instead, he simply grabbed the first normal-looking one and opened it. Then he unrolled it as quickly as he could. There was something about this woman that made him feel out of control. Like the last time they'd been together, he doubted he could wait.

He slid inside her. *Oh, God.* Fuck, yes, that was what he needed. Why the hell didn't he find himself a girlfriend? He wouldn't have to wait so long in between times like these.

And talk about putting a damper on things. He knew exactly why, but the next thrust pushed the idea out of his head. All his thoughts were focused on that throbbing engine down below, the one that drove him to move on instinct. He pumped as long as he could stand it, long past the time she cried again, cursing and screaming and begging him to let her have it, until he had to let it all go. It was intense and mind blowing, and afterward he closed his eyes so she wouldn't talk to him, because his thoughts were once again on the girl he couldn't be with.

CHAPTER THIRTY-SIX

AS THE DAYS grew colder, Brad's thoughts intensified. He was happy so far with the progress Fully Automatic was making, but there were several problems. The first one was that he was already damned sick and tired of living in that dinky apartment. It wouldn't have been so bad if he hadn't had two roommates who were always either fucking loudly or fighting even more loudly. Ethan and Val had taken to arguing constantly, and he supposed that was their passion playing out. It wasn't just over Ethan's drug use, though. He wasn't sure what else they fought about, and he didn't want to know, but their relationship was filled with drama, and it was pissing him off.

So far, it hadn't spilled over and affected the band, but he *would* get involved if it came to that, and they wouldn't like it if he had to.

As it was, he saw a need to pull the leader card anyway. The guys seemed to be resting on their laurels. No one had written anything new in weeks, and no one was practicing anymore. It was like they felt they didn't need to practice nowadays, like they were good enough. And if they thought they were earning enough money just playing gigs, they needed to think again. He felt like no one was taking it seriously.

So he called a meeting. They sat in the living room in a circle. "Guys, money's tight. I don't think you have any idea. You should think about getting jobs, each one of you."

Zane said, "But I thought we were making enough off merch and our gigs to pay the bills."

He shrugged. "Yeah, but I gotta tell you, I'm nervous about handing you over your money and then you go blow it on shit and then we don't have enough for the rent."

"So keep what you need, like you used to when we went on the road." Nick cocked his head and continued. "You know...how you'd save money for the motel and gas. Why can't you do that now?"

Everyone in the circle nodded. Brad shook his head. "It's no problem for *me*, man, to withhold your part of the rent, utilities, and groceries, and then give you what's left." In fact, that alleviated most of his worries right there. As long as they could pay the bills, then the money from his job could go to other things that would eventually progress the band.

Ethan, in his typical fashion, rolled his eyes. "So just *do* it. If we need more money, we'll figure it out."

Yeah, he wanted to ask exactly *who* the *we* in Ethan's sentence was, but he took a deep breath instead. "You better hope I'm able to keep booking enough that it *does* cover all that shit. Otherwise, I'll kick your ass out."

The problem was they all *knew* he would. Why would he start slacking now? They knew Fully Automatic was his life, his dream, and there was no way he was going to start screwing off. They counted on it. He didn't know that his lecture had done any good, and he didn't care. They'd given him license to hold back money for the bills. He'd tack other things on too, the things he always had—gas, paying for new merchandise, and things like that. He'd have to come up with a budget and list and hold back what he needed. If they complained, he'd have it in writing for them to look at, and then they'd have no arguments.

As far as his feelings toward Valerie went, he had good days and bad. She got her first tattoo, a tribal armband on her upper right arm, and it was damned hot. Now that she was toned and tight, the tattoo accentuated the curve on her slender arm. He caught himself looking at it more than he should when they were onstage. They were playing another show with Last Five Seconds headlining, and Ethan was more blitzed than usual. He'd managed to hold it together for the show but was wasted by the time they had to unload. Brad almost hated giving the guy his fair share of the money, because he knew where it went. But he had to remind himself of the same thing he always told Val—Ethan, no one else, had to decide he was done.

As they cleared their equipment off the stage, Val tried to talk Ethan into resting in the van. She was holding his arm, begging him to listen to reason. "Val, stop acting like my mom. Jesus Christ, this shit gets old."

Brad couldn't hear Val's response as he walked past them, but he was ready to tell them to pull their weight. Zane bumped Ethan on the head "accidentally" with a cymbal, and Ethan growled at him but didn't do anything in retaliation. Instead, he told Val, "I'm not laying down in the van, and that's final." And then he walked off to hang somewhere in the crowd.

Once they'd loaded all their equipment, Val stopped Brad before he could head back inside. She asked, "Brad, should we find Ethan and try to talk some sense into him?"

He loved this girl, but she was like a broken record. "He's a big boy, Val. He makes his own choices, no matter how fucking stupid they are. So you track him down in the crowd. *Then* what? You make a scene, telling him he's too jacked to be out there? That'll go over well. Yeah, why don't you guys have another obnoxious fight like you always do, but this time why don't you do it in front of the whole crowd? That'll win 'em over and make 'em fans for life."

Oh, shit. He hadn't meant to let that all slip out. He'd been holding in too much for too long, and it just flooded out of his mouth. She nodded and he couldn't quite read the look on her face—it might have been one of shame or upset or partial anger. But she said, "Okay," and looked down, walking back inside.

If it would actually sink in with her, it would have been worth causing the pained look on her face.

The band spent Thanksgiving in Denver, but Brad didn't book any shows right around Christmas, insisting they needed to spend time with family. They were back before the new year, though, both because of his and Val's jobs and scheduled gigs. Still, they had three days with their families, and they came back recharged and refreshed.

Jo called him once in a while, usually about once a month, and she learned quickly that Thursdays through Sundays were bad days. She hadn't known until she'd tried to get him to come to her place on a Saturday night that he was in a band, so she asked him to bring a guitar the next time and play something for her. He wasn't sure why chicks dug that, but they did. And he couldn't resist another opportunity to make her go crazy.

Sex with her was insane and unbelievable. Brad also knew it was unsustainable, particularly because she supposedly had a boyfriend, but the way she rocked his world was dangerous. It was way too intense. He never would have thought that would seem like a problem, and it wasn't, but he didn't know that he would have been able to do it long term.

Ethan was cheating on Val, and Brad was sure she was in denial for the most part. He wasn't going to educate her and rub her nose in it. Like Ethan choosing to admit he had a problem, Val too needed to see that she and Ethan were dysfunctional as fuck. It was absolutely insane. Brad wouldn't have expected that, but Val allowed herself to get sucked into Ethan's toxic world, and she just played into it. Brad wouldn't have expected it from Ethan, either, because even though the guy was a hothead on occasion, he'd never had a bickering relationship with a woman. Even with Heidi, the girl he'd been with longest pre-Val, he'd get pissed at her, and the girl would bat her eyelashes at Ethan, and he'd let it go, focusing his anger on someone or something else, not always the true target of his fury.

With Val, though, he fought and argued and yelled, and that was when Brad realized that Ethan really did love the girl. It was a poisonous, unhealthy relationship, but Ethan did care about her in some weird, warped way.

He just had no fucking clue how to treat her right.

Brad knew the drugs were partly to blame. He'd get so hammered, he wouldn't even know where he was. Brad knew the shit Ethan took removed all his friend's inhibitions and any moral leanings he might have had.

And it killed him to see Ethan break Val's heart, but it wasn't his place to step in, and he wasn't going to. He'd had his heart crushed by the two of them enough—no fucking way was he getting in the middle.

It just hurt seeing her get slapped in the face with the undeniable truth. They'd played a great show at one place in January, and Ethan had barely made it through. At the end, he could barely walk himself offstage and he almost passed out. Nick helped Brad get him out to the van.

Brad hadn't been there to witness it, but Nick told him that Ethan later made his way back inside and found a girl willing to suck him off in the bathroom. Val had gone to check on Ethan in the van to make sure he was okay. When she didn't find him there, she looked everywhere else she could think of, and somehow she'd figured out where he was and caught him in the middle of the act.

Brad didn't know until the show was over. They looked all over for Val and couldn't find her, and that was when Nick told him. He hoped that didn't mean Val had decided to do something equally stupid. They decided to check the van and she was there. Brad could tell she'd been crying—her face was red and puffy and she talked like she had a cold. "We've been looking for you everywhere."

She shrugged. "Sorry."

"You okay?"

She nodded. She didn't want to say anything else. God, he wanted to take her in his arms and hold her, let her cry as much as she needed to, but he couldn't. It wasn't his place and—more than that—he knew it would make him a doormat. No way was he going to do that.

He heard Val and Ethan having a long talk the next day in her bedroom, and he was sure it was over. He also heard Ethan do something he'd never *ever* done with anyone ever before.

He heard him tell Val he was sorry.

Ethan even admitted he was wrong.

That alone knocked Brad down. His friend rarely admitted he was in the wrong and, even when he did, he didn't apologize for it. It was another sign for Brad that his friend really did love Val. He just had no fucking clue how to treat her.

And so it didn't surprise him when they stayed together. Their relationship even seemed stronger after that.

For a while anyway…until it didn't.

CHAPTER THIRTY-SEVEN

SOMETIME IN FEBRUARY, Jo tugged on Brad's leash, summoning him for another booty call, and he gladly obliged. They had just finished that evening when there was a loud banging on her door.

She panicked. "Don't say a word."

Brad gave her a look and, as she scrambled out of bed and threw on a thin red robe that barely covered her ass, it dawned on him.

The boyfriend.

She closed the bedroom door, but he heard the front door open at almost the same time, which meant the boyfriend also had a key. Holy shit. He was fucked. Even if he got dressed at this point, he was in her goddamned bedroom—he couldn't really act innocent there, could he? Still…if he had to fight for his life and bail, it would be easier with his clothes on. For once, he'd taken them all off in her bedroom, so he could get dressed while she finagled with the guy.

The dude had a loud bass voice. Brad imagined him as six-foot-five, weighing in at two-hundred and eighty pounds, solid muscle.

"I called you three times, Jo. I need you at work tonight."

"I *am* working, you moron."

"No, I need your ass onstage. Diamond bailed."

"Okay, I'll need a little bit."

Brad couldn't hear what else Jo said, but he'd managed to fasten his jeans by the time the bedroom door burst open. "You a customer, mister?"

So...the guy wasn't six-foot-five, but he *was* a big dude and taller than Brad. He caught Jo behind the man nodding, signaling Brad that answering *yes* would likely save his life. He needed to play it super cool—he knew that much. He grabbed his t-shirt off the floor (wondering if a customer's shirt would really wind up there) and slid it on and said, "Yeah, and I'm thinking this is shitty customer service."

The guy examined Brad. Something inside Brad wanted to challenge him—stand up to him, puff out his chest, take a jab or two if need be, but he mostly just wanted out of there. Jo was never going to be more than sex for him, so fighting over her would have been stupid and senseless. The only part of him that wanted to unleash on this guy was something primal and instinctive and had nothing to do with the girl. He'd remembered her telling him one time that her boyfriend *was* her boss, and from some of the things she'd said since, he gathered she loved the guy, but their relationship was pretty messed up. Sounded like another couple he knew.

"You gettin' smart with me?" Brad ignored him, finding his socks and boots and sitting on the edge of the bed, trying to act pissed off. The guy grabbed Jo by the elbow and took her back out of the room. "You know you're not supposed to bring 'em back here. What the hell's the matter with you?"

He came back in the room, watching Brad finish tying his boot. Brad stood and was just going to try to walk past the guy, but he blocked the door. "I'm afraid there's the matter of payment."

Brad's heart sunk. Yeah, he had cash, but it wasn't slated for a hooker. The man wasn't budging, though, and Brad knew if he didn't cough up some dough, he'd probably wind up paying that money in medical fees. So he glared at the guy and pulled out his wallet. He took out a twenty and handed it to him.

"You fuckin' kiddin' me, pal?"

Brad felt his blood growing hot. He was going to have to dig into the money he was saving for a new tattoo. He grabbed a hundred and prayed that was enough. He had to follow it up with some balls, or the guy would wind up taking all his money. What sucked was he had no idea what a girl like Jo—Sugar, the sexy stripper—would cost. "Look, dude. She gave me a helluva blowjob, okay, but we didn't discuss rates and, frankly, I've had better for less. So take the money and get the fuck out of my way." Brad clenched his jaw and set his brow. He allowed the earlier need to respond to a challenge take over, and he invested in his words. Yeah, it was all a lie. They had fucked like animals, another crazy romp, but he knew that would cost a lot more. He also knew he'd never had a blowjob like the ones

Jo had graced him with. The girl was talented. But the only way out alive, near as he could see it, was by putting on this show.

The guy backed up a little, allowing Brad to pass through, and Brad spotted his jacket. His eyes barely crossed with Jo's, and he thought he could see relief in them. He was glad, because he had, for a moment, started to wonder if this scenario had been her ultimate goal. He didn't think so, though, because he'd been getting "free" sex from her for months by this point. It would have made more sense to do it right from the beginning, so he didn't think she'd set him up. He picked up his jacket without a word, feeling in his pockets for all the things he wouldn't be able to come back for if he'd lost them. As he stepped out the door, he heard the big guy saying to Jo, "That's why you arrange it all at the club and you need to discuss rates first."

The cold air outside helped him get his bearings. He walked to his car, still smarting over losing a chunk of money but grateful that he'd survived. The sex was good…but he liked having all his teeth intact. He decided at that point no more strippers. Jo had proved to be hazardous to his health and finances.

Brad tried to keep his twenty-first birthday in March low key, especially since he had to work that day, but his mother had sent money and Val and the guys made a big deal out of it. They made steak and baked potatoes, followed up with a sheet cake. And, because he could, he went into the liquor store and bought his first twelve-pack of beer.

It inspired him, though, and he told his bandmates that, Saturday after the show, they were going to host a party to celebrate their successes thus far. He was feeling good about his band again. They were making solid music, playing to energetic crowds, molding and jelling and evolving.

And, maybe, if he had a party, he could get to know more people. He worked mostly with guys at his day job and, yeah, he met a few girls at the shows, but he didn't *really* get to know them. He thought a party might afford him the opportunity to meet real women.

Their place was small, so he planned to keep it small and invite the bands they were going to play with as well as any guests the bands wanted to bring, and he told his bandmates to not invite too many people. He also talked with neighbors, explaining that they'd be celebrating his twenty-first birthday and so they might be loud for a while. The neighbors were cool with it, especially since they all wound up being invited. He spent way more money on alcohol than he should have, but he thought, for a change, he was worth it. He wanted to have fun.

The show that Saturday was insane, probably the best one they'd ever had up to that point. The audience was completely plugged into them, and they were on. It had been magic.

He was on a high when they got back to their apartment, and it wasn't long before the place filled up. It was nice to have his neighbors over, because he'd seen some of them in the hall for months. Now they could actually act neighborly. After mingling for a bit, Brad saw Val walking toward the living room. "Hey, Val, come with me for a sec." She smiled and followed him to the kitchen. Along the counter, he had lined up several drinks and filled the sink with a bag of ice. There were plastic cups and cans of beer, enough for everyone there. Brad thought she might be a little upset about something, but she smiled just the same. He picked up a bottle and held it out to her. "I know you're not comfortable drinking, Val, but I bought this with you in mind."

"What?"

"Butterscotch schnapps."

"Why for me?"

"It's smooth. I thought you might want to get a little buzz on. You helped propel us to where we are now."

She grinned. "Why do you want me trashed?"

"I don't. I just want you to feel good…just a little. You deserve it."

"Okay."

He held up the bottle. "One shot, you and me?" She smiled again and nodded, and Brad poured a shot's worth in two cups and handed one to Val. "Bottoms up." As he poured the shot down his throat, he felt grateful for one thing—that, in spite of Ethan's douchebaggery, Brad and Val remained close friends, and he knew, even if just from this act alone, that she trusted him. That meant a lot. She set her cup down and he asked, "How's that feel?"

"Pretty good."

"Okay. Just one more. As tiny as you are, I don't dare let you drink more than that." He even wondered if a second one was a good idea, but he'd go easy on the second one. She wouldn't have to know he wasn't giving her a full shot. He just wanted her to enjoy herself, and he knew alcohol usually relaxed him, so he hoped it would help her too.

When she set her cup down, he said in her ear, "Now…half an hour from now, you don't feel like you've got a buzz on, come back. I'll hook you up." Being that close, he couldn't help himself. He pulled her into an embrace. In just those few moments, he remembered how much he cared about her, how much he wanted her. He had to let it go, though. Friends only. He hoped that was all she got out of the hug, and so he let her go quickly and grabbed another cup to divert her attention. "In the meantime, though…" He placed some ice inside the cup and filled it with water. "Nurse this."

She smiled and said, "Thanks, Brad. See you in a while."

Brad had already seen a stacked blonde getting friendly with Ethan, so he hoped he wouldn't be seeing Val crying later. She looked pissed as she spied Ethan across the way, and he suspected she was going to grow a spine tonight. If she didn't end up in a catfight with the groupie tonight, he'd be surprised.

But he couldn't worry about that. This was *his* damn party, and even though he didn't plan to get laid tonight, he was hoping to lay some groundwork. Things were going pretty well, too. He felt like he was forging strong bonds with a lot of band members—not quite friendships. That wasn't a bad thing, though. Friendships weren't quite what they were, but they were more than just acquaintances. Business relationships and mutual understandings, maybe. And he also talked for a while with several different women. He hadn't gotten any phone numbers yet. He didn't want to seem too eager, and he didn't want to be a dick either. If he went around asking for every girl's number in the place, he'd look desperate and none of the women would want to have anything to do with him either. No, he had to take his time. By the end of the evening, he would choose one and get her number.

When someone found the stereo and turned it up, Brad was counting his blessings, grateful that he'd invited his neighbors to the party. Even if they left later, he hoped the good will he'd earned would prevent them from tattling, would instead have them come back and ask him to turn it down if it came to that.

He was talking with the lead singer of one of the bands they'd played with earlier that evening when, in spite of the volume of the stereo, it felt like the room grew quiet. The guy he was talking to shifted his gaze and got a bit wide eyed. He nodded his head toward the hallway entrance and then said, "Isn't she your vocalist?"

Brad turned around. Sure as shit, Val was standing in the entryway to the kitchen, her shirt off. She covered herself just as he looked over, and then his eyes looked at hers. She was completely out of it. But how? Two shots wouldn't do that.

Would they?

"Sorry, man." He walked away from the singer, setting his cup on the kitchen table as he made his way toward Val. When he got there, he rested his hands on her shoulders and got close. "Val? You okay?"

Her eyes told him she wasn't. He had to get her out of there, away from the gawking eyes in the room. He led her to her bedroom and had her sit on the bed while he glanced around. She had a robe hanging on her closet doorknob, and he draped it over her shoulders. He sat next to her and asked, "What happened?"

She looked up at him and said, "I don't know." She started crying—a waterfall of tears—and he pulled her close, resting her head on his chest, letting her sob. She'd tell him when she was ready. When she was able to get herself under control, she said, "Ethan had this slutty girl with him."

"Yeah, I saw her."

Her breaths were a little jerky. "I feel really weird, Brad."

"Weird how?"

"Like I'm not totally here. It started earlier. I went over to see what was up with him and that girl. They were awfully cozy." Brad was pretty sure he knew what was on Ethan's mind because it often was. He was going to see if he could once again cheat on his girlfriend and get away with it. Brad nodded, though, and let her continue. "So I sat right next to Ethan on the couch, and he kissed me. It was strange. Not just a little kiss—a huge display. I'm surprised he didn't start grabbing my boobs. And then he introduced me to that girl, and she started squeezing my thigh and playing with my hair, telling me she *really* liked me. It was kinda creepy. And right after that, it was like everything was turning black. Everything looked fuzzy, kind of surreal. I felt like I wasn't totally in my body. Things around the room were starting to move, things that shouldn't have. You know, like that Eiffel Tower print in the living room. And then—" She started crying again. He knew she'd let it out eventually, so he just continued to hold her, hoping he was giving her the comfort she needed. She started talking again, through the sobs, and he couldn't understand the first few words that came out of her mouth until she said, "—into the bedroom, and I was so out of it. Then the next thing I remember, my shirt's off and they're both all over me, you know, wanting me to…"

Brad got it. They were trying to get her involved in a threesome, and Val was in no shape for it to be consensual. "It's okay, Val. You're here." He let her cry more, letting her wind down. It seemed to be what she needed.

But then her voice was stronger than it had been. "Brad, what the hell kind of proof is that schnapps?"

"What? Why?"

"Because…it wasn't real, Brad. It was so weird, so dark, so fuzzy. I didn't have full control of myself." She gasped and started sobbing again. "Oh, my God. What if I'm allergic to schnapps?" If Brad hadn't been so worried, he might have laughed. He'd never heard of anyone being allergic to liquor before, but he supposed anything was possible. "What if I die? What will my mom and dad think?"

And then it dawned on Brad. It wasn't alcohol. Hell, no. Yeah, it might have loosened her up, maybe even caused her to black some things out, but it wouldn't make her feel like she was out of her body or hallucinating. The truth of it finally hit him…and he was *pissed*. "What'd Ethan give you?"

"Nothing."

Maybe nothing that she knew about. It would have been easy enough to slip it in a drink. "Bullshit." He stood up. He didn't want to leave her, not in this fragile state, but he needed answers. He leaned over. "You okay here by yourself?"

"What are you gonna do?"

"Find out what the fuck he slipped you."

"He didn't..." But he saw a look cross her face as she accepted that it must be true. He rose again and stomped through the door. He couldn't even think straight anymore. He walked to the other bedroom. The door was closed, so he was certain Ethan and that girl remained in there.

He threw the door open, and it wasn't until the light flooded in that he realized Val was right behind him. As his eyes adjusted to the semi-darkness, he realized that Ethan and the girl were, in fact, still in the room, and Ethan was giving it to her doggy style on the bed. He looked like the epitome of the drugged, crazed, out-of-his-mind rock star. His t-shirt was on, and he was holding a bottle of vodka. His free hand gripped the blonde girl about her waist. At least he had the decency to stop and look at Brad and Val. At first, Brad had thought he was going to have to slap him to get his attention.

The bimbo on the bed said, a whine in her voice, "Fuck me. God, why won't you just fuck me?"

It was all Brad could do to not pull him off the bed and start beating the shit out of him. But he wanted answers, not blood. Ethan continued eyeing him with that dull stare, so Brad got a little closer and asked through gritted teeth, "What the fuck did you give her, Ethan?" Ethan raised his eyebrows but looked stupid and senseless. Brad took a deep breath, feeling more anger surge through his veins. He leaned over so he could get closer to Ethan, and his voice was low. "Goddammit. Answer me, man, or I'll beat it out of you."

The bimbo looked up at Brad, a tearful look on her face,

and then she looked at Val and burst out laughing. "She's tripping. Don't you feel great, sweetie?"

That confirmed his suspicion. "Acid?"

The dull look on Ethan's face continued stoking Brad's anger, and his stupid answer didn't help. "I guess."

The bimbo piped in again. "Yeah. Now would you please either get out of here or help him fuck me?"

Brad felt like he was going to grind his teeth out of his head. He was ready to toss the blonde out the door. He got close to Ethan again. "What the fuck is wrong with you, Ethan?" The same thick look was Ethan's only response. "I should beat you anyway, just on general principle."

Ethan raised the arm that had been holding the girl in position out in a Jesus Christ pose, inviting Brad to pummel him into pulp. Brad was at a crossroads. As angry as he felt, he was afraid if he got started, he wouldn't be able to stop. He'd held back so much anger for his friend for so long that letting it out at this point could prove dangerous.

Val got right next to him, and he was amazed at how much clarity her presence gave him. Before he could say a word, Val stuck her finger out and held it inches away from Ethan's nose. Her voice was stronger than it had been since the beginning of the episode and she said, clear as day, "We are *over*, Ethan Richards."

"Babe—"

"Go fuck yourself." Inside, Brad felt a weight lift. He'd never seen Val stand up to Ethan like that before. He knew she did and often, because the two of them were constantly bickering, but for her to cut him off like that…that took balls. He was proud of her.

At that point, he didn't feel like beating Ethan anymore, because Val was taking care of it. She pulled the robe back over her shoulder and turned on her heel, leaving the room before Ethan could say another word. He backed away, tempted to shake his head, but he instead just turned too and closed the door. And, as he followed Val back to her room, he thought about it. He was pretty sure Ethan was finishing up what he'd started with the blonde girl, in spite of (or maybe because of) Val giving him walking papers.

In the meantime, Val was crying again and she needed him. He wasn't going to let her down.

CHAPTER THIRTY-EIGHT

VAL FELL ASLEEP in Brad's arms that night. He'd always dreamed about that moment, but it certainly wasn't the way he'd envisioned it or even wanted it.

And he was worried too. Brad had never taken LSD, never planned to. It sounded way too freaky. He didn't ever want to lose that much control. He was anxious about leaving her alone. He'd have to for a bit, though. So, after he was sure she was in a restful sleep, he left her room and closed the door. A few people had left but not many. He looked for Nick, because Nick was someone he trusted, but Nick was nowhere to be found. Scoring again, no doubt. He found Zane in the kitchen, doing shots. He told him Val was fucked up, and he was afraid to leave her alone. Zane raised an eyebrow, reminding him of why he hadn't wanted to tell Zane in the first place. "No, we are *not* doing anything you need to be worried about. She is completely fucked up, and I'm pretty sure Ethan or that bimbo with him slipped some acid in her drink. I'm going to be with her. If you need something, come get me, but, otherwise, do you mind running the show?"

Zane grinned. "Want me to just get rid of people?"

He shook his head. "Nah. Not fair to them." He made his way back to the hallway and considered telling some of his guests *goodbye* but thought better of it. He didn't want them feeling like they had to leave.

He stood outside Val's door. Yeah—happy fuckin' birthday.

Still, he wouldn't have had it any other way. He was glad he'd been the one to find her.

He went back in her room. She was restless—mumbling in her sleep, tossing, whimpering. He pulled her to his chest and held her close, and she seemed to relax then. He lay there, running his hand over her hair, talking quietly to her on occasion, half expecting Ethan to come in at some point. Much later, the party died down, and when it finally got really quiet, Brad felt himself getting sleepy. But he wasn't going to leave her.

Much later but before it got light outside, she startled awake, muttering something about some wild animal in the bedroom ready to pounce. It took him a little time to convince her everything was okay. She rolled on her side, and he wrapped his arm around her. He wanted to protect her for the rest of her life, and he was angry that she'd had to deal with such seediness.

When she woke up the next morning, her motion in the twin bed awakened him too. He was exhausted. He sat up. "How you feeling?"

She shrugged. "A little strange, I guess. Still kind of out of it." She rolled her neck. "Pretty pissed."

He nodded. "Understandable. You gonna be okay now?"

She looked at him, a small smile on her face. "Yeah. Thanks for making sure I was okay, Brad."

"I was worried about you."

"I appreciate it." She stood. "I think I really need a shower." He had so much he wanted to say to her…but he somehow knew that now was not the time. It was too early, too fresh, and he wasn't ready. He knew she wasn't either.

He wanted to get more sleep and that had been the plan…until he saw all the people sleeping on the living room floor. Well, a party had been a stupid idea. He wouldn't do *that* again. He decided to make coffee and clean the kitchen. It was trashed. Making noise might get the people up and at 'em, and then he could take a nap later if he needed to.

While he cleaned the kitchen, he heard Val in the shower singing. She was belting a song they'd written last summer, one called "Let You Go." He knew why. It was about ending a toxic relationship. Maybe she was thinking along those lines. That was his hope.

But as the week progressed, he saw that Val and Ethan hadn't broken up any more than the oceans had evaporated. Ethan was on his best behavior, yeah, but they were together. Either Val had forgotten she'd broken up with him or she'd forgiven him. Either way, they were back at it, and even though Ethan was behaving himself, Brad knew it was just a matter of time before they started fighting again. They were just one of those couples. And they'd make everyone around them miserable.

Brad decided he had to talk to his friend about it. He couldn't sit back anymore, so he asked Ethan out for dinner one night when Val had to work. He didn't want her—or the other guys—to see it. If Ethan chose to tell her after the fact, fine, but for now, Ethan was his to deal with.

Ethan knew something was up but found it difficult to turn down a free meal at Wendy's. They got their food and sat down and Brad figured he shouldn't pussyfoot around. "I know you know something's up, so I'm just going to get it off my chest."

Ethan shrugged. "Okay." Ethan had been in one of his phases where he was high more often than not, but he was lucid right now. Brad was grateful, because nothing he had to say would matter if Ethan's head was shoved up his ass.

"You know Val loves you, right?"

Ethan could barely hide what he was thinking. He was irritated. "Yeah." Brad wasn't sure exactly how to word what he wanted to say next, and before he could speak, Ethan started talking. "You think it's one-sided?"

That took the wind out of his sails. Yeah, he had, actually. He'd assumed all along that Ethan was playing with Valerie, enjoying pulling her strings, especially because of the way the guy had treated her early on. Brad had never considered that Ethan might really care for her. He knew that on some superficial level Ethan cared, but he didn't think it ran that deep. "Is it?"

Ethan put his burger down and took a sip of his drink. Then he took a deep breath and looked Brad in the eyes. He shook his head. "I care about her. I—love her. I can see it in your eyes. You don't think so, and I really don't give a shit what you think. But you need to know she's important to me."

Brad nodded. He had to rethink the discussion. He'd planned to tell Ethan to treat her well because she loved him and he needed to try to reciprocate; instead, if his friend really did love Val, then maybe he could reason with him. "That's good, man. I'm glad to hear it. Just…your actions don't always show it."

After a long moment of silence, Ethan nodded. "I know." He shrugged and took another sip of his drink. "I know. But I also know I'd be worse without her."

"You think?"

"I guarantee." And that was when Brad decided to back off entirely. He'd had no idea. If they loved each other, he wasn't going to get in the way, and he wasn't going to fuck things up. But one thing that worried Brad—if Ethan would be worse without Val in his life, what the fuck would he have been like? The thought scared the shit out of Brad and made him fear for his friend's well being. Val had a lot riding on her shoulders, and Brad doubted she had any clue.

As spring marched forward, things around their apartment seemed smoother. Brad didn't know why—maybe Ethan was trying harder or he and Val had learned to get along better. He had no idea, but it was a welcome relief.

Jo called again, apologizing to Brad for what happened the last time, and told him she was dying to see him. He tried to be as gentle as possible but told her he thought her boyfriend would flat-out kill him if he caught him with Jo again. It was a risk he wasn't willing to take.

One thing Jo *had* taught him, though, was to not go so

long without a woman in his life. So, now that he was of legal drinking age (and none of his fellow band members were yet), he made it a point to go out one night a week and have a beer. By himself. And half the time he got lucky. There were no strings, nothing permanent, but he discovered that there were a lot of girls out there feeling just as lonely as he was, and even a quick connection was better than languishing. He had to get his head on straight, and one way was to stop denying his sexual urges. Sure, he could have had groupies constantly. They weren't a huge band, but they already had their fair share of girls who loved the idea of rock stars. Still, he didn't want to go there. Ethan, Nick, and Zane had no issues with it, but Brad hesitated. He felt like it was shitting where he ate.

Jet called Brad one day and told him he'd read a review of a recent Fully Automatic concert. Brad looked it up on the internet but found that the review was only available in the hard copy. He asked if anyone wanted to go with him to check it out, and Val and Zane took him up on the offer. So they got in the van and drove to a nearby Chipotle. The restaurant wasn't open yet, so they sat in the van for a while talking, waiting for the doors to open.

The paper was free. They all got drinks and then huddled around a table, each of them with a copy, leafing through the paper. Val examined each page, afraid she'd miss it, but Zane was zipping through and said, "Found it. Page forty-four." Brad and Val flipped through their papers until they found that page.

Brad noticed the picture first. It was a typical newspaper photo, black and white and pixely. But it was cool—it was the first time his band was mentioned in the press. He stared at it for a while, taking it in. He'd seen a couple of fan-recorded videos on YouTube, but they hadn't prepared him for this.

He slowly took it in, paragraph by paragraph. At first, he couldn't tell if the reviewer liked the band, because he was using words that could be either positive or negative, depending on the context. Descriptions like *gritty* and *unpolished* could be good or bad. But before he could find that context, Val said, "Oh, God…I can't read anymore." Well, that made him think the review wasn't good.

Zane started reading out loud, so Brad searched the text to try to find where he was reading from. "At first, Quinn seemed to be holding back. By mid-show, however, her vocals were strong. Her style alternates between singing and screaming, and she can hold her own doing either. By the third song, Quinn had the audience eating out of her hand, whipping them into a headbanging frenzy."

He continued and Brad gave up trying to find where he was in the paper. He talked about how talented Nick was—his performance was grueling, almost painful to watch, but he was precise, and he said a tiny blip about Zane too. He talked about Ethan, stating the guy was talented as hell but didn't seem to be present. Well, that was no surprise to the band members. He mentioned some of their songs too, and Brad started to think maybe this guy was becoming a fan. He felt relief.

Zane kept reading. "However, the best part of the show was guitarist Brad Payne. Payne showed precision beyond his years, whether he was involved in brutal shredding or impressing the audience with masterful melodies. His energy seemed to be one of the driving forces of the band too." Zane kept reading and, while Brad was grateful that the guy had liked him, he was also a little embarrassed that the rest of the band hadn't been on the receiving end of more praise. And he didn't quite believe it, either. He knew they had a long way to go to be perfect.

Zane looked at him, nodding and smiling. Brad shook his head.

Val said, "Brad, you should be proud. Everything he said about you is true."

He looked down. "Not everyone in the band is going to be as enthusiastic as you, Val." Ethan would likely be pissed. He'd hardly gotten a mention, and it hadn't exactly been a compliment.

"Yeah, well, he needs to get the fuck over it. It didn't say anything bad about him, and you deserve every word the article said." Val smiled and rested her hand on his. "I'm proud of you and glad to be your friend." He smiled. What could he say that wouldn't sound asinine? She turned her attention to Zane and he was relieved. "And you too, Zane."

"Yeah, but the article didn't gush about me like it did Mr. Guitar Man. I know. I get it. Guy who plays bass is the low man on the metal totem pole." He started laughing. "At least it doesn't affect how much pussy I get."

Val said, "Yeah. God forbid."

Brad cleared his throat. More than anything else, he didn't want the praise getting to anyone's head, especially his own. Until they were signed, a review didn't mean shit. It might bring a bigger audience, though, so he wasn't going to sneeze at it. "Let's get the fuck out of here and let the guys know. This is just one of many things that will help us get recognized. No time to rest on our laurels, ladies."

And he meant it. Until success was in their hands, there was no time to rest.

CHAPTER THIRTY-NINE

A COUPLE OF days after the review, Jet called Brad again with a proposition. "Hey, dude, we've set up a couple of shows out of state, and we were thinking about going balls out—invite a couple of other bands, make a huge show. You know, we could contact lots of venues close together but get exposure to people who've never seen us before."

"When are you thinking?"

"We already have a couple shows booked for late spring, so we're gonna see what we can come up with. But before we start booking shows, we want two solid bands with us. I'm pretty sure Spanky's Kids is on board. You play with them before?"

"No, but I've heard they kick ass."

"That they do. And they have a huge following—probably more people than you and me combined. What's your schedule look like?"

They discussed particulars, and Brad was stoked. He loved Denver crowds, but expanding their audience could only help them.

When he told the band, they too thought it was a great idea. Of course, the questions started. He tried to remind them of the times—not even a year earlier—when they would do weekend shows on the road. This would be the same, only it would be longer. The best part was that Brad wouldn't have to book any of the shows.

He wound up pitching in, though, and all three of the bands on board did a little asking around. Brad wound up securing one venue on his own. When all was said and done, they had nine new venues spread out over fourteen days. As soon as Jet had told him about it, Brad asked his boss if he could have the time off. The guy had been really accommodating, and all Brad could figure was it was because he'd never missed a day of work. He'd asked for time off, but he'd never called in. Not once. Yeah, he hadn't even been there a year, but turnover for the place was pretty high and, of the employees who stayed a month or two, attendance wasn't always the best either. When Brad thought about it, he was surprised too. In just eight months, he was the senior employee, aside from his boss.

When the dates were solidified, Brad also told Val to ask for the time off. Her place of employment wasn't quite so understanding, though, and told her that her job might not be waiting for her upon her return. Val decided that, even though she found it distressing, she was going to do the tour anyway. Her future wasn't in sandwiches. It was in music. She could get another sandwich-making job when she got back if she had to. Brad even offered to bring her back during the part of the tour where they had a couple of days off in the middle. Fortunately, she saw the foolishness of it and told him she'd get another job if her boss decided not to take her back.

In preparation, they worked on a couple of new songs and switched up their set list. They were going to debut the new songs on the road. They'd make them perfect and then share them with their old fans back home.

And, just in time for their road trip, Ethan and Val began bickering again. Oh, they were quiet and contained about it at first, but it was there just the same. If they got vocal or out of hand, Brad was going to have to say something. Nick and Zane never complained about it, but he could see on their faces that they hated it as much as he did. It was stressful. When he'd been making their accommodation arrangements, he told them they'd be sharing a room and the three guys the other—a small shift in what they used to do, but that would give the three other guys a break. Still two rooms among them, but it would feel a little roomier.

All three bands met at Village Inn a few days before the tour started to iron out the last few final details, and Ethan made a huge display. He was obviously on something, and he was all over Val. She let him, but his friend was acting possessive and alpha for no good reason. It was ridiculous and embarrassing. All Brad could figure was it was because Ethan was trying to send a signal to all the guys on tour that Val was his. Brad could halfway understand it. Val was beautiful *and* hot, and she was the only woman in their baker's dozen. Ethan felt the need to let the other men know she was his and they'd better not lay a finger on her.

Still…he could have been more subtle about it. Instead, when they continued talking out in the parking lot, Ethan pushed Val up against the van and let her have it full on. Jesus. It was awkward and uncomfortable. If he started feeling her up or some shit, Brad was going to have to step in. Ethan stopped just short of it. And instead of saying anything, Brad took a deep breath and continued talking to the other people in their group, trying to ignore Ethan's territorial display.

Once they got on the road, though, he grew excited. New audiences, more fans, new sights. Brad planned to do all the driving for his band. They would only be driving during the day and, other than the first day, it didn't seem like they'd be on the road more than six hours at a time, so he knew he could do it. When it came to the van, he was a bit of a control freak. Hell, he was a control freak about everything, because he felt like he could ultimately only trust himself. It had paid off thus far. He didn't think it bothered any of his bandmates for the most part—sure, some of them bitched once in a while (like when he organized duties at their apartment), but they got over it. He decided if he got super tired, he'd ask Val if she wanted to drive, but she was the only one he'd trust to do it.

It was just two days into the tour, and Brad sensed a weird shift in the dynamics of the group. He wasn't sure exactly what was going on, but he knew something huge was happening between Ethan and Val. Neither of them said a word, but by day three, they weren't talking to or looking at each other—and yet Val looked like she was having a hard time not smiling.

Maybe that meant that she'd finally told Ethan goodbye for good. But the last time she'd done it, she'd been miserable until they'd gotten back together. Something serious and heavy was going on, but he didn't want to get in the middle of it, so he wasn't going to ask. As long as the band was functioning okay, he'd keep his nose out of everyone else's business. And, if he knew Ethan and Val as well as he thought he did, he'd find out soon enough.

Turned out he was right. Ethan was angrier than usual but didn't say a word. He knew it was because, when it came to Val, the guy didn't trust Brad. Maybe he'd had every reason not to a year earlier, but in the present, he had nothing to worry about. Brad had made a promise, and he wasn't about to break it.

He started putting two and two together, though. First, Ethan started sleeping in the room with the other three guys, confirming the split. But then Brad noticed that Val and Jet were hanging together—*a lot*. And when Jet draped his arm over Val's shoulder after one of the shows and whispered in her ear, Brad thought he'd figured it out.

It was a little disheartening. Brad was glad Val had managed to escape the toxic hold Ethan had over her, but she'd jumped right into another relationship. He knew Jet might just be rebound guy, but it bothered him. Still…he and Jet had always gotten along. Jet was a good guy. A bit of a party animal, but he respected the hell out of the guy, and if Val kept smiling like she was, he guessed he'd find a way to live with it.

Val confirmed his suspicions not long after he'd figured it out. One night, they were loading up their equipment after another great but exhausting show, and she pulled him aside when they'd finished. Whatever it was, it was making her nervous, so he tried to look calm. "We're spending money on an extra room, but I'm not using it. Well…I'm using it to put on makeup and get dressed, but that's it."

He didn't want to jump to conclusions, even though he was pretty sure he knew what she was saying. "Why? What's wrong with it?"

She blinked and said, "Nothing. I've just...been spending the night in someone else's room. And I figured we were wasting money. You can either just not get it, or one of you guys can share it with me."

Even though he'd known, the admission felt like a wrecking ball to the chest. He forced air into his lungs and hoped his expression was as neutral as he was aiming for. He tried to sound casual and upbeat. The truth was the rooms were already reserved, so he figured they were stuck with them. "That makes it mine now, and I'm kinda glad. It was hard enough sharing a room with two other guys, and now we're back to four in a room...well, mostly." Since she'd broached the subject, he had to know for certain. "So...you and Jet...pretty serious?"

She blinked again and then shrugged. "For now, I guess."

He nodded. "Come here." He put his arms around her. He needed to hide his face from her. They were close friends, but he loved her. He fucking loved her, and it was hitting him fast and hard. He needed a few seconds to pull his shit together. "You know I'm always here for you, right?"

"Yeah. Same here." He had to let her go or she'd figure out things weren't right with him. So he did and then she asked, "It's okay if I leave my stuff in your room, right? And if I dress and all that stuff, but the bed's yours?"

So...she was sleeping with Jet but leaving her shit in

another room? That didn't make sense. So he wouldn't be able to just ignore it. He'd be reminded of it constantly. But what the hell else could he say? So he said the only thing he could. "Yeah, we'll make it work."

All their conversation had done, though, was open a wound he thought had healed. No, it had just scabbed over, and Val had ripped it back open. It was raw and painful again, and Brad felt like breathing was an effort. He had to do something to get her off his mind. He wasn't going to survive if he couldn't find a way to let her go for good.

A few nights later, several band members were partying together again, and a few fans had joined them. A gorgeous brunette was flirting with him, telling him how much she loved the band, the show, and especially Brad himself. She kept touching him and leaning in to whisper in his ear, and he decided maybe *she* could get his mind off Valerie.

He barely saw Val anymore. He saw her during shows and while they drove from one venue to the next, but her free time she was spending with Jet. He couldn't blame her, he supposed. She was infatuated with the guy. He made her feel loved and wanted, and he suspected that he gave Val everything in him, unlike Ethan. Even when Ethan was faithful with Val, he kept a part of himself closed off. Brad understood why, but that didn't make it easy for Val to accept.

Yeah…the girl named Brittany touching his arm. She would be a one-night thing, but it would be a good first step. Awesome sex managed to alter the course of his thoughts enough that he knew it would at least make the whole *I love Val* revelation a little less fresh. So when she asked, "How many girls ask you for a private concert?" he took that as his opening.

"I think you're the first."

She bit her bottom lip and then smiled. "Well…?"

He shrugged. "Come on." He crushed the empty beer can and tossed it in the trash on his way out. He was glad no one commented on the fact that he was leaving with a girl, but he wasn't going to act all cute about it. He put his arm around her shoulders. She wanted to feel special for the night with him; he would give that to her.

He led her out to the van and unlocked the trailer, pulling out his guitar case. She could only see what the parking lot lights illuminated inside, but she could tell it was full. "Holy crap. You guys have a lot of stuff."

"I guess people don't realize what all goes into making music. It's more than just a guitar."

"Yeah, I guess you're right."

They walked up to his room, the one that was only his…and the place where Val stored her luggage. He'd felt a little guilty at first for having an entire room to himself, but he justified it in his mind. He was, for all intents and purposes, not just their guitar player; he was also their manager. He deserved to be spoiled a little once in a while. And, as he led this beautiful girl into that room that was only his, he was glad he'd decided to be selfish. Nick—hell, even Zane and Ethan—might not care if they found a girl who didn't mind fucking in front of other people, but Brad wanted a little more privacy…and he wanted to be with a girl who didn't feel the need to be an exhibitionist.

When they got to his room, Brad invited her to sit on

one of the beds. On the other, he laid his guitar case down, opened the snaps, and pulled out his newest baby. He'd bought it for himself for his birthday—a beautiful work of art, tight and cherry-colored, and she had the loveliest tones. He'd fallen in the love with her the first time he played her, and she made playing onstage a treat.

He knew too that girls got off on guys playing their guitars. He couldn't quite understand why, but he wasn't going to question it, especially not now. He sat next to her on the other bed and started strumming a song no one else had ever heard. Without an amp, he couldn't really give her the "concert" she was wanting, but the song he was playing—one he'd written about Val—was one that sounded better on an acoustic, and an unplugged electric mimicked (although poorly) the sounds of an acoustic. Still, it didn't do the song justice.

That didn't matter, though. He looked up at her and he thought his jaw would hit the floor. She really *was* getting turned on by it. She was rubbing the back of her neck and fluttering her eyes, acting hot and bothered. He wanted to throw the guitar down and start fucking her, but he wasn't going to. He was going to keep playing until she either asked him to stop or he couldn't take it anymore. It was definitely a turn on.

He could have sung to the song too, but he didn't want to break the mood. Even if the song hadn't been mournful and sappy (and probably what Valerie would describe as *generic*), the words would have pushed her away. They were about his pining for another woman. He doubted that would keep her aroused.

When the song was almost over, she said, "Kiss me."

That was all he needed to hear. He slid the guitar off his lap and onto the bed and placed his hands on her cheeks. Oh, she tasted sweet, and Brad didn't know if it was because he'd once again waited too long. She raked her hands down his chest but then he realized her hands were no longer on him. She was unbuttoning her blouse.

Holy fuck, it was gonna happen fast. Yeah, that was what he needed. A girl who wanted to call the shots. He decided he'd kiss her until she was ready for him to take over.

Only it never happened. She took her bra off next and, before Brad could even touch her, she was feeling herself, moaning into his mouth. Okay...still a turn on, but he wondered when he'd be able to step in. Then she stood, leaving Brad sitting on the bed with his cock straining against his jeans, and she kicked her shoes off. Next she peeled her tight little red vinyl pants off, followed by tiny little thong panties. She flashed a seductive smile at Brad and crawled up on the bed, but she did it beside the guitar. He turned more on the bed to look at her. She brushed the headstock with her hand and then slid her palm underneath, lifting the guitar up at an angle, its body resting on the bed. She lifted the headstock close to her face and then started licking a tuning peg. Goddamn. He had no idea why he was finding this so hot, but he was. This chick was fucking making out with his guitar, and it was insane the way his body was reacting.

She wasn't done, though, and Brad wasn't sure if she wanted him to take over or just watch. He was mesmerized. Brittany slid the guitar further down the bed and then lay down, her head resting on one of the pillows.

She lifted a leg so that the shaft of the guitar was between her thighs, and she rested a foot on the body. Part of him wanted to tell her to stop, because he was afraid she might hurt his guitar, but he was frozen. He was wired too, so close to losing his load, it wasn't even funny.

She wrapped one hand around the fretboard, lifted her foot off the guitar body, and brought the headstock to her pussy. Her legs were spread wide, and she bent her knees and tilted her pelvis to meet the very top of the headstock with its smooth, curved, polished wood, and she rubbed it against herself. She moaned and then shoved a finger in her mouth, biting down. She kept rubbing his guitar up and down her slit, and she got louder as she did it. She slid her hand down her neck and chest to play with a nipple and Brad was entranced. He couldn't move. All he could register was that he was more aroused than he'd been in ages and it was almost painful. She rubbed one more time and gasped again, then lay the guitar down and let her fingers take over. She cried in ecstasy while Brad sat there and watched in agony.

Could he jump in now? Would she even let him? He wasn't sure what move he should make.

Fuck it. His cock told him to try. Unlike Brittany, though, he felt his guitar was precious, and he gently lifted it off the bed and laid it on the other one. Then he pulled off his shirt and lay next to her. Her eyes were closed and she looked peaceful, and he almost didn't want to disturb her. He rested a hand on one of her breasts and brought his lips to hers, giving her a soft kiss.

"No, no," she said, pushing against him with her hand. "That was perfect."

How'd he manage to pick them? She kept shoving him hard, though, and then she forced him down on the bed. By the time he felt her hands on the waistband of his jeans, he was sure he was going to explode. He didn't, though. Then she pulled his underwear down and spat on her hand, taking his cock in her fist and massaging it vigorously. If he hadn't been so aroused and so close to the edge, he would have had trouble, because she was aggressive—too aggressive. But it wasn't even a minute and he let it go, a burst of pleasure exploding in his mind and making him forget everything else—five glorious seconds of nothing but happiness, and he was going to ride that wave.

CHAPTER FORTY

AFTER BRITTANY FELL asleep, Brad cleaned his guitar with a damp washcloth. He had no problems with bodily fluids, but he did know that guitars had to be treated with respect and love and had to be kept clean, something he did with his religiously. He knew the oils and grime from his fingers weren't good for the finish, so he figured it was better to not take a chance with anything else. He'd never say a word to her about it.

That had to be one of the most bizarre sexual encounters he had ever experienced. Uh, yeah, he got off and so did she, but could it even be considered sex, considering his cock got nowhere near her female parts? Hell, all he'd had to do for her was play his guitar. Weird.

So he lay next to her on the bed and had a hell of a time falling asleep. She hadn't rocked his world like he'd hoped. He needed someone to drive the image of Val out of his mind for good, and he had yet to find the right woman for the job.

He managed to doze off, but he didn't sleep well. He finally got up around seven and turned the TV on. He flipped through channels, finding nothing that grabbed his attention, but he was passing the time. He wanted to sleep but knew it wasn't going to happen.

He started drifting off, though, and that was when he heard his phone go off. He got a text. He picked the phone up off the nightstand and read it. It was Val. She'd been coming over every morning to shower and dress after spending the night with Jet, and she wanted to again. He mulled it over for a few minutes, trying to figure out how to tell her nicely that he didn't want her there.

He decided not to text her back, because he'd taken too long thinking about it. She'd be knocking on the door any minute. So he jumped out of bed and threw on his jeans that were on the floor beside the bed. Then he grabbed the t-shirt he'd thrown on the other bed. He snatched the card key and stepped out the door. Sure enough, Val was already there.

She had a big grin on her face. "Look at you." He frowned, not sure how to ask what he needed to. No matter what hadn't happened between him and Brittany the night before, he wasn't going to have Val traipsing through the room until Brittany was gone. "What?"

He took a deep breath. There was no easy way to say it. "Would it be too big an imposition to ask you to come back in a while?"

She considered it and said, "I'll do you one better. Can you just bring me my suitcase? I think I have everything else I need."

That was cool and had wound up being easier than he'd

expected. "Be right back."

He went in the room, closing the door behind him. Her luggage was next to the dresser, so he picked it up. Jesus. It was heavier than it had a right to be. He stepped back out into the hallway. "What the hell do you have in here, Valerie? Lead?" She laughed. "Seriously…you need me to carry it?"

"No. I've got it. It has an extending handle and wheels."

"Okay." He had to find a way to let her know he appreciated her attitude. "And, uh…thanks."

She grinned again. "So what's gotten into you, Brad?"

He smiled back. Truth—always the truth. "I got needs, Val, just like any other guy."

"I know. Just givin' you shit. You know I respect the hell out of you, right?"

Well, hell. No, he didn't know that. She might have even said it once or twice, but it had never sunk in. He and Val had a solid friendship, but he had never thought of respect before. He was pretty sure the other three guys in their band didn't feel the same way. So he said, "I think that's the nicest thing anyone's ever said to me."

She pulled the handle out of her suitcase and started wheeling it down the hall, away from him. "Well, don't let it get to your head. Get back to your lady friend."

He almost told her the girl in the bed might have been a lot of things, but she was *not* his lady friend. He chose not to. Brittany seemed nice enough.

He went back in the room and managed to get another hour of sleep before she woke up. And when she did, she gave him a real ride that helped erase the strange memories of the night before.

Brad declared the tour a success. They had a few more Facebook fans, but they'd sold lots of merchandise (they'd need to order more t-shirts) and the crowds were wild. It invigorated him, refreshed him, made him want to try twice as hard to push the band to new heights. He wanted to make sure his bandmates felt the same fire burning inside, and so he called a meeting.

He had other things he needed to discuss, and he'd already laid the groundwork, but he had to have them all on board before moving forward. This meeting would tell him what he needed to know—was Fully Automatic fully committed, or did he need to draw up a new game plan?

"Guys, we just finished something huge. Did we make a lot of money? Hell, no. If you're feeling like me, you're tired and can't even begin to settle back in. I'm sorry about that. But I hope that taste makes you hungry again. I feel like we've just kinda been sittin' on our laurels the past few months."

Val nodded, but then he saw a shadow cross her face and she frowned. "In all fairness, Brad, I haven't stopped writing. I'm constantly coming up with new stuff."

"Yeah. I give you that. Hell, we're *all* doing some writing. I don't think that's the hard part." It was time to get down and dirty. He was going to have to say some things people didn't want to hear, but he was tired of feeling like he was carrying the heavy load. It was time to get their attention. "But how many of you are contributing around here?" Ethan acted like he wanted to say something, so Brad wanted to nip it in the bud. "I'm not talking about doing the shit on the chore chart. That just keeps you in. I'm sayin'...how many of *us*—myself included—go around promoting our shows, trying to sell advance tickets? How many of you guys ever even log onto our Facebook page and post to our fans? Did you guys know we actually have over five hundred fans?"

Zane asked, "Fuckin' serious?"

Brad nodded. "Yeah. But we can do better. Val and I are busting our asses earning extra cash for if we need it. Don't want a job? Fine. Then represent us...on Facebook. Get a Twitter account going. Make flyers and pass them out around town. Ethan, you have that fuckin' sick computer and software, and I've seen some of the shit you can do. You should be all over that. But then get the word out there. Talk us up. Find new cool merch for us to sell. That's a steady stream of money, even when we play free gigs. But I can't keep doing it all, guys. I book us the shows. Help me out." There. He'd said it. He'd been feeling like he was the only one trying. He knew it wasn't true, but there was so much the other guys could be doing, and he hoped his words settled in, even if they felt defensive about it at first. He could see in their eyes that they were taking him seriously, taking his words to heart, so he continued. "I'm not saying the music's not important, but if we don't do this other shit, no one will care what we're writing."

Zane added, "We need to record more of our stuff too."

"That we do, so why don't you find a place for us to record on the cheap?"

"On it."

There was one other thing he had to say, and his feelings

had become evident after having his own room on the road for more than a week. "As for our living arrangement...I just can't take this anymore. It's too close, too tight. I feel like I'm constantly on top of one of you motherfuckers. I need some space. This just ain't cuttin' it."

Zane nodded. "Agreed, man, but you know the price of rent. No fuckin' way we'll survive here in separate apartments."

"That's not what I'm saying. You guys know we're on a month-to-month here. I found a three-bedroom apartment. It's more than what we pay here, but I don't give a shit. I can't do this anymore. This new place is also unfurnished, meaning we'll have to buy our own stuff, but these bedrooms will fit twin beds. That means we'll all have a real bed. I need that, guys. I really do."

"Yeah...that'd be nice."

Everyone seemed to be in agreement, so he kept going. "A lot of the shit we'll need we'll have to go to secondhand stores to get or buy some of that cheap-ass assembly stuff at Walmart, but I need this. You guys already got some money from the past two weeks, right? I socked away the rest. We actually made a lot, even after the motels, gas, and food were taken out, and I think it'll get us started. Well, you know what I mean. Not tons, but enough."

Ethan finally spoke. "Do it, man. Do it. You want me to do shit on my computer? If we had a bigger place, I could find a spot to set it up and actually do something."

Brad smiled. "That's the spirit." He made the call and they started packing that day and moved the beginning of the following month. Seeing the solidarity of his friends when they knew he needed it most told him everything he needed to know. Fully Automatic would move forward with their current lineup, and they'd be better than ever.

Before they moved, though, Brad got confirmation that Val and Jet were continuing their relationship past the tour. Hell, Jet even helped with part of the move. He didn't know why he'd expected it to be a fling simply relegated to the tour. Maybe it was because it seemed so intense and consuming while it happened. He'd tried to ignore it, but it was difficult, because every spare moment they'd had on the road Val and Jet had spent together. It seemed too hardcore to last.

And, yet, there was Jet at their door one Thursday night early summer. "Hey, Jet. You here to see Val?"

"Yeah." Brad and Jet had always gotten along. Brad respected the guy's musical abilities—he was a hell of a guitarist. Amazing, in fact, and Brad was surprised their band hadn't already been picked up by a label. Seeing him through Val's eyes made him see the appeal to women too. The guy's tattoos put Brad's to shame. He was inked from shoulder to wrist on both arms, but that wasn't all. He was pierced all over too. He knew Val also had a thing for long hair, and Jet's fit the bill. He just wasn't sure about it all, though. Not only did it bother him that Val had run straight from Ethan into Jet's arms, but he knew Jet was a bit of a playboy. He didn't want the guy breaking her heart. Still, he had to let Val make her own mistakes. He would never say a word to her about what he thought.

Goddamn, he had to let her go. He wasn't going to be able to find his own happiness if he continued mourning the fact that he'd never had her enough to consider her lost to him.

"She was in the shower. Let me see if she's free. Come on in." Before she'd gotten in the shower, she'd acted upset, and now he was putting two and two together. Lovers' spat already? Jet stepped in the door and stood to wait. Brad figured he wouldn't make himself at home, because it had never been a secret that he and Ethan weren't friends. The bathroom was free, so he went to Val's room and knocked on the door.

"Yeah?"

"Val? Jet's here. Did you wanna see him?"

"Yeah, okay."

Brad peeked out of the hallway and motioned for Jet to join him. By the time he made it over, Val opened her bedroom door and she took Jet in her arms. Brad backed away.

And he prayed for strength. Strength to let her go so she could live her life and the will to live his own. He had to find a way.

CHAPTER FORTY-ONE

THE DAYS BEGAN to fly as Brad renewed his goals. He liked lists, and so he made a list of priorities, all leading to the same main goal. The first was to continue booking shows. More than that, though, his focus changed a little. If he had a choice of more than one show (which happened more and more often), he would choose the one that had bands they hadn't played with before (if that was an option). He was constantly looking for new venues too. The point was more exposure, because he figured he'd never know when they'd get noticed by the right person.

The second goal was to keep writing music. He'd noticed that every new song he wrote was better than the last. In fact, the stuff he was writing that summer put the first few songs he'd ever written to shame.

The third goal was to get laid more often. Thoughts of Val continued to linger in his head, and he felt like he was in perpetual grief. It wasn't healthy. He was twenty-one, for fuck's sake, and he should have been having sex every goddamn night of the week. But he wasn't, and that was going to change.

He still didn't over the summer. He found a girl once in a while and made sure he always had condoms at the ready, but he just couldn't get into it. When he would, he'd picture Val in his mind. He knew it was unhealthy, but he didn't know how to let her go.

By fall, he managed to find a girl now and then, but more than that, his feelings for Val were simmering down again. She broke up with Jet, but he wasn't going to allow himself to make a move. Every time he had in the past, he'd gotten his heart crushed. It wasn't going to happen again. So he was going to bury those feelings for her, and the music was key. He poured everything into it—his heart and his soul. It was therapeutic. Sometimes he wrote lyrics too. Sometimes he shared them with the band, but he usually didn't. Most often, he'd keep the words to himself so Val could write her own and make the song hers too. She didn't have to know the song had meant something else to him entirely.

As an extension of his objectives, he kept doing things that real rock stars did. He got tattoos when he felt like it; he kept growing his hair longer (although he had to tie it back in a rubber band for work); and he would go to pawn shops once in a while to buy cool pedals for his guitar to try new sounds.

The best thing, though, was Zane had suggested a studio where they could record a high-quality CD. He checked it out and was impressed. Yeah, Fully Automatic had a CD, but it sounded amateur (which it was), and he knew they needed something that sounded professional. It was going to cost a lot, though, but he didn't know how much. It all depended, first off, on how much time they'd have to spend in the studio recording. What also factored into the cost was how many songs they wanted to record. So, by September, he'd set another goal for himself. He was going to set aside so much money a month until he had enough. Since moving to the bigger place, though, it was going to take longer. At the rate he was going, it would take at least a year to save up enough money—unless, in the meantime, they started earning more with their shows. That didn't seem likely, but he could always hope.

In fact, hope was the one thing that often kept him going when nothing else would.

They had a show in October, one that at first made Brad feel like they'd gone off the rails. It was intense and energetic, far above and beyond anything they'd experienced before, but he didn't like how they'd gotten there.

They were setting up for the show, just like they had hundreds of times before, and he noticed that Val was wearing a trench coat. Yeah, it had been raining earlier and it was cold, but the long coat seemed to be impeding her motion. She'd been acting secretive anyway, so he wondered if she'd gotten a new tattoo or something she was wanting to unveil for the show. He said, "Val, you'd have an easier time with your coat off. Are you still cold?" She just smiled.

Later, though, when they were getting ready to go up onstage to play, Val asked, "This time, would you guys start playing? Then I'll come out after the music starts."

That confirmed his suspicions. She was going to do something but was afraid of sharing it with them beforehand. The fact that she wouldn't tell them made him nervous, like it was something they might hate. Still...he kept his mouth shut. Ethan wasn't going to be quiet, though. "Why?"

"I want to try something new."

"You're not gonna ditch out on us, are you?"

"No, of course not. Just trust me."

Trust her. That was going to be tough. They were getting ready to play his newest song, one called "Primeval," and he was nervous about it. He didn't need to fret over some shit Val had up her sleeve in addition to worrying about how the new song would go over.

Didn't matter. They went onstage and started playing, and he let the music fill his soul. This was a song he didn't have any secret lyrics for; it was one where he'd simply let the music speak for his emotions, and it was full of anger. It was how he could keep his daily emotions in check, by pouring out all the negativity into his guitar. He felt anger at his bandmates for not pulling their weight; at Ethan for not getting or keeping his shit together; at Val for making stupid decisions; at himself for not finding a way to let her go.

When he played the song, he felt a weight lift, and he just let himself feel it. He was going to trust Val, just like she asked. Ethan had the notion that she was going to bail, but why would she? They'd been playing together for over a year. She had as much invested in the band as the guys did. And he decided to not worry about whatever the hell she was going to do.

After they started playing, Val made her entrance, and Brad thought he was going to die. She strutted onstage in red heels and little else. She was wearing matching panties, bra, and a fucking garter and hose. That was it. She was wearing less than a lot of Victoria's Secret models he'd seen. He took a deep breath and felt grateful that his fingers and the instinctive part of his brain knew what to do, because his conscious mind was losing it.

He heard Ethan hit a wrong note, and it sounded like nails on a chalkboard. The guy had done it before, especially when he was blitzed out of his gourd, but this was one even the audience couldn't help but notice.

Brad wondered if the guy did it intentionally to make a statement.

Didn't matter. The crowd went wild. He'd never heard that kind of reception for one of their shows before. Yeah, he knew they had fans and they made for kick ass audiences, but now he realized how important Val was to them. She fronted their band—she was their face…and now she was their body too. Brad had to give her credit—it was ballsy. But he also felt like it meant that she didn't believe in herself enough as a singer to trust that her vocal chops and stellar songwriting skills could pull in the audience.

Instead, she felt like she had to rely on sexual appeal.

He wasn't sure why, but it pissed him off. It pissed him off hardcore, and he was even more glad they'd chosen to play "Primeval" first. He let his emotions build and tear through the song, and by the time they got to the solo, he felt like he'd melded with his guitar. The solo was not only flawless (the goal he'd been aiming for during the days he'd been practicing), but it felt effortless.

The entire show was amazing, full of frenetic energy, and he knew if they could play shows like that all the time, it wouldn't be long before a label snatched them up. He could barely remember it, though, because his mind was in a dark place for the whole show. He wished he could have enjoyed it, because he believed it was their best show ever.

He decided, as they took their equipment off the stage, that he wouldn't say anything for a while. He was going to wait until he could be rational. Maybe in a few days, he could trust himself to be reasonable and explain to Val why what she was doing was a bad idea. For now, though, he wasn't going to say a word.

He should have known that the guys wouldn't keep quiet, though. During the drive home, Ethan was the first to say something. "What the hell inspired *that* shit, Val?"

She turned in the seat to look at him. Brad kept his eyes on the road. "The outfit?"

"Yeah. Not that any of us are complaining."

"I dunno. I just thought if I looked kinda sexy, it could only help us."

Zane said, "It worked. I think half the audience had hard ons for most of the show."

"Okay, I didn't need *that* visual, Zane. Thanks."

Brad bit his tongue. Fucking goddamn. He was having a hell of a time. He wasn't ready to talk, because he didn't think he'd be able to say what he needed to say without sounding like a jealous asshole…which he was right now. He could feel Val looking at him—*why?*—but he forced his eyes to stay on the road. She said, "I guess I might as well warn you guys—there's plenty more where this came from."

He could hear Ethan. "Jesus Christ. Please just tell me you don't have any more garters. My heart can't take it."

Zane laughed. "I think I'm gonna ask Tanya to buy something like that."

Val said, "Why don't you buy it *for* her, stud?"

"Wouldn't she find it insulting if I bought her something and then asked her to wear it? Like she's not good enough on her own?"

"I dunno. Why don't you go shopping together?"

"That's a great idea."

The chatter died down and Brad almost turned the radio up loud. He couldn't keep quiet anymore, though, because the rest of the band had weighed in. He included Nick in the weigh in, because his silence wasn't atypical. He needed everyone else to know how he felt, and then if she still chose to do it, he'd live with it. But he couldn't keep quiet. "Val, I'm not gonna tell you what to do, but are you sure you want to go down this path?"

"What do you mean?"

He shrugged. Truth be told, he loved seeing her body, and if he hadn't cared about her so much, he would have loved it even more. But he didn't want her selling herself short. "There's always a chance people won't take you seriously. They'll think you're just a cupcake."

She giggled. "A cupcake? Why would they think that? I sing and rock out."

"I'm just sayin'. It's a chance you're taking."

"So what should I do, Brad?" She was looking at him—hard. He couldn't look back. He couldn't. She would know how he felt; they all would. So he kept his eyes on the road while she continued. "Was it just me, or was the audience insane tonight?"

He knew it was because of her, but he didn't want her to get cocky. "You think that was all you?"

"You think I had nothing to do with it?"

"I didn't say that."

Of course, Ethan would defend her. In spite of her summer with Jet, he knew Ethan still thought of Val as his girl. "Bradley, man...you know they were eating it up because of Valerie. I know you don't want to hear it, but she stole the show. And goddamn. If we get that kinda reaction just 'cause she's showing a little skin, then I say we let her."

Nick, the last holdout, said, "I'm for it."

Zane added his two cents' worth. "Me too."

He wasn't going to say another word. She—hell, *they*—knew how he felt. His objections had been duly noted. So he took a deep breath, clenched his jaw, and drove. It was all he could do...all he'd been doing, and he wasn't going to stop now.

CHAPTER FORTY-TWO

VAL CONTINUED TO surprise Brad and the band with lots of provocative outfits. Brad tried not to let it bother him, but underneath it all, it did. It would have eaten at him even if he hadn't had deeper feelings for the woman. He hated that she felt like she needed to use her sex appeal to boost the band. He would've been pissed if any of the guys had done something similar.

He knew, though—it bothered him worse with Val *because* it was her and because of how he felt about her.

He wasn't going to say another word, though, and he tried to get over it.

In November, a couple of weeks before Thanksgiving, they played their first show with Last Five Seconds since touring with them. He had been planning to talk with Jet a little bit, since they were solid acquaintances, because Jet and Brian, their bassist, had been talking, and it sounded like they might have a recording deal. Brad was eager to talk with Jet, because if their band could make it, he knew

Fully Automatic had a great chance. He knew Jet wouldn't bullshit him. He wanted to ask him what they'd done to get noticed.

When he went backstage to find him, though, he found Val sitting on Jet's lap, and things were pretty hot and heavy between them. Goddamn. Not only was he going to miss the opportunity to get information from Jet, but he had to find Val back in the guy's arms. He clenched his jaw and turned. He'd go watch the last band of the evening and try to put that scene out of his mind.

He couldn't find any of the guys, so he just found a place to stand in the crowd, away from the moshing but close enough to have a good view. It turned out the band only had a couple of songs left. They were good and Brad enjoyed what he saw of the show. In a way, he was glad he'd found Val and Jet in an embrace, because he wouldn't have appreciated the band if not.

The lights came up and he decided to find everyone else. As he started walking toward the stage, though, he felt a hand on his arm. "Brad?"

He turned around. The blonde in front of him was familiar, and it was a few seconds until he realized it was Leah. Holy shit. He hadn't seen her in over two years. She was all grown up. Still beautiful, but she was no Valerie. That was when he knew Val had infected him deeply, when his former flame couldn't even take his mind off the woman. "Leah. How are you?"

"Great. I had no idea you and your band had gotten so big."

Brad smiled. "Oh, so you saw us performing?"

"Yeah. Gosh, you and Ethan look so different."

"Time changes everything. You too." He cleared his throat. "What have you been up to?"

"I'm a junior now, so halfway done with my bachelor degree."

"How's that going?"

"Really well." A clean-cut kid with brown hair and a neat goatee came up behind Leah and put his arm over her shoulders. Yeah...that was the kind of guy Brad had pictured she'd end up with. He'd always known he wasn't her type, but she'd wanted to play around with the bad boy on the other side of the tracks. He could tell from her smile that she hadn't regretted her choice. She wanted the rich kid. He couldn't blame her. He just didn't understand why someone like Val—someone who didn't take issue with his hair and tattoos, someone who loved their music and the lifestyle—would continue to reject him.

No, that wasn't true. He was instead questioning why he continued expecting her to love him. She'd made it clear more than once that he was not the guy for her, so why did he find himself pining for her still, still after all this time?

It was a question for the ages.

Winter kicked into high gear and brought with it snow, ice, and cold. By January, Brad had managed to let his feelings for Val cool off as well once more, but he feared that they would still be there, just like they always had been. There was a pilot light in his soul for Val, and most of the time, he didn't even notice it was burning. Something would inevitably happen, though, and it would rekindle his heart, setting the whole goddamn thing aflame until it died down again, leaving a charred mess behind.

She dressed warmly for the trips to their shows, but once she got there, she'd strip down to her skimpy outfits. He wasn't minding them as much, because he appreciated that she had a great body. She'd grown into a beautiful woman, and as she'd become more comfortable with her position in the band, she'd gotten a few tattoos and piercings, and Brad was pretty sure she'd started working out a little too. She had definition where there'd been none before, and if he'd thought she was sexy before, he'd had no clue.

The new year brought with it new behaviors. He wasn't quite sure how it had happened, but he and Val started flirting onstage. They didn't do it much at first. Val had said something to someone in the audience and Brad had responded. The crowd had found it funny, and the applause was amazing, reinforcing for them the idea that they wanted to do it again. Ethan would get pissed sometimes, but that was just more reason for Brad to want to do it. When Ethan was angry, he was fully present, something they weren't always blessed with. He was happy to take angry Ethan. Zane would get in on it once in a while as well, and it just became something fun they did.

In March, though, Val kicked it up a notch. It went from being cute, funny, and flirtatious to being pretty serious. At least, it was starting to feel that way to Brad. And he was pissed, because every time they'd gone there in the past, Val had wound up shitting all over him.

Maybe that wasn't completely fair. Maybe it was partly his fault too. After all, he'd promised both her and her father that he'd keep his hands to himself. If she kept up the onstage antics, he didn't know that he could stop himself from making a move on her either. He assumed, though, that the flirting was simply another thing she was doing to try to boost their audience participation and get more fans, just like her lingerie trick had been, so he was trying hard not to get his hopes up. He'd been disappointed one too many times before when it came to Val.

Bottom line…Val had been through two incredibly intense relationships in the course of a year. She'd loved both Ethan and Jet hard, and even though her reunion with Jet had seemed to last for one night only, he knew her feelings for both of those men had run deep. He was convinced that Val considered him only a friend and that was all they ever would be, in spite of their past.

But they were playing a show on his birthday. He hadn't minded when he'd scheduled it. His birthday was on a Friday and he couldn't turn down a show. But—mid-set—Val had stopped the show and sung "Happy Birthday" to him, just like the old Marilyn Monroe version the blonde bombshell had sung for JFK. It wrecked him. She was breathy and seductive, like Marilyn had been decades ago, but unlike the actress, Val was hardly wearing a thing. It was insane. And she called him her "hot guitarist," no less. She was fucking killing him.

A guy in the audience yelled, "Whatcha gonna give him for his birthday?"

She said in the microphone without missing a beat, "I bet you'd like to know, but it's not something we should talk about in public."

If only. The problem with all the flirting was he lost his eye for other women. Again. He just couldn't do it.

It was fucking stupid.

And, yet, there wasn't a goddamn thing he could do about it.

Since the birthday song, Brad started thinking about Val again all the time. He had it bad. And all he could do was try to bury it like he always had.

She wouldn't let him, though. She'd been teasing him onstage so much, it had started to spill over into their real lives, and he wasn't quite sure what to think about it. Part of him toyed with the idea of pursuing her in earnest, but then he remembered the promise he'd made her...*and* her dad. He didn't want to mess up the band, and he'd promised her father her honor would remain intact with him. He didn't plan to go back on his word, no matter how deep his desire.

Still...she was making it difficult. He wasn't even *looking* at other women anymore. If there really was such a thing as lovesickness, he had it. He had it bad.

He wasn't about to stop flirting, though, because he was having fun and the audience seemed to enjoy their banter. One night at a concert in April, someone threw a handful of condoms onstage, and they appeared to be aimed at Valerie. Well, having things thrown at them wasn't completely unusual. Some girl had thrown a pair of panties at him last fall. As long as the fans weren't throwing rocks or tomatoes, he was cool with it. On this particular evening, Valerie had picked up one of the wrapped condoms. She held it up and started wagging it toward the audience. She said, "Glad to see you folks are practicing safe sex."

He didn't even think twice about joining in. It had become their *thing*. He stepped up to the mike and said to her, "Not very safe if they're throwing them up here instead of hanging onto them." He'd considered saying…*more*, but he respected Valerie too much to be too crude onstage. He didn't want to give all the perverts with their tongues hanging out any ideas. Just the thought that half these guys would be whacking off later thinking about her made his blood grow cold.

Speaking of perverts, some asshole yelled, "Let me at 'em. You'll never be the same, Valerie."

Brad saw red and couldn't think straight. He wanted to go beat the shit out of the moron, but he instead grew even calmer. He'd never keep fans if he went around kicking their asses. Instead, he was going to play it cool. He could do that. So he smirked and said, "Now why the hell would she want *you* when she's got my sexy bod?" The women in the audience started screaming. He hadn't expected *that* reaction. It felt nice, though. So he pushed it further. "And she's never been the same since." Really, it wasn't difficult. They'd been engaging in this sort of repartee for weeks now.

Wow. That look. He hadn't seen her look at him like that in a long damn time. She was checking him out. For reals. She was literally eyeing him up and down. He swallowed hard. No. He must have been imagining it, right? Val didn't think about him that way anymore, did she? *Did she?*

She winked at him then and started flopping that stupid condom around. She breathed into the microphone, "You know, Brad, I don't think this would fit you anyway. You need the large size, right?" After a beat, he started laughing. He couldn't believe she'd said that. It was an ego booster, even though she had no idea the size of his cock. The girls in the audience started screaming again and he swallowed once more. He yelled into the mike, "Hit it, guys." And he didn't know what overtook him, but he walked the short distance over to Valerie who stood center stage, and he cupped her cheeks in his hands and pressed his lips against hers.

It was fucking electric. He didn't know why he was surprised by her reaction, but it was as though no time between them had passed. He wasn't content with just a short platonic kiss, either. He brushed her lips with his tongue and when she responded by opening her mouth, he didn't hesitate to claim her. And when he let go, he knew he'd left her breathless, and that meant one of two things— either she *was* starting to feel the same way again, or he'd shocked the shit out of her. How he managed to play his guitar on cue, he'd never know.

And the rest of the show he played by rote. His lips couldn't forget the feel of hers against his, and he could remember how she'd smelled up close—sweet, like vanilla, and her skin had been warm and soft. That had been a stupid fucking move, planting a kiss on her, because now he'd never get her out of his head. He could remember every time he'd ever touched her, every time he'd tasted her, and his obsession would begin all over again. There would be no stopping it.

He was pissed with himself then, and he was deep in thought as they loaded up their equipment. He didn't say a word, though, and he was glad none of the guys did either.

Val acted like nothing had happened. He felt a little relief at that. Not much, though.

Later that evening as they were driving back to the apartment, he finally found the words. He looked over toward the passenger seat where she was sitting and he said, "Hey…sorry about earlier."

Val had been looking out the window but she turned to him. It was dark but he could see her expression thanks to all the streetlights they were driving past. "Hmm?" She seemed lost in thought. "What?"

Saying it again was going to be hard. "Onstage. Kissing you. Sorry about that. I know you weren't expecting it."

She smiled and giggled. God, she was so cute when she did that. "Hey, the audience liked it. That's what matters, right? It didn't bother me."

Yeah…but now he wasn't getting the sense that she felt the same way. Of course, she didn't. It felt like a fucking punch in the gut, but yeah. Stupid ass. She was still in love with either Jet or Ethan. Of course. Brad's kiss hadn't meant a thing. To her, it had just been a stunt. An effective one, but a stunt nonetheless. So he nodded and tried to keep the disappointment out of his voice. "Yeah, I was just kind of rolling with the punches."

She smiled again. God, she was beautiful. She had no idea. He'd been angry when at first she'd decided to dress provocatively onstage, but she'd bloomed and embraced her womanhood, and he was okay with it now. But he had to keep reminding himself she wasn't for him, no matter how badly he thought he wanted her. He tried to keep his eyes on the road. She said, "It worked." She turned to look back out the window.

He nodded, acting as casual as he possibly could. Yeah, he had to bury it deep. Really deep. And pray this time it stayed there.

But, try as he might, he didn't know if he could keep up with the charade.

CHAPTER FORTY-THREE

BRAD MANAGED TO arrange a mini-tour much like the one they'd enjoyed a year earlier. It was set for mid-July. It was four shows only but four bands on tour, and the venues were all new. Brad had managed to book bigger places than they were used to playing, and he arranged it early enough that (he hoped) the venues could generate a lot of interest.

Because their schedule on this tour was tighter and the locations farther apart than the tour the year before, Brad created several lists, including a driving schedule. He, Val, and Zane would take turns driving. No one questioned it, except for Val, asking why it was only the three of them. Brad simply told her the truth. He knew if Val or Zane had to get behind the wheel, they'd be sober. He knew for a fact that both Ethan and Nick had driven when they shouldn't have, and Brad didn't want to risk their lives or his van just because one of them was being irresponsible. He only planned to give Val or Zane the keys when he needed sleep, so he had to know the van was in good hands.

The tour was fast and frenetic. It was energizing, something their shows had been lacking for the last few weeks. He wasn't sure why.

Their last show was in Texas and it kicked ass. They made more money from that show than any other on their tour, but the entire tour had amazed Brad with the money it brought in. He and the other bands had hoped for that, though, and they'd planned ahead in anticipation. They'd sprung for three suites the final night, because he knew they'd want to party hard before heading back home. Val, of course, still had her own room and it was down the hall, and when the guys complained about that, saying she could sleep on a couch or something, she paid for her own room and told them to "shut the fuck up already." She apologized to Brad for making things difficult, and he said, "Val, you know I've always supported you having your own room. No need to tell me you're sorry. I'll slip you a little extra cash to pay for it."

"No, I got it. It's cool."

The suites were bigger than he'd imagined, and the accommodations were a little nicer than they were used to. He just hoped they wouldn't trash them and get bills for damage later. They hadn't had that problem on the road thus far, but they'd always stayed in lower-rent places that wouldn't notice any damage the band happened to inflict.

He showered before joining the party. It was hotter there than he was used to anyway, but add to that the stage lights and playing his ass off, and he needed a long, cool shower to feel normal again.

When he got to the party, all the bands were there, as well as lots of people he didn't know. There were lots of girls around, so he knew someone had decided to spread the word—it was no longer a bands-only party. That was probably better, though, because otherwise Val would get all the attention of all the horny twenty-something guys there. He looked around and didn't see her, so he figured maybe she'd decided to call it a night. Probably a smart move.

He looked around and spied all manner of fine women. It was a shame he didn't feel like making a move on any of them. He'd realized over the past year that picking up women was getting easier, but he didn't think it was because he'd gotten any better at the process. He figured it was because they were starting to view him as a rock star, and rock stars got women. It was as simple as that.

The problem was he didn't want any of them. There was only one woman he wanted, and the feeling wasn't mutual. He was growing angry with himself for not finding a way to let her go, but he knew that as long as they kept up the flirtatious stage act, he'd never get her out of his head.

He needed psychiatric help. He doubted other guys carried a torch like he had. And he knew it was fucking stupid but he had no idea how to just let it go.

Maybe he'd drink a lot tonight. They weren't leaving until sometime the next day, and checkout was late morning, so if he partied a little harder than usual, he'd be okay. If Val was sleeping (as he suspected), he could ask her to drive the first shift if he needed to catch a few extra Zs.

He decided to chat with various band members. Thus

far, networking had not let him down. He never knew when a person he'd met could help him along the way. Sometimes, by simply knowing other bands and asking them to commit to a date, he could book a show because he'd lined up several bands for it. He had only managed to do that because he had taken the time to get to know the people in the bands, and he had a good rapport with them. They had come to realize that Fully Automatic (and Brad in particular) was reliable. They did what they said they were going to do. So they had a good reputation. Brad saw no reason to not keep up the streak, and he would do it by befriending people in the other bands. Some of the guys he already knew, but a few of them were new additions. It happened. In the world of indie metal, line ups changed all the time, and some groups simply disbanded when they couldn't get along anymore or had a difference of artistic opinion. Last Five Seconds was one of the few that was going to make it. They'd found recognition and were going to the next level, and Brad suspected they'd never play with those guys again because of it (or until Fully Automatic made it as well). Spanky's Kids, the other band they'd toured with the year before, had already split up. There were too many egos involved. The singer and drummer had since started up a new band, but Spanky's Kids was no more. Brad had seen that happen a lot. Sometimes, it made the individuals stronger, but they were starting over at the bottom. At least if your band had a name, you had a fan base and recognition. He didn't think their fans loved him personally. It was his band. If they had to replace a member, they'd move on, but he couldn't imagine starting from scratch. Fully Automatic was *his* band and always would be. The guys knew it too.

But Brad was feeling happy with his band right now and the other bands they'd played with, and discussing music with any one of the guys of any one of the other bands was in order. He was chatting with two of them when he spied Valerie just across the room. She too was mingling, chatting with people here and there. Goddamn...she was just like him in that respect. She knew how important it was to get to know people and establish good will. He couldn't remember anymore whose idea it had been to bring her on board, but it was a damn good idea. The best.

And that thought alone made the vice around his heart clamp down again. God, he ached for that woman, and she had no idea. He knew, though—he knew deep down that it would end in heartache, and he didn't know if it would be worse than the pain he felt now. He didn't know if he was willing to take that risk with her anymore.

Of course, he knew he wouldn't act on any attraction he felt anyway. He'd promised her, promised her dad, and the band was better for it.

It didn't stop him from feeling, though.

He forced himself to concentrate on the conversations he was engaging in, but after a while, he was alone again, and that was when he noticed she was in the kitchen. It looked like Ethan was giving her a hard time, and the guy was holding her on his lap. That meant Ethan was stoned, drunk, or both, and he hadn't found some girl willing to suck his dick for the evening. That was unusual for Ethan, because he usually had a line of girls ready and willing.

By the time he got to the kitchen area, he heard Val say, "You're my friend, Ethan. And you're drunk." Brad sat in the chair next to Ethan's. "Let me go."

Ethan was out of control. Brad hoped he would listen to reason. "There a problem here?"

Ethan scowled and barely made eye contact with his friend. "No problem. Just tellin' my girlfriend what she means to me." What the fuck was the guy taking? He and Val had been split up for over a year.

Val tried pulling away. "I'm *not* your girlfriend, Ethan. I haven't been in a long time."

"Why can't we be again?"

"Why don't you ask me when you're sober?"

Enough. He didn't want to have to get physical with his brother, but he would if he had to. He hoped he'd listen to reason with whatever part of his brain was still paying attention. "You heard her, Ethan."

"Fine."

As soon as he let go, Val stood up. She grabbed a glass of water on the table and Brad saw her whisper to him, "Thanks."

"Aw, c'mon, babe."

Smart girl. She kept walking. Brad looked in his friend's eyes. "You gonna be okay?"

Ethan smirked. He was fucking wasted. "Getting there."

Brad felt helpless again. This was one of those times where his friend had gone overboard, and there would be nothing he could do except watch the guy make an ass out of himself. There was no saving him until he decided to take care of himself. Brad stood and patted Ethan on the shoulder. "Let me know if you need anything." He knew Ethan wouldn't take him up on his offer, never had, but it didn't stop him from wanting to say it.

He wanted to find Valerie and make sure she was okay—both physically and emotionally. He grabbed the bottle of spiced rum off the counter that he'd bought and forgotten about and a shot glass and moved toward the love seat in the living area where he saw her sitting. She was sipping her water and she looked introspective. She was probably questioning what she ever saw in Ethan. He knew, though, that when Ethan was sober, he was one of the most charming people a girl could ever meet and fall for. It was temporary, but Val looked like she needed a friend just the same.

He sat next to her and said, "Sorry Ethan was being such a dick."

She laughed. "Like you have any control over him. But seriously…thanks for the save. I appreciate it."

"That's what friends are for." He poured a shot and asked, "Want one?"

She shrugged but said, "Yeah…just one, though." When he handed it to her, she gulped it down.

He poured another shot. "Sure you don't want more?"

"Positive. But thanks."

He swallowed one himself. Damn…that felt good. He needed a little liquid steel and this felt about right. He was going to ask a tough question. "So…you still love him?"

She looked shocked. "Ethan?"

"Yeah…who else? Jet?" Oh, fuck. Did he really want to know the answers to any of these questions? Yes…and no. And he couldn't even blame the liquor because he hadn't had enough yet.

Still, she smiled and considered the question. "Ha.

Love is a thing of the past. I don't plan to ever give my heart to a man again."

That was when he knew she was lying to him. "Oh, stop that shit, Val. You're talking to *me*. I'm your friend, and I know better. I know you've been hurt and you're afraid of risking love again. Am I right?" He read her lyrics and they were like a lifeline to her heart. She was afraid of taking another chance, but she hadn't closed off her heart.

He knew exactly how she felt.

Her eyes searched his for a few seconds before she answered. "That's not it. I just don't have a place in my life for a man. That's all. Especially right now."

"You forget...I actually *read* your goddamned lyrics, Val. And I sing some of them. I don't just give them lip service." He couldn't look her in the eyes anymore and he needed another shot, so he concentrated on tilting the bottle over the shot glass. "You are a romantic, whether you want to admit it or not."

"Okay...so I'll admit it. All right? But...so far, all real life romance has done for me is break my heart."

"Makes for some good songs, right?" He felt an opening, like it was time to have a tête-à-tête about something that had bothered him for a long time. "And so now you're playing this sex-starved goddess onstage. Does that validate your feelings? Or do you think you'll find the perfect man by doing that?"

"What? Are you drunk too?"

He wished, but he was a long way from it. No, he was saying something she didn't want to hear. Still, he couldn't help but laugh. "Hell, no. Not even close."

"Well, bottom line...I'm not looking for the perfect

man. I don't *want* a man right now, perfect or not. That's not on my agenda."

That was good, but it didn't explain the provocative persona she'd been wearing for a while now. "So what is?"

"Making our band successful, and..." She wanted to say something more, and so he raised his eyebrows, encouraging her to spit it out. "And having fun."

Maybe the alcohol *was* loosening him up, because he couldn't stop the words before they spilled out of his mouth. "What kind of fun?"

He saw her eyes grow wider as she said, "Any kind."

Holy fuck. Was he understanding what she was saying? If he wasn't mistaken, she was full on flirting with him, and not like the shit they'd been doing onstage lately. He should have walked away or taken another drink or laughed. Instead, he tried to get his bearings. He took a deep breath and rested his elbows on his thighs, his hands pressed together as though in prayer, and he rested his lips on the tips of his fingers. Yeah, he might have been slow on the uptake once in a while, but she was definitely flirting with him, and he couldn't resist. Just couldn't. Valerie had never been his, never would be his, but he couldn't resist just once, now that they were adults, playing back. He smiled and said simply, "Any kind, huh?" He turned his head then and looked her in the eyes. He wanted her to know she needed to stop right there because what she was doing wasn't fair. "That could get you into trouble, Valerie."

Instead, she sat up. He could barely hear her voice. "Don't I know that." Her eyes drifted down to his lips, and he felt his blood start to rush and swirl. The rest of the room stilled at that moment. He couldn't hear the music playing anymore, couldn't hear the cacophony of voices, didn't sense anyone or anything but Val at that moment. And it was as though he was watching a movie and not his own life in the moment. She set her glass of water down and leaned forward, touching her lips to his.

He didn't—couldn't—stop her.

She grabbed his shirt in her fists and pulled him close to her, and it was as though he'd lost all control. All the years of every pent-up emotion he'd felt for Val came through that kiss, and there was no stopping it. He pulled her close and kissed her as though the world was ending and it was the last thing he'd ever do. He couldn't stop his tongue from entering her mouth, but he fought against the rest of his body because another few seconds and he was going to have a massive hard on. He had to stop, had to quit this. It was wrong. He and Val would never work and he knew it. He couldn't let it continue, because it was going to hurt even worse if he did. So, even though he didn't let her go, he broke his lips from hers and opened his eyes. "We can't do this, Val."

She took a breath. "Do what?"

"This. Us. We can't."

"Why not?"

"Ethan, for starters…and he's right over there."

"Are you kidding? Ethan? The guy who fucked around on me more than once? We haven't been together in a long time, Brad. That ship sailed a long time ago."

He'd have to dig deep. She was resisting his arguments and that was making it even harder for him to think rationally. "And then there's Jet…"

"Jet? Seriously? Brad, he and I broke up…almost a year ago."

"Bullshit. You guys hooked up again last…November or December, wasn't it?"

She sighed. She barely kept her voice from sounding like she was dealing with a child. "We made out. That was it. And we decided friends only."

Why was she doing this? Did she not know how this could wreck him? "And the band, Val. That's why we stayed away in the first place."

"That was *your* idea, and if mine and Ethan's fucked-up relationship hasn't ruined the band…" He saw a shadow pass over her eyes, and she grabbed her glass of water. She took a drink and said, "Know what? You don't want to, just grow a fucking pair and say so." Holy shit. She was pissed. Where the fuck had that come from? She stood. "Jesus."

Oh, God, she had no idea how he felt about her. He wanted to. Hell, yeah, he wanted to. "Val, that's not it—"

"Good night, Brad." She walked straight out of the suite without looking back.

This was one of those crossroads moments. He could let her go to bed mad at him, let her sleep it off, and the next day, he could buy her a cup of coffee and they could have a rational discussion like they always had, and he could tell her why—really why—he didn't want to.

Or he could go talk to her right now…and let the chips fall where they may.

CHAPTER FORTY-FOUR

BRAD'S LEGS WERE moving before his brain had fully engaged. He wanted to believe. Maybe this time it was meant to be, right? Third time's a charm or some shit like that?

No, whether or not anything happened, he felt compelled for some stupid ass reason to explain himself to her. She was pissed off at him, like she'd thought he was rejecting her, and that wasn't the case. He needed to make that clear.

No. He didn't *need* to. He wanted to.

He went to her room and knocked. It was quiet. He didn't hear any motion and wondered if she'd even gone to her room. In her anger, she might have stormed out of the building. But he wasn't leaving—not till he was sure.

Val opened the door finally, and she didn't look happy. Worse, though—she was just wearing the t-shirt she'd been wearing earlier and nothing else. No pants, no shoes. Maybe this had been a bad idea. But he was already committed, and he wasn't leaving until he'd said his piece. "Can I come in?"

She nodded, inviting him in and then closing the door once he was inside. They were standing in the center of the room. He took a deep breath, found the words, and then just spat them out. "I *know* you're not with those guys now, but that doesn't mean your heart's not. And I promised your dad."

After staring him down, she started laughing. "That was over two years ago, Brad."

She was killing him. "I don't know what's so funny."

She was too close to him as she cocked her head and lowered her voice. "Seriously? Brad, he was worried about my virtue and of some guy forcing me to do something I didn't want to do." She looked at his lips and then into his eyes again, and he could feel his resolve crumbling. "Do I look unwilling to you?" She got even closer, so near to him he could feel her body heat, and he clamped his teeth together. "I might not remember what he said word for word, but three words stuck in my mind—*without her consent.* Know why I remember that?" He shook his head, trapped, mesmerized, lost. "Because up until that point in my life, I'd been told how premarital sex was a sin, and I should save my virginity for marriage, although my mom decided to spring on me right before college that if I loved a boy, it would be enough. For my dad to throw in that he'd kill anyone who touched me without my consent…well, that kinda blew everything else out of the water." Her eyes pierced his when she said, "So give me one *good* reason why we shouldn't do this."

That was it. He was done. She would be his downfall,

and he didn't give a fuck anymore. He wanted to do this, had to do this. His voice was a whisper when he said, "I can't."

She wrapped her hand around his neck, and he bent over to kiss her. He felt so much with that one kiss—it was an onslaught of emotion and hormones rushing through his body. He could feel his heart beating faster as her nails dug into his neck. If they were gonna do this, they were gonna do it, and he felt like he had already signed his own death warrant and was being dragged into the depths of perdition. And he didn't care anymore. This was Val, and now she was his, even if it was only for a little while. She could be the death of him. He was willing to accept it.

He was afraid he was being too rough with her, but he couldn't stop himself. Now that he'd decided to just go with it, he could hardly contain himself. His kisses were hard and demanding, but she didn't seem to mind. In fact, she was pulling his t-shirt up before he could register it. His brain wasn't keeping up with his body or his heart.

He grabbed his shirt to help her get it over his head, and then he felt her hands on his chest, and he knew he had no control. The train was on the tracks, and there was no stopping it till it reached its destination. He took the bottom of her shirt in his hands and she pulled it the rest of the way off, throwing it to the floor. His brain was turned off now, and he was operating on instinct. He bent at the knees and lifted her up, wrapping her legs around him and walking toward the bed.

Because he knew he had no control, he had no idea how long he'd last, and he didn't want to take the chance of being a shitty lover the first time he and Val were together.

They had so many reasons to not be together, to not do it, that he didn't want to give her another reason to toss him out on his ass. He was going to do something he knew he was good at. So as he lay her down, her knees draped over the bed, he kissed her on the lips but then moved to her neck, then to her collarbone and her breast, reaching behind her to undo the clasp that held the bra together. She sighed and arched her back, assuring him that he was on the right track.

Her hand was in his hair, and she'd twisted some of the strands around her fingers. He loved the way it felt—kind of possessive, kind of demanding. He pulled the bra off her shoulders and just tried to appreciate the moment. He'd seen her breasts before, yeah, but that was a time when she was distressed and needed his help, and he hadn't gawked, much as he'd wanted to. Now, though, he could look upon her beauty and appreciate it, and he was going to. Yeah, he'd imagined what she'd looked like under those bras and corsets she'd worn onstage, but he was seeing the real deal now. He bent over and took a nipple in his mouth, tonguing around the circle as it hardened against his touch. She let out a loud sigh as her fingers tightened against his hair.

He kissed down the mound of her breast and then drew a line down her belly with his tongue as he grabbed both sides of her lacy black panties and pulled them down her legs. He slid off the bed then and glided his hands under her ass, pulling her down to the edge of the bed. Her legs were on either side of his head and she was right there. He was actually looking at naked Valerie, and he could hardly believe it. He parted her folds with his fingers and then ran his tongue up the middle. She was already making noises, and he wasn't surprised, because she was wet. She was wet...*for him*. It hit him like a ton of bricks, that maybe the feelings weren't one-sided. Maybe for some stupid reason she'd avoided him too. Maybe this had been inevitable.

And that made it beautiful. He felt another wave of emotion rush through him and realized he just needed to concentrate on her. The emotions were too much—too raw, too fresh, too un-fucking-believable, and he kept expecting himself to wake up from a stupid dream.

If it was real, though, he wanted to make it a night to remember for her. He stroked her with his tongue again and then turned his head a little so he could suck on her clit. He could hear her sucking in a deep breath of air through her teeth, so he kept it up. One hand was on her thigh, massaging it, while his other hand held her apart and let his mouth do the rest.

He could feel her legs start to shake, as though she were cold, but then she cried aloud. He decided then to switch tactics, increase the pressure, so he stroked her with his tongue again, and he could tell from her cries that he was on the right track. He moved his hand to her belly underneath her breast, almost as though to hold her steady. She kept going and so he did too, and she called his name, not once, not twice, but more times than he could remember, and so he didn't stop until he was sure she was finished.

She relaxed then, almost a puddle of jelly compared to how tight her muscles had been just moments earlier. Because he and Val had never been together, he didn't know what she was like in contrast to other women. Oh, he knew as a person, but not in bed, so he didn't know if he should give her a few moments to rest or if she would be ready right away. The only way to find out would be to move forward, get in closer, and see what she had to say. He thought if she was ready to go, she would want him to take his time.

He climbed on the bed, straddling her on all fours, ready to kiss her and move forward. She said, "I want to feel you inside me, Brad." That was music to his ears, all he'd ever wanted to hear from her. He reached for his wallet and pulled it out of his back pocket. He threw it on the bed and started feeling inside for a condom while Val's fingers playing on his chest distracted the shit out of him.

Not good.

It felt empty.

And he thought back as he kissed Val. When was the last time he'd used one? When was the last time he'd needed one? Was it possible he was unprepared? *Fuck.*

He stopped kissing her. "Just a sec." He sat up enough that he could pry the wallet apart and looked inside, feeling behind the bills. "You fucking kidding me?"

Val propped herself up on her elbows. "What?"

He was hoping against hope, but he had to ask. "I don't suppose you have any condoms, do you?"

She frowned. "No." She paused and then said, "I could—"

He knew what she was thinking—either he could pull out or she could give him a blowjob. Yeah, either would be fine, but he wanted it to be as perfect as possible. No, though. He'd already fucked that up. Still, maybe he could salvage the evening. He shook his head and unclenched his jaw to talk. "No. I can go buy some. I wonder if there are any here in the public restrooms in the hotel." He could ask one of his bandmates—he knew one of them would have one—but then they'd know. No fucking way.

"I bet the gift shop would have some."

"They're long since closed, Val. Gotta be."

"Well, uh…a convenience store, maybe? There's gotta be one nearby. I saw a Walmart too. They'd have one for sure."

"Yeah. Okay. You don't mind waiting?"

She smiled. "I'm coming with you."

Oh, God, how could he not love this woman? "You will?"

"Yeah…only fair, right?" She kissed him and then asked, "You sure you can drive?"

He nodded and looked at her a few seconds longer. God, she was beautiful, and even more so now that she felt satisfied and alive. He sat up and Val got off the bed, throwing her clothes back on. He found his t-shirt and pulled it over his head and then waited for her to finish. His mind wandered back over the last fifteen minutes, and so much had changed. And it hadn't escaped his notice that she'd said his name not once but multiple times while he brought her to the zenith of pleasure. In all the times he'd accidentally overheard her with Ethan, he hadn't heard her say his name once. That made his heart swell. So, yeah…he could wait a little while longer.

Val slipped some shoes on while Brad tried adjusting himself. Goddamn, his balls hurt and his cock wasn't letting up. Jesus Christ. Val noticed his discomfort and asked, "You gonna be okay?"

He laughed. He was amazed. She probably wanted nothing more than to curl up in bed and snuggle and here she was coming along for the ride. "Thanks for being a good sport, Val."

She snatched her room card off the dresser and shoved it in her back pocket. She grabbed his hand as she walked toward the door. "*I'm* the good sport? Do you not know what you just did to me?"

God, she knew how to make him feel like a man. Yeah, he could wait even longer when she said shit like that. He turned her around so that her back was against the door and pressed into her. He hoped she could see the desire in his eyes when he said, "I'm gonna do it again."

Yeah…he wanted to make her feel so incredible that the idea of any other man tumbled out of her brain for good.

CHAPTER FORTY-FIVE

HE COULDN'T BRING himself to hold a coherent conversation on the way to Walmart. In fact, he had to put all his free thought into remembering exactly where they'd seen it. It wasn't too far, but all he could think about was burying himself inside Val.

She was quiet too. She must have known. She confirmed when she thought they were going the right way, but she didn't say anything else. All she did was find a radio station playing Of Mice and Men and turn the music up a little.

He'd managed to will his cock down but his balls fucking ached. He needed some relief. He knew it was coming, and he wasn't going to complain, but it was starting to get to him.

They went into the building and found what they needed. Val was like a kid in a candy store. She thought it was a fucking riot that it was obvious what they planned to do based on their purchase. He loved that. She was having so much fun, he couldn't help but smile. And she was beautiful. Her hair was a little wild, but she was sexy and gorgeous. God, he loved her.

When they walked outside and started heading toward the van, she let out a long, loud laugh. He grinned at her and then unlocked the van. He walked over to the other side to open the door for her, but she laid her hand on his. She had a devilish smile on her face. "Let's get in the back."

At just the thought, his cock started to swell again. They weren't parked by any of the bright overhead lights, so it wouldn't be like they were obvious. "Seriously?"

She nodded. She was turning out to be his dream girl, just like he'd always known. He slid the door open and waited for her to get in. Then he joined her and closed the door. She said, "This feels kinda familiar, doesn't it?"

He smiled. He'd never forgotten the steamy encounter they'd had in the backseat of this very van over two years ago. He never would. "It does." He sat down next to her, and she straddled him. "You're not wasting any time."

She whispered in his ear, "Nope. Time to take care of *you*." He felt the air escape his lungs as his cock strained against his jeans once again. She kissed him—slow and sweet—and then she nibbled on his lower lip. Fuck. It was finally gonna happen. About damn time. He touched her lip with his tongue and then moved inside her mouth, taking over, wanting to possess her. And as he allowed himself to fully engage with the idea that he was going to at last be able to feel himself inside her, he felt emotion wash over him. It was deep and raw. He'd felt it for her for so long, but now it released itself and came full force. Yes, he loved this woman, loved her with everything in him, and now he knew he could never not love her. She was everything, and this act made him feel like they were soul mates, like they should have always been together, like they should always be. There was no escaping that fact in his mind. His heart would always, always belong to her, no matter what happened. And now he was happy to give it to her.

He couldn't taste her enough. His kisses were deep but slow and soft as he explored all that lay between them. He felt her hands moving up underneath his shirt, up his abs to his pecs. She moved her lips to his ear and asked, "You ready?"

Hell, yes, he was ready. He had been eons ago, but he wasn't going to say it. Instead, he said, "Whenever you are." She sucked on his earlobe and then kissed on his neck while she played with the buttons on his jeans. Just feeling her fingers outside his jeans pressing against his cock upped the ante even more.

He was wearing button fly jeans, and she unfastened the first button, then the second, and said, "Oh, what have we here? I think there's something down there that desperately wants out." He loved the sense of fun she was bringing to round two of their lovemaking. It was going to be even better because of it. "Maybe I can help." He sighed as she opened another button, and she sucked on his lower lip. "I think I need to let him out." Oh, fuck, yes, please. She kissed him hard then and slid her hand inside his underwear. She wrapped her hand around his cock and *oh, fuck*. He thought he was going to lose it right then and there.

He couldn't concentrate anymore. All his focus flew to her hand and what it was doing to him. He'd been in an aroused state for far too long, and nothing—aside from orgasm or a war breaking out around them—would get his mind back on anything else. Val kissed him, but it was even difficult to concentrate enough to kiss her back. Then she said, "Shit."

"What?"

She was unbuttoning her jeans and got off him. "I'm gonna have to take these all the way off."

"I'm not complaining."

She smiled. "I didn't figure you would." As she messed around with her jeans, he grabbed the Walmart bag and fished out the box of condoms. It was time, and he opened the box and took one out. He unwrapped the package and started rolling it over his cock.

She straddled him again. "Scooch forward a little." He was her willing slave at that point and did as she asked. She tilted and slid his cock inside her. He closed his eyes, letting himself become absorbed in the moment. Shit. She felt like heaven. "Ah…" She must have felt the same way. It felt so damn right when she shoved her fingers into his hair and pressed her lips into his. Yes. This was what they should have done years ago back here, but he wondered if it tasted sweeter because he'd had to wait so long.

He could barely focus. It was all he could do to grind—as slowly as possible—and not lose his load. Not yet. He had to maintain…just a little longer.

He grabbed the bottom of her t-shirt and asked, "Mind if I pull this off?" He wanted to feel all of her against him—no cotton between them. And it was sweltering in that van. If she was going to sweat, he wanted to feel it on him. Her skin on his, all of her body on him. Without a word, she lifted her arms, and he pulled the shirt over her head. Holy shit. She hadn't put her bra back on. Her tits were right there in his face and his concentration flew away again. He left the shirt hanging on her wrists, taking a breast in his hand and sucking her nipple into his mouth.

She was so fucking hot, and she was grinding into him. He didn't know how much longer he could hold out, but he was going to do his best. She took her hand out of his hair and slid it between their bodies. She started fingering herself. Holy fucking shit, that was hot, and she gasped as her eyes closed, and she rotated her hips into him again.

He couldn't take his eyes off her. "Let me help." He stuck his thumb in her mouth. She started sucking on it, and he was sure then that he was going to blow. He couldn't leave it there or he would. He pulled it out and replaced his hand with hers. He searched for her clit with his thumb and her breathing grew erratic. That was the sign he'd been looking for. Now she was close too.

That was the moment he'd been waiting for. He kept up the pressure and the motion with his thumb. She sucked a big gulp of air in her mouth. "Oh..." She was still riding him, but he could tell her concentration was now shit too—she had one goal in mind now and that was hitting the mark. She gasped a couple of times and then he felt her thighs quiver against his hips. "Oh, God, Brad..." His hand rested on the small of her back to steady her, and he refused to let up on her with his thumb until he was sure she was done. But then, hearing her cries again, he couldn't hold it back anymore. He let it all go and it was fucking magic. A burst of pleasure unlike any he had ever known, and it filled him with light and bliss…and more love than he'd ever known before.

It took a minute or two for him to get his bearings, but he was holding her close to him. She could never be close enough for him to feel like she was. His breathing slowed and then he realized that it was fucking insanely hot in that goddamn van. They were both sweaty. It didn't bother him much, but he was sure she didn't care much for it. He mourned the fact that he was going to have to let her go. He prepared himself for it, and, moments later, she got up off him and got dressed.

He took that as his cue to put his clothes back on too.

They were quiet on the drive back. He was suddenly exhausted, but his emotions were battling with him now. All the love, all the emotion he'd felt before was now replaced with doubt and insecurity. He knew Val as well as he knew himself, and as much as he'd wanted to believe she now thought he was the guy for her, he wasn't too sure about it. Val had run back to Ethan more times than he could count, had spurned Brad more than once as well, and he was afraid he had more invested here than she did. He knew he cared about her a hell of a lot more than she did him. And it left him feeling empty when he should have felt like he was on top of the world.

He decided then and there that he would just enjoy the moment. He couldn't control what she would say or do tomorrow, so he had to appreciate what they had tonight. It killed him to think that way, but he knew it was what he had to do.

Still…inside of him, a war had been waged and he was a

fucking hot mess.

When they got to the hotel and got out of the van, he kissed her as soon as he'd helped her out. If his kisses could erase the memories she had of old lovers, he was going to do it. Or if this was the only night they would ever have together, he wasn't going to let it end already. So when they were in the elevator, he pressed her up against the wall and kissed her until he heard the bell ring and the door opened. He kissed her right outside too, and then he held her around the waist before they started walking down the hall. She asked, "You're coming to my room, aren't you?"

He realized that he'd expected her to tell him *good night* and send him on his merry way until she'd asked. Her question was a bit of a reassurance, but the doubt still nagged at him. "Sure." They walked past the suites occupied by all the other band members and noise was drifting out of the doors of the one in the middle. Brad hoped they wouldn't get in trouble, because it was late, but he wasn't going to worry about it. He had his own concerns right now, and the partying wasn't one of them. He knew Val was thinking the same thing he was, hoping that no one would come out of the room as they walked past. It would have made their time together awkward and uncomfortable.

They got to her room and she opened the door. As soon as they got inside, Val started giggling. She was looking at the Walmart bag that contained the box of condoms. He smiled in spite of the storm of emotions brewing in his chest. "What? I couldn't leave that in the van for the guys to see."

She placed the card key on the dresser. "It's not like they've never seen a condom before."

"Yeah, but you know they'd ask where it came from. Would *you* be able to keep a straight face?"

She shrugged and changed the subject. "I want to shower. I feel all sticky and gross." Yeah, he did too.

"Can I join you? No hanky panky if you don't wanna. I just feel pretty sweaty myself."

She nodded and walked toward the bathroom. He took a deep breath and clenched his jaw. Jesus fucking Christ. He'd never felt as insecure in his life as he did right at that moment. He knew—just fucking *knew*—this was a dream. It couldn't be real. He swallowed hard. *Get a grip, Payne.* Enough. He had to stop trying to jinx the night. He took a deep breath and pulled his shoes off, then started walking toward the bathroom. She already had the water running by the time he got there. She was pulling her clothes off and so he pulled his t-shirt over his head and threw it on the floor.

She grinned, fully naked again, and said, "Meet ya in there!" She hopped in the tub and pulled the curtain closed.

He pulled his jeans off and took another deep breath. Fuck. Why the hell was he letting this whole thing get him down? He should be happy right now. He'd dreamed of this for how long? Why couldn't he just let it go and enjoy the moment?

He pulled the curtain back and stepped in. Val was rinsing soap off her breasts. Things didn't feel right and he didn't know why. He thought she could sense his mood, because she grabbed his hand and slapped the tiny motel bar of soap into his palm. She said, "Turn around."

"What for?"

"I'll wash your back." He turned around, giving the soap back to her. He closed his eyes as a few trickles of warm water splashed onto him, but he felt her sliding her hand over his back, gliding because of the soap on it. He loved the feel of her hand on him, and he wanted to imagine years of that, but something in the back of his mind tickled at him, told him he shouldn't get his hopes up.

She announced, "All done," and he turned around, trying to force a smile on his face. She could sense that all was not right with him, though. "You okay?"

He was a fucking idiot if he thought he could hide from Valerie. Still, he wasn't going to tell her what he was thinking, so he nodded. "Yeah."

"You're probably as tired as I am." She held the soap out for him and said, "Trade places? I'm gonna get out."

She stepped out of the shower and closed the curtain. He braced himself against the wall of the shower and let the water rain down on his head. He wanted to wash it all away—all the doubt, the fears, the lack of faith he felt. He wanted to believe in Val, believe in them, but he couldn't shake that feeling.

More than that, he was aching. He knew he should be filled with love, and he was, but it should have been a feeling of wonder and happiness. Instead, it was a feeling of dread and worry, complete disbelief. He took a deep breath and found his resolve. No matter what tomorrow brought, he was going to be for Valerie what she needed tonight. He could do that. He just had to let go. And so he did his best—he let it all wash down the drain and let the

overwhelming love he felt for her take over.
It was the best he could do.

CHAPTER FORTY-SIX

BRAD WALKED OUT of the bathroom and found Val already in bed, a pillow tucked under her head, her eyes closed. He walked over to her and got under the covers beside her. He felt a little better after the shower, but he could feel the lingering doubts hovering in the dark corners of his mind. Still, as he'd promised himself, he was going to try to get out of the funk he was in and enjoy their time together.

He looked at her. God, she was beautiful. Her long brown hair, damp from the shower, lay on the pillow behind her. Her skin was flawless, a peach color, and it was even more beautiful without the makeup she usually wore. The sexy tribal armband on her upper arm accentuated the definition she'd worked into her arms. His eyes raked over her again, loving the eyebrow piercing that drew more attention to her already striking eyes. He was rubbing her arm absentmindedly, and she opened her eyes. She smiled up at him. "You okay?"

He lied. "Yeah."

Goddammit. But she knew. Of course, she knew. This was Valerie, a woman that he did think was his soul mate, even when she seemed bound and determined to deny it. She knew and she wasn't going to let it go. "Is something wrong?"

He forced a smile. "No." He could be honest and tell her at least part of the emotions running through him. He looked in her eyes and made himself say some of what he'd been gnawing on. "You…are so…special, Val." She blinked and said nothing, sensing he was working through the emotion. "I just…never expected this, I guess." There was more to it, but he didn't want her feeling guilty about something she hadn't even done.

She stroked his cheek. "Do you regret it?"

God, he didn't want her to think that. He could never regret anything he'd ever done with her. "Oh. No. Fuck, no. I just…didn't expect it." She tilted her head, and he knew then that she understood. She knew how deep this all went for him and so she didn't have another word to say.

All he could do then was kiss her.

He loved this woman, loved her more than life itself, and he now felt whole for the first time in his life. She knew; she felt it too, and as he continued kissing her, she got closer to him, winding her fingers through his hair.

She was full of desire—he could feel it. Was he ready to make love to her again? Yes, he was, but he didn't want to rush this time. He wanted to savor her, taste her as though she were his last meal. She was demanding, though, moving at a hurried pace, and he was bound and determined to take his time.

He could feel her swallow as he kissed her neck. He could feel what she was feeling. It was deep and soulful, and there were no words for it. It wasn't just love. It was more than that. It was deeper than anything he'd ever known, and he knew then that it wasn't just him. She felt it too. By the time they joined again, he felt as though they were on a cloud, ethereal, and being inside her was where he belonged. It felt so right, so pure, so perfect.

Her orgasm wasn't as intense as it had been earlier, but she cried his name, consumed him, buried him inside her.

And as she fell asleep in his arms, he was finally able to say what he'd needed to say all night. "I love you, Val." He kissed her forehead and whispered, "And I always will."

He awoke to a loud banging, and it felt like he'd just drifted off to sleep. Then he heard through the door, "Val? Val! Are you in there?"

Yeah...it really had happened.

He took a deep breath, trying to get his bearings. He heard Val say, "Yeah. What do you want?"

"Can I come in?" It was Nick.

Val sighed and looked at Brad. She raised her voice. "Can't it wait till morning?"

"No. Please hurry up."

Something was going on. Still...he wanted to respect Val's wishes, so he whispered, "You want me to lay low?"

"Think he'd freak out with you in here?"

Brad smiled. "We're talking about Nick. Yeah. He'll freak. Or not." He ran his fingers through his hair. "I dunno." He didn't believe so after giving it more thought. Nick was pretty laid back—usually—but whatever was going on had the guy rattled, and it made Brad tense and he projected those feelings onto their drummer.

"Then just be quiet." She wanted him silent. He could do that. "Just a sec." She kissed him and then started dressing. He rested his head on the pillow.

But as she started walking to the door, he decided he should prepare as well. Something was seriously wrong. He could sense it. He went into the bathroom and found his jeans, pulling them on. He was able to hear Val open the door and say, "Yeah. What's so frigging important it can't wait till morning?"

"It's Ethan."

Oh, fuck. Yeah. Brad headed toward the door as Val said, "What? What, Nick? What the fuck?"

"I'm sorry to bug you, Val. I tried to find Brad. But—"

Their worst fear. Brad said, "Spit it out, man. What the fuck happened?"

"He won't wake up, man. He's like—"

"Where is he, Nick?"

"He's in the suite. He's passed out."

Brad pushed past the two of them, heading down the hall, Nick right behind him. He entered the suite. There were people surrounding one of the couches, and that's where Brad's gaze focused. Zane was beside Ethan. Fucking A. He knew before he even got all the way to his brother. It was just a matter of time, right? It was bound to happen, the overdose that had been lingering on the horizon. Leave it to Ethan to do it on the most important night of Brad's life, though.

The back of his mind told him maybe Ethan knew what was going on and had done it on purpose.

As soon as he thought it, he grew angry with himself. Of course, Ethan didn't do it on purpose—not the overdosing part anyway. This was what Ethan did, and it wasn't the first time. And it would keep happening until he gave the shit up for good.

Or died. But he couldn't think that way.

Brad had to make his way through the people standing around gawking to get to the couch where Zane and Ethan were, and he sensed that Nick and Val were right behind him. Ethan's head was reclined on the back of the couch. Brad asked Zane, "How do you know he's not just sleeping?"

"He's not. *You* try waking him up."

Val cut in front of him and sat next to Ethan. "Ethan. Ethan? Wake up." Ethan didn't say a word. He didn't blink or stir, and Brad saw panic wash over Val's face. She grabbed Ethan's shoulders and started moving him, but his head just swayed with the motion. He wasn't there. "Ethan. Wake up." Brad could tell from her voice that Val was starting to lose it. "Damn it, Ethan. Wake up. Wake up..." Zane grabbed her hands. Brad was grateful for that, because he had some decisions to make and didn't need her being hysterical.

"How long has he been like this?"

Nick said, "I don't know. We just tried to get him up a while ago."

"What'd he take?"

"Hell if I know, man. With Ethan, it could be anything."

Zane looked up. "Or everything." Yeah, Brad knew that.

Someone in the circle of people standing around added, "I'm pretty sure he did some smack." Again, with Ethan, that was pretty much a given.

Brad took a deep breath and muttered, "Fuckin' heroin." He wanted to add, *the evilest shit on the planet*, but that wouldn't have been productive. Instead, he nodded and asked, "What else?"

Zane let go of Val's wrists and looked up at Brad. "He was drinking. We all were. But there might have been more. I don't know. He was with a couple of guys and a girl a while ago, and they're gone."

"Do you know their names?"

"You're kidding, right?"

Val finally spoke. "Shouldn't we be calling the ambulance?"

Brad looked at her. He'd already been considering the same thing, but he had other ideas. "Do you think they'd get here in time?"

"We have to do *something*."

He nodded. "Zane, help me load him in the van. Nick, you still have that GPS app on your phone?"

"Yeah."

"Then you're comin' with."

Zane said, "I'm comin' too."

He leaned over and grabbed his friend. Seeing Ethan's face up close and feeling the dead weight of his body filled Brad's gut with dread. Jesus. This was bad. Ethan had never been like this before. It made all the other times he'd scared them look like a day at the beach. He didn't say a word, but when Zane got on the other side of Ethan to help move him, Brad could see it on his face too. This was fucking serious...and *real*. Brad clenched his jaw. He had to push those thoughts out. Now wasn't the time. He had to keep his shit together or they'd all lose it. He sucked in a deep breath. "Nick, get my keys too, would ya? They're on the dresser in our room."

By the time the elevator doors opened, Nick and Val had joined them. He saw that Val had his jeans and shoes with her and he felt gratitude—not just for her thoughtfulness, but how they all banded together for their friend. Over the past couple of years, they'd had moments, but it was now—when it mattered most—that everyone was completely on the same page. And, really, it wasn't for the band. In a roundabout way it was, but it was instead for their brother. They were family now, and they were doing what they had to to take care of Ethan. There was nothing selfish about it.

They laid Ethan down on the middle seat, and Brad felt a fresh new wave of fear overcome him. His friend felt cool to the touch and clammy, but his body on the seat looked dead. He swallowed it down and took the t-shirt and shoes from Val without a word and put them on. Nick handed him the keys and said, "I've got the address for the nearest hospital."

Val climbed up in the van and sat on the floor next to Ethan. That was good, because he needed Nick in her usual seat. "Nick, I need you riding shotgun as my navigator." Zane got in the very back. Brad caught the guy's eyes again and then saw Nick's as they got in the front. They were all as scared as he was. They knew like he did that this was something special.

He turned off the radio when he started the van. He

could hear Val behind him saying something to Ethan. It felt then like he had put himself on autopilot. Nick gave him directions and he followed them without question. He sped when he felt like it wasn't dangerous to do so. The only good thing about it being early morning was that the traffic was minimal. He didn't have a clock in the van, but he knew it was sometime after four.

Once they got to the hospital, things moved quickly. The staff there took Ethan's health seriously and whisked him away on a gurney, leaving the four of them to answer questions. They were all the same questions Brad had asked his bandmates when they'd pulled him out of Valerie's arms, but the nurse with the clipboard asked more. And none of them were able to answer many of them.

After some time, they were shooed off to the ER waiting room, and the nurse promised to give them information as soon as possible. After they settled in, she asked Brad back up to the desk. "I noticed that we failed to get insurance information for you."

Shit. If Ethan had insurance, Brad didn't know about it. "I don't know if he has any insurance." She frowned. "Do you need some kind of copay or something?"

"Well, I can't really assess it without knowing what insurance he has."

Brad pulled his hand through his hair. It was damp from the shower, but the ungodly heat on the drive to the hospital had dried out all of it except the part closest to his head. He drew in a deep breath and shrugged. "I don't know. I wish I could tell you, but I don't know. Can't you get that information from him when he wakes up?"

He had almost said *if—if he wakes up*. She said, "Will you

be guarantor of payment?"

Brad didn't know why, but it felt like a threat—like they wouldn't help Ethan unless they knew money was coming. What the hell else was he supposed to do? He shook his head but said, "Sure." He decided, though, that if they didn't save his brother, they wouldn't get shit from him.

And he felt himself grow numb as she started telling him costs of procedures.

Inside, he was raging. They were putting costs on his friend's life. If Brad had had oodles of money, he and the nurse wouldn't even be having that conversation. So when he joined his friends in the waiting room, he wasn't just worried; he was angry.

Sometime later, another nurse came out and asked for Brad. When he stood, she told him that Ethan was in stable condition and said they would be moving him to a room. She wasn't going to tell him what room until he got pissed and demanded it. "I'm paying the goddamn bill, and we might not be blood brothers, but make no mistake. We *are* brothers. You tell me the room number or let me speak with your supervisor." She looked nervous for a few minutes but finally caved and told him. They wouldn't be allowed in there for a while, so Brad shuffled them all off to the cafeteria and they all drank coffee.

It didn't escape his notice that no one wanted to eat.

As he sipped at the liquid, he talked with his friends, but he wasn't really paying attention. His mind was on Ethan, and if his friend made it out of this shit, they were going to have a long conversation, because he couldn't keep doing this. It was fucking killing him.

CHAPTER FORTY-SEVEN

THAT AFTERNOON, ONLY Brad was allowed to see Ethan. The nurse he'd gotten firm with before said, "It's because you're his brother, sir." The look in her eyes told Brad that he had to follow along with the story—if he said anything about not really being Ethan's brother, the jig was up. "These other people aren't family."

It was stupid, and he could have kicked his own ass for saying it, but he couldn't stop the words from flying out of his mouth. "What about Val? She's his fiancée. Shouldn't she be allowed to see him?"

Val looked up at him, but her acting skills were superb. Instead of protesting or denying it or even looking shocked, she got a look of indignation on her face, challenging the nurse to tell her no. The nurse nodded and Brad suspected she might have been onto them but agreed nonetheless. She wrote Val's name down and then led them both to ICU, and—once they were there—introduced them to the nurses in charge who then told Val and Brad a list of dos and don'ts. They weren't allowed to spend much time with Ethan, and there were only certain hours they could be there.

Brad asked, "What's next? I mean...is he in a coma or what?"

The pale thin-lipped nurse sitting at the desk gave him a look. "Yes, he's in a coma." Brad didn't say anything, but he had more questions. She saw that in his eyes and said, "He'll be in ICU until the doctor says he's stable enough to be moved."

"But how long will he be like this?"

She shrugged. She wasn't unsympathetic, but her words were clipped and cold. "There no way of telling. He could wake up from it in the next five minutes, or it could be five years from now."

Brad's heart sunk, but he put his arm around Val's shoulders, and they went in to spend as much time with Ethan as they could.

The guy looked like shit. His skin was almost white, making the dark circles under his eyes all the more noticeable. His cheeks looked sunken in, even though Ethan hadn't lost any weight recently. Val started crying when she saw him and sat in the one chair in the room, pulling it up close to the bed. She took Ethan's hand in hers.

It destroyed him, seeing her in such pain over something stupid and foolish Ethan had once again selfishly done to himself, and he couldn't do a goddamn thing to make her feel better. He rested his hand on her shoulder and squeezed, hoping to comfort her.

But then he felt a cold shiver worm its way up his spine.

No. He wasn't hurting just because of Val's helpless feelings or because Ethan had done this to himself. It started to dawn on him that there was a lot more going on here, and that realization felt like a hot knife in the chest as soon as it hit him.

Val still loved Ethan.

The next day they moved Ethan to another room, but he was dead to the world. Before that, though, Brad sent Zane and Nick to the hotel. They were in charge of checking them out of their rooms, Val's included.

They were all in the room with Ethan when he was first moved to it. Because it was during visiting hours, they were all allowed in the room, but the new nurse in charge made it clear that only Brad and Val could be there once visiting hours were over, and *only* if they didn't get in the way. Brad didn't see how they *could* be in the way. A nurse came by once in a while to check his vitals and the IV drip, but that was it.

There was another bed in the room. It was empty for now, but Brad knew another person could be put in the room at any time. He knew it was because the hospital had no idea how they were going to pay Ethan's bill (aside from Brad's signature on some papers), and a semi-private room was cheaper than one alone.

When Nick and Zane were told to leave, Val asked, "Brad, should we call June?"

Brad had already thought of it. There was no reason to tell her, because her knowledge wouldn't change a thing. The only thing it would do to his mom would be to make her worry. And he wasn't ready. "She'd flip out, Val…and there's really nothing she can do."

"But what if he stays in the coma forever, Brad, and we don't tell her? Then what?"

"And how the hell do you think she could even get here?"

"The same way we did."

He relented. She was right—his mother should know. But he hoped to give Ethan time to wake up. He was torn. "I'll make you a deal. If he's still like this in a week, I'll call her." Val seemed satisfied with the answer. He asked, "You wanna come with us to get something to eat?"

"I'm not hungry."

And that was the answer he got from her every time he asked her to eat a meal. He started bringing food to the room, though—a slice of toast or a banana from the cafeteria. She'd eat at it without even paying attention, but she did eat, in spite of her insistence that she wasn't hungry.

When it was evident that Ethan wasn't going to wake up anytime soon, Brad gave Nick and Zane a wad of cash and asked them to find a cheap ass motel with two beds and a shower. That way they could sleep and shower when they needed to.

He called his boss on the second day, because he was scheduled for work the following day and, even if Ethan miraculously awakened that afternoon, there was no way in hell they'd make it back in time or that Brad would be in any shape to work. His boss was cool about it but asked him to keep in touch. He also canceled their shows for the following weekend, because even if Ethan was okay by then, he probably wouldn't be ready to perform. He'd need some time to himself.

But Brad didn't know how long he could keep all their lives on hold.

Val continued refusing to leave Ethan's side as the days wore on, and it became evident that he wasn't just going to sit up in bed and start talking. Brad knew what was going through Val's mind. She was feeling guilty. She thought that if she and Brad hadn't spent the night together, she somehow could have saved Ethan. Or, just like the thought he'd entertained himself, maybe she believed that Ethan *knew* what had happened with them and done it on purpose.

It was possible. It was something Brad had considered more than once.

It seemed like forever ago now, but he was sure he remembered them kissing in the suite, and that was what had prompted him to put her off and make her pissed off. Ethan could have seen that. And then he felt chills, because Ethan had, just that evening, been telling Val how much he loved her and wanted to get back with her. If Ethan had seen what had transpired between his best friend and the woman he apparently still loved, he very well could have decided to overdose. Ethan took everything in life hard, *everything*, and it was a possibility.

Yeah, Ethan made his own choices (and they were shitty choices at that), but if Brad and Val had pushed him over the edge like that?

God, that revelation hurt. It hurt badly. And he was never going to say a word to Val about it. It would be something he kept to himself for eternity.

A couple of days later, Brad, Nick, and Zane came back to the room, having finished breakfast, loaded with a couple of snacks for Val. When they walked in, Val was holding a cup of water up to Ethan's mouth, her hand resting behind his neck.

Brad freaked out at first, thinking Val had finally gone over the edge. The woman hadn't bathed in days, had hardly eaten a thing, and looked like hell. If that wasn't guilt, he didn't know what was. But when he first walked in, he was convinced she was fooling herself into pretending he was awake and was forcing water down his throat. As he got closer, though, he saw that Ethan's eyes *were* open. He whispered to Nick to ask him to get a nurse. And it wasn't long before they were all whisked out of the room so the staff could tend to Ethan.

Relief washed over Brad, and he excused himself to find a restroom. He found a tiny one down the hall that looked like one used for urinalyses. He locked the door and let the past week's emotions overtake him. He hadn't cried like that since he'd been a kid, and he hoped he never would again, but he had a lot of shit to let go and no punching bag around to beat the shit out of, so he sat on the toilet, rested his arm against the sink, dropped his head on his arm, and let it all out.

Somehow, he knew his life would never be the same.

They got back to Denver and tried to settle back into a routine, but it felt fake to Brad. None of them talked about it. Yeah, he understood that they felt relief that Ethan had pulled through, and it was a horrible thing, but no one wanted to talk about it. It was tucked away in a seemingly safe place.

It was like a time bomb.

Brad wanted some reassurances. He was at the end of his rope. Ethan was his brother and a brilliant musician, but Brad didn't want to wonder and worry when the next time would be.

He felt like he was walking on eggshells, and he considered calling another team meeting to talk about what had transpired. But then he thought first that he should talk to Nick to see how he felt. Nick was the most reasonable of the bunch, the one most likely to tell him what he thought. So when he caught Nick outside the apartment after work, he asked him to take a walk. He was still wearing his work coveralls, but he needed to feel everyone out. "How you feeling?"

"What do you mean?"

"The past few weeks have been pretty emotional. You holding up okay, man?"

"Yeah." Nick shrugged. He was quiet for a little bit but then said, "Things have been a little weird, though."

"Yeah." He cleared his throat. "I was thinking about calling a meeting."

"You think that would help?"

Brad took a deep breath. "Honestly? I have no fucking idea. But…I hate the idea of waiting for the next time, you know? I'd like a promise from Ethan that we're done with this phase of our lives."

"You don't really think he'd make a promise like that, do you?"

"No. Wishful thinking."

They walked in silence for a minute and then Nick said, "You know what's going on with Val and Ethan, right?"

A ringing started in his ears, and he felt dread as a shiver tickled his spine. He knew he wasn't going to like what Nick had to say, but he needed to know. "What?"

Nick stopped walking and Brad turned to face him. "I'm only telling you this because it's only fair to you. I'm not sure what all is or was going on between you and Val, but I don't want—anyway, uh…Ethan proposed to Val."

It felt like the air had been knocked out of his lungs. When he got his bearings, he sucked in a deep breath of air. Had he heard Nick right? "What?"

"Ethan asked Val to marry him. I, uh…don't know if it's totally official yet, but…"

Brad couldn't hear him after that, and it felt as though the world turned black. He already knew. If Ethan proposed, he knew Val accepted. He felt numb.

Somehow he had the presence of mind to say, "Don't say anything about me and Val to Ethan. That shit's over."

"Yeah. No way. It's not like she was cheating on him."

Brad felt like he was going to throw up. He grew quiet, walking back to the apartment with Nick, but his mind was trying to find a way to deal with the worst news it had ever received.

CHAPTER FORTY-EIGHT

BRAD SAT AT the bar nursing the mug of beer. His forearm still stung, but it was a temporary irritation he'd grown used to over the years.

He thought back over the past two hours. He'd been sitting in a chair getting new ink. He'd asked his tattoo artist to design a new one for him, something that had been begging to be part of his permanent story for a while. So now he glanced down at his left forearm to look at the spot that stung—the representation of an arrow. It looked much like what Brad imagined a Native American might have used hundreds of years ago. It was beautiful and colorful and fit right in with all the other tattoos on his arm.

They all held meaning for him. One of his first had become part of the montage on his upper right arm when he'd been eighteen. It was a small banner that was a cliché, but it said *MOM*. He'd shown it to his mother to soften the blow that her son had gotten an entire half sleeve of ink in less than two months. Others were simply cool designs that became borders around and between the pictures. Another in the initial half-sleeve was a bullet, meant to signify the first name of his band. It was a cool tattoo...dark with no color. Only his skin created the lighter areas of shading. But he also had a tattoo of a revolver, and underneath it were the words *Fully Automatic*. He'd had that one done just a month or so after meeting Val. What was it about that woman? What had it been about her then? Sure, she was pretty, but for a while now he'd been surrounded by pretty girls who wanted to feel like they were dating a not-too-dangerous bad boy. He'd never understood how he'd gotten that rep. He had his suspicions, though. The main reason was probably because he'd always hung out with Ethan, a guy who *had* earned the reputation...between his bouts with drugs, drinking, fighting, and a couple run-ins with the law in high school, not to mention the fact that he'd broken a lot of girls' hearts too. The only thing Ethan ever seemed to give a shit about were himself, his mom, and his guitar. Brad sometimes.

So when Ethan had walked into Brad's house with Valerie all those years ago, Brad had expected a girl who was more Ethan's flavor...trashy. He'd never said anything and hated feeling judgmental, but Ethan wound up with skanky girls. Valerie...she was different. She was sweet, intelligent, friendly. But, more than that and something he couldn't understand, he felt like they had some kind of connection. He'd been drawn to her from the moment she said *hi* and then stared at the beginnings of what would become a full sleeve on his right arm.

He knew they'd had...*something*, and for a long time both of them had just pretended it was a best friendship. And they'd finally consummated that burning, consuming need they'd always had for each other and denied. That was it, he'd thought. *Finally*...years later, they could be together and no one—Ethan included, the guy who'd shit all over her and pissed away any chance he should have had—could say anything about it.

Brad downed another swig of beer. Exactly how had it happened, though, that Valerie had once more wound up in his friend's arms? But this time, they were engaged to be married. Brad had figured out that Val still loved Ethan because she hadn't left his side, not once, while he was in that goddamned coma. She loved him in spite of the fact that the guy had jerked her around for way too long. Brad had thought Valerie was really done with his friend. She'd broken up with him, had finally had enough, had even dated a good guy who'd treated her well...a guy Brad would have hated to lose her to. No, Brad hadn't been too happy about that one either, but at least Jet had treated Valerie with love and respect.

So he'd spent the last week watching Ethan somehow pull her back, like she was a fish with a hook in her mouth. And Brad realized then that what he'd told her all those years ago was true...that he'd wait for her, forever if need be.

What a fucking lovesick dumb ass.

While he'd been sitting in the chair earlier as his tattoo artist permanently colored his skin yet again, he looked at that arrow that he'd asked her to draw. It signified what Valerie had done to him. Somehow she'd struck him in the heart. It felt like an arrow, piercing clean through, and if he pulled it out, he'd die. He knew that. So he'd be happy just so long as she was in his life.

He'd known Karen had had a crush on him ever since he'd had her ink her first tattoo on him—one of a jaguar on his lower abdomen. Earlier tonight, she'd touched his arm more than usual, more than she'd needed to, but she'd finally given up flirting. He knew he'd been sour and quiet. But maybe he should take her up on her offer. He was considering it as he knocked back the remainder of the beer in the glass. He needed something—*anything*—to drown out the fresh pain he felt from losing Valerie again. Yep…Karen could maybe be just the distraction he'd need.

And he'd continue to wait.

In the meantime, he had to prepare to engage in a difficult conversation, likely to be the hardest one of his whole goddamned life.

He waited for the perfect moment. If nothing else, Brad really was a patient man. He'd always believed good things came to those who waited, and he had to keep believing it.

Several weeks later, Val was in the kitchen brewing a cup of coffee on a Saturday morning. He'd just gotten out of the shower. He leaned against the counter next to her and said, "Let's go to Starbucks." She started to protest. "Don't worry—the guys will drink it."

She considered it and nodded. "Just give me a minute." She went into her bedroom and pulled her hair back. He wondered if she was telling Ethan what she was doing and decided not to worry about it. If Ethan needed to be a part of it, he'd get some news he wouldn't have wanted to hear.

But Val came out alone, and they walked in silence to his car. He drove the short way to Starbucks and they went inside. She started pulling out her wallet. He knew she was working again, but he wasn't going to invite her out and then make her pay. "I got this."

"You sure?"

"Yeah. Mocha, right?" She nodded. They decided to sit outside where it was warm but not yet hot under the umbrella. Brad pulled his sunglasses out from where they dangled off the front of his t-shirt. He needed to hide his eyes from her. He took a deep breath. Prolonging it wouldn't make it any easier. He and Val had always had an honest relationship, and it wasn't going to stop now. He just had to force the words out. "Val, I don't want you to feel bad, okay, but we need to talk."

She nodded. "Yeah, we do." He was glad she agreed, so he decided not to pussyfoot around the subject. He was going to hit her with the big guns.

"That night…did it mean anything to you?"

She looked pained, almost on the verge of tears. It almost made him angry. *She* was sad? Seriously? She spat it out, though. "Yes."

Well, that was more than he'd hoped for. He hadn't expected her to say that. He was expecting her to tell him it was a one-night thing, something she'd always wanted to get out of her system, and now that she had, she was free to marry the love of her life. He searched her eyes for truth, and he believed her. She meant it. But now for the harder question. "Do you love him?"

She acted like this conversation was hurting her as much as it was him, and he wanted to get on his knees and beg her, asking *why*? Why, if she cared so much, was she doing something so fucking stupid? But he wasn't going to. If she wanted to marry Ethan, he didn't need to make it harder on her. She sounded desperate. "Why? Why do you want to know?"

He had to stay cool. He couldn't let on. "I *need* to know."

"Why?"

He couldn't tell her, no, but he didn't have to lie to her. He had to know her answer, though. So he took a deep breath. How he managed to keep his voice steady and calm, he would never know. All he could figure was it was due to all those years of playing the diplomat, keeping peace amongst his friends and bandmates. And he heard himself as though he were listening to someone else. The words echoed in his head as they escaped his throat. "If you love him, I'll support your decision, and I'll never say anything about that night again. Ever." He took off his sunglasses then and stared her down. This was the most vulnerable she would ever see him and, based on her answer, she might not ever see this part of him again. Because if she loved Ethan, really loved him, then Brad had no business being in the picture at all…and he'd make damned sure he wasn't. And before he could stop them, his heart made one last bid for hers. "But if you tell me you don't, I'll fight for you."

She inhaled sharply and stared at him, her mouth open, her eyes watery. It took her some time to get the words out, but when she did, it felt like a sledgehammer slamming into his heart. "I love Ethan."

He nodded and looked out on the traffic. He had to process, but he couldn't let her see what he was feeling. He sucked more air into his lungs and sipped at his cup of coffee. He didn't trust himself to say a goddamned word.

Val, smart girl that she was, kept her trap shut. She knew it was heavy. She looked down at the table and said nothing.

She'd just set him on the path he'd follow for the rest of his life. It even sounded melodramatic in his head, but he knew—he knew he'd never love another woman like he loved Valerie. She was the perfect woman in his mind, but her heart would never belong to him. He'd been fucking stupid to ever even hope she could love him. No, she was hopelessly addicted to Ethan. But he couldn't point a finger, because he was hooked on her just the same.

It was something he had to accept, though. And he'd survive. He always had.

More than that, though, he didn't want to hurt Val anymore. She'd told him the truth, and he appreciated it. He couldn't torment her over it. If he really loved her, he'd let her go and let her try to pursue happiness however she needed.

So he took another deep breath and slid his sunglasses back on. "Thanks for being honest with me, Valerie." He stuck out his hand to shake hers. "Friends?"

She put her hand in his. "Of course. Forever."

And Brad then knew he had to find a way to live out the rest of his life. Fully Automatic. That was it, all he had left, and he was going to make it if it killed him. He didn't need a woman.

He hoped it wouldn't take the rest of his life to convince himself of it.

CHAPTER FORTY-NINE

WHEN HE WASN'T driving Fully Automatic forward, he spent the next few months trying to fuck Valerie out of his brain. He'd had more mindless sex in the last three months than he'd ever had before. He was still discreet about it; he couldn't help but be. Unlike Nick who "didn't give a fuck *where* (or who) he fucked," Brad didn't need it plastered on a billboard.

He *did*, however, hope it would do the trick.

After those few months, though, he started feeling hollow, and it bothered him that he'd gone on a path of self-destruction. Sure, he knew it could have been much worse, but he would have derived just as much satisfaction from jerking off in the shower. And some of the women actually made it more difficult, because they didn't want a one-time thing. He didn't either, but none of them fit the bill.

None of them would ever fit the bill, and when he realized that, he decided to stop.

It wasn't fixing a goddamn thing.

He knew, too, that in the back of his mind, he was expecting the next big Valerie-Ethan breakup. Only it never came. This time, there was no arguing, no screaming and yelling matches, no loud, obnoxious fights. And, for the first time ever, he saw Ethan trying to be sober. He was going to classes and staying clean.

As much as Brad wanted to deny it, he knew Valerie was responsible.

It was hard making the transition back to friends only with Valerie. He knew he had to find a way to do it, but it was difficult. The woman didn't realize how much she'd broken his heart.

By November, his fire had died back to the slow burn it had always been. There was no way to cool it off any further.

One day, he got a text from Jet asking when he had time to talk. He texted back *Now*, and it was minutes later that Jet was calling him.

"What's up, man? How you doing?" In a way, he felt like Jet was a better friend today than ever before, because they now had something else in common. But at least Jet hadn't been dumped so Val could run back to Ethan.

Jesus...he had to stop doing that to himself.

Jet said, "Great. We just finished recording our first album. It's in post right now, and in a month or so, our first single is going to hit the airwaves."

"That's great, man. I can't think of another band who deserves it more." Aside from Fully Automatic, of course, but he wasn't going to piss on Jet's good news. Brad wondered why he was calling, but knew he'd get around to it in good time. Jet was a lot of things, including cocky, but he wasn't the kind of guy to flaunt shit in other people's faces. Brad knew he wasn't calling just to brag.

"Thanks, Brad. That means a lot coming from you." Brad heard him take a deep breath. "That's why I'm calling. I'm sure you know I don't have a lot of pull, but if you guys are game, I'm going to see if you can play one or two shows with us when we're around your area. Kind of like the opening act to the opening act?" Jet chuckled.

Brad smiled. "Yeah, we'd definitely be up for that shit. We play all the time anyway."

"Don't I know. You drive your band into the ground."

"You really think so?"

"No…but you have to be the hungriest guy I know. If you don't make it, there's something wrong with the world."

Brad laughed. "Believe me—there's *lots* wrong with the world." God, he was gonna be a downer. He had to shut his mouth. "Seriously, thanks for thinking of us, even if it doesn't pan out."

"I'm also plugging you with the powers that be, if you catch my drift. You guys need to be heard from coast to coast. I'm serious. And if these guys listen to reason, you will be."

"Thanks for that. Sincerely."

"Least I can do. You made me step up my game." Brad laughed again, this time long and loud. Jet was one of the best guitar players he knew, and while it was flattering that the man said Brad challenged him, he highly doubted it. "I'm dead serious. I was just fuckin' around, playing our shows but getting pretty lackadaisical. Then here comes this kid, fresh outta school, playing the guitar like he was born with it in his hands. I watched you. Your goal was never to be the fastest or the loudest. Your goal was precision—you never miss a beat; you never hit a wrong note, even when you're improvising. You're good, man, and you made me shoot for that kind of accuracy onstage. You're impressive as hell, and I shouldn't be the only one noticing that."

The air had evaporated from his lungs. He had always liked and respected Jet before, but apparently it went two ways. "Thanks." He repeated exactly what Jet had said moments earlier. "That means a lot coming from *you*."

And, for the first time in a long time, hope was going to fuel the hunger Jet had mentioned.

Brad wasn't ready for another tattoo, but he wanted an excuse to see Karen. He was tired of hollow non-relationships. He wanted to give real dating a try again. It had been far too long, and he was beginning to think he'd forgotten how. Hell, yeah, his heart still ached, but Val had made her choice for all eternity. It was time for Brad to move on.

So he headed into his favorite tattoo shop one Saturday afternoon. Karen was working. She was with someone, and the girl at the counter told him another fifteen or twenty minutes. So he walked around, looking first at the body jewelry under the glass counter and then finally sitting down and staring at the television in their sitting area.

When Karen was done with her customer, she sat next to Brad on the couch. "My favorite customer. What's up, Brad Payne?"

He smiled. Karen's dark hair was pulled into a high ponytail, showing off a delicate neck tattoo under her right ear. Her personality was rough around the edges, a little too tough and cold, but looks-wise, she was hotter than hell. She was heavily tattooed and pierced and wore a lot of heavy makeup. Hell, she was more Ethan's type than Brad's. But the woman had obviously been interested in him for a long time, and he needed to get back up on that horse.

"I'm thinking about getting another tattoo."

"Yeah? What'd you have in mind?"

He shook his head. "Not sure. I want something on my left shoulder blade. You know, to kind of balance things out back there. I was thinking maybe you could surprise me."

"How much money we talkin'?"

He smiled. "Let's see what you come up with. Then you can tell me."

"Pretty big?"

"Yeah."

"Bad ass?"

"Of course."

She smiled at him and nodded. "Give me a week."

He smiled back and then took a deep breath. "I wanted to ask you another question."

"What's that?"

"You seeing anybody?"

She cocked her head a little and her smile widened. "Nobody important."

"Wanna go out sometime?"

"I'd love to." Yeah, he hadn't misread her. So he asked

her for her number and promised to call her within the week.

And not a moment too soon, because Ethan and Valerie started planning their wedding.

One thing Brad could say about Karen—she managed a lot of the time to keep his mind off the impending wedding. Ethan had already made Brad agree to be his best man. He didn't know that he was the right guy for the job. Yeah, Ethan was his brother and he loved him. The problem was he also loved the bride.

But he agreed, and that was that. The entire Fully Automatic crew would be at the altar on that fateful day. Valerie chose a date in July, because she didn't want it to interfere with any shows.

The wedding itself *wasn't* going to interfere with shows—Brad made sure of that. No, but the fact that there was a wedge between him and Val did. He didn't know that things would ever feel *normal* between them again, but, more than that, they had to change things onstage again. Oh, Val continued wearing her skimpy little outfits, but there was no flirting between them anymore. No way was Brad even going to try it, and he was glad Val wasn't attempting it either. It would have felt awkward and weird…and, no matter how he felt about the whole thing, it would have seemed like they were slapping Ethan in the face. Brad might have thought their marriage was the stupidest, most misguided act in the history of the world, but he respected the idea that she and Ethan were engaged.

Most days, he blamed himself. It was so fucking stupid, and he should have known. Valerie always, *always* ran back to Ethan. Every fucking time. Sometimes it was almost immediate; this last time, he'd actually believed it would never happen again. What a dumb ass he'd been.

By the time the wedding rolled around, he and Karen were only seeing each other casually. He was glad, because he wasn't ready to bring a woman to the wedding.

It was hard, but he asked the bride for a dance at the reception afterward. Val looked so fulfilled, so beautiful, that he couldn't deny her happiness any longer. He wanted her to know things were okay between them.

Val looked almost ready to cry when he asked, and that was when he knew he'd done the right thing. He really had been missing her friendship. He knew, though, that that friendship would never be the same. She was now a married woman and her loyalty would lie, from this point forward, with her husband…exactly where it should. Brad knew he would do well to remember that.

CHAPTER FIFTY

KAREN'S HEAD RESTED on Brad's chest, her dark hair flowing down her back. She rubbed his uncovered pec with her fingers. Brad felt himself getting sleepy. He needed to get up because he had to work the next day, but he wasn't ready to leave, not yet. He didn't want to just fuck her and run, even if his feelings for her didn't run deep. Karen had a brash personality, but Brad was starting to suspect it was to cover up deep insecurities.

"You know I really like you, don't you?"

He smiled. "Yeah. I kinda like you back," he joked.

She lifted her head to look at him. "Seriously, though. I know…" She shifted her eyes to look at something else. She was having a hard time saying what was on her mind. "I know in your business that you probably get plenty of…girls. And I'm not asking for a commitment, okay, but I just want you to know I'm here."

He wasn't quite sure what she was saying. He was going to let it slide, but then she looked him in the eyes. She needed something from him, and he wasn't sure what. "What do you mean exactly?"

She exhaled, then inhaled again, both visible and full of effort. "I mean…" She swallowed. "I mean I know you probably get pussy thrown at you day and night and it's hard to resist. I get that, and I don't want to interfere with it." Brad raised his eyebrows. He wasn't going to correct her. Yeah, he had offers, but it wasn't a constant barrage of women approaching him with their legs open. Ethan got way more offers than he did. He was okay with that, because he didn't want to fuck everything that was "thrown" at him simply because he had the opportunity. He was trying to figure out how to respond when she said, "I'm just happy to be with you whenever."

"What are you saying?"

"I'm saying I'm perfectly fine being a friend with benefits."

At first he thought he'd never been in that position before, but that wasn't true. His brief relationship with Jo (or "Sugar") had been that kind of thing, even though they'd never called it that. She'd call him when she wanted him around, and he wouldn't hear from her for weeks. If the sex hadn't been so damn hot, he might have felt used. And now, here Karen was *asking* for that. He didn't want her to feel like she was a second choice. No one deserved to feel that way…and yet she was. Unless and until he could find a way over her, Val would always be number one in his heart. Karen might have thought it would be his success in snagging groupies, but that would be the least of her worries. On some level, she must have known his heart couldn't fully engage.

He struggled inside. He thought maybe he wouldn't say anything, but—in a way—that felt dishonest. He sat up. "Karen, you are a great girl. I'm glad I met you. And I enjoy the time we have together."

Her mouth screwed up in a grimace. "But no way, huh? Just not good enough?"

"Oh, no. No. That's not what I was going to say at all. No. There's something you need to know, though." He took a deep breath. Her brown eyes searched his. "There's a woman—just *one*—I've known her for a long time and, as stupid as it sounds, I have loved her for almost as long."

"Not reciprocated?"

"No, not really. We hooked up once and things just didn't work out."

Karen smiled and scooched up so her lips were close to his. "Ah…so *my* job is to push her out of your mind, and then you can just focus on little old me."

Brad wasn't going to tell her that he doubted it was possible. He hoped it was. And he felt better, knowing that he wasn't harboring that secret from her. If she wanted to try pursuing some sort of relationship with him, she had to know what she was up against.

He didn't know that he was ready, but he also knew that he probably never would be.

It was a good thing he'd been socking money away again. He'd always wanted to record a higher-quality CD, but now he *had* to. Jet called and asked him to deliver something as soon as possible. Last Five Seconds now had *connections*, but Jet said he needed to move pretty quickly. Brad called around to studios in the area, because the one he'd settled on before had changed its rates. Even the least expensive studio he talked to was more than he had, so he sat the band down and told them what was going on. They'd probably instead have to cut an EP—two or three of their best songs—and just make sure they couldn't get the songs any better. But Val said she had some money too and Ethan said he had some money. If Brad didn't know better, Ethan was going to hit up his grandfather (either that or they had money they'd received as wedding gifts that they'd socked away). Ethan hadn't asked the old guy for money in a long time, but Brad knew Ethan's grandfather had a little nest egg and was happy to share with his grandson when he asked. Brad almost told him not to, because he was pretty sure Ethan was still paying for his Texas coma (and Brad was grateful for that, because, otherwise, he would have had to come up with the money). The only thing that saved the guy was that Val's parents paid for the wedding.

But the entire band agreed to forego concert funds if it meant they could put together enough money for a decent CD. Zane said, "Besides, even if this falls through, we can sell it at our merch table." Brad knew that was right, and they could sell it for lots more than the shitty CD they'd been selling for the last couple of years.

Knowing they had the money after another few weeks, they decided to go balls out. They couldn't settle on a few songs and wound up with fourteen. The cost of putting the CD together would depend upon how much time their asses were in the studio, so Brad stressed perfection. "Practice your asses off first, guys. When you go in, you need to nail it the first time." They knew what was at stake.

If they fucked up on studio time too much, they wouldn't be able to record all the songs. It was as simple as that.

It started with Nick. They bought an hour here, an hour there, and booked the studio for those times. After Nick laid down the drum tracks, Brad and Ethan took turns doing guitars. Ethan was rhythm on some, lead on others, and vice versa with Brad. Zane followed up with bass. They finally got all the music down and were happy with it.

Val had a problem, though. Her voice hadn't been up to snuff for a month or two, and Brad was afraid it was going to affect the quality of the CD. He didn't say anything, but she was starting to sound like crap—hoarse and raspy. It might have sounded sexy on a song or two, but it didn't work for some of the sweeter melodies she had to belt out. At first he thought maybe she was coming down with something, but he lost that notion when she was even worse a month later.

No one wanted to say anything, but Brad was sure they were all thinking the same thing.

They were *fucked*. No studio executives in their right mind would want Fully Automatic sounding like that.

Still, Brad intended to give her a chance. She'd been with them for the long haul and had propelled them to new heights. He didn't want to just shit on her. But he was worried. This was their big chance, everything he'd ever hoped for.

He'd let her record and then they could discuss it—as a group—and decide together.

The first song she recorded was "Metal Forever," one of her favorites. It was one that highlighted Val's emotional depth as well as her range. But, right out of the gate, her voice was raspy and harsh.

She spent an hour recording and rerecording, because she wasn't happy with it. He wasn't either, but he wasn't going to say anything even though he could feel the money bleeding out the door. He and Ethan were in the studio. At the end of the hour, she broke down in tears.

Ethan was being a good husband. Brad was glad for that. He pulled her in his arms. "What's wrong, babe?" he asked.

"You guys have noticed, right? Something's wrong with my voice. I rest it and it just doesn't snap back."

Brad wanted to be encouraging. "It sounds okay, Val."

Ethan patted her back. "Yeah…works for the song."

Her voice was scratchy sounding, like she'd been yelling in a football stadium all day. "Maybe so, but it'll never work for 'Just Another Stupid Love Song.' My voice has to be clear for that." Brad agreed, but he was glad she'd said it instead of him. Ethan started to say something, but Val interrupted. "No, Ethan, you know it and I know it. I can't sound like I took a fucking emery board to my vocal cords for that one. I have to sound sweet and soft and sexy, or it doesn't work when I scream at the end. Goddammit." She started crying again.

Brad wasn't willing to give up on her yet. "So you take it easy tonight. You drink extra tea and don't say shit. Nothing. If your voice is still fucked up, you go to the doctor."

"I—we can't afford the doctor."

"Bullshit. You're goin'." Why the fuck was she being so stubborn? Did she *not* want to do this? She acted like she was going to argue with him. "You're going, Val.

Don't piss me off." He looked at Ethan. "Talk some sense into your wife, please."

"Yeah, because I'm really good at persuading her." But Ethan looked at Val, his eyes sympathetic. "Val, he's right. If your voice is still sucky tomorrow, you should go."

"And then what? You know how much money it'll cost just to be seen? And then what? What if—"

Brad needed her to be rational and quit stressing her voice out more with her emotional outburst. "Stop it. We cross that bridge when we come to it. For now, you go home and rest."

And, even though Brad wasn't a religious man, he considered praying that night.

CHAPTER FIFTY-ONE

IT WAS A few days later before Val was able to get to the doctor. She came home in tears, Ethan holding her close, and they said they wanted to have a band meeting.

Ethan did most of the talking because Val was struggling to hold it together, but Brad suspected he was talking because of her voice too. She was holding out hope.

They sat in the living room and Ethan said, "Bad news, guys. The doctor said Val has some pretty brutal scar tissue. He chewed her ass for not getting vocal training, said she had shitty vocal techniques. He said the cure is surgery—laser would be best—and vocal therapy. The two of us have talked, and we don't think Fully Automatic has the time or the money."

Brad looked over at Val. She reminded him of a water balloon filled past its breaking point, her eyes springing leaks, tears starting to fall down her cheeks, because he knew how much this meant to her. Fuck. He was the one who'd talked her into being their lead singer in the first place. He'd had no idea she'd been stressing her voice so hard for so long. He'd give her credit—he could tell she was sad, but she was doing a great job of holding it together.

He started to protest. It was killing him seeing how this whole mess was eviscerating her. He too wanted to hold her close and tell her everything would be okay, but it wasn't going to be. She had to have surgery, and Ethan was right—they didn't have the money and they probably didn't have the time. If healing from the surgery was like other operations, they were talking weeks. And therapy on top of it? They didn't have that kind of time, not if they wanted in on the opportunity Jet had offered. So he stopped himself from giving a knee-jerk response, trying to spare Val's feelings, and instead asked, "So what are you proposing?"

Ethan shrugged but Val steeled her face—Brad could see it—and she said, "I think you should sing lead vocals."

Brad knew he could do it, but he hadn't expected her to say that. He too was feeling emotional, and so he blurted out, "No. No way."

Val nodded and reached over to grab his hands. "Please, Brad. You know I can't do this."

Zane added, "They're right. If we weren't under the gun, it might be different, but…"

Nick nodded too but didn't say a word. Brad sighed. "Val, you sure you want to do this?"

She hadn't taken her hands off his. In spite of the tears threatening to fall, making her eyes glisten, she smiled. She whispered, "Yes."

Ethan said, "You've been singing most of the backup of all the songs since Val took over."

Zane said, "You've got a great voice man."

Brad took another deep breath. Being their leader meant he'd take responsibility, even when it might hurt others. So he nodded. But then he said, "Okay. But no fuckin' way am I rerecording 'Metal Forever.' That's Val's song. It stays as is or we scrap it."

All three of the guys agreed and Val started crying then. She couldn't hold it together anymore. It was as though her tears ducts had been cracks in a dam, and they had weakened to the point that they just couldn't hold the water back any longer. It was torrential. She excused herself and went to the bedroom she now shared with Ethan.

Brad asked Ethan, his voice quiet, "Think she'll be okay?"

Ethan, his voice equally low, said, "I don't know, man. I've never seen her like this. I'm worried about her."

Nick said, "This sucks. Totally sucks. Can't we wait?"

Ethan shook his head. "No way. We're talking thousands of dollars for this surgery. We just don't have it. We're still paying for my hospital stay in Texas. We don't have the money, and we don't have the time…right, Brad?"

"Yeah—Jet made it sound like if we wait too long, we might as well just kiss it goodbye."

Nick sighed, looked at his feet, and then shrugged. "Poor Val."

Brad knew they all felt like total assholes, but they knew what had to be done. Brad wanted to practice in the apartment that night so he could go in that Saturday and bang them all out, but he wasn't going to rub Val's nose in it. Instead, he sang one song on the way to work and coming back home, then the next, and the next. He had a few days before the next studio slot. And he sang each song until he went through it once without any mistakes and sounding the way he wanted it too. Sometimes he could get through three songs going one way.

He couldn't hold a candle to Val. She'd perfected the songs. But when he sang, he dedicated each song in his heart to her.

He wasn't sure how he did it, either, but he had all thirteen goddamned songs recorded in a few hours. Lots of water and not stressing his voice. He was nervous now, though, wondering if he should get vocal lessons. He didn't want to suffer in the future like Val was today, and maybe a little prevention now would save him from pain and surgery later. So he decided he'd get a little vocal training on the sly over the next year.

He felt like such an asshole. It should have been Val's voice on the CD. Everyone listened to the CD and loved it, including the track with Val's vocals. It sounded great.

And that made Brad feel guilty as hell, but there was nothing he could do about that.

He shipped it off to Jet, but not before talking to him on the phone. "Man, Val's only on one song."

"Why? What the hell happened?" Brad told him about what had been happening with Val's voice and that she was going to need surgery. "That sucks."

"Yeah, so we decided I should do the vocals. We knew we had to get this done and get it done quickly. If Val could have had the surgery…"

He heard Jet sigh. "Frankly, she was one of the selling points. But I'll see what I can do. You guys kick ass." Brad suspected that if Ethan had done the vocals, Jet wouldn't have touched it with a ten-foot pole. It had never been a secret that Ethan and Jet couldn't stand each other, but he and Jet had a good working relationship, and Brad trusted him. If he said he was going to try, Brad believed he meant it. And, after he paid the clerk at the post office, it was out of his hands. Their fate rested in others' hands, and Brad decided to put it out of his mind. Thinking about it would just stress him out.

Now came the time to tell their hardcore local fans about Val. And he knew that wasn't going to be easy, because she had a lot of fans. Still, it had to be done. The weekend before, they'd said she was ill (half true) and couldn't perform, so Brad was covering for her. Now, though, they had to tell the truth and pray the fans didn't throw shit at them.

Brad was talking to the guys about how to do it and Val said, "Let me do it. I want to."

Val had been teetering on depression. Her telling her fans could go one of two ways—it could, in one way, give her closure and also let her know how well loved she was. It could at least make her feel better about leaving. On the other hand, it could just make her feel worse, knowing how much she would be missed. Still…if she wanted to, he wanted to let her. And, coming from her, he was sure the fans would understand better.

All three shows that weekend, she opened. She sang "Metal Forever" first, and she was able to hold it together for the most part. But then she said a tearful goodbye to her fans, telling them what had happened. Each night the fans screamed and hollered and cheered for her, and the last night, one good-hearted fan even started collecting money for her. At the end of the night, the girl gave Val a coffee can filled with bills. Val didn't want to take it, but the girl insisted. It held over three hundred and seventy dollars…not nearly enough for surgery, but it made Val cry fresh tears nonetheless.

If Brad had any say in it, someday he'd make sure Val got her real shot. But he had to make sure Fully Automatic made it first.

Ethan's dad died a couple weeks later. Ethan pretended like he didn't care, but Brad knew from his long-standing friendship that Ethan had a lot of daddy issues. As much as he acted like he didn't give a shit, Brad knew better. And, worse yet, Brad saw the signs that indicated a new cycle of drugs and alcohol abuse were just around the corner. He didn't know if Val recognized the signs, but he did.

Brad was surprised, because Ethan indulged for about a week and then got his shit back together. Just in time, too, because their dream came true. They got *the* call and were signing a contract within a week. Ethan got pissed at Brad because Brad read every line on those papers and even questioned a few. Ethan just wanted to sign and be done with it.

The next year was a whirlwind. They rerecorded some of their songs and the label took over. The label tried to talk them into changing the band name, but they let the guys keep it. Brad argued that they already had a fan base—it might not have been huge, but those people knew who Fully Automatic was and would hype them from the get go. The band had little say in the cover or what songs went on the final album, and they had no say in the first single. The label chose one of Brad's least favorite songs, one called "Scream Loud Enough." It wasn't a bad song, but it was one he'd written early on. Everyone else in the band had always loved it and apparently the label did too, thinking it would be a song that would get people's attention. He disliked it because it was nothing more than a hate letter to Ethan. No one had ever seemed to pick up on it, but Brad knew. It had been cathartic when he'd first written it, but as he grew older, he felt like it lacked the love and support his brother needed, and singing it over and over reminded him of that fact. It wasn't as meaningful now as it had been, and maybe playing it over and over for the video and then on the road constantly could make it mean even less.

It was a good song, though, as far as showing off their chops. There was some mean axe work in the song, some good vocal stuff—from low to high and a lot of death growling. It really highlighted a lot of the cool things Nick did as a drummer too, so once Brad let go of the fact that he didn't much like their choice for the single, he knew it would be good for the band.

They had barely wrapped the video than they were on the road. Ethan asked Val if she wanted to come along, but it was evident that it continued to be a painful subject for her. She stayed at home with her mother for a few months, and then, when the band had a week hiatus, she spent the entire time with the band. It was then that she and Ethan started looking at homes, because after only two months of being on the shelf in the music store, Fully Automatic was getting recognized and money was already starting to pour in.

Their new manager and everyone at the label told them all the same thing—now was not the time to rest. They needed to work their asses off. That meant they spent two-thirds of the following year on the road. Some of the bands they opened for bitched about the grueling schedule, but Brad loved it. He wasn't having to change oil in cars anymore. He was doing what he loved several days a week. He was seeing parts of the country he'd never seen before. He wasn't having to worry about spending money either. He loved every second of it. And being in that position made him all the more creative. He was writing more songs than he ever had before.

He was proud of the guys too. They really stepped up their game. They played one flawless show after another, and the crowds were amazing. They appreciated the effort they put into it.

One night, somewhere in South Dakota, they were wrapping up their set before exiting for the next band, and he got to the edge of the stage, a little away from the lights, so he could see the audience. It was like an ocean, not like the tiny audiences he'd been playing for over the last few years. There were hundreds—*thousands*—of people out there. He couldn't see their faces, but even near the back, he could see arms waving, cheering, signing. He felt his heart swell with emotion, and that was the moment when he knew he'd finally made it.

CHAPTER FIFTY-TWO

BRAD STARTED FEELING like the tour for their first album would never end. As it was, they were recording their second album during mini-breaks from the tour. But their manager had told them "no rest," and Brad was taking it seriously. He was still hungry—in fact, he was even hungrier, because he'd tasted success. He was not going to be just a flash in the pan.

It was sometime during their recording process that Ethan announced he was going to be a dad. That hit Brad like a ton of bricks. He'd thought fame and fortune had wiped Valerie out of his mind, and while achieving his dream had helped push her to the back of his mind, knowing that Valerie was carrying Ethan's child pretty much sealed the deal. A child made their relationship permanent. There were no take backs when a child was involved.

Ethan had fallen into his usual addictive ways once they'd hit the road. Still, it seemed that once he'd found out about the pregnancy, he was trying to be a good husband. He bought a house for Val with his newly earned spoils, and she put her heart and creativity into it. It was an older house in need of TLC, but that was what Val said she wanted. And, yeah, Ethan seemed to try to get his drinking and other illicit activities under control when Val told him she was pregnant, but—like always—Brad suspected it would only last so long.

There were only two things he knew for certain—if Ethan was involved, Val would always run to the guy, and if drugs were involved, Ethan would show up at some point in the party. Those were the two givens of Brad's life, and if he hadn't finally started experiencing success with the band, he would have had to find a way to break out from their dysfunctional madness.

Ethan grumbled some at the nonstop touring and writing as well, but Brad, Zane, and Nick talked sense into him. They could rest when they knew for certain that they were solid. Until then and as long as there were any doubts, they were working their asses off. Brad did not plan to become a grease monkey again. Ever. No fucking way.

Karen was a blessing in disguise. He didn't see her much, but when he did, she made him feel special. She still had that hard edge, but she seemed to worship him and gave him more attention than he'd ever asked for.

Brad broke down and bought a house as well when they were in the middle of writing their second album. He saw no reason not to. Zane and Nick decided to keep the old apartment for a while since they had plenty of room at that point—two guys, three bedrooms, price of rent locked in for a while. They knew they wouldn't be there much anyway, if their grueling tour schedule kept its pace.

Brad loved the idea of having a house to come home to, but there wouldn't be anyone there and, if left unwatched, there might not be anything left either. So he invited Karen to move in with him. She was enamored with the idea, and Brad felt like a real asshole for getting her hopes up. Then he wanted to kick himself for thinking *that*, because he and Karen got along okay, and she accepted him for who he was. What more did he want? Did he feel a fire burning inside for her? No. Was the sex the best ever? No, but it was enjoyable enough; he wasn't complaining. Did he picture himself with her forever? No, but he didn't think that was possible with any woman. Karen wasn't perfect and neither was he, and as long as she wanted him, fucked in the head and all, they would be together.

He thought she was starting to question her decision, though. Even though she was able to decrease her hours at work *and* Brad brought her a new car, she was beginning to feel like she was getting the short end of the stick. He wouldn't have known it if she wouldn't have started grumbling about it. One morning before he had to go to another recording session, they sat at the table in his new kitchen eating breakfast, and she said, "It's Valerie, isn't it?"

He swallowed, forcing the bacon down only half chewed, making him uncomfortable. He grabbed for his coffee and took a big swig. It was a little too hot but he managed. He took a deep breath and hoped he sounded calm. He'd been dreaming about Val the night before. Her pregnancy was weighing heavily on his mind. He hadn't seen her in months and hoped she was okay. He imagined her in that big old house all by herself, hanging cute wallpaper in the nursery, crying, wondering where her husband was and what he was doing. If she and Ethan hadn't been married, he would have called her. They remained friends, after all. But somehow that kind of contact nowadays felt inappropriate. So, yes, he'd been worried about her, but how had Karen figured it out?

Once he felt he could control his response and keep emotion out of it, he asked, "What do you mean?"

"The woman you said you've always loved." He blinked. Karen had only ever met Val in person once before, and that was at a Fully Automatic Christmas party. It was intimate, not a lot of people, but each guy had a gal on his arm—not just the band, but roadies and other important people now a huge part of the band's life. How the fuck had Karen made that connection? He and Val hadn't said more than twenty words to each other since the band had gone on tour. He thought about denying it, almost even shook his head, but before he could even pretend, she said, "You were saying her name in your sleep last night."

He made sure his voice sounded strong in spite of how he felt inside. "I was?"

She nodded. "It's okay, Brad. I told you we were cool from the beginning, and thank you for telling me the truth." She frowned and picked up her coffee cup. "I just wonder how her husband feels about it."

Brad almost said Ethan knew, but he wasn't so sure about that. Ethan *should* have known, but Ethan wasn't always present. Ethan knew Brad had been interested in Val long before the guy decided to pursue her. Ethan knew Brad and Val had been intimate more than once. Brad knew, though, that Ethan had no idea that Val and Brad had slept together right before they took him to the hospital in his comatose state. And, if Brad had any say in it, Ethan would never know. That said, the guy was a fucking idiot if he didn't know that, at least in the past, Brad cared very much for Valerie.

Of course, Ethan excelled at being a fucking idiot sometimes.

Bottom line, though—Brad wanted them *both* happy—and that meant he'd stay out of the picture.

He wasn't sure what Karen was looking for. Did she want to make Brad mad? Sad? Make him grateful for her? He wasn't sure what her angle was and, because of that, he didn't know what kind of answer to give her. He shrugged and drank the rest of the hot coffee and then stood. He scraped his plate in the trash and said, "Gotta go," kissing Karen on the forehead and then leaving the house as quickly as he could. He wasn't prepared to talk about his feelings for Valerie, especially with the woman who was supposed to help him forget about her.

Brad had convinced the powers that be to let the band be home around Val's due date. It was her first baby, for God's sake, and she would want her husband nearby. The band worked on the last couple of songs for their second album while they were homebound so their time wasn't wasted.

Ethan grumbled on occasion about having to attend childbirth classes with Val. Brad hoped he was just whining about it because it wasn't the most exciting thing he could be doing; he hoped Ethan wasn't entirely serious. This was his first child. He should be thrilled. Ethan had mentioned that the baby was a boy too, and he and Val were trying to choose names.

It was then that Brad felt the familiar old ache. Ethan didn't seem to appreciate her as much as Brad thought he should. He wanted to be there for Val. He tried telling himself, of course, that Ethan appreciated and loved his wife and was thrilled to have a child on the way. He was just expressing himself in typical Ethan language—bitching and pissing and moaning, even when there was no reason to.

It was probably because he was maintaining his sobriety, and he felt like it was against his will.

Well, being clean wouldn't kill the guy.

Neither would being a father.

The time came, though, and Brad, Nick, and Zane got a group text from Ethan that baby Christopher was born, inviting them to come by the hospital the next day.

It was delicate. He was going to go, with or without Karen, but he wanted to invite her. He didn't care if she came, but he needed her to know he wanted her along if she so wished. So when she came home from the tattoo shop that night, he told her that Ethan and Valerie's baby had been born, and he was planning to visit the next day. "Do you want to come with me?"

She smiled then. Brad had no way to know for certain, but he thought maybe it made her feel better that he wanted her along. "Yeah, okay." She paused. "Should we get something for the baby?"

Brad smiled. "Yeah, I guess so." He realized then that Val must have had some kind of shower but she hadn't invited Karen. Maybe it was time she and everyone else knew he had a steady woman in his life. And having Karen choose a gift for the baby was the perfect time to start.

CHAPTER FIFTY-THREE

WHILE THEIR SECOND album was in post-production, Fully Automatic did some touring, but it wasn't as intense as the past year, because Ethan actually wanted to be home with his wife and baby. Brad knew they'd be full-blown touring soon and hardcore. It was too soon to quit. He was hungry enough for all of them, and he knew they got sick and tired of hearing him say they couldn't "rest on their laurels," but it was true. He knew it and, even if they were tired, they knew it too.

He wanted to be number one in his fans' hearts. He wanted to be number one on the charts that mattered. And there would be no resting till they got there.

Part of him started to question if they were releasing their second album too soon, but his manager assured him it was time. They'd milked four strong singles out of their first album, ones that got solid airplay on some of the hottest metal stations around the nation, and it was time to give them new songs to play. Brad wasn't going to argue, and he had so many songs inside his heart and his head and even on paper that there would always be more to share.

As the money started rolling in, Karen asked Brad if he would mind if she only worked one day a week. She loved tattooing, but she wanted to become an exclusive artist, in demand. Eventually, it would drive her prices higher, she said, and the quality of her art would be even better. But she couldn't stop working without support. Brad didn't mind. She cleaned around the house, not that there was much *to* clean with just the two of them, and she was a solid companion. His only complaint was that she was starting to act jealous once in a while. She didn't even have reason to be jealous. He wasn't fucking around on her, even on the road. Yeah, he hadn't been able to resist all the pussy thrown at him while touring for the first album, but since Karen had moved in with him, he couldn't bring himself to do it. She cared about him on some level, and he wanted to respect that. Besides, he'd had enough groupie sex to last a lifetime from their first tour alone. It made him feel dirty and disrespectful, and he couldn't do it anymore.

All the touring became a blur. They were on the road a lot. They had time home here and there—a few days once in a while or even a week at a time—but they were on the road constantly. Brad promised they'd slow down with their third album, but one night when Zane and Ethan were bitching, he sat them all down and said, "If they don't know us or love us, they won't want a third album. We'll write it and no one will give a fuck. So help me make sure they never forget us. Then you can have an entire goddamn year off for all I care."

The looks on their faces told him they understood.

They were home for a one-month break about the time Ethan's son was a year old. Yeah, Brad had planned it with the folks in charge so Ethan could celebrate his kid's birthday. Brad knew too that Ethan wouldn't even notice or appreciate it (probably), but he knew Val would. While they were home, the guys met a couple nights a week, beginning to write songs for the next CD. Ethan was lapsing into his old ways big time, and once in a while, he wouldn't show for their practices. It sucked, too, because Brad had finally converted one of the old bedrooms in his house into the perfect space—soundproof walls and everything.

One night, Karen was out with some of her friends and Brad's cell phone rang. He didn't think much about it until he saw that it was Val. That was weird. They hadn't talked on the phone in well over a year. It was stupid, the way his body reacted. His heart rate increased and his senses became more acute. He wasn't sure if it was because he had never lost his feelings for her or if he was worried that something had happened with Ethan or the baby. Either way, his reaction was real and palpable. He couldn't ignore it. "Val. How are you?"

She sounded concerned. "I'm doing fine. What about you?"

He was beginning to wonder about the nature of her call, but he knew she'd get around to it when she was ready. "Can't complain. And what about the little guy?"

"Well, actually, that's why I'm calling. He's been really sick tonight, and I can't get hold of Ethan. I wondered if you could pass a message on to him."

So why was she calling *Brad?* He was not and never had

been his brother's keeper. Val knew that. But then he realized...Ethan must have *told* her he was with him. Best to just get it over with. "I haven't seen Ethan since Tuesday, Val."

He could hear it in her voice. "Uh, well...if you see him, would you please ask him to call me right away?"

"Yeah, sure." He paused. "Hey, do you need me to help you out with the baby?"

"No, Brad. I couldn't ask you to do that. Just—have Ethan call me please."

"Yeah." He hung up. Both of them knew damn good and well he wasn't going to see Ethan anytime soon. Brad knew exactly what was going on. Ethan was off somewhere, probably shooting up or getting completely wasted on Jack, fucking some slutty woman, some chick who somehow satisfied his needs more than Val. Goddammit. What the fuck? Ethan had a thing for slutty chicks, and, try as she might, Val just couldn't *be* what he needed—so he sought it out when he couldn't take it anymore.

He called Ethan then. It didn't even ring. It went straight to voicemail. Brad felt himself growing angry. "Ethan, your wife is looking for you. She needs you. Your kid's sick, all right?" He stopped himself. He wanted to lecture Ethan and tell him to be a man and take care of his family, but for all he knew, Ethan was lying in a ditch, bleeding to death.

He wanted to call Val again, ask exactly what she needed, but he forced himself to put the phone back on the coffee table. She hadn't asked for his help. She didn't want him. She'd chosen Ethan...and Brad had to stand back and let Ethan do what Ethan was gonna do. And he couldn't say or do a goddamn thing about it.

It wasn't long before Fully Automatic was back on the road again, this time with international dates later in the tour as well. That made it feel real to Brad. That meant they had made it. They were there.

Like before, Brad thought he'd never forget a single day, a single concert, but—while he could remember some specifics—overall, the days, the events, the cities blurred into each other. They did other things while they were on the road too like the first time, because he and his friends had never traveled much before. So they tried to see the sights too. They also had fan events, meet-and-greets, appearances on local radio stations, and the like. They were just as busy on the road as they were off, and the days flew by.

They did a lot of partying too. They were living life, having fun, enjoying their success. Zane and Nick had no ties at all, and so women were a big part of their parties. Of course, being a husband and new father didn't stop Ethan either. Brad was being faithful on tour, though. Karen might not be his soul mate; he knew he didn't even love her, but he was committed to her. He wasn't going to cheat on her, even if the woman herself had given him carte blanche to do so when they first got together.

There was a party one night in the great state of Washington. They'd been on a mental high for days. He could see it in his bandmates' eyes—they were *there*; they'd made it. There would still be no rest, but they had done it. Brad had started feeling that way anyway, but seeing it on the guys' faces only reassured him that he wasn't imagining it.

Ethan, though…the guy didn't know when to stop. He'd been partying harder and harder, and Brad had resisted the urge more and more to pull him aside and beg him to get his shit together—for the band, for his kid, for his wife. He wouldn't listen anyway. And why would he bother to get his life on track now? He never had. Yeah, the guy was a brilliant musician, but Brad was starting to see him as a liability.

For the first time, Brad started wondering if he could front the band and play lead guitar. He started asking himself if he could do it without Ethan if he had to.

He didn't say a word to anyone else about it—not to Zane or Nick and certainly not to the man himself. But it was an idea that started circulating in his head.

And it was something he started preparing for. The truly great artists died young—Kurt Cobain, Jimi Hendrix, Layne Staley, Mitch Lucker. If he didn't get pissed at Ethan and finally kick his sorry ass out of the band, the man could very well kill himself off. Brad knew it was a very real possibility.

If that happened, he couldn't ask Val on board. Fully Automatic had a man's voice now. Fans would never accept Val as their singer, even if she had been their voice for years before. The world didn't know it. Wikipedia did, though, and even though there was no hyperlink for her name, she was listed as a previous member.

In the meantime, though, Brad would hold out hope and save the lectures for when Ethan was sober and of a mind to listen.

Washington, though—they had an epic party. The drugs were flowing as freely as the breasts were spilling out of girls' tops. He wasn't sure how that had happened, but the girls at that particular party were freer than others, and half a dozen of them started out with a striptease. Brad stepped out in the hallway. His excuse was that he wanted to get some ice for the party. In reality, though, he wanted those girls to sit on someone else's lap, and he didn't give a shit whose, but it wasn't going to be his. Most of their roadies were single, and they loved being with the band *because* they scored—a lot. He understood that, even appreciated it, but he didn't want to be put in any awkward positions. If he hadn't wanted to be around people, he would have just gone to bed.

When he got back to the room, there was a cluster of people around the couch. He didn't want to look. He figured it was something weird or gross like he'd seen groupies do before—like pulling something ungodly out of her snatch or doing some weird trick, like putting on lipstick by holding the tube in her cleavage. But as he stepped farther into the room, he didn't sense fun or lightness. No, something serious was going on. Something seriously *bad*.

And then he realized he'd been here before. More than once.

Sure enough, Ethan was fucked up. His eyes were rolled in the back of his head and he looked dead. Brad pressed his way inside the crowd. "Excuse me." He put his finger under Ethan's nose to make sure he was still breathing and then he dialed nine-one-one on his cell phone.

It wasn't until later, when they were at the hospital and it looked like Ethan wasn't getting out anytime soon, that Brad called Val. Fucking A, he hated Ethan at that moment. He was angry at his friend because Brad had to call his wife and give him the bad news. He had a hard enough time dealing with Valerie anymore, and to have to tell her...

Well, he had no choice. He stepped outside in the cool air and then called her number.

Her *hello* sounded panicked. And she had every reason to *be* panicked. Val was no dummy. She knew her husband better than she wanted to.

There was no easy way to say it, but he didn't want to blurt it out with no finesse. She needed a few minutes to wake up and get herself oriented. It was after two where they were, and it was an hour later in Colorado, so Brad knew she had to have wakened from a deep sleep. "Sorry to wake you."

She was ready. There was no hesitation when she asked, "What's going on? What's wrong?"

There was no sense prolonging it or beating around the bush. "He OD'd on H."

She was quiet for a few seconds. "So...how is he? Is he—?"

"They've got him stabilized now. He should pull through, but he's in a coma right now."

"Coma?" Brad could hear the baby in the background. "What the hell happened? He told me he wasn't using."

He sighed. Was Val really asking him that stupid a question? "Apparently he was lying. Like that's a first. You know him as well as *I* do, Val. Ethan's gonna do what Ethan's gonna do. We were partying, and you know Ethan parties harder than anyone else."

He heard Val soothe the baby with a quiet *Shh*. Then she asked, "Where are you guys right now?"

"Spokane."

"I'm gonna book a flight. Not sure when I'll be there."

He considered telling her not to, but he knew she would. When it came to Ethan, the woman was stubborn. More than that, what if this would be Ethan's last coma? What then? He couldn't tell her not to come.

It turned out that by the time Val got there the next day—that next afternoon—Ethan was out of the coma, sitting up in bed, sipping at a bowl of soup. Brad offered to hold the baby while Val had a heart-to-heart with her husband.

Brad was nervous at first, holding the little guy in the waiting room. But Chris could toddle and made baby noises. He asked, "Mama?"

Brad said, "Mama's with Daddy. I'm Brad."

Chris nodded his head and then pointed at Brad's Metallica shirt, tracing the line of the words with his finger. He wasn't with Chris for long, but it was long enough for him to realize that the little guy was pretty cool. Maybe he'd want to be a dad someday too. It made him even angrier with Ethan. His friend was pissing away his son's infancy and trying to kill himself in the bargain. What the fuck was wrong with Ethan?

No…Brad knew, had always known Ethan had issues. Lots of issues. For some reason, he'd hoped Ethan would grow up, though. The guy had a wife and kid to worry about now. It was time for him to stop acting like a kid himself and being selfish. It was time for him to think about someone besides himself for a change.

But Brad was starting to wonder if Ethan would ever figure out how to do that.

CHAPTER FIFTY-FOUR

THE TOUR FINALLY ended, and—aside from canceling Fully Automatic's part in one show—no harm was done because of Ethan's little stunt.

Before they headed home, though, Brad made sure he had a chance to talk with Ethan. It was a few months later, so his head had cooled, but he had a few things to say to his friend, and he was tired of holding them in. He'd bitten his tongue for years, hoping Ethan would decide he was done. Enough, though. Enough. Not only did Brad want to talk to him for the sake of Val and Chris, but also for Fully Automatic...and his friend himself. Ethan was killing himself, and Brad was tired of watching it happen.

He texted Ethan early in the morning, and they were due to leave at eleven. Ethan texted him back before ten, so Brad called. "Yeah, I just wanted to talk to you about a couple of things. Wanna go find some breakfast before we hit the road?"

"Yeah. Give me ten minutes."

The hotel where they were staying had a little restaurant on the ground floor. He didn't know if Ethan had packed or anything, so he figured he'd save them some time by keeping it close by. After a few minutes, he waited outside Ethan's door.

No, it shouldn't have surprised him when a blonde with double-D tits wearing a skimpy dress emerged first, giggling. Ethan was smiling and slapped her on the ass as she started bouncing down the hall. She turned around and blew him a kiss through red lips and then turned back around, making sure her hips swayed more than they needed to.

Fuck, no. He wasn't going to talk about *that*. He was pissed that Ethan was still fucking around on Valerie, a woman who adored him and had given birth to his son, but Brad started to suspect all of it was interrelated. Ethan was drunk and high—numb to the world—and the women were a part of that. The guy had no self-control when he was under the influence, and he'd always been a sucker for a slutty girl. Until he could maintain sobriety, the women would be a part of it.

And *that* was what Brad intended to address. Ethan asked, "Where we goin'?"

"Downstairs. There's a restaurant on the premises."

"Convenient."

"Yeah." They walked to the elevator together. Brad was glad that Ethan at least seemed lucid this morning. He noticed, though, that the guy was wearing sunglasses, probably to cover up a multitude of sins. Brad could only imagine: bloodshot, red-rimmed eyes, dark circles. He'd seen it before. All he asked for was attentiveness. Fine if the evidence of his hard partying was mapped on his face. Brad didn't give a shit. He just needed his friend present and accounted for this morning.

They got to the restaurant. It wasn't busy. There were only two other tables with customers, so the waiter met them at their table almost immediately with menus and asked if they wanted coffee.

It wasn't long before they'd ordered and Brad could talk. He took a sip of his coffee and said, "No sense beating around the bush. I wanted to talk to you about something."

"Goddamn. I knew it was too good to be true."

"What?"

Ethan shook his head and took off the sunglasses. "We can't just be old friends anymore. You gotta ruin it with a lecture."

"*A lecture?*" Brad inhaled. Maybe to Ethan it *would* seem like a lecture, and maybe that was why the guy wasn't taking any of his words to heart. That meant one thing—Brad had to strike hard. "No, not a lecture, man. We're way past that. Think of it more as an ultimatum."

Ethan's nostrils flared. "An ultimatum?"

Ethan was riling up, and this conversation wouldn't be productive if he was pissed off and tuning Brad out. He took another deep breath. "Fuck it. Let's start over." He shook his head. "I'm worried about you, man. We all are. And we're *tired* of worrying about you."

"So don't. I've never asked for your concern." Ethan picked up his coffee and took a big swig.

"Ethan, you are my brother, man. We're all like brothers. There's no way we can turn that off. You're killing yourself."

Brad saw Ethan's jaw clench, but he didn't talk right away. "I look dead to you?"

"Not yet. But how many comas now? How many more before you decide enough? I'm not talking to you as a guy you play with in a band. I'm talking to you as a friend, Ethan. I'm not the kind of guy to stage an intervention. You know I don't believe in that shit. You gotta decide you're done. But I'm afraid you're going to discover it in the afterlife, 'cause I haven't seen you have a revelation here."

Ethan started to say something and then blinked. He took another drink of coffee. At first, Brad expected his friend to be bristly and crusty as he often got whenever anyone questioned or challenged him. Instead, his voice got quiet and he looked into his cup of coffee. Then he said, "I can't do anything anymore. Not without something. You know…a joint used to make me feel kinda peaceful, but it can't touch shit anymore. H, though—it drowns it all out, and when it doesn't quite work, I drink too. It's the only way I can hang on."

Brad hadn't expected Ethan to be so forthcoming. His friend wore chainmail made of hate, anger, and indifference to cover all the scars, but now he'd taken it off and was standing bare in front of his friend. That was a cry for help if Brad had ever heard one.

He hadn't even had to pull out the you-have-a-wife-and-kid card.

"What are you saying?"

"That dying doesn't sound so bad."

Brad felt like a wrecking ball slammed into his chest. It made sense. Ethan really was trying to kill himself with the poison he took. He'd known Ethan for years and, for some reason, he thought distance and time from his painful past would heal the man's wounds. Not so. Apparently, now that Ethan *was* an adult, he was finding ways to cope with the hurt inside. Brad thought he'd understood...but he must have had no idea. "Are you serious, man?" Ethan looked at his friend and shrugged but said nothing. "We've finally made it. We're not rich, but you know it's comin', right? And you have a wife who loves you, a beautiful son. You have—"

"—everything anyone would ever want. Yeah, I know that, and that's just another notch of guilt to add to my frayed belt."

Oh, fuck. Ethan was way worse than he'd ever let on. And then Brad felt like a total shitheel for never having noticed. He sucked in another breath of air, now almost painful. His friend was hurting, and he'd never seen it for all it was. "What can I do?"

Ethan shook his head again, clenching his jaw. "Nothing really. There's nothing you *can* do. Just...just stay out of my way and let me do what I gotta do."

Brad was quiet, and the waiter brought their food out, asking if they needed anything else. When they told him they didn't, he poured more coffee and walked away. Brad wasn't hungry anymore and his mind was racing. Ethan was squirting ketchup over his hash browns when Brad was finally able to ask, "Have you ever thought about seeing somebody?"

Ethan smirked. "What? Like a shrink?"

Slowly, Brad started to nod his head. "Yeah, I guess. Like a shrink. You know, somebody to talk to, somebody who can give you ideas of how to handle what you feel."

"I don't need someone to tell me what to do or how to feel."

Brad let the air out of his lungs. He had to find a way to say what was on his mind. "They're trained to help, Ethan. This shit's way outta my league. Hell, it's outta your league too. Aren't you tired of suffering?"

Ethan shrugged. Brad could tell he'd already put the coat of armor back on. "I do what I gotta do. It's what's made me who I am."

Brad looked at him, waiting until Ethan at last looked up from his plate. "Seriously, man. If you need help, I'm here."

His face was steel. "I'm good. I got this."

Brad swallowed and picked up his coffee cup, nodding. As he brought it to his lips, he wondered if Ethan would be around a year from now…and if there was any way Brad could stop the man's imminent self-destruction.

CHAPTER FIFTY-FIVE

WHEN THE BAND returned to Denver, Brad said they needed a break. They'd worked their asses off the past several years, and now they could enjoy the spoils a little. He insisted they meet once or twice a month to discuss plans, but he told them to focus on rest. Write if they had to, he said, but rest.

He considered urging his friend once more to consider visiting a psychiatrist, but he knew it would fall on deaf ears. He'd mentioned it once, and Ethan knew how he felt. If he said it again, Ethan would ignore it or actively decide to *not* do it.

Brad wanted to talk to Val and tell her about their discussion too and then thought better of it. First of all, it was crossing the line she'd drawn between them when she'd accepted Ethan's proposal of marriage. Secondly, though, it would feel like he was betraying his best friend. Ethan didn't need them ganging up on him. Brad hoped that being home around the people he loved who loved him back would be all the stimulus he'd need to decide to pursue professional help with all his demons.

That was all Brad had now—hope. He'd led the proverbial horse to water, but he knew there was no way he could make the goddamned beast drink it. Ethan had to decide for himself that that was what he wanted.

As the months passed and the band members met on occasion, though, Brad saw Ethan's health declining instead of improving. He was pasty looking. He'd started getting a little chubby on tour, but now he'd been losing weight, and his cheeks were starting to look sunken in. The dark circles under his eyes appeared permanent.

Brad bit his tongue, though. He had to hope against hope that Ethan would get his shit together. The man didn't know it, but Brad had put him on probation. If he was still in this shape in another five months—when the band planned to get together to start recording—the four guys were going to talk...and Ethan would maybe get the boot. Brad just didn't know that a dysfunctional Ethan was good for the band anymore.

He kept those thoughts to himself, though, even with Karen. Karen should have been his friend and confidant, but she'd been growing more distant lately. Brad suspected it was because he couldn't give her what she wanted. She'd been spending more and more time away, in spite of working less. Sometimes she said she was hanging out with friends, but that didn't explain her nights away.

It bothered Brad on the surface, but deep down, his thoughts were with Ethan, Val, and their child. Brad stopped by once in a while to check in, but it got harder and harder to see the family in their natural habitat. It was obvious to Brad that they were all suffering on one level or another. Yeah, even the toddler. His dad didn't give him the attention and affection he was starving for. Brad hoped his occasional appearance let them all know he supported them, but he started to wonder why he was tormenting himself.

He knew then that he couldn't visit them anymore—not till Ethan was clean.

They ended their hiatus, trying to meet three times a week to write and rehearse, and things weren't going well.

One night, Brad was taking out the trash and saw a car parked in front of the house. Karen had been itching for a fight all day. She'd been picking and grousing, and Brad finally told her to shut the fuck up and slammed himself in his practice room. After a while, he was hungry, though, and went to the kitchen. Karen was chattering on her cell phone, oblivious to the state of the room. It was a mess. The dishes were dirty and the trash was overflowing. He decided to take the trash out and then he'd wash the dishes…or go out for a bite to eat. When he stepped outside, it took him a little bit, but he thought the car in front looked like Val's. He took the trash can back inside and set it inside the kitchen. Karen was still sitting at the kitchen table gabbing with one of her friends, so he wasn't even going to tell her what he was doing. He walked back outside and toward the car in front. As he got closer, he was sure he saw a person sitting inside.

He leaned over and got close to the passenger window. He was positive it was Val, so he rapped on the window. No Ethan. That was odd. She rolled the window down and smiled. It was dark and he wasn't sure, but—smile or not—she didn't look happy. She seemed quiet too. "Val, what the hell are you doing here?" What shitty manners. He couldn't let his shock make him a bad friend or crappy host. "Why don't you come in?" He saw Chris in the backseat. "Oh, you brought the little guy." He glanced at Val and said, "Come on in." Then he opened the back door. Chris was looking at him, wide-eyed and smiling, and he unbuckled the car seat. "Hey, little buddy. How've you been?"

Chris smiled and said something that Brad couldn't translate. Brad laughed, lifting him out of the car. They walked up to the house in silence.

Once inside, Brad undid the straps holding Chris inside his car seat and lifted him up and out. The kid looked so much like Ethan, it hurt, but he had a little Val in his features too. He was a cute kid. Chris touched Brad's cheek with his hand. Brad said, "Boo!" and Chris started giggling. He set Chris on the living room floor and said to Val, "Have a seat." Val looked strange—almost timid, something he'd never seen from her. She was closing herself off from him too. What was she hiding?

He got closer, and that was when he saw marks on her neck. "What happened?"

Karen came in then. Perfect timing. He could feel her eyes on his back, burning a hole through him. She said, "Valerie." Her words were cold. He didn't need her being all weird, not right now.

Val gave her a tentative smile. "Hi, Karen."

She didn't want to beat around the bush. "Brad, can I talk to you?"

He didn't even turn around to look at her. "Just a

minute." He focused on Val. He looked her in the eye, because he wanted honesty. He feared he knew the answer, but he needed confirmation. And if he was right, he was gonna fuckin' blow. "Did Ethan do this?"

He saw her eyes start to glisten, and that was all the answer he needed. *What the fuck had Ethan done?* It explained why she was here…and without her husband. Karen said, "Brad. I need to talk to you, please." *Now?* What game was she playing? He knew, though—she knew Val had been number one in his heart, always would be, and the fact that she had come running to him told Karen probably everything she would ever need to know. Her voice was almost a growl, and she was tired of waiting. "Fuck it. I'm outta here."

Letting her leave wasn't fair to her, though. She'd been his companion for a while, had kept him focused and sane, and she was a friend if nothing else. It wouldn't be fair to just let her walk away. But he wasn't happy about it. "Karen…goddammit." He looked at Val, hoping she would understand. "Give me a minute, Val. I'll be right back." He turned and looked at Karen, tilting his head toward the kitchen. If she needed to talk, he didn't want to do it in front of Val. Val had enough of her own bullshit to deal with. She didn't need theirs too.

They got in the kitchen, and he was glad for the first time that it had a swinging door. Karen could get loud and ugly when she was angry, and he could see it all over her face. She'd been gearing up for a rager all day. That was usually her excuse to leave and party all night with friends. They'd done it enough that he knew, and he just didn't care enough anymore to fight about it, especially when his friend was hurting and needed him. Still, if he could help Karen through whatever shit was going on with her, he'd try.

It was hard, though, seeing the look on her face. She was wearing a hell of a scowl. "What's going on, Karen?"

"Like you don't know."

"You think I'd ask if I did?"

She gritted her teeth and got close. She pointed her thumb toward the living room. "What? Val didn't do shit. And I didn't invite her over. She needs something, and I was trying to figure out what it is. She's my friend, Karen. I've never told you who could be your friend, so don't start with me." She rolled her eyes. "Besides, you were on a tear long before Val got here. What the fuck's going on?"

"Whatever."

"Don't give me that."

She got louder. "I'm done, Brad. I don't need this shit."

In direct response to her volume, Brad lowered his. "Look, Karen. You and I both know now's not a good time. Can we talk about this later?"

If Karen hadn't let off steam like this in the past, blowing on occasion like Old Faithful—regularly and without fail—her next words might have seemed to come out of the blue. She took a few seconds, seeming to consider her response, but then she blurted it out. "You're an asshole."

"Really? Is that all you have to say?"

What she said next he hadn't seen coming, and it told him all he needed to know. "You know...I thought if I stayed, you could love me. I thought you could forget this stupid hang up you have over that...*twit*, but you can't.

You just can't let it go, and this is the final straw."

Yeah. Oh, God, he should have known. Karen had grown to love him, and he didn't know why. He cared about the woman, yes, but he'd never love her the way she wanted, and seeing Valerie at her most vulnerable—that had been the confirmation Karen had been looking for. She wasn't willing to stick around when there was no way she'd be able to turn Brad's heart around. It had been her wish, her goal, and part of Brad had hoped she would be able to do it. Having Val here now, though, hurting and needing him—it was all fresh again, like not a moment had passed, and Karen must have been able to see it on his face. Still, he would live up to the title of *asshole* if he didn't at least try. "Karen…"

"No, I'm done."

"Karen."

"Fuck you, Brad. I am sick and tired of competing with the memory of someone else. I'm outta here."

He shook his head. He'd hurt her, pretty badly, it looked like. "I'm sorry."

She pulled her snug t-shirt down to her hips and blinked. "It doesn't matter. I called Jimmy anyway. He's already waiting for me."

And those words confirmed the suspicions he'd been harboring for weeks. Now he knew for sure she'd been fucking around on him with a new tattoo artist who'd started working in the shop she did a few months earlier. He couldn't half blame her, though, and it was technically part of their original agreement. Still, he knew when she'd moved in that she'd expected fidelity, and he'd made sure he was faithful to her. He couldn't just let it lie. "You're sleeping with him, aren't you?"

Under her breath, she said, "So fuckin' what?" Then she flipped him off and shoved the kitchen door open, storming through the living room toward the bedroom. God, she was ugly when she was pissed. Her eyes were dark and venomous and he was frankly glad she was leaving. For how long, he had no idea. She'd done this before, though never quite on this level.

He stood in the living room looking at Val. God, he felt like a dumb ass. Karen was acting like a child, but he wasn't about to apologize for her. He winced but kept his eyes on the baby after his initial eye contact with Val. She picked Chris up off the floor and sat him on her lap, probably afraid Karen would storm through the room again and knock her child on the floor. He took a deep breath, feeling uncomfortable, just waiting for Karen to leave. He wasn't going to discuss Val's personal business until she was gone.

Karen was in the room in a matter of moments. She was carrying a suitcase. Wow. She *was* serious this time. She'd never packed before. She got close to Brad and said, "Don't bother trying to stop me." He wondered if that meant that she really *did* want him to stop her, but he wasn't going to. He was tired of the drama she'd whisked into his life. He didn't need it, especially because his heart wasn't in it. She stomped over to the closet, pulling out her purse, and then walked to the door. "I'll be back tomorrow to get the rest of my things." She slammed the front door with as much strength as she could muster, and Brad breathed a sigh of relief.

And, after all that, he wasn't sure where to pick up with

Val. He leaned against the wall for a few moments, looking at Chris. Finally, he said, "Hey, little buddy." He smiled at the little guy, glad he was too young to understand what had been going on—with his parents or his "uncle," as Val liked to call him. He looked at her and asked, "Can he have a cookie?"

"Yeah…I think a little spoiling by Uncle Brad would be fine."

He smiled and waved his arm toward the kitchen. As they entered the room that felt like it continued to reverberate with Karen's nasty little diatribe, he said, "Sorry you had to hear that shit." He pulled out a chair for Val and then started searching inside cabinets. It didn't take long until he found a box of vanilla wafers—good enough. He pulled a couple out and walked over to the table. He handed them to Chris, who smiled and took them. Brad couldn't help but grin back at the cute kid and he tousled his hair. Then he sat down and said, "So…tell me what happened." He didn't know that he wanted to know, but he needed to.

Val looked down, avoiding his eyes. "I don't want to talk about it."

She might have said that, but he knew better. Why else would she have come running to him? She needed some encouragement, but he knew she'd tell him. "Come on, Val. I know Ethan did this. What the fuck was going on?" He noticed then that she had bruises on her arm too, and he wondered why he hadn't caught it before, but then he remembered she'd been wearing a jacket and it had covered them up. He started to feel angry. What the fuck had Ethan done? He touched the bruises as though to confirm their existence. "What the hell? Did you call the cops?"

She started crying, and that told him all he needed to know. Ethan would have to answer for this, but for now, Val was hurting. He brought his chair closer to hers and brought her head to his shoulder. She let it all go, wailing and sobbing like he'd never heard her. It made him imagine all the horrible things the man who'd felt like a brother had done to her. Chris was still on Val's knee, working on the wafer, and he tugged on Brad's hair. He looked down at the boy and smiled. The little guy had short hair, but his dad and his dad's bandmates all had long hair. He wondered what kind of confusing message that would send to the kid as he got older, because long hair wasn't accepted in mainstream society. Ah, maybe the kid would realize that meant they were *cool*.

He felt like tousling Chris's hair again, but he instead rubbed Val's back. He loved this woman, would always love her, but they were destined to be apart. All he could be now was her good friend and stay by her side while she needed him. When it seemed like she was starting to wind down, he got up and grabbed a box of tissue out of the living room. He came back and set it on the table near her. He sat down again and asked, "Sure you don't want to talk about it?"

"No. I don't even want to think about it anymore."

"You need some sleep." He tilted his head toward Chris. The little guy looked sleepy too. Without giving it any thought, he said, "You can sleep on my bed."

"Oh, no. I don't want to take your bed."

"I have a couch, Val. It's no biggie." He would have had a guest bedroom or two if he hadn't converted the damn things. He'd bought the house on a whim, because he'd wanted a home. Honestly, he wanted a bigger place, but for now it worked. And the couch was comfortable.

"I can stay at a motel."

"Damn it, Val, just say *yes*."

She looked concerned. "What if Karen comes back tonight? I get the feeling she doesn't like me very much."

"Don't worry about her. Just get some sleep. You need it."

He knew Karen wouldn't be back. Even if she changed her mind about the permanency of this breakup, she wouldn't return that night. She never had before. He was confident that she wouldn't tonight either.

So he wanted Val to sleep, because he had plans. Not so nice plans. And they involved her husband. He was going to have to leave the house, and he didn't want to have to explain to her why or what he was going to do.

CHAPTER FIFTY-SIX

BRAD HAD NO idea what he was going to say to Ethan, but he was angry as fuck. He'd never been this mad in his entire goddamned life.

Traffic wasn't as heavy as during the day, and by the time he got there, he wondered if he'd ever made it to Ethan's house that quickly.

He couldn't even fucking think straight.

He stormed up to the door and banged on it. Then he remembered the doorbell and rang it. Several times. Banged again.

Rang the doorbell once more.

"I'm coming. Chill the fuck out."

Good. Ethan. Brad noticed his breathing was out of control and his fists ached, they were clenched so tightly.

It was seconds later and Ethan opened the door, an unlit cigarette hanging out of his mouth. He wore a dirty white t-shirt and jeans. His hair was disheveled, his eyes bloodshot. When he saw Brad, he was pissed. "What the fuck do you want?"

Brad threw the screen door open and walked in. Ethan backed away a little and then stood his ground. "Why did you do it, Ethan? Why? Were you trying to kill her?"

"What? You gonna be the fucking knight in shining armor, Bradley? You think she didn't have it comin'?"

That was all it took. Brad pushed him back against the wall, and the mirror hanging behind Ethan fell. His hand wrapped around Ethan's neck too and he said, "How you like it, motherfucker?" Ethan struggled a little and Brad let go of his neck, following it up with his right fist in Ethan's face. One...for what he'd done to Val. Then his left fist for Chris. Another for all the hell he'd put Brad through. Another for the band. Another...another...another.

He felt tears falling down his face and saw the blood spilling from Ethan's nose and cheek. What the fuck had he done? It had been red then black in his head.

Ethan hadn't resisted, hadn't fought back. He'd *wanted* Brad to hurt him.

Brad backed away, holding his hands palms out at Ethan. "Fuck. I'm...I gotta go."

His hand was on the doorknob when he heard Ethan ask, "Is she okay?"

"She'll live." He had to leave. "I'm sorry." He turned around. "You have a week. *One week*, Ethan. Get your shit straight." And then he stumbled to his truck. His vision was blurry and his knuckles were throbbing. He got in his truck and drove and drove and drove.

But it didn't make the pain go away.

He'd had a hell of a time falling asleep. His hands hurt,

but the pain was nothing compared to what was in his heart. He felt bad about what had happened to Val, but he felt even worse for what he'd done to Ethan. As he'd left, he saw his friend's lips, cheeks, eyes swelling, and he knew Ethan. He'd get rid of the pain with drugs, alcohol, or both, and now it was Brad's fucking fault. What the hell kind of friend was he? His friend needed help and he'd instead beaten him mercilessly.

So he lay on the couch, immersed in guilt. He looked back, though, and didn't know what or how he could have done anything differently. He'd been too angry for too long.

He was starting to awaken, these thoughts in his mind. He'd heard the front door open, and it had started him on the path to wakefulness, but he was trying to fall back asleep. He heard a baby fussing, though, and that made him wake the rest of the way. Well, no, it wasn't a baby. It was Chris. He wasn't so much a baby anymore. He heard him making noise, winding up to start crying. He sat up. He wasn't sure where Val was—outside somewhere—so he decided to check on Chris.

He was wearing jeans under the sheet on the couch, but he'd taken his shirt off and thrown it in the dirty laundry. He hadn't checked it closely, but he was pretty sure it had blood on it. He knew it had tears. It was painted with shame, and he didn't want to see the goddamned thing.

He walked in his bedroom and Chris spotted him. The child babbled and smiled and Brad said, "Hey, there, little buddy. Let me get a shirt on and then we'll go see your mama. How's that sound?"

"Mama?"

Brad nodded while he opened a dresser drawer and grabbed the first shirt he touched, pulling it over his head. Chris sat up in the bed, surrounded by pillows, and Brad came over, holding his hands out. He picked up the little guy and brought him to his chest. "Let's go see that beautiful mama of yours." He was praying that Val hadn't done something stupid, but he hadn't heard a car start up. He wouldn't have been surprised if she'd run back to Ethan, but he hoped he was wrong. Ethan needed to seriously get his shit together, and until he did, Val needed to stay away.

He wouldn't say that to her, though.

He was talking to Chris as they moved through the house. "Where'd your mama go, buddy? What's she doin'?"

He opened the front door, expecting to find her on the phone with Ethan. He didn't know what else she would be doing out there. Instead, he found her sitting in one of the chairs he had on the porch. She was just looking at the trees, lost in thought. The sun was starting to lighten the sky. As soon as Chris spotted Val, he said, "Mama!"

Brad sat in the chair next to Val, ready to hand Chris over to her, but he seemed content in his arms. "How'd you sleep?"

She shrugged. "What about you?"

"Probably about the same."

"Did I wake you up?"

He lied. "No. Chris did. He might be hungry."

"Yeah, probably." She touched Chris's nose. "My little pumpkin."

The child smiled at his mother and touched his nose

too, imitating her. "Pukkin." Val started laughing.

Seeing the smile on that woman's face made everything seem better. She really was the most beautiful woman he'd ever known. No, it wasn't her looks. If it were looks only, she'd have stiff competition. Yes, she was beautiful on the outside, but it was the person he saw inside too. She was a beautiful soul—caring, giving, passionate, even if she was sometimes stupid in love. Since he'd met her, he'd felt like she was his other half, like she could see inside his soul and knew him, really knew him, and he felt the same way. He would read her lyrics and feel like she'd reached inside his heart to pull out his raw emotions and slap them on the page. But, more than that, he would read her words and know what the catalyst was for a particular song.

That was why he'd known at one time she'd considered loving him but had held herself back.

And why was he letting himself feel these things so deeply *now*? It would never work. He knew that. He was just fucking putting himself through the wringer if he deluded himself into thinking otherwise.

Still...he was going to allow himself this moment to enjoy her and her son. No pressure, no thoughts about tomorrow. They'd get there at some point, but for now...for now, he wanted to enjoy her beauty, let it wash over him, and maybe—just for a second—he could pretend that Val had chosen him and not his fucked up friend. How different their lives would have been if...

No. He couldn't go there. Instead, he let her laughter wash over him and he smiled at her. "I can put some coffee on, or would you rather grab some breakfast somewhere?"

"I just want coffee right now." She frowned. "I hate to bug you, but do you have some cereal or something Chris could eat?"

"Can he do scrambled eggs and toast?"

"Yeah."

"Then let Uncle Brad make some breakfast too."

She touched his arm then, and that made the psychic scar he'd been fiddling with all the more painful. "Brad...thanks for everything. You've always been my best friend. I can always turn to you. Always. And...I'm sorry I always get you involved in the middle of all my bullshit."

His mind flashed back to last night, his fist in Ethan's face over and over. He tried to laugh, but he really wanted to cry. "Jesus. You have no idea." She grimaced. She'd misunderstood, and that was his fault, because she had no idea what he'd been up to the night before. He shook his head. "Come on...I'll explain over breakfast."

They got inside and Chris then decided he wanted his mother. She took him in her arms and said, "Oh...he needs a diaper change. Be right back."

She went back to his bedroom and he felt like a heel. He probably could have changed that diaper, but he'd never changed one before. He could tell Chris was soaking wet, but he didn't even know where Val had put the baby stuff.

He was being way too hard on himself. He made his way to the kitchen and grabbed some eggs out of the fridge. He melted butter in a skillet and then scrambled a few eggs before dumping them in the skillet. Val came in then, setting Chris on the floor with a toy. She had a bottle of juice that she took the lid off of and then screwed on a nipple, handing it to him. She asked, "Want me to make coffee?"

"Sure." He needed it.

He glanced over at her while she looked around the kitchen. "I don't have a high chair for the little guy."

"Maybe a stack of books or something to sit on?"

"If you don't care if he's standing, he could just eat in the living room, and we could put his food on the coffee table."

She smiled at him. God, he'd do anything for that smile. "Have you seen the way he eats?"

He shrugged, removing the skillet from the hot burner. "Fuck it. You only live once, right? I own a vacuum."

"Your house. If you're sure."

He pulled a saucer out of the cupboard. "Little guy's gotta eat. You want any?"

"No."

He pulled a plate out of the cabinet as well, just as the bread popped out of the toaster. "Suit yourself." He filled both the plate and saucer with eggs and then buttered the toast for Chris, placing it next to his eggs. "A spoon for the little guy?"

"Yeah, but he'll probably just use his hands." He smiled and opened the silverware drawer, taking out a spoon for the kiddo and a fork for himself. The coffeepot started to sputter and Val asked, "Sugar and cream?"

He nodded, and then took the food to the living room. Then he went to the linen closet in the hallway and took out a bath towel to spread out where Chris would be eating. He didn't want Val to fret about Chris's eating habits. It would be easy to clean up if it all landed on the towel. By the time he returned to the kitchen, Val had two cups of coffee doctored and ready to drink. "Want me to get the coffee or Chris?"

"If you don't mind getting Chris…"

"Come on, buddy." He bent over and picked Chris up, grabbing his bottle of juice with him. When he got to the coffee table, he stood Chris right in front of his food. Brad touched the top of the scrambled eggs—not too hot. Then he sat on the couch on the other side and Val joined him, placing a cup of coffee in front of him on the coffee table but out of Chris's reach. Chris was already shoving eggs in his mouth, using his hand just as Val had predicted.

Brad touched his fork but didn't pick it up. "I don't know why I made any for me. I'm not that hungry. Sure you don't want any?"

She nodded, sipping her coffee. "I'm sure." She took a deep breath. "So what were you going to say about being in the middle of my crap?"

He shook his head. Part of him didn't want to tell her, because he didn't know what she'd think of him from that point on. She'd know he had a dark side, a horrible secret. He'd pummeled her husband, for Christ's sake, and she might not find it easy to forgive him. "It's not what you think." He had to force the words out, though. He'd never lied to Valerie, and he didn't plan to start now. He took another drink of his coffee and said, "I went to your place last night."

She looked at him for a bit before saying, "You *what?*"

He couldn't stop now. "Yeah, Val." Hurting Ethan had been the culmination of *years* of shit, but seeing what his friend had done to Val had caused the dam to break—he hadn't been able to hold it in any longer. He didn't know how to explain that...but he had to try. "You're not the only one having Ethan problems. And...what he did to you yesterday. That's it. We're supposed to be rehearsing three days a week, and we're lucky if he comes to one. And when he bothers, he's argumentative and asinine. Nick, Zane, and I have been considering kicking his ass out, even though he was a founding member." He took a deep breath, looking down at his hands. "He's a wrecking ball. He doesn't create; he destroys. He tells us our new material *sucks*, but he won't do anything to help. And know what? He couldn't, because it's the most perfect stuff we've ever written. But he wasn't involved in it, and that's why he hates it."

"That's his fault for not being there."

"Damn right." It didn't make him feel any better about what he'd done, though. "But he doesn't see it that way, and until he does, he'll never change." He grabbed his coffee and forced himself to look at Val. "I was lying here on the couch last night, and I was pissed. Pissed about what he did to you, even though you haven't told me exactly what happened. Pissed that he doesn't give a shit about his friends, his band, his kid. Nothing. He's so goddamned self-absorbed. When we were kids, you know, that was fine, but Ethan never grew out of it. I'd stood by and never said a word, but I'm done.

"So...I just told him he has a week to get his shit together or he's out."

"That's fair."

"I don't want you worrying about income, Val. You're still writing most of our lyrics. You're in the loop. We'll take care of you."

"I'm not worried about that."

"I know. But…" He took a deep breath, clenching his jaw together. He was *not* going to fucking lose it again. "I also beat the shit out of him, Val." He hung his head, resting his forehead on his fist. "I'm sorry. I just…am so angry."

She touched his shoulder. God…she forgave him. She'd already forgiven him when he didn't know how to forgive himself. "I know, Brad. I know."

He looked at her. "If he ever touches you again, I'll probably kill him." It scared him, but he knew it was true.

"He won't. Ethan and I are done. Forever."

Oh, God, if only he could believe it. But they'd been there…over and over and over again. Val had told Ethan she was done more times than Brad could remember. And he couldn't—*wouldn't*—believe it ever again.

CHAPTER FIFTY-SEVEN

BRAD AND VAL started texting like the old days, but he stayed away. Yeah, four months and Val and Ethan were still apart, but he knew they'd been apart longer in the past, only to get back together. Brad would be a fucking fool to make a move, and he knew it.

He and Karen were definitely done. As promised, she had come by later that day to get her things. Val had called her parents earlier that day and decided to visit them for a week or so. Brad called Ethan a few days later and met him for lunch. He apologized and Ethan said it was cool. Brad could tell the guy was in the worst shape he'd ever been in, but he didn't know what to do.

Ethan moved out of his house, letting Val and Chris have it. And he tried twice to show up to rehearsals, but he was blitzed out of his mind. Brad went to the powers that be and told them Ethan was out of the band. They weren't pleased. Ethan was publicity, plain and simple, and no publicity was bad, they said. He kept the band in the spotlight. After Brad yelled, asking them if they were out of their fucking minds, they asked him and the other two guys to sit tight for a few more months. Money was still pouring in, not only from album sales but also merchandise. There was no rush. The band's manager and label agreed, but the label was not amused with Brad's demands.

They didn't know Brad very well. Brad felt the need to make sure he was still on top. Number one. It wasn't about the money.

To quell his fury, the label let him, Nick, and Zane release a single, something to keep fans interested and eager, and they'd have no idea Ethan wasn't involved.

Ethan was in bad shape, though. He was living with a woman who was draining him dry, and Brad decided not to deal with the guy anymore. It hurt too badly. If the goddamned label wanted Ethan, they could fucking deal with him.

A couple months later, Val called him and asked if he'd come over for dinner. He expected her to want to talk to him about Ethan. They'd been down this road before too. When she'd worried about Ethan in the past and hadn't known what to do, she'd ask Brad. This time, though, he'd washed his hands of the guy. Until Ethan cleaned up his act, Brad couldn't go there anymore. It hurt too much. He couldn't watch Ethan kill himself anymore.

Reluctantly, he agreed to visit Valerie. Before he left his house, he stood in front of his mirror. "Don't you fucking give in to her, Payne. Not again. If she says Ethan's name once, shut her down, right then and there." He nodded his head and walked out of his room toward the front door, continuing the thought. When she mentioned Ethan, he was going to tell her to seek psychiatric help. He'd be sincere about it. He believed she and Chris had a lot of healing to do.

He had managed to talk her into getting her long-overdue throat surgery now that she had the money to do it, so maybe she'd listen to him again.

He drove slowly to her house. He was looking forward to seeing her and Chris, but he was afraid too. Val had more control over him than she'd ever know, and he still felt like a major asshole for unleashing his fury on Ethan.

He almost bought her flowers and stopped himself from doing it. They were *friends* and that would be all they'd ever be.

It didn't matter that his heart was crying out to him, telling him he needed to tell her how he felt.

Fuck that. Every time he'd ever come close, she'd driven another knife into his heart. He had to stop torturing himself with those thoughts.

He rang the doorbell to her house and waited. He could hear dried, dead leaves rustling on the lawn behind him as the breeze blew them around, and he took a deep breath. He wasn't cold, but he could tell the night was going to get colder.

Val answered the door, her hair pulled up in a ponytail. She looked harried and overheated. Chris came to the door too. "Hey, come in." Chris tilted his head. "You remember Uncle Brad, don't you, sweetie?"

He nodded. "Uncka Brad."

"Oh, you're getting better at that." He closed the door behind him and stuck out his hand. "Give me five." Chris grinned and slapped Brad's palm. "Atta boy." He started following Val to the kitchen, Chris walking beside him. He noticed she had flour on the back of her jeans where she'd wiped her hands. "You look a little stressed."

"Let's just say nothing has come out according to plan." They walked in the kitchen. The entire table was covered with flour and Chris handprints. The kitchen was muggy, and the windows were fogged with condensation. "I wanted to make cheese ravioli, but it's all fuck—er, *messed* up." She gave Chris a quick glance. He was eyeing the table, no doubt ready to rake his fingers through the flour again. "They hit the water and fall apart, so I've got what looks more like mini lasagna noodles and boiled ricotta." She grabbed a raw ravioli off a plate on the stove and dropped it in the boiling water. "See?" No, he couldn't see. He was halfway across the room, but he could tell she was at the end of her rope. "And I still haven't made the garlic bread or the salad."

Brad pulled his jacket off and draped it over the chair in the kitchen farthest from Chris. He didn't want flour all over his black leather jacket. He'd live if Chris managed to get it, but if he could avoid it, all the better. "What can I do to help?"

She shrugged. "Wave a magic wand?"

He laughed. "I have a better idea. Turn off the stove. Take a deep breath. Then hand me the phone and I can order a pizza."

"But—"

"Or we can eat your mini lasagna noodles. I bet your sauce is awesome."

She started laughing hysterically, almost near tears. "I haven't even made the sauce. Chris kept getting into everything and I just wanted it to be perfect." She frowned, pulling her lips together. Shit—she really *was* about to lose it. "I wanted to have it ready by the time you got here. I didn't even have a chance to shower. He—"

Brad was standing in front of her then, and he put his hands on her shoulders. "No big deal." He didn't know what possessed him then, but he kissed her on the forehead. "Go take your shower. Relax. I'll call in a pizza, okay?"

Her beautiful blue-green eyes searched his and then he saw her let go of her tension. "Okay."

"Don't come out till you feel better."

She smiled. "Thanks." She started to say something else, but she took the apron off and tossed it on the counter.

Brad watched her walk down the hall and then turned off the burner. He looked at Chris who now had his hands in the flour on the table. "You kept your mama busy today, didn't you?"

Chris grinned. "Ravi."

Brad laughed. "Yeah, ravi. Crazy, dude."

"Dude."

Brad pulled out his cell phone and looked up nearby pizza places that delivered to her neck of the woods. He placed an order for a large, half pepperoni, half extra cheese, and a salad. He spied a bottle of red wine on the counter and popped it in the fridge to cool for a little bit. He knew there was some rule about not putting wine in the fridge, but he didn't give a fuck, and he doubted Val did either. That woman was going to want a glass of wine when she got out of the tub, and it would taste better cool.

He filled the sink with hot soapy water. "We're going to clean up for your mom, buddy."

"Keen."

"Yeah, keen." Chris left the room and Brad wondered if he should check on him. He figured he would after he got all the excess flour off the table. So he found the trashcan and wiped the flour off the table with the rag into the trash. Then he tossed the cloth back in the sink and walked down the hall. "Chris?"

Chris emerged from his bedroom with an electronic drum set. "Wanna come with me back to the kitchen? Show me how that works?" The child nodded and walked beside Brad. He played the noisy toy while Brad cleaned the rolling pin and pot. He left the plate of raw pasta and bowl of cooked alone so Valerie could decide what she wanted to do with them. He finished cleaning off the table and was wiping down the counter and stove when she joined them.

She was a vision. Her hair was damp and a little curly, but she'd combed it out. She wasn't wearing much makeup—just a little around her eyes—but she was stunning. She seemed relaxed too, just like he'd hoped. "Oh, my God, Brad. You didn't have to do that."

"I know I didn't."

Crash! Boom! went Chris's drum toy. "And I am *over* that stupid thing." He laughed. "Only Ethan would think that was a cool toy to give a kid."

"Aw, Val, he's learning music. That's a good thing, right?" She shrugged and kissed Chris on top of his head. "Where are your wine glasses?" The doorbell rang. "Ah, that'd be the pizza. I stuck the wine in the fridge. Be right

FULLY AUTOMATIC

back."

They wound up eating in the living room, Chris in his portable high chair and Brad and Val on the couch. They watched an animated movie—one of Chris's current favorites—but Brad was simply enjoying their company. He and Val chatted off and on during the movie until a song would start. Chris would "sing" to it, and they enjoyed listening to him.

Long after the meal was over and Chris was out of his high chair, they talked and talked, and it felt like old times to Brad. Not once did he worry about Ethan or the future. It was like he and Val were old friends, long ago when he was crushing on her but before he'd fallen into deep love with her. He realized that when she excused herself, picking drowsy Chris up off the floor so she could tuck him into bed. She was gone for a few minutes and Brad allowed himself to think about all that.

He picked up the plates off the coffee table and took them into the kitchen, then headed back to the living room and carried the high chair back too. He wound up cleaning it off and putting it back where Val had it before they'd taken it to the living room. Then he headed back to the living room and poured himself another half glass of wine. He knew it wasn't the best idea because he'd have to drive, but he suspected it was contributing to his warm feelings. Then he carried the glass to the kitchen, determined to take care of the dishes.

He spied the dishwasher under the counter next to the sink and opened the door. There were already a few dishes inside, so he loaded in the ones they'd used for dinner. Val walked in the kitchen then and said, "Holy crap. You're feeling productive. Guess I should invite you over for dinner more often. I didn't even have to cook."

He turned around, smiling, and he took a drink of the wine. She walked over to him then and just looked in his eyes. She grabbed the glass out of his hand and placed it on the counter and then rubbed his cheek with her hand. "Thank you…for everything."

He closed his eyes then. He wanted it to happen—he did—but he knew it was wrong. It would never work. It was a bad idea.

But then he opened his eyes and looked in hers, and when she brought her lips to his, he couldn't shut himself off.

His arms wrapped around her as he kissed her back. This woman was all he'd ever wanted, and he knew now that she was going to be the death of him.

Fine—let him die. He kissed her again. He didn't care. She'd been all he'd ever dreamed about for almost as long as he could remember. She would make him complete…or she'd kill him.

But his heart protested. It didn't want to ache anymore. When they finished kissing, he opened his eyes and looked at her. "Ethan…"

"Ethan is going to be my ex soon." She must have seen the doubt etched in his eyes. Oh, yes, he'd heard it before, dozens of times, and he couldn't hide that fear from her. "You don't believe me." He didn't want to say anything. He felt too exposed and raw. One strike and she could fell him like a mighty oak. She smirked and then he felt weak. She knew. She knew the power she had over him and she didn't care. She let go of him then and walked across the room to the tiny desk tucked in an alcove. She opened the second drawer on the side, pulling out some folded papers and walked back over. She unfolded the papers and held them out for him to see. It took him a little bit, but he was able to put two and two together, thanks to words like *Dissolution of Marriage* and *Ethan Allen Richards, Respondent*.

He took a deep breath, and she set the papers on the counter. "Something I've been thinking about...*a lot*. Brad, you've been my friend forever—through thick and thin, good times and bad, and you've put up with a lot of shit from me." He smiled and she said, "Don't deny it. You know it's true." He started to say something, but she placed her finger on his lips. "I was so blinded by my feelings for Ethan that I never gave you a fair shot. And that was stupid, because...what you felt for me was pure and—"

He laughed. "Oh, Val, my thoughts were *so* not pure."

She giggled then too. "You know what I mean." He took a deep breath. "I was blind to what was in front of me the whole time." He felt hesitant but she said, "I love you, Brad. God, I love you, and I was so stupid to not see it. I can't regret Ethan, because I have Chris, but—"

She loved him?

He took a moment as it sunk in. She *loved* him. She'd said it. The words his heart had ached for so long to hear, and he could feel the emotion swell inside his chest. The woman he'd loved for so long was saying what he'd longed to hear for more years than he could remember. He could barely believe it.

He kissed her then, this time his passion unrestrained. He continued to feel a niggling doubt at the back of his mind, but he had to let it go and trust her. Yeah, he knew...he knew if she trashed his heart again, he'd be done for, but he couldn't not try. If he didn't trust her and walked away, he would always wonder.

The kiss ended but he held her close. "I love you too, Val. I always have."

He heard her breath catch in her throat and then she swallowed. She inhaled and said, "*Always?*"

He nodded. Now she'd know what a fucking dumb ass he was. But it didn't matter. It was the truth...and he wasn't going to lie to her. "Yeah."

She blinked and touched his cheek again. What was she thinking? He could see something in her eyes—not a question but something. She finally said, "I had no idea. I knew..." She shook her head. "But I—I didn't know."

"It's okay. I didn't publicize it." He kissed her again then, because he didn't have to wait anymore, didn't have to worry, and she *fucking loved him back*. He wanted nothing more than to take her, right then, right there, but too many things were holding him back. The first was her child sleeping not too far away from them. The other was that niggling doubt. The one and only time he and Valerie had spent a night together, Ethan had taken hold of her heart the next day harder than he ever had before. She'd snapped back to the guy like she had a bungee cord wrapped around her heart. If Brad made love to her, he would spend the rest of the week waiting for the other shoe to drop. He kissed her once more and then said, "I should probably go."

She wrapped her fingers around his neck, shoving her fingers into the hair at the nape, and said, "No...don't leave." His eyes searched hers, and he wasn't sure what to say. "Please. Stay."

How could he say no to her sweet request? It wasn't just desire, though it was there, thick and heavy as it flowed through his veins.

He answered her with another kiss. He couldn't say no to his sweet Valerie, the woman he'd wanted for so long he couldn't even remember what it was like to not need. As they stayed in that embrace kissing, he heard her breathing change, signaling that she felt the same way he did. She needed him as much as he needed her.

She broke away from his kiss and looked in his eyes. "Do you have any condoms, or do we need to run to Walmart?"

He started laughing, in spite of the fact that he did not. "No, Val. I didn't come over here tonight planning to get laid."

"Shit." He could tell her gears were turning, but he was considering driving to a 7-Eleven. "Actually, hold on." She grabbed his hand and they left the kitchen. She walked into the bathroom and let go of his hand as she rifled through a drawer under the sink. "Aha!" She pulled out a box of Trojans.

"Better check the expiration date."

She turned the box over while she talked. "After I had Chris, I didn't want to get back on the pill since I was breastfeeding. And I could never rely on Ethan to make sure he had any, and, well…I felt like I needed to protect myself in more ways than one—if you catch my drift."

He did, but he wasn't going to say a word. He knew exactly what Ethan was like, and at least Val hadn't been a complete idiot.

She held the box up to his face, grimacing. "They expired last month. Think they're still okay?"

He shrugged. God, he wanted her, but he wasn't about to make that decision. "You willing to take that chance?"

She grinned and grabbed his hand. "Fuck, yes."

She led him to her bedroom door. He asked, "What about Chris?" He'd had plenty of sex with plenty of women, but children sleeping nearby had never been part of the equation.

"It's fine. Just…we'll close the door almost all the way, and lights off. That way if he *does* come in, we have a little warning."

"He can't reach the light switch, can he?"

Val giggled. "No." She walked over to the nightstand and placed the box of condoms on it. Brad stood near the doorway, almost in disbelief that this was even happening. She strode over to him, all confidence, and *fucking hell* was she sexy. She was *the* woman for him and here she was…

She reached over to the light switch near his right shoulder and shut it off. The door was already all but closed and it was dark. He felt her lips on his as she pulled her shirt up and then broke from his kiss to pull it over her head. He placed his hands on her lower back, feeling her warm flesh, and that was when he felt the blood rushing to his cock, filling it with that familiar need. It got even worse when he heard the zipper on her jeans slide down, and she bent down to peel them off.

That was when he figured he'd better undress too. He started pulling his shirt over his head when her fingers attacked his jeans button and her lips assaulted his chest.

Oh, fuck, he was gonna have a hell of a time making it, because she had him completely wound up already. His cock was throbbing, dying to be inside her again for the first time in years.

They got the jeans off and then she pulled him toward the bed. He felt blind in the near dark of her room, but somehow it made it hotter, feeling for her instead of seeing her, and he felt behind her back for her bra so he could undo the straps. He got them undone but then she pushed against him, urging him onto the bed. "I need you inside me *now*."

Another surge of blood to his dick and all coherence flushed from his brain. He wasn't about to argue with her, because that was what he needed too. He reached down to yank off his shorts, and he felt her peel her panties off. She shoved a condom in his hand, still wrapped. "Can you take care of that?" He started to answer when he felt her hand on his cock, and he couldn't help the low groan in his throat. He hadn't expected her to touch him yet. It felt insane, so fucking good, and she was gonna make him come right this second if he didn't stop her. So he moved in with the condom and rolled it on.

She moved into position, poised over him, but he knew there was no way he was gonna make it through the ride. He was too turned on, too far past the point. So he slid his finger down her slit. Oh, fuck, yeah, she was wet. That was good. She probably wasn't too far from climaxing either, but he wanted to make sure she came before she rocked his world. He slid his finger up and down over her clit and she paused in place at first, just enjoying what he was doing to her. She started to move, at first, he thought, to bury him inside her, but no. She was moving against his finger, and so he responded by applying a little more pressure, a little more speed, and a little different motion.

She made it so easy. He could tell she was getting close, because her breathing was erratic and her knees were digging into his hips, her thighs tense, and she kept making little noises of pleasure. He wanted to say something, to urge her to let it go, but he didn't want to break the mood. He didn't want to rush her either. Her nails were digging into his chest, and she took a deep breath—followed by a loud moan. "Oh, God, Brad." She kept moaning, clenching against his sides, burying her nails deeper in his pecs, and he wasn't gonna stop.

She groaned one last time and then, before he could even move his finger, she lifted her hips and slid him inside her. He'd been on the verge anyway, but hearing her cries had taken him to the brink. Having her slam his cock inside her as far as he could go was the final straw, and he saw fireworks inside his head. Yeah, him and Valerie together at last. It was definite cause for celebration.

CHAPTER FIFTY-EIGHT

THE NEXT COUPLE of months, he spent the night at her house, but once in a while, she and Chris would come to his. He kept waiting for the rehearsal when Ethan would show up and he'd have to tell his friend what was going on. But the guy hadn't bothered.

Ethan and Zane were pretty close, though, and he knew Ethan had heard it from Zane. He didn't think there was any malice on Zane's part when he told Ethan, and the guy was gonna find out eventually.

He did get a (probably drunken) text from Ethan accusing Brad of moving in on his wife. But he knew Ethan knew better. Sure, Ethan had had Val's heart for a long time, but he also knew that Brad had loved her first.

And, unlike Ethan, he would treat Val right.

He and Val realized it was stupid, just spending the night when they wanted to spend every waking moment together, enjoying the love they'd denied for so long. They didn't live close by each other either, so it wasn't just two minutes to be in each other's arms. So Val asked him to move in with her. He was going to protest and ask her to move in with him, but she had the bigger house, and it was already Chris friendly. He loved his sound studio, but he loved Val more and packed his shit, putting his house up for rent.

He'd go back to practicing in a garage. He didn't care.

And Chris—that little guy. He'd always loved the kid, but living with him placed the little boy in Brad's heart forever. The more time he spent with him, the more he saw Valerie in the child. More than that, though, he saw the part of Ethan that he'd always wanted to save. It was the innocence, the wonder.

Val acted like she was starting to hate Ethan, and it killed Brad to see it, but he also knew why. First, his friend hit bottom like he never had before and was ordered into an inpatient rehab program. Brad was sure when he got out, he'd be like his old friend.

Only, no. He was worse. He might have been sober, but he was an asshole to the extreme. It was like Ethan *wanted* Val to despise him. He was being a real prick, fighting the divorce and threatening to sue for full custody of Chris. Brad wanted to sit down with his friend like old times and talk sense into him, but he knew those days were past. He doubted Ethan would ever forgive him for being with Valerie.

He didn't know that Ethan and Val would ever have an easy time from this point forward either. Ethan finally got his shit together, apologized for being an asshole, stopped holding up the divorce, and quit threatening for sole custody of his child. Then Valerie let him see Chris, and he first took the boy for a few days. Val was a nervous wreck the entire weekend, and when Ethan showed up, he had a gorgeous redhead with him, but she definitely looked like someone more his type. Yeah, she was wearing professional clothes, but she had that air about her that Ethan liked. Val felt the same way too, because she asked to speak to him in private and chewed his ass, only to find out she was way off base. The gal was Ethan's drug counselor-turned-girlfriend, a woman named Jenna.

So they both allowed themselves to hope that maybe, *maybe* Ethan was getting better.

And, with Val's divorce on the horizon, Brad was inspired to let her know exactly how he felt. One morning when she was in the shower, he took the ring off the sink that she always wore on her right ring finger. It looked like a cord wrapped around her finger but on the front was a microphone, a reminder to Brad that she missed that part of her life. Someday he'd find a way to get her back there, but first he wanted to ensure their permanence as a couple.

He took the ring and traced it, inside and out, on a piece of paper and returned the ring to the bathroom sink. She'd never suspect a thing. He had a date with the jeweler's.

And while that goddamn ring was being created according to his specifications, Val told him she had a little news.

She was pregnant.

He felt like an idiot. He couldn't even remember the last time they'd used a condom, and he was more than okay with it. She knew he loved Chris, so to have a child of his own put him out of his mind. He kissed her tummy and asked if he could go with her to her first doctor appointment. "You need to go to the ultrasound too. That shit'll blow your mind."

Knowing he was going to be a father, he would have thought everything would have changed, but it didn't. He was already like a father, for all intents and purposes. The baby would simply be another child he would love in his life.

Val had been right, though. When he saw the baby's heartbeat on the weird screen, its little limbs moving around, he felt his eyes grow wet. That baby was part of him. That was huge.

He woke up early one morning, Val and his new baby heavy on his mind. He rolled over and pulled Val close, her back up against his chest. She wasn't completely asleep, because she muttered a *Morning* to him and he started kissing the back of her neck. Before he knew it, they were making love, not changing position, but hot and sweet just the same.

She rolled over then, kissing his chest, and he held her close, rubbing her back, grateful to have her there.

Chris threw the door open. "Mommy, mommy!" He ran over to the bed.

"Come on up, sweetie."

She rolled onto her back. Chris touched her belly. It had been a source of fascination for the boy ever since Val and Brad had explained to him that he had a little sister on the way. "Baby?"

"Yes, baby, honey."

"We love baby."

"Yes. We love baby."

Chris looked up at him. "Daddy Brad?"

"Yeah, buddy?"

"You love baby too?"

He laughed. That kid cracked him up. "Yeah, of course, I love the baby."

His kissed Val and then picked Chris up, bringing him over to the other side of the bed and giving him a big hug. Val asked, "So what are we doing today?"

"I'm doing band practice this afternoon." Ethan wasn't involved...*yet*. The two of them had talked on the phone and the conversation had been promising. Ethan and his girlfriend were going to be picking Chris up that weekend and Brad planned to find out if Ethan was for sure in or out. Either way, they had an album to make. It had been way too long and the powers that be who had been patient and indulgent and had said that Ethan's rehab woes and bad behavior were good press had since changed their tune and told the band they needed something—*soon*. Brad had considered bringing Val on board for a duet too, but she'd been hesitant. It'd be a shame to waste her new vocal cords, though.

She asked, "So...breakfast in or out?"

Chris chimed in. "I want pana-cakes."

Val ran her fingers through her child's hair, grinning. "With maple syrup?"

"No. Boo-berry."

"Well..." She looked over at Brad. "Does Daddy Brad have all that stuff?"

"Nope. I think we'll have to go out for *boo-berry*."

"I get my shoes," Chris said. He slid off the bed and ran back to his room.

No better time than the present. Brad slid over to Val

and kissed her. "So...we're getting the little guy pancakes. What're we gettin' his mama?"

"A cup of decaf, I think."

"Is that all?"

"I'll figure something out."

"Uh...there's something else I think you should get."

She grinned. "And what would that be?"

She'd fallen for it. He rolled over and opened his nightstand drawer to pull out the little box from the jeweler. "Close your eyes."

"Do you have hash browns over there?"

"Close your eyes, Val." When she did, he opened the box and took out the ring. The woman at the jeweler's had promised that any woman would love that ring—it was simple but stunning, she'd assured him. He took her left hand and held it by her ring finger. They'd only talked about it once and she'd dismissed him because she'd thought at the time that Ethan would never give her a divorce. She'd told Brad it didn't matter, that she was married to him in her heart. That told him all he'd needed to hear. "Will you marry me, Valerie Quinn?"

She opened her eyes, stunned at first. She took in a breath and then smiled. She looked up at him and stroked his cheek, then kissed him. "Yes, yes, I will, Brad Payne. I will marry you."

He slid the ring over her finger just as Chris bounded back in the room. He set his shoes on the bed and climbed up. Brad almost laughed because he was still wearing his pajamas. He didn't know that he'd ever felt this happy in his life, and Chris was a part of that joy.

Chris grabbed his shoes and finished making his way to

Val's side. Instead of asking her to help him, though, he touched her cheek. "Why are you crying, mommy?"

"Because, I think, my life is finally perfect." Brad touched her belly, and Chris smiled, placing his hand on top of Brad's. "No, I take it back, sweetie. I don't *think*. I *know* my life is perfect."

Brad leaned over and kissed her on the cheek. "Fuck it. Let's get dressed. We're gonna have breakfast and then we're gonna go to the Justice of the Peace."

"What?"

"Why not?" He could tell she was giving it a lot of thought. She wasn't sure. He would give in—if she wanted another big wedding, hell, yeah, he'd do it for her, but he didn't give a shit. She was already his girl. He'd seen it in her eyes the moment she'd said *I will*. That was enough for him. That would last forever.

EPILOGUE

ETHAN HAD RECOMITTED to Fully Automatic, and the band's third album exceeded everyone's expectations. It was amazing.

And the baby...little Hayley Marie. God, she was his pride and joy. A beautiful baby and more than he could have ever asked for.

For all the joy Val had brought to his life, he needed to repay her. He managed to convince her that his plan for her was brilliant.

And that was why they were here now, performing in front of a sold out crowd in San Antonio. Val was at the helm, and they'd just finished a kick ass song.

She was the front woman of a new band called Val Hella. She was back. Most Fully Automatic fans didn't know her from the girl next door, but they knew Brad and they knew Nick. After Fully Automatic's third album, the four guys announced they wanted to branch out into side projects. Fully Automatic remained intact and they would release another album in a couple of years, but they wanted to pursue other projects. That was good, because Ethan and Zane wanted to go completely death metal, something Brad had resisted. They wanted a side band so they could unleash the darker, heavier pieces Ethan had been writing, and Brad was convinced it was fueled by the demons Ethan was finally learning to let go. It was a good thing for his brother.

And it gave him the perfect opportunity to get Val on her feet. He'd barely gotten the words out of his mouth when Nick said, "Hell, yeah."

Brad knew it was because the guy liked the idea of playing percussion with a female bassist.

The three of them auditioned lots of women before settling on one who seemed the perfect fit.

Watching Val tonight—the third night on tour—made him realize it was the smartest move he'd made since proposing to her. Her voice was in fine form. The surgery had changed her singing voice a little—it sounded more mature, deeper, throatier, but he knew too that part of that was due to the music lessons she'd invested in. She didn't want to lose her voice again, and so she was doing all she could to ensure its health.

She'd also learned guitar big time, and she was playing rhythm to his lead. It made her sexier than ever to him.

She yelled into the mike, "San Antonio! How we doin' tonight?"

The response was amazing. He knew most of the fans were there for the headliners—Last Five Seconds—but they had accepted Val's band with open arms.

She really did belong up there. She knew how to work a

crowd and they were eating her up. "You guys might know this tune. Fully Automatic plays it on tour, but they've never recorded it. I used to sing this back in the day, and it's one of my favorite songs. So here you go—'Metal Forever'." Brad had never had the heart to record it when their label had rejected the one song Val had sung for the demo, but he'd always loved it and couldn't resist playing it on tour. He convinced Val to put it on her band's first album.

She looked over at Brad and he smiled. He loved hearing her sing the words, because he'd long considered "Metal Forever" her theme song. Nick cued them up and they started.

She was beyond beautiful. The lights beamed down on her as she leaned into the mike, and she was vibrant, fully alive. He knew too that the same light in her eyes would be shining later that evening when they met up with the nanny and their kids after the show, but for now, her job was entertaining thousands of people—doing something she was born to do.

The fine people of San Antonio might not have known that "Metal Forever" was actually Val's song, but they loved it, and it was so good hearing her sing it again. It summed up all she was.

At the end of the song, Brad spoke into his mike—in place for singing back up. "God, I love this woman."

As he walked over to her and kissed her on the cheek, the screams from the audience ensured him that they too loved her…almost as much as he did.

ABOUT THE AUTHOR

Jade C. Jamison was born and raised in Colorado and has decided she likes it enough to stay forever. Jade's day job is teaching Creative Writing, but teaching doesn't stop her from doing a little writing herself.

Unfortunately, there's no one genre that quite fits her writing. Her work has been labeled romance, erotica, suspense, and women's fiction, and the latter is probably the safest and closest description. But you'll see that her writing doesn't quite fit any of those genres.

And Jade is a-okay with that!

Printed in Great Britain
by Amazon.co.uk, Ltd.,
Marston Gate.